A Little Primitive

JOSH LANGSTON

2nd Edition

Cover model image
Copyright 2012 by Photoshow/Shutterstock.com

Warrior silhouette
Copyright 2012 by Tatiana
Oleshkevich/Dreamstime.com

This is a work of fiction. Names, characters, places and incidents either are the product of the author's imagination or are used fictitiously, and any resemblance to any actual persons, living or dead, events, or locales is entirely coincidental.

ISBN-13: 978-1735373379

A Janda Books publication, Canton, GA

Books by Josh Langston

A Little Primitive
A Little More Primitive
A Primitive in Paradise
Primitives in Peril
Resurrection Blues
Treason, Treason!
Greeley
The 12,000-Year-Old Whisper
Zeus's Cookbook
Oh, Bits!
Voices
Garden Clubbed
A Season Gone to the Dogs

With Barbara Galler-Smith

Druids
Captives
Warriors
Under Saint Owain's Rock

Textbooks on Writing

Write Naked!
The Naked Truth
The Naked Novelist
Naked Notes

Josh Langston

Dedication

This book is dedicated to the five littlest people in my life (though I know they won't stay that way very long): Alexis, Anabelle, Nicolas, Knox, and Adam. I love you all and eagerly await the day when you're old enough to read this book without your moms and dads going nuclear.

—Pop

Chapter One
Meet and greet

Tori had seen the cat chase something under the cabin earlier that morning. Mice were always getting into the decrepit log structure, and Tori's early efforts to keep them out failed utterly. Hence, the cat. The mice still got in, but they probably developed ulcers in the process. Tori didn't especially like cats. Most of them treated her with indifference, just like the gray tom at work under the cabin. They shared some space, and that was about it. The cat didn't have a name, which suited them both just fine.

When the cat screamed, Tori went looking for it. She hurried out the cabin's only door and knelt to look beneath the building. Rocks piled under the corners and at strategic locations in between held the cabin off the ground and helped to keep vermin at bay. Some of it anyway.

Tori peered into the darkness expecting to see the cat torturing a rodent. Some folks thought that sort of thing was cute. Tori rated it somewhere between bear baiting and dog fighting. She didn't like mice, but she had no desire to see them suffer.

The cat screamed again, and this time it flew out from beneath the cabin as if strapped to a rocket. Score one for the mice, Tori thought. Damn cat was getting way too uppity. Then she heard a faint coughing sound. The heavy shade made it impossible to see anything clearly. She heard the cough again. It seemed almost human, but higher pitched.

A child? She abandoned the thought as easily as it came to her. There were no children out here. Hell, she hadn't seen an adult in over a week. That was the whole reason she'd bought the cabin in the first place. The town of Charm, Wyoming, was a good twenty miles away, and she could count on one hand the people she knew there: Caleb Jones, a pleasant old cowboy who owned the town's grocery, Chet Andrews, a horny realtor she hoped never to see again, and Maggie Scott, a park ranger with a penchant for pinochle and whiskey sours.

Another cough.

What the hell was it? Coyote? She'd seen and heard them often enough, but they never came near the cabin. It would have been different if she kept chickens or other livestock, but she had no interest in ranching. Her freezer was full, as were her cupboards and liquor cabinet. She had plenty of gas for the generator which supplied all the power she needed to live in comfort *and* solitude. She had satellite connections for her phone and computer. She could play her stereo as loud as she wanted, and usually did. Just then, however, the only thing to complement the cough was silence.

~*~

Mato squeezed himself into the darkness. A menacing shadow moved about the edges of the building, searching for him. It moved in a clumsy sideways shuffle that would have made him laugh if he weren't in pain. He dabbed at the open wounds on his chest and abdomen with an amazingly soft garment he'd found while exploring. It consisted of two roughly triangular pieces of thin, supple cloth connected at the corners. The widest edge was made from some sort of stretchy material. Reyna would love it. He imagined how delicious it would feel to curl up with her in the sensuous fabric. Unfortunately, the steady flow of his blood suggested he might not have the chance to realize the dream.

How stupid! He should have known there would be an animal on guard. Though tiny compared to the great cats that roamed the mountains, this one moved just as swiftly. And just as quietly. He hadn't had time to draw his weapon before the beast knocked him to the ground. Sharp talons had raked his upper body leaving deep gashes. Messy, but survivable if he could get home. That didn't seem likely with the other monster lurking beyond the shadows. It wasn't too big to crawl in and grab him, but it moved so sluggishly he knew he could evade it if he stayed awake.

He leaned back against the stacked stone supporting the building. He wanted to sleep. He needed to sleep. And it would have been easy. Too easy. The cat would eventually return. Though he had stabbed it, the wound was superficial, and he'd had no time to properly prepare his weapons. Without such preparations it would have taken three or four hunters to kill the beast and haul away the meat.

What had he been thinking? Hunters were supposed to know better! One didn't go alone into a strange place, especially not one occupied by a giant. He rubbed his face with both hands. Little Reyna would never know what happened to him. He hated that thought. But what he hated even more was the thought that someone would try to take his place and claim Reyna for his own.

Mato coughed again. The pain in his lungs was a match for the ragged furrows in his flesh. He was doomed. It didn't matter much whether he was consumed by the cat or the giant. Logically, he knew it would be better for The People if the cat got him. Then, he'd just be food. If the giant got him, however, it might be tempted to look for others of his kind. The People would never allow themselves to be caught, he knew. Outposts would sound an alarm, and The People would disappear into the wild, away from the dreaded giants once again.

They'd move without him—without a thought of his heroic efforts to discover the source of the amazing music the giant produced. It's what attracted him so close in the first place.

He leaned forward and peered around the edge of the piled stone. The giant was nowhere to be seen. Nor was the cat. Had they both given up? His heart began to beat faster. He might get away after all!

The music started once again. Amazing, ethereal sounds drifted down from the cabin overhead. They lifted his spirits and gave him new strength. How could they make such music? The giants were insanely clever with their machines; everyone knew that. But making music—real music—required a soul. And a voice. This wasn't voice music. No harmony could match the breadth and depth of these amazing sounds. If only Reyna could hear them, and feel the emotions they stirred, she would be his forever.

He closed his eyes and smiled. He would rest a little. Then escape. As soon as the sun went down. But his world went dark before the giant's did.

~*~

Tori hadn't completely given up on the idea of finding what was under the cabin, especially if the cat failed to drag it out and leave it by the door as he usually did. The last thing she needed was something bleeding to death and then stinking up the place. Lord knew what kind of creatures would come to investigate. She shivered involuntarily, then pressed shuffle on the CD player. Saint-Saëns' "Organ Symphony" poured out of the six speakers mounted around the cabin's interior. Tori smiled in sheer delight as the music rolled over her, all thoughts of the cat and its prey relegated from "act now" to "screw with it later."

She sat in the lounge chair that filled the area she'd dubbed the living room. It was also the kitchen, bedroom, library, and writing studio. There actually was a separate room for the toilet and bath. She'd insisted on that before she moved in. She didn't have to bathe *every* day, but having the option was essential. She wanted remote, not primitive.

Eyes closed, she ignored everything as the lush strains of the symphony suffused her world. When it finally ended, replaced by a haunting Gaelic soprano, she eased herself out of the chair and back toward the door. Though concerned at first by the cat's cry, she could see only a small wound on his chest as he squeezed past her into the cabin. No limp, very little blood, and thankfully, no little dead surprise in its mouth. That was likely still beneath the cabin.

Grabbing a stout flashlight from beside the door, Tori started back outside. Her hand drifted toward the shotgun, and briefly rested on it, before she snorted at her own fears and left it behind. Lowering herself to all fours, she clicked on the light and peered into the shadows. Nothing moved. She strained to hear another cough, but only heard the warble of a meadowlark. An odd bird, she thought.

Kinda like me.

She swept the beam of light from one side to the other but saw nothing of interest except a snake skin. It looked huge. Which suggested its former occupant was well fed. Goosebumps formed on her arms as she forced the thought aside. She had no time for snakes. Dead ones, anyway. She kept the shotgun near the door in the event one of them ever showed itself. With wildlife, she tried to observe a simple live and let live policy, but she had no intention of sharing her home with a snake. Any snake.

Something moved.

Suddenly tense, Tori moved the light even slower, concentrating on the spot where she thought she'd detected movement. There was still no sound. After a solid minute of silence, she worked her way around the corner of the building, still splaying her light on the footing she thought might be hiding the cat's prey. Please let it be something without teeth, she pleaded, though to whom she couldn't say.

The cat reappeared. It passed her and slowed to a slink a few feet ahead of her. Head low and tail pointed straight up, the tabby moved in creepy silence.

"Go away," Tori said.

The cat spared her a glance, then went back to the search.

"I mean it." Tori flicked a pebble at him.

The cat jerked back and crouched low, hissing and showing its teeth.

Tori threatened it with the flashlight. "Attitude? You're giving me attitude? I don't have to feed you, y'know. I could leave you to fend for yourself. Maybe let you tackle the monster that left that thing over there." She pointed the beam of light at the desiccated snake skin. The cat was clearly unimpressed. It straightened up and walked away as if it had declared itself above the fray.

"Uppity little prick," Tori muttered. "I should've gotten a dog."

She continued working her way around the cabin and soon reached the back side where the ground sloped away leaving a bigger space. She could sit comfortably and probe under the building with the flashlight. The theme from "Riverdance" had just begun when she rolled the circle of light to a stop. She squinted at what she'd found.

Where in hell did that come from? She scratched her head in bewilderment. This wasn't the first time she'd inspected the underside of the cabin. She had to crawl under it when installing insulation and a thick layer of plastic sheeting to keep the insect world at bay. She would've noticed an abandoned doll. Especially one dressed like an Indian.

~*~

Pete Sutherland considered himself a decent assistant district attorney. Neither showy nor superbly intelligent, he had nonetheless produced more wins than losses, for which his boss had been grateful. In retrospect, if he had been brilliant or produced uncanny legal victories, the Bibb County DA might have feared him as a potential rival. But Pete sought only what was rightfully his: a comfortable retirement. In the process, he'd delivered a number of bad people to prison and thereby made Macon, Georgia, and society in general, a better place.

It would have been a significantly better place if his wife, Bonnie, hadn't succumbed to cancer the summer before he retired. With his kids grown and on their own, the four-bedroom colonial they'd occupied for so long seemed more like a mausoleum than a home. Which is why Pete spent very little time there. He preferred the "fishing shack" he'd purchased with the insurance money he received after Bonnie's death.

The stylish A-frame overlooked a trout stream in the north Georgia mountains and offered a different kind of solitude. Not only did the place sport every comfy convenience he desired, but he could toss a line from the back deck or stroll along the carefully designed stone steps that meandered down the hillside to a short pier which bordered the stream. He had installed small refrigerators to store his beer in both locations. Pete Sutherland had thought of everything. Except uninvited visitors.

The car which pulled into the driveway looked familiar. It was identical, in fact, to his wife's bright yellow, late-model Chevy, which had occupied his Macon garage for the two years since her death. Pete's oldest son, Chad, would take the car for a short spin from time to time, mainly to insure it still ran. An investment advisor, Chad often suggested that Pete sell it and put the money in something for himself or his grandkids, but Pete wasn't ready to let it go. Bonnie had loved the ugly car, corny as that was, and he wasn't eager to part with it.

And here it was at the fishing shack. Pete squinted at the vehicle. *Chad?* No; the driver was too old. *And what in hell was he doing in Bonnie's car?*

"Mr. Sutherland?" The man walked around the car and straight toward Pete who was standing at the front entrance to the building.

"Yes? Who're you? And what are you doing with my wife's car?" He almost waited for an answer before reaching into his pocket for his cell phone. Naturally, it wasn't there. It sat, batteries dead as stones, on the kitchen counter.

"I hoped you wouldn't mind," the visitor said. "I thought I'd drive up here so's we could have us a little chat."

Pete's eyes narrowed still further, his suspicion unimpeded by fear.

"Do I know you?"

"You should," said the visitor. "Or do you just forget the names of people you send to prison?"

~*~

Tori crawled under the cabin slowly. From the back, there was plenty of room, but she didn't want to give up the flashlight, and she certainly didn't want to put her hands down on something crawly. She'd heard about scorpion stings and had no desire to acquire firsthand knowledge. Besides, the doll wasn't more than ten or twelve feet in.

She didn't pay much attention to the doll while working her way toward it. She wasn't even sure why she bothered. Curiosity mostly. Close enough to reach out and touch it, she put her hand on the doll's leg, fully expecting to feel hard plastic. Instead, she felt warm flesh and jerked her hand away.

A kid? The damned cat had chased a child under her cabin? Where had it come from? She didn't have neighbors. Nobody drove by on their way to somewhere else. The nearest paved road was miles away and the dirt track which connected it to her parking spot was barely navigable.

"Hey, you okay?" she whispered, not wanting to frighten the little kid, and little it most definitely was. Tiny. Maybe two feet long, or tall, if it had been standing.

It didn't respond.

Tori crawled closer and again put her hand on the child's leg. Still no response, but she felt sure it continued to breathe. Thank God for that she thought as she slid her hands carefully beneath the body and lifted. It was significantly heavier than she anticipated. Working backwards like a sniper exiting an ambush, she made her way out from under the cabin. She paused when she reached the light and stared down in shock at the body in her arms.

It was no child. Not even close. She held an adult, male Indian in her lap, his chest and stomach swaddled in a blood-soaked pair of her panties. Weird didn't even begin to describe the thoughts flying through her head, not the least of which was the need for better clothes pins. When he moaned, she forced all such thoughts aside and concentrated on his wounds.

The cat had done quite a job on him. Four long, deep gashes crossed his bare chest at a slight angle. Two more decorated his back. She couldn't help but note that he had an impressive physique, despite his diminutive stature. She was tempted to peek beneath his breechcloth, then mentally slapped herself. That's just... icky, she thought. Yet the idea lingered.

She stood with the Indian in her arms, his weight still surprising, and carried him into the cabin. The cat materialized at her feet and stalked her burden as she went.

"Get out, you little monster," she said, pushing the cat toward the door with her foot like a soccer player laying the ball off to a shooter. Except the cat wasn't having any of it. He gave her an unambiguously disgusted meow and crowded closer, tail aimed at the ceiling, eyes tracking the Indian like radar.

Tori looked for some place to put him so she

could throw the cat out, but the little bugger was intent on finishing the job he had started. She settled for the top of a waist-high bookcase and snatched the cat out of the air as it launched itself up from the floor. Tori ignored its struggles and hurried toward the door, clutching the cat firmly to her chest and doing her best to ignore the claws that raked her arm.

In a move so swift that they were both surprised, Tori sent the feline on an arcing heave ho that the cat probably survived. But since she'd slammed the door before he landed, she couldn't be sure. Not that she cared.

Thankfully, the Indian hadn't stirred, else he'd have rolled off the bookcase and splattered himself on the floor. Tori grabbed a towel from the door handle of the stove and spread it, one-handed, on the duvet as she relocated the slumbering Indian. He certainly didn't take up much space, and once again she applauded herself for choosing a full-size mattress rather than a single. Her objective had been comfort, rather than elbow room, in the unlikely event she invited someone to spend the night.

With the Indian sprawled on his back, Tori gingerly removed his leather vest to get a better look at his wounds. Wincing for him, she slipped his arms free of the supple leather and left it beside him on the towel. The bleeding had slowed, but the wound hadn't closed. If he lived, he'd have scars profound enough to earn the sympathy of biker gangs. Poor schlub.

She retrieved a first aid kit and flipped it open. Surely there was some hydrogen peroxide in here somewhere, she thought. And then she found it.

"Here goes nothin', Tonto," she said as she opened the bottle and poured it on the little Indian's chest.

Instantly, his eyes popped open in obvious shock.

~*~

Something cold splashed on Mato's chest and jolted him awake. The bright light blinded him, and he crossed his arms over his face. *What was happening?*

His heart raced as he looked up into the face of a she-giant. Whatever she had poured on his chest was bubbling like Winter Woman's cauldron. He looked quickly from side to side to find an escape route when it occurred to him that whatever she had poured on his chest *didn't hurt.* Or rather, it hurt no more than the cuts he'd suffered from the cat. *What was she doing?*

He looked her squarely in the eyes. But whether he was ready to die or not, he wasn't sure. He only felt profoundly defiant. She might be big, but he wasn't going to give up without a struggle. His hand slipped to his belt, then to his knife. She was so confident she hadn't bothered to disarm him. The obsidian blade was small, but the edge was sharp. Big as she was, he could make her feel pain.

Staggering to his feet, he waved the knife, daring her to make a move. Instead, she merely smiled. She made soothing sounds, like those a mother shared with an infant. She spoke softly. Calmly. He had no idea what she was saying, save that it wasn't threatening.

He stepped back, surprised at the give in the surface beneath him. Springy and soft, at the same time. Extremely odd.

The she-giant hadn't moved, though her expression changed. She looked concerned and had fallen silent.

"Who are you?" he asked.

She looked at him quizzically but made no answer, so he repeated the question.

"I am Mato," he said, lightly touching his chest. "Mato. Hunter. Stalker of beasts, and dreams."

"Mato," she repeated.

He nodded up and down. "Mato. Mato! Who are you?"

She tapped her own chest and said, "Tori."

Stupid name, he thought. What was a *tory?* It made no sense. He glanced at the central wall of the cabin and down at the remains of a wood fire. Sitting, he edged toward it, careful not to fall from his perch. When he could go no further without dropping to the floor, he paused. Digging his fingers into the fabric covering the platform, he lowered himself to the floor.

The pain which accompanied his short climb nearly caused him to black out again. The she-giant watched him, her expression of concern deepening when he straightened and groaned.

She reached toward him with something white and fluffy smashed between her thumb and index finger. When he backed away, she stopped and pretended to use the ball of fluff on her own chest. Then she pointed at him and dropped the ball at his feet. Suddenly it dawned on him that she meant to stop his bleeding. Since he had no spider silk handy, he reached for the fluffy thing with both hands and used it to blot the blood on his chest.

Again she spoke to him, her voice soft, low, and reassuring. She pushed another of the fluffy wads toward his chest. This time, he held his ground and let her clean his wounds. She was strangely gentle, her touch far from what he expected of a giant, though in truth, this was the first one he'd ever met face-to-face. Still, the treatment was not without discomfort. He tried not to show his pain, but a groan escaped his lips from time to time despite his best efforts.

Each time, she pulled her hand away and frowned. Still weak, he lowered himself to the floor and leaned back against one of the wooden supports that held up the platform, which he surmised was what she slept on. Soft and springy. Truly a marvel.

She turned away for a moment and removed something from the box at her side: a glass bottle. Though similar to other such containers the giants often left behind when traveling through The People's land, this one was smaller and darker. The giant removed a white covering from the end of it and extracted another soft, round, fluffy thing, only this one was wet with an orange fluid. It had a strong smell, almost as bad as some of the potions Winter Woman made. He held his arms straight out as if to ward the giant away.

She paused and smiled again, murmuring more soft, unintelligible words. If not for her gentle eyes and patient approach, he would have tried to escape rather than allow her to apply her medicine. The giants knew many secrets and had many machines. What chance did he have on his own? He lowered his arms.

She dabbed the liquid on his open wounds. There was a short, sharp sting all along the cuts, and he gasped in surprise before he could stop himself. But the pain quickly subsided.

"Mato," she said, and then added something he couldn't understand. When he didn't react, she pretended to lift something from the floor. It dawned on him that she wanted to return him to the platform, where it would be easier for her to treat him. When he nodded his assent, she gently lifted him in both massive hands and carefully lowered him to the same spot as before. She then went back to the box at her side and produced a length of thin, white cloth. She wrapped his torso with the white strips and then secured them with a shorter piece of sticky, white material.

When she was done, he lowered his arms. He still held the knife and smiled sheepishly at her as he put it back in his belt. "Mato thanks you," he said formally.

She smiled and said something in response. Though he'd never heard such words, he felt certain he knew what she meant.

He lay back on the sleeping platform as she stood and collected her healing kit and cleaned up after him. He watched as she produced a huge rectangle of cloth which she folded in half twice and placed on the floor in front of the fire pit. She then pointed at him and gestured toward the cloth. Now they both had something to sleep on. When he struggled to sit up, she hurried to him and gently carried him to his sleeping mat.

Where was the cat, he wondered, wishing he knew something of the she-giant's tongue. It was painfully obvious she couldn't understand his words. Moving slowly, he approached the fire pit and extracted a length of partially burnt kindling. She watched intently as he sketched a cat on the hearth, then set the stick aside and shrugged at her.

Again she smiled and pointed at the door. Then, as if to be sure he understood, she acted out the process of grabbing the beast and throwing it outside. Mato laughed. Briefly, because it hurt. They both settled for smiles of understanding.

Chapter Two
Everyone's got something to hide

"Some of the people I've sent to prison are worthy of being remembered," said the former assistant district attorney. "Obviously, you aren't one of them."

Shawn Donlevy, the man who'd arrived at the outrageously misnamed "fishin' shack," chuckled. "I 'spect you're right." He raised a 9mm automatic and aimed it squarely at the former ADA's face. "Why don't we step inside and have that chat?"

Pete Sutherland finally got the message. *Deep shit.* And he was in it up to his chin. "Right," he said, trying to remain calm. "C'mon in."

Shawn waved Sutherland inside, ahead of him. "You can't imagine how long I've been looking forward to this."

~*~

Tori gazed at the Indian sleeping in front of the fireplace. Though tempted to cover him with something—a bath towel or a kitchen cloth—she hesitated lest she wake him. Better to let him sleep, she thought. And then she smiled. Did looking at him make her a voyeur? *Good Godamighty, what a body!* Too bad he was so damned small. She shook her head. It had been way too long since she'd spent the night with anyone, let alone a 24-inch-tall savage with a body out of a Gold's Gym flyer. Sometimes life sucked. Really hard.

What was she supposed to do with him? Nurse him back to health, of course, but after that— what? Where had he come from? And, wherever that was, was it logical to assume there were more just like him? If he'd been blue, she'd have called him a Smurf. If he'd been hairy, she'd have called him a hobbit. He was neither. And as she recalled from a National Geographic program she'd once watched, he wasn't even big enough to be a pygmy.

Obviously, he was from outer space.

She groaned. Of course. Where else did primitive little men come from?

She tried to sleep, but the best she could muster was half snooze/half conjecture about the little Indian. *Mato.* Short for to-mato? She couldn't help but smile. If the shoe fit....

By the time the first kiss of morning slipped through the window, her visitor was awake. He sat still, perusing the cabin.

"Hey," she said, conversationally.

He squinted at her, then said something guttural. No surprise there; everything he said sounded guttural.

Tori merely smiled and rolled to a sitting position that mimicked his. She stretched, keenly aware of his eyes on her and the fact that her long, thin T-shirt did little to disguise her breasts. Men were all alike, no matter how tall. Chuckling to herself, she shuffled to the modest bathroom appended to the cabin. Once inside, she closed the door and sat on the toilet.

Within seconds it occurred to her that Mato would need to relieve himself, too. What did she expect him to do, stand on the toilet seat? Go in the sink? Not bloody likely. He would just have to go outside. Like the cat.

The cat!

Christ on a crutch! Where was the damned cat?

~*~

"I'm not a wealthy man," Shawn advised the ADA. "But if I was, I think I'd be content with just one house."

"Yeah, well, different strokes," Sutherland said.

"Seriously. I don't think I'd feel the need to have a great big house in town, and a snazzy hideaway in the mountains, too." He waggled the automatic at him. "I've never understood rich folks."

Sutherland laughed. "Rich? Me? Right."

Shawn looked around at the plush furnishings of the "shack." The living area was full to bursting with coffee tables and a sectional sofa. A gigantic, hi-def, flat screen TV occupied center stage, and vibrantly colored prints decorated the walls. Framed photos of kids and grandkids graced most of the remaining open spaces. "I really like what you've done here."

Sutherland squinted at him in surprise.

"It's so much more... I dunno. Masculine. Your other house—"

"My *other* house?"

"Yeah. The one in Macon. Where I got the car." He motioned Sutherland into a kitchen chair, then seated himself with the table between them. He kept the gun pointed at Sutherland's chest. "I spent several nights there." He laughed. "You've got a nice, roomy bed."

Sutherland's face purpled, but he kept quiet.

"I brought in a lady friend," Shawn said. "She liked it, too. In fact, we spent a lot of time in it. And that big TV in the living room? Awesome! But that reminds me. Don't be surprised when you see some charges for pay-per-view movies on your cable bill. We really had a great time. That high-def shit is something, ain't it?"

"You ordered *pornography* in my name?"

"Well, yeah. But, I gotta tell ya, I don't think it was worth the price."

"What do you want from me?" Sutherland asked.

Shawn regarded him carefully before responding. "You sent me to prison."

"Not me," Sutherland said. "A judge and jury did that."

The ex-con waved the handgun disdainfully. "That's bullshit. You tried the case."

"I wasn't the one who broke the law. You chose to do that. You earned whatever you got."

Shawn aimed just past the former ADA's ear and pulled the trigger.

Sutherland dropped backwards as if hit by artillery. He scrambled to a sitting position and rubbed his ear. "What the hell was that for?"

"Practice," Shawn said. "Let's go for a walk."

"A walk where?"

"Outside."

~*~

Mato felt as if he were stuck in some strange, demented dream. He was trapped in a giant's lair, and had no idea how he would ever get away. He had watched the she-giant carefully from the time he awoke, hoping she might slip up and reveal an escape route. Instead, she walked through an opening to another room, leaving him all alone.

Obviously, his escape wasn't worthy of her concern.

Almost as quickly as she had left, she returned, mumbling. Not that he could have understood her if she spoke more clearly. She waved him toward the door to the outside.

Was she letting him go? He couldn't believe his good fortune.

She knelt in front of him, and held her arm out as if fencing him in, then opened the door. The cat bolted through the opening without sparing Mato even a look. The woman moved her arm out of his way and motioned for him to go outside. He left without waiting for any further gestures.

Once outside, he ducked back under the building and jogged to one of the supporting piles of stone. He relieved himself there and tried to make sense of all that had occurred since the previous afternoon.

He had seen much but learned little. Clearly, the giants possessed magic, although that was hardly a revelation. The People had seen the giants from afar and were acquainted with their cunning machines. Most operated on the ground, rolling along at great speeds, throwing up dirt and dust in their passage. But more wondrous still were their flying machines, some of which flew so high Mato could barely see them above the clouds. Why the Spirits of the sky ignored them he could not guess. If he were such a Spirit, he felt sure he would flick them out of the air with a vengeful finger. The machines made much noise, and those on the ground left ugly tracks, but simple to follow—and more importantly—easy to avoid.

He had learned two things at least: she-giants could smile, *and* they didn't always eat any of The People they might catch. This had come as a surprise. His entire life seemed to consist of warnings about which creatures ate The People, and which could be eaten. There seemed to be far more of the former than the latter. Giants, of course, ate anything, and could never be trusted. There were legends about them, told over and over again around council fires and hearths. Children weren't the only ones who learned from these tales.

Fortunately, there were tales of heroism, too. Had not Snake Eater once stumbled into a giant's camp? Snake Eater was not only brave, but cunning. He tricked the giants into letting him go, but only after showing him some of their magic. That was how The People learned to harness fire. It had been many, many years since the days of Snake Eater, and now the giants had even stronger magic while The People still made fire in the old way. Perhaps if Mato captured some of this giant's magic, The People would tell his tale. A smile slowly worked its way across his face. Such a thing would bring Reyna to his tent forever. And maybe others. Reyna would not like that, but she would not dare say anything about a warrior of legend. Mato would earn great honor, and all he had to do was out-think the she-giant.

How hard could that be?

~*~

Tori feared she had made a grave mistake letting Mato wander alone outside. Though she'd locked the cat in the bathroom, there were other predators to consider. Coyotes and foxes were plentiful in the rugged terrain surrounding her cabin. So were eagles and snakes. She had never seen a mountain lion, but it wouldn't surprise her to learn they were out there as well.

Of course, the little primitive had almost certainly lived his entire life out in the wild. He was probably far better equipped to survive alone than she was, assuming she didn't have her house, her shotgun, her truck, and about a thousand other things that made her solitary world not only livable, but comfortable. Mato could take care of himself, provided his wounds didn't become infected.

He hadn't seemed particularly dirty. She thought back to the previous afternoon and evening when she tended his injuries. She didn't recall smelling him. No musk or hint of perspiration remained where he slept. She stood and walked to the door. The sun was still low on the horizon, but that wouldn't last long. Shadows would eventually disappear as the heat of the day asserted itself. She gave herself a virtual pat on the back for having the foresight to install a window air conditioner. Though it put a strain on the generator, it made the worst of the summer bearable. The choice between a dryer and AC had been so easy!

Mato might be okay with crawling into the shade of a rock somewhere, but that wasn't an option Tori cared to contemplate. She'd have a beer or a soft drink with her cool air, thankyouverymuch. And if the AC ever crapped out, she'd throw the unit in her air-conditioned truck, haul it down the road to Charm or Ten Sleep, and either have it repaired or replaced. Little things like that, she could afford. Thank God for royalty checks.

She sat on the stoop and drank her coffee. She'd started a pot just after opening the door for Mato. Now she missed him. Would he like coffee, she wondered, and what could she put it in to serve him? There were no demitasse cups in her cupboard; she had no great love for espresso or much of anything else from the yuppie world she had escaped. *A shot glass? Maybe. No handle.*

"Mato?" she called. "You want some breakfast?"

When he didn't answer, Tori stepped back inside. Maybe the smell of food would bring him around. She shrugged. For all she knew, he was out hunting for his own breakfast. Maybe he'd leave some disgusting trophy on her doorstep like the cat did. A conversation materialized in her head:

"Ugh. I kill rabbit. You cook. Me hungry."

"You betcha, Tarzan. I'm on it. You want fries with that?"

He'd damn well better like toast and eggs, she thought, 'cause that's what we're having. She flipped on the CD player as she made her way to the corner which housed her fridge and a gas stove. She left the cabin door open, and strains of "Sweet Home Alabama" filled the air.

~*~

"I'm not stupid," Sutherland said. "If I go outside with you, you'll shoot me."

Shawn looked at him in mock surprise. "You've got it all wrong. I'd have no problem shooting your sorry ass right here. I just thought it might be nice to enjoy the sunshine. It's a pretty day. I missed a lot of pretty days because of you."

"You're not going to kill me?"

"I didn't say that. But to be honest, I haven't decided." Shawn smiled. Lying was so easy. He could do it in his sleep. Best of all, it almost always worked. He watched as the former ADA got to his feet and walked to the back door. The man was obviously worried, but by dangling a little piece of hope in his fucked up, middle-class head, Shawn virtually guaranteed his cooperation. It truly didn't matter to him whether he killed the jerk indoors or out; the decomposing body would start to stink pretty quickly either way. His big concern was to make it look like a suicide. He didn't want anyone searching for him while he was busy tracking down everyone he needed to find. Still and all, he was in no hurry. Sutherland had a nice cabin. He was looking forward to spending a few days in it.

He certainly didn't want to share it with a dead guy.

~*~

It was the music that really convinced him to turn around and risk going back into the she-giant's lair. The sound rolled out of her cabin and soaked into Mato's head like the morning mist from a lazy river. A melody danced around a subtle drum beat, complemented by other instruments he couldn't identify. Giants were so unimaginably clever. How had they ever conjured such amazing sounds?

He moved cautiously back to the door and peeked in.

The giant—Tori, she called herself—stood facing away, busy at some task on the other side of the cabin. She was cooking something, and the smells made his stomach rumble. She couldn't hear it over the sound of the music and the clatter of pottery. She spread dishes on a table, then scraped something fluffy and yellow into two of them. She put a pile of bread on the table as well, and glasses of an orange liquid. She drank from another vessel, but he couldn't tell what it was. Blood, perhaps? It didn't seem likely, but he wasn't ready to trust her, even if she did smile at him. A smile was the trickster's greatest weapon. Perhaps she was a trickster among the giants. How would he know?

She seemed to notice him for the first time, and smiled again. As if he were an old friend! Did she think him completely stupid? Then she gestured for him to come to the table. She pulled out a chair for herself and sat down.

Mato realized he had come to a moment of truth. If this was a trap, it was the most elaborate one he'd ever seen. There were weapons on the table, made of metal. The giants used so much metal! How easy his life would be if only he could make things from metal like they did. Sadly, The People had no such magic.

Tori patted the table and gestured for him again. She lifted some of the yellow stuff to her mouth with one of the metal weapons and chewed contentedly. It didn't seem possible that she would poison the food they both ate, and he had seen her serve it with his own eyes. Maybe he could trust her.

He entered the room, walked to the table, and climbed up onto the chair. While she sat, he stood, the edge of the table touching the lower portion of the bandages around his middle. She pushed a plate toward him, and he reached a tentative hand out toward its contents.

She said something, then jiggled one of the metal weapons lying beside the plate. Though large, like everything the giants used, it didn't look very fearsome. The edge was rounded and dull. He could lift it with one hand, but using it the way she did was out of the question.

She sighed and pushed the plate closer to him, then gently removed the weapon from his hand and set it aside.

He dug into the hot, fluffy food. *Eggs!* He recognized the taste instantly. Mixed in were mushrooms and something orange colored and sticky. It had a wonderful flavor and melted in his mouth. There was far more than he could ever eat.

She pushed a piece of the bread at him. It was soft and hot and had something made from berries smeared on it. The taste was easily as amazing as the egg stuff. Sweet. Oh, how Reyna would love it! He wondered idly how he might carry some with him when he left. It wasn't the magic he originally had in mind, but The People would sing his praises just the same if he managed to bring some of this home to them. It saddened him a little to think that he would reward Tori's hospitality by stealing from her.

Tori watched the little Indian with amusement. Everything he touched seemed new and fascinating to him. Clearly, he had never experienced cheese. Or toast and jam. Or eating utensils. She could have kicked herself for trying to make him use a spoon. What was she thinking? It might have been different if she had offered him one appropriate for his size, but she had no baby spoons. He handled the tableware like a pitchfork and shovel. At least she had the presence of mind to pour his orange juice into a shot glass, and he was gulping that down like a drunk with a bucket of muscatel.

"Slow down there, Mato," she said.

He paused at the sound of his name, then lowered the glass to the table. His response was another word she'd never heard before, but she suspected it meant something like "good" or "yum." He followed that with a tremendous belch and smiled at her in satisfaction.

She took a stab at repeating the same word

he had used, pre-burp, and was rewarded with a smile and a nod. This led to an idea she couldn't resist. Motioning for him to stay, she reached to the counter and grabbed eggs, cheese, and bread. These she placed on the table one at a time, identifying each as she went. He caught on very quickly and repeated every word she used.

When they'd finished with those, she grabbed mushrooms, butter and jam, and repeated the process.

Mato had words for some of the things, but not all. Whenever he offered one of his own words, Tori repeated it, often struggling with the pronunciation.

They worked their way through knife, fork, spoon, glass, and cup. She poured a bit of her coffee into the shot glass when he'd emptied it. They both quickly discovered Mato was not a coffee-drinker.

"Hey, no problem," Tori said. "It's an acquired taste. Kinda like beer." Her lips formed a wry smile. "Beer is probably a bad idea. I'm going to leave that in the fridge for now."

When they had exhausted the words for everything on the table, Tori opened the door to the refrigerator and gestured for Mato to investigate. Wincing only slightly as he climbed down from his chair, the little Indian gazed at the contents of her aging Kenmore. There wasn't a great deal inside that hadn't already been part of some other meal. Tori never claimed to be a great cook, but she knew enough to make extra because leftovers were fine with her and a damn sight easier than cooking something new for every meal. Mato seemed more interested in the fact that the fridge was cold.

While he poked around there, Tori pulled a pad and pencil from her desk, which occupied the space beneath one of her three windows. A small desk, it was barely large enough to accommodate her computer and an ancient monitor. She quickly jotted down the names Mato had given her for eggs, mushrooms, plates, and a few others. She had no idea how the words might properly be spelled and merely used a crippled form of phonetics. She didn't owe *Webster's* anything. This was her dictionary, by God. She could write it up any way she pleased. The thought made her laugh.

Mato looked at her quizzically.

This was going to work out okay. After all, the little guy liked her cooking. Not an altogether bad way to begin a relationship.

~*~

Shawn counted himself fortunate that Sutherland maintained a cabin in the boondocks. A big city would have crime scene investigators, cops who were paid to be suspicious of everything, especially suicides of former prosecutors. Georgia, which had more counties than any other state in the union—159 at last count—had raised "small town" politics to an art form. There were even a few counties so small, their biggest towns weren't really big enough to *be* towns. At least, not in Shawn's estimation. If a place didn't at least have a restaurant and a motel, it wasn't a town. He would've added a requirement for a whore house, too, but they had become all but extinct outside of Nevada, a place he'd wanted to visit all his life.

Sutherland's body sat propped at a slight angle against the base of an oak tree overlooking the little trout stream that gurgled past his A-frame. Shawn tucked the 9mm automatic in the dead man's hand and tried to imagine how his arm would have fallen if he had really shot himself. He tried several poses, then settled on letting the arm fall by itself. The damned gun wouldn't stay in his hand, but he reluctantly decided that's the way it would have been if he hadn't shot Sutherland first.

Sometimes it was hard to do things right. Still, he had to make the effort. Lord knew, nobody else was looking out for him.

He decided to shorten his stay in Sutherland's country place. There was too much risk involved. Better to hit the road and go on to step two: finding Vicky Lynn's mother. He had some ideas how he would accomplish that, but if Sutherland maintained the same kind of freezer and liquor cabinet here as he did at his city place, Shawn would take the time to enjoy it before he continued his mission. He was a patient man after all. That was a lesson he'd learned from the Georgia Department of Corrections.

He patted Sutherland's corpse on the cheek and headed back to the A-frame, a distance of roughly five hundred yards. Surely the smell wouldn't drift that far before Shawn pointed the hideous yellow Chevy toward his next stop.

Steak for dinner, he thought. Steak and potatoes. And beer.

He wondered where he might find a hooker in these parts. Did they advertise in the Yellow Pages?

~*~

Mato's stomach was full. Almost painfully so. He recalled a few feast days when there had been such quantities of food. The People were happiest then. There was dancing and singing and story-telling. Laughter was plentiful among them, as was love-making.

But here, in the she-giant's lair, Mato felt no warmth of family. Tori had been generous and gentle, nothing like what he had feared. And yet, she was alone amid such vast wealth. It puzzled him. Why would she not have a mate and children by the score? Perhaps her mate was out hunting, and when he returned Mato would go into the larder with whatever else he had slain.

As quickly as such thoughts arose, they subsided. There were no males living here; this was a woman's place. It bore Tori's strong, clean scent, and it was neat, organized, and efficient. She thereby doubled the power of her magic. Most males couldn't, or wouldn't, do that.

Sitting on the sleeping pallet Tori made for him, Mato watched as she emptied an enormous basket of clothing on the table where they'd eaten.

She carefully picked through the pile, smoothing and folding various items before stacking them neatly. When she found some of the wondrous cloth he'd used to staunch his wounds the previous day, she merely balled them up and tossed them on a chair.

He noticed her looking at him, and she winked, a sly smile drawing her lips to one side. She said something to him, then waggled her finger and laughed as if she'd just heard the most clever story ever told. Mato, naturally, had no idea what had set her off, but assumed it was somehow connected to the mysterious fabric. She was staring at him, the same odd look on her face, when she blew a few strands of hair from her forehead and abruptly stood up. Had her cheeks taken on an extra bit of color? And why was she chuckling? Females, whether giants or of The People, could be utterly incomprehensible at times. Still, he pondered, if—

Moving so quickly it startled him, Tori turned completely away and raised the hem of her long sleeping shirt well above her waist. But rather than merely exposing her woman parts, Tori wiggled her bottom to display one of the garments like those piled in the chair. She looked over her shoulder at him and snapped one of the elastic side strings. All too quickly, she lowered her top and turned to face him. She was more than a little flushed, but still laughing. Mato laughed, too.

There was more joy in this place than he had thought. He wished this gigantic female were closer to his size. He wished he could talk to her. He wished....

But wishes were for children and old people. Mato was a warrior. Still, he counted himself fortunate that Tori would so easily share her secrets. Giants were, by far, the strangest creatures.

Chapter Three
Faces from the past

The drive south had been uneventful. Shawn observed all the traffic laws, and acted the part of a fine, upstanding citizen. Like Sutherland. Well, like Sutherland used to be.

Getting to the big city was easy. It happened almost too quickly. But after only a few hours driving the streets of Atlanta, Georgia, Shawn came to a startling discovery. The only peach trees in Atlanta were parts of street names. He hadn't seen a single fruit tree of any kind all afternoon. Not that he'd been looking for any; his real quarry was a woman. He'd met her once, back when things were good, before he went to prison. Her name was Edna, or Emma. Something like that. An old style name. Last name: Pruett. He remembered that distinctly because it was so different from Vicky Lynn's last name. The two didn't share a single letter.

He remembered the old woman as being slender, like her daughter. They had the same hair color, too—light brown. Only Edna/Emma's hair was short. Vicky Lynn's hair was long, the way he liked it. He never let her cut it, not even to "trim the split ends," which he knew was just her way of trying to get around him.

Edna/Emma lived in Atlanta on some street with the word "Peachtree" in it. Naturally, the bitch couldn't have found a normal street name, one that you could remember. Or find. He took a long, last pull on his cigarette, which had burnt down to the filter, and flicked it out the window at a panhandler. The retard didn't even move out of the way.

It seemed his task might be harder to accomplish than he'd first thought, but Shawn was nothing if not persistent. Fixed on his ultimate goal, there was no way he would deviate from it. He was out to recover what was his, and pity the fool who got in his way. Sutherland had certainly learned that. Shawn had proven it in prison, too. Twice. Once when an old con named Smiley was assigned to share his cell. Smiley wanted the bottom bunk. Shawn's bunk. Said he had bad knees or ankles or something. Like that made a difference. He pissed and moaned so much, the CO made them swap beds.

Smiley died in his sleep the next night. So sad, Shawn thought, laughing. Nobody gave a shit about cons, so nobody bothered to figure out what made old Smiley stop smiling. Or breathing.

Then there was the time some hotshot black

kid stole his smokes. Devontay they called him, and he was some big deal on the outside. Had a gang. Scary. "Devontay, he bad," they said. He stupid, too. And now, he dead. Shawn caught him on the crapper the day after the theft. It was one of those rare opportunities that put two cons in a room without witnesses.

Shawn told a joke, something he'd heard in the yard. They were both laughing right up until Shawn smashed the kid's head against the wall with a plunger. It wasn't a fatal blow, but it stunned him. Then Shawn shoved the handle of the plunger down the little bastard's throat. All the way. It stopped when the rubber part hit his lips. The other end may have poked out his ass, but Shawn wasn't curious enough to check. Bad ol' Devontay survived a couple days but couldn't say who attacked him. It's hard to talk with your mouth full. Shawn laughed at that. Life was funny sometimes. Laughing was good. Shawn liked to laugh.

He would really laugh hard if he could just find old Edna/Emma. There had to be a better way.

~*~

Tori had surprised herself. She'd never flashed anyone in her life. That was the province of boys in junior high, and evidently, young women living alone in the Wyoming boonies. What would her mother think if she knew Tori had just mooned a midget?

Mato didn't look too much the worse for wear because of it. If anything, he might have begun to develop a little erection. She giggled, thinking, what other kind of erection *could* he have? Thank God her momma wasn't here now!

She put her hands on her hips and contemplated the little Indian. Just because he was small didn't mean she could treat him like a toy or a garden statue. He was a human being. And he certainly *acted* like a human, albeit one of the untamed variety. She motioned for him to turn around. She wasn't interested in expanding the floor show for him while she got dressed. He didn't get the idea.

"This isn't some cheap nudie bar, Bucko." She pointed at the opposite wall and pantomimed turning her head. He still didn't get it.

"Look that way," she said, a little more forcefully, then carefully turned his makeshift bedding in a slow circle, which left the cross-legged Indian staring at her over his shoulder.

Tori pointed again, then shaded her eyes in another pantomime. Eventually, he looked away, but he was clearly puzzled by the demand.

The only way she'd gain any privacy was to dress in the bathroom. She gathered up jeans, clean panties, and an Atlanta Braves T-shirt. In a belated second thought, she grabbed a rarely worn bra from the bottom drawer of her dresser—the same drawer where she stored her shotgun shells.

Mato watched her over his shoulder, no doubt wondering why she wanted him to turn his body away from hers. Hadn't she already flashed him? What possible difference could it make if he ogled her while she dressed? Well, she decided, it mattered to her. She had no interest in entertaining Mato's fantasies, or anyone else's for that matter. That sort of crap was firmly in the past where it belonged. Her self-esteem once again restored, Tori threw open the door to the bathroom. And let the cat out.

The animal streaked past her, a silent flash of gray fur which headed for the door, then stopped as suddenly as it had charged. Tail twitching, the cat visibly switched modes from "bail the hell out" to "what's for dinner."

Mato hadn't wasted any time watching the feline. He'd already made a move to high ground and stood on the short counter beside the sink.

The cat began stalking him, moving with graceful, soundless steps. Mato merely watched, expressionless.

Tori opened her mouth to shout at the cat when the little Indian waved her to silence. What did he think he was going to do? The cat weighed at least as much as he did, and probably more. The cat had teeth. And claws. Size, strength and speed were all in the cat's favor, and would have been even if Mato wasn't still recovering from the previous day's attack. He was going to be mauled and eaten unless she intervened.

While Tori was occupied by such practical and reasoned thoughts, the cat leaped up on the chair and in a single, fluid motion continued on toward the counter. Before she could utter a sound, the cat let out a screech that would have scared her shitless if she'd been the target.

The cat's banshee wail ended abruptly in a brief, high-pitched yelp when Mato bashed him on the head with the business end of a wooden serving spoon. The blow not only halted the cat's flight, but reversed it. Mato stood in triumph, looking down at the stunned animal with the handle of the makeshift war club clutched in both hands. The dazed cat moved away slowly, taking an occasional step to the side like a drunk searching for balance.

"Well, damn," Tori said, appraising Mato with new respect. "Nice goin'."

Mato leaned on the spoon and stared down at the cat in triumph, muttering something as it made a wobbly retreat. The Indian looked for all the world like a TV wrestler, demanding to know if that was the best the promoter had to offer.

She would have to keep an eye on the cat in case it sought revenge. But, based on her admittedly limited knowledge of the species, cats rarely made the same mistake twice, especially if the first experience was unpleasant. And Mato had seen to that.

~*~

"Go, lick your wounds, and trouble me no more," Mato said quietly. He waited until the cat left the cabin before he discarded his club. Such animals could never be trusted. As long as he knew this one was around, he would be on guard. It was no mere chance that caused him to climb to the she-giant's workspace to defend himself. He'd thought through the plan long before she opened the door to the room where she'd left the cat. Chance certainly played an important role in the lives of The People, but those who planned ahead lived longer, happier ones.

Mato missed The People, especially Reyna. He wondered if he would ever see her again, or if he merely fooled himself with his crazy dreams of a triumphant return, giant magic in hand.

Tori soon re-entered the main cabin, the outside door of which still stood open. She approached him casually, a look of concern on her face. Reaching a tentative hand toward his bandages, she asked him something. He presumed she was interested in his wounds. He put his hands on his hips, and with legs shoulder-width apart, faced her.

She retrieved her medicine kit, and by gesture, offered to lift him to the table. He declined, making the short hop from counter to chair to table on his own. Tori seemed genuinely surprised by this, though he failed to understand why. He sat cross-legged on the table and waited for her to indicate her intentions. In one hand she held a metal instrument which resembled two flat knives attached in the middle. By spreading the handles, she also spread the blades. Reversing the process brought the blades together. A most cunning arrangement. He allowed her to touch him with the tool, then bent sharply away. She could cut him in half!

She sat back and smiled at him again, then picked up a piece of the thin, gauzy material from the box and held it up for him to see. With one quick movement, she cut the cloth in half. Then she pointed at his bandages.

Mato felt foolish. This woman meant him no harm. If he truly had the heart of a warrior, he wouldn't act like such a baby. He lay back and allowed her to cut away the bandage.

He relished the feeling of the cool air on his bare skin. Looking down, he could see that the scratches were healing nicely. The scabs were thin. Movement was still somewhat restricted, but nothing like it had been the day before.

Tori, however, appeared shocked. She stared at his chest as if something were about to burst out of it. He frowned. What troubled her so? Curling upward from the waist, he crossed his legs and sat upright. She toyed briefly with the contents of her medicine box, then shook her head and put it away. Were all giants so peculiar, he wondered. He was healing like a dreamer—like *all* dreamers—what else did she expect?

~*~

Shawn pulled to a stop in traffic in a part of Atlanta the locals called Buckhead. He had no idea where the name came from. It was pretty much like the rest of the city, if a little trendier. It had the same big buildings, lots of cars, and busses everywhere. Residential streets flourished a couple blocks from the main drag. Mostly big houses.

The pleasant weather seemed to have coaxed half the population out onto the sidewalks. He took a side street to escape the Mother of All Peachtrees, and ended up in still more traffic. He glanced at a building out his side window. A library. Why hadn't he thought of that? Libraries had computers. Better still, they had people who knew how to use them. If cops could use computers to find people, why couldn't he? All he had to do was find a place to park.

Life would've been so much easier if Edna/Emma had lived in some little out of the way place, like the one where Sutherland had his A-frame. He wouldn't have needed a freakin' library or a computer to track her down in a place like that. He could just pop into a gas station and ask somebody. A small town had been plenty good enough for him and Vicky Lynn. He hated cities. Except for the strip clubs. Those were pretty nice, and Atlanta had a bunch of 'em.

He wondered how Vicky Lynn would have done working as a stripper. She was pretty enough. Had great legs, too. Most strippers seemed to have big tits, which would've put Vicky Lynn at a little disadvantage. Shawn wasn't a big boob man himself. They were okay, but a woman needed more than a monster rack to get his attention. As he pulled into a parking lot and handed the attendant a five-dollar bill he'd taken from Sutherland's wallet, Shawn decided he wouldn't have let Vicky Lynn dance naked in front of anyone but him. There was no reason to share. None at all. In fact, he decided he'd get her to dance for him as soon as he tracked her down. They had an awful lot of catchin' up to do. And the sooner he got to Edna/Emma, the sooner he'd know where to look for Vicky Lynn.

He wondered if she still had the crotchless panties he'd given her for Christmas way back when. She was always funny about wearing 'em. He never could quite understand that girl.

~*~

Tori sat at her computer, struggling to concentrate. Mato didn't help. He managed to stay relatively quiet while poking around the cabin, but would occasionally mutter something or voice surprise when an object didn't behave as expected. Tori's attention bounced between thoughts of Mato's amazing recuperative ability and the possibility that he'd kill himself digging through her stuff.

"Why don't you go outside and beat up the cat or something?" she suggested.

He gave her his ultra-macho, inscrutable Indian look, and went back to deconstructing her stereo.

Finally, Tori admitted defeat. There would be no progress until she resolved the Mato issue.

Fortunately, she was ahead of schedule on her current project, a sequel to the novel she'd sold two years previously.

The book had garnered great reviews and flirted briefly with a couple Bestseller lists. Her contract required her to produce another book, and she'd jumped into the work as soon as she'd gotten settled in her new home. That had taken far longer than anticipated. Notoriety made it more difficult to disappear, not that anyone in Charm had ever heard of her, or her book. She wasn't worried about them anyway; they were the people of her future. The ones she wanted to avoid were from her past.

Mato located the knob that controlled the base on Tori's amplifier and demonstrated his preference for beat over harmony. Then he found the one marked "Volume." Tori leaped to his side and commandeered the controls. After restoring the base and volume to levels that wouldn't damage their hearing, she attempted to show him what each of the knobs did. Mato, however, preferred the discovery method and wasn't shy about it.

It dawned on her that he was very much like a child when it came to exploring her cabin. That made sense, especially if the technology of his world ranked well below the Pez dispenser level.

Who on Earth was that sadly backward? She recalled as a child reading about a primitive tribe on a remote island. Near Indonesia? She couldn't remember. There had been a huge flap about whether missionaries should be allowed to contact them. At the time, she couldn't understand why there was an argument at all. Those people were running around naked. They mostly died young. And toothless. The children were filthy, and the adults went to great lengths to mutilate themselves. She shuddered just thinking about it.

No books? No music? No advertising. Well. Maybe it wasn't all bad.

She looked at Mato, testing various sound styles on her amplifier: stadium, theater, in-home, etc. She wondered what he would make of the treble knob, though it would certainly be anti-climactic after his encounter with volume.

Abandoning all thought of working on the book, Tori went to shake out Mato's bedding. When she lifted the folded blanket, she revealed the sketch he'd done the night before. Though slightly smeared, the few simple lines he'd drawn offered a remarkable rendering of her cat. She looked at him with newfound respect. Why hadn't she noticed it before?

"Mato?"

He looked at her, and she pointed to his drawing. Frowning, he joined her at the fireplace.

"This is really quite good," she said, knowing he wouldn't understand her words, but hoping he'd pick up on her positive tone.

Instead, he retrieved the dish rag from the sink. She halted him before he could get down on hands and knees to clean the floor. Laughing, she took the damp cloth from him and tossed it back on the counter. She then pulled a few sheets of paper from the printer beside her computer. Wishing she also had a box of crayons to give him, Tori put the paper on the floor and pretended to draw on it.

Mato inspected the paper, held it up to the light, and sniffed it. He smiled back at her. Then, just as he had done the previous evening, he stuck his hand in the cold ashes of the fireplace and withdrew a partially burnt stick. This he used to make another drawing of the cat. As she stared in wonder, he sketched the animal in motion. Two converging lines became a leg; another became the tail. Ears, eyes, whiskers—all grew from mere suggestions of lines. Her mind filled in what Mato left out, and the final result captivated her. He was an artistic genius. People studied for years to be able to produce such quality. She wanted to hug him. If only she had some real art supplies! She tried to imagine what he might be able to accomplish with paints and brushes. Where could she find some? In Charm? She doubted it. More than likely she would have to drive to Ten Sleep, a significantly larger community. The drive there and back would take over an hour.

But, what the hell, she didn't have anything else to do.

"Hey, Mato. You up for a little road trip?"

~*~

The librarian treated Shawn as if he had the plague. Shawn knew the type well. Timid little assholes who assumed that since they got a paycheck, they were somehow superior to everyone else. Nothing could have been further from the truth, especially for the joker staring at him now.

"I'm sorry," the 20-something librarian said, blinking steadily behind a pair of granny glasses. His name tag proclaimed him *Morris, Assistant Librarian*. "I don't have time to show you how to do a search for an individual. If you had a full name or an E-mail address...."

"I already told you I only know her last name and part of her address. Her first name is—"

"Edna or Emma. Right. I got that," Morris said. "Why don't you just google her? Something's liable to turn up."

"*Google* her?" That sounded... interesting.

The librarian frowned at him, a look so insulting and dismissive Shawn was tempted to kill him right there. Maybe strangle him with his pony tail. Maybe shove the keyboard up his ass. That'd do it. But there were too many people around, and Shawn knew better than to attract attention.

"Wait here a second," Morris said. He minced away in a flurry of tiny, silent footsteps.

Shawn glared at the computer screen. Google my ass, he thought. He wouldn't mind googling the assistant librarian, right between the eyes. Or—

"Here," Morris said, appearing from behind a bookcase. He handed Shawn a thick, paperback manual. "You should be able to find everything you need in here. I gotta go."

He walked away as Shawn looked at the book, his anger barely in check. The title read: *Idiot's Guide to the Internet.*

"Can I help you?" asked a young woman who appeared at the computer next to his. She looked to be about the same age as Morris, but it was hard to tell with chubby girls like this one. She certainly smelled good. Vanilla, he thought.

"That'd be great. I'm not— I don't know much about computers."

"No problem," she said. "Morris can be a little prickly."

Prickly? Well, she got it mostly right. "Yeah, I noticed."

She stuck her hand at him. "I'm Daphne."

"Shawn," he responded.

"So, what is it you want to do?"

Amazed by his good fortune, Shawn summoned his most charming smile. "I'm trying to find an old friend. I've been, uhm, overseas for a long time, and she moved away. Her mother still lives around here, though. She's the one I'm trying to find. I think she can tell me how to find my friend."

"What's her name?"

"Edna Pruett. Or Emma Pruett. I only met her once, and my memory isn't all that great."

Daphne typed while Shawn talked. Several

screens went by so fast he couldn't pick out any details, much less follow what she was doing. "I can't keep up," he said. "Maybe—"

"Oh, don't worry," Daphne said. "It's no big deal. I'm just— Wait. When I get to a useful page, I'll stop. I promise. You can take all the time you need."

"Good," he said, wondering if it was.

"Do you know what she looks like? Maybe we could find her on social media."

Shawn tried not to look at her as if she'd just stepped out of a spaceship. "I might recognize her. I dunno. It's been a pretty long time."

Daphne brought up a page full of small images, one of which featured a naked female.

"Oops!" Daphne laughed as she zipped the pointer around the screen, pulling menus out of thin air and clicking options faster than he could read them. "Sorry 'bout that. Somebody turned off the 'Safe Search' mode."

"Uh, right."

"It's no problem. I fixed it."

"Good."

"Little kids use these machines, too. Can't have them pulling up dirty pictures!"

Shawn wondered why that would be such a bad thing. Kids were going to be exposed to stuff sooner or later. Who cared?

"Okay," Daphne said, "do any of these folks

look familiar?"

They went through several screens before he saw a face he vaguely recognized. "Stop." He tapped the photo on the screen.

Daphne worked her magic and eventually produced a larger version of the photo he'd spotted. "Is that who you're looking for?"

The woman's name was Emaline Pruett, and she was pictured on a page with several of her aging siblings.

"Yeah," he said. "I think it is." How had she found the old broad so fast? "Does it give her address or phone number?"

They both read through the page, but Daphne was by far the faster reader. "No," she said.

"Damn."

"At least we have the correct name," she said. "We can work from here."

Within minutes, Daphne had located Emaline Pruett's address and E-mail information. "If I had more time and was willing to spend the money, I could probably dig up lots of stuff on her."

"Like what?"

"Oh, you know—credit report, public records, stuff like that."

"You're kidding, right?"

She shook her head. "You'd be amazed how much information is out there. And most folks don't have any clue how easy it is to get."

Shawn gave her a sly smile. "You're not a crook, are you?"

"Do I look like a crook?" she asked, genuinely amused.

"You look like someone who could use a drink," he said. "My treat."

She overcame the temptation, but he sensed it was a struggle for her. "I'd better not; I've got stuff to do."

Slinging the strap of her oversized purse on her shoulder, Daphne smiled at him and walked away. She stopped briefly to look at a book lying on a display table near the door, then made her way to the exit.

Shawn pocketed Emaline's address, then followed the same route Daphne had just taken. He even glanced down at the book that captured her interest. The title also captured his interest. **Uncle Bob—Memoir of a Rebel**. It couldn't be, he thought. *Uncle freakin' Bob*? He grabbed the book off the table and examined it. On the inside back cover he found a photo of Vicky Lynn! He was certain of it. Only she didn't call herself that. The author's name was Tori Lanier.

But she couldn't fool him. Even with short hair. He'd know that lying, faithless bitch anywhere.

Chapter Four
Missions

Mato followed Tori out of the cabin. Sunrise had long since come and gone, but the air was still cool, the sky cloudless. Tori had put on extra clothing, but Mato had nothing more to add than his vest. He was satisfied with that, but the she-giant tried to wrap him in a heavy cloth, pinning his arms at his sides. How would that help if her stupid cat tried to attack him again? She seemed disappointed when he shrugged out of the material and let it slide to the floor.

She took long strides away from the cabin, which he was unable to match. But rather than run to keep up with her, he moved at a sedate pace, which also gave him time to evaluate his options, since he had no idea what she was up to.

The woman stopped beside an enormous machine and reached for some sort of handle. When she pulled on it, a door opened in the side. Mato crept closer for a better look, while Tori walked around to the far side and opened yet another door. Mato could see through the two open doors to the woman. He watched as she climbed in and sat behind a large black wheel, which was angled slightly away from her. She gripped the wheel with one hand and gestured for him to join her. Mato stepped closer. But as he prepared to climb up and sit beside her, she did something which made the machine growl like a great mountain cat. He leapt backwards, away from the danger, and landed on his feet.

Tori put her hand to her mouth and looked very surprised. She said something to him, but he was quickly learning to ignore her. In many ways, she acted much like Reyna—so emotional, and at times so... irrational. When she gestured to him again, he turned away from her and headed back to the cabin. He was content to practice with the music magic. He had watched her insert the shiny discs which held the captured sound. And there were so many, many discs to examine.

~*~

"Well," Tori said, watching Mato stomp away from her and go back to the cabin. "Just... shit." She cut the engine and sat back in the seat of her cramped, two-door Nissan pickup. Maybe it was better she didn't take her guest into town right away. How might the citizens of downtown Charm react? Or, if she ignored them and drove on to Ten

Sleep, would the reaction be any different? Better? Worse? Ten Sleep wasn't exactly a cosmopolitan metropolis like Atlanta or New York, but then, folks there, too, would likely freak out if she popped into a store with Mato at her heel.

What, after all, did she know about him? He was an Indian, there was no doubt of that, but at two feet tall, he wasn't exactly cut from the same cloth as the native Americans she'd met thus far in Wyoming, or anywhere else for that matter. She stepped out of the truck and walked to the edge of the bluff to clear her head.

The internet had yielded tidbits—stories of small-statured folk who either helped or tormented the local Indian populations, depending on which source one listened to. Various tribes had legends, like the Cherokee, Choctaw, Yakima and Mohegan, but all sounded about as believable as the Irish tales of Darby O'Gill. Even William Clark—of the famed Lewis and Clark expedition—had journaled that the Sioux and other plains tribes were wary of 18-inch-tall warriors with "large heads," very sharp arrows, and a perpetually pissy disposition. Not exactly an accurate description of Mato, but who was she to say if his people had toned down their attitude in the intervening 200 years?

She got back in the truck and cranked the engine, convinced that Mato had made the right decision for her. She needed to know a great deal more about him before she mentioned to anyone that he even existed. It seemed particularly odd that

Uncle Bob, her long-dead benefactor, had never mentioned little Indians in his journal. A keen observer of his surroundings, Robert Lanier would surely have known about them if anyone did. Shifting into first gear, Tori let the clutch out and roared away from the cabin. The dirt road that connected her to civilization was a good ten miles long. With any luck, the recent rains hadn't completely washed it away where it crossed the seasonal streams and run-off beds that crisscrossed her valley.

Robert Lanier, a former officer in Robert E. Lee's Army of Northern Virginia, had migrated to Wyoming after the "unpleasantness." Though the current mining operations in the "Equality State" consisted of mostly coal and uranium, Lanier was interested in gold and silver. Years of searching yielded nothing shiny. According to his notes, however, he found something more valuable. Sadly, he never actually said what it was, but his discovery had been made while he lived in the very cabin Tori now occupied.

Her move to the remote vastness of north central Wyoming had been prompted partly by greed and partly by self-preservation. The only person who knew where she was living was her editor, and Tori had sworn her to secrecy. That was a story in itself.

Clearly, Cassy Woodall didn't put much stock in the oath. That's when Tori showed her the scars her loving hubby had left her before the State of

Georgia arranged to feed and house him for ten years; slightly less if he behaved himself.

Tori thought back to the scene in a posh Manhattan restaurant. It had been a long day, capped by a pitcher of margaritas. Cassy had paced herself, but Tori had felt no such compunction. The book was done; her advance was in the bank; her ex was behind bars, and life was sweet. Tori, at long last feeling safe enough to relax, got snockered. And when Cassy pressed her about the need for secrecy, Tori swiveled in her seat and pulled her blouse over her head, revealing Shawn's handiwork.

A nearby waitress had rushed forward to restore order, but Tori's objective had been accomplished. She put her blouse back on. When she once again turned to face her editor, the woman's face was ashen.

"Your *husband* did that?" she asked, her voice a whisper.

"Yeah. Cute, huh?"

Cassy merely shook her head, her hand still hovering near her mouth.

"Why, for God's sake?"

"He claimed I disrespected him. That I said things no woman was allowed to say to her man."

Cassy was shaking her head. "Like what?"

"I told him no."

"No?"

"He wanted sex," Tori said. "I didn't." She poured herself another margarita. "He used a belt to make me change my mind."

"What did you do?"

"Aside from bleeding? I cried. And I waited. I doubt I looked real sexy. Eventually, he got tired and left. I called 911."

"They arrested him, I hope."

Tori nodded. "Oh, yeah. And was he ever pissed. The guys who cuffed him weren't very gentle about it. Said he was resisting arrest, which he was. Got his head smacked into the roof of the squad car when they helped him into the back seat. Big bump; no blood. What an asshole. Seeing some of his blood would've made me feel better, if I hadn't been in so much pain myself."

"You pressed charges, I hope."

"Damn skippy! I wanted him shot. Or hung. Castrated at the very least."

"I'm sorry, Tori," Cassy said. "I had no idea."

"He's going to be up for parole one of these days," Tori said, "and he'll get out. He can be a real charmer. When that happens, I don't want him to be able to find me."

Cassy promised she'd never reveal Tori's secret. But somehow, that pledge didn't apply to the marketing department which designed the cover of Tori's book. They were only too happy to feature her face on the jacket.

The truck took a savage lurch as the front tires caught in a deep rut, nearly tearing the wheel from her hands. Tori concentrated on the dirt road. If Shawn ever discovered her cabin, he'd have to break the door in and work his way past the shotgun. Tori smiled the way she imagined the grim reaper might. She had no problem with the idea of burying Shawn way out here, although leaving him for the coyotes appealed to her more.

Not for the first time she wondered about getting a dog. She'd never owned one, even as a little girl, and had reservations. On the other hand, she'd known lots of people who did own them, and they all seemed like normal folk. Shawn didn't like dogs, and that was almost reason enough to get one. What would Mato think if she brought a dog home? Maybe a little one? She grinned thinking what Shawn would say. "Bull shit," she exclaimed. If she was going to get a dog, she wanted a *real* dog—a serious dog, something on the order of Cerberus.

In the ensuing quiet, she heard something moving in the narrow space behind the passenger seat. She quickly pulled to a stop and leaped out of the truck. Snakes had been known to sneak into vehicles, she'd heard, and she had no intention of sharing her ride with a sidewinder. Whatever it was moved again, the sound barely audible. It was still behind the seat. Tori searched for something she could use as a weapon. A handgun would've helped, but she didn't own one. She picked up a fist-sized rock. The rough edges ground into her fingers as she tightened her grip. Toeing the door open as wide as it would go, she raised her arm, ready to crush the life out of whatever had crawled into her vehicle.

~*~

"Hey, Miz Pruett. 'Member me?"

The woman stared at him through a screen door on her front porch. The building was as old as she was, and in about the same state of disrepair. If Vicky Lynn made much money off her book, Shawn thought, she sure as hell wasn't sharin' it with her momma.

"I know you," the woman said, then coughed. "Go 'way."

"That any way to talk to your son-in-law?" Shawn asked. "It's been years. You should be glad to see me."

"I'll be glad to see you leave," the old lady said. "We ain't related anymore."

Shawn held up his left hand and pointed to the thin gold wedding band he still wore. "I never took it off."

"Well, Vicky didn't have that problem. Hers came off easy. Now, you go on. Get outta here." She started to close the inner door, but Shawn moved faster than she could. He yanked open the screen and shoved his foot into the opening. Emaline Pruett tried to slam the door on him, but the cheap, hollow-core door bounced off his shoe. He pushed his way into the room beyond.

Mrs. Pruett backed away from him with her

hand on her chest, as if he might try to tear her ugly, pink bathrobe off and rape her. The thought almost made him puke. Emaline Pruett hadn't improved since the last time he'd seen her. Between the cigarettes and whatever she had been drinking, she'd aged about thirty years while he'd only given up ten.

"I need to find her," he said.

"I do, too," she responded.

"Where's she livin'?"

"Beats hell outta me," the old woman said. She stuck a cigarette in her mouth and used two hands to hold her lighter steady. Shawn helped himself to her smokes, lighting one, then pocketing the rest of the pack.

"She give you a phone number?"

"She calls every now and again, but it's from a cell phone. She could be any damn place."

Shawn let that sink in.

Mrs. Pruett reached toward him and retrieved her cigarettes. "You're old enough to buy yer own. I don't owe you nuthin'."

"Does she ever write? Send you a card?"

The old woman fixed him with a pale, watery eye. "Did she ever write to you?"

"No."

"Me, neither. 'Course, I wasn't sittin' in jail."

"That's all behind me," Shawn said. "I just have a couple scores to settle, and then—"

"Then it's not all behind you." She dropped into an overstuffed chair partially covered by a flowered sheet. There was little light in the room, but Shawn could see well enough. Mrs. Pruett was not living in the lap of luxury.

"You got a copy of her book?"

"Nah, but I've seen it. They wanted twenty-sumpthin dollars for it. For a damn book. Can you imagine?"

He shook his head. "No ma'am. That's crazy." He paused and looked at her, trying to see if she'd gone shifty-eyed, like she was trying to hide something. "Doesn't it make you a little mad?"

She squinted at him. "Doesn't what make me mad?"

"Her book. The whole Uncle Bob thing. You were closer to him than she was."

The old lady took a long drag, then let it out slowly. "I looked at his journal. Some kinda dang code. Didn't make any sense to me, but Vicky Lynn... She always thought she could figure it out, and she did. You think that makes me stupid?"

"Just 'cause you couldn't figure it out? No way. It didn't make any sense to me, neither."

She stubbed out her cigarette in an ashtray already full to overflowing with squashed and twisted butts. "Guess we're both stupid."

"She should have shared it with you. And me, too. I'm family."

"Hold on," she said, rambling around in a drawer in a little table beside her chair. "Oh, good. Still got it."

"Got what?"

"This," she said, pointing an ancient derringer at him. She pulled the hammer back and aimed it at the center of his chest. "This belonged to Uncle Bob, too. Called it his 'boot gun.'"

"That thing's more likely to blow up in your hand than actually work," Shawn said, no trace of pleasantness lingering in his voice.

"I'll take that chance," she said. "Will you?"

Shawn was already backing away, hands extended, as if he could deflect any bullets that might come his way. "There's no need for that."

"Really? I told you to go away. You ignored me. I told you we ain't related anymore. But you're still wearin' a wedding ring. Seems to me you don't know how to take a hint." She wiggled the gun at him. "I'll tell the cops you forced your way in, which as I recall, is exactly what you did. They'll drag your sorry dead ass outta here, and I'll never hear another word about it. Then, when Vicky Lynn calls, I'll tell her she can come home, 'cause you'll be dead as roadkill."

"I don't believe you've got the brass to pull that trigger," Shawn said. "But if you do, you'd better

A Little Primitive

kill me. Otherwise, I'm gonna make sure you don't live to piss off anyone else in this world."

She was holding the little gun with both hands. The barrel wavered, but significantly less than her lighter had a few moments earlier. "Get out. I won't tell you again."

"You're makin' a big mistake."

"Not half as big as the one you'll make if you don't get outta here," she said.

Shawn left.

Imagine that, he thought once he'd gotten back into his—or rather, Mrs. Sutherland's—car. There's a little spine in that girl's family after all. He doubted he could get any useful information out of the old lady, even if he beat her half to death. Besides, she hadn't taken anything that belonged to him. She was just ornery. Stubborn. And now he knew where Vicky Lynn got her own mean streak.

There had to be someone who knew where she was. He just had to figure out who.

~*~

Mato began to suspect there were drawbacks to the magic the giants had harnessed. He had listened to several of the shiny silver discs that Tori had available. It was impossible to tell by looking at them whether the music was good or not. Some of it was bad enough to frighten the Spirits, he thought. But then, why would the Spirits allow such to be captured in the first place? It made little sense.

He had mastered the control which made the sound louder and discovered that some music sounded better when played softly. Not all of it, by any means, but a significant portion. He had also learned that by touching a couple of other controls, he could summon voices. They did not speak the language of The People, and therefore were probably giants just like Tori. The more he listened, the more he wished he knew what they were saying. It must be important, for the voices never stopped. Some never even paused to breathe.

When the leaders of The People spoke, everyone listened, for in most cases what the leaders said made sense. But it was a rare man who could start talking and not stop. Females often did that, but it was unusual when one of them was elected to lead. Reyna was a good example. Strong and cunning, she knew the world as well as he, and was often more comfortable out in it. She would be a good mother someday, and if he had his way, she would bear his sons and daughters. He would teach them the ways of the giants and share the magic he would steal. If only, he thought, he could figure out how to do it.

Tori's music machine weighed as much as he did and was bulky besides. He would need a stout cart to pull it. And there was other magic he would need, too. He had found a tail coming out of the machine. It was much thinner than a snake but easily as long, and it ended in a head with two dull teeth. The teeth attached to a pair of openings in the cabin wall. The machine would make music only when the snake was putting its venom in the wall. When Mato yanked it free, the magic fled. It would take some clever work to bring the part of the wall the snake needed.

There were many machines in the she-giant's cabin. Another he found particularly interesting was the one in which Tori kept her food. It had a thick, white door with a long handle. He had seen her open it many times. He was able to open it himself and was shocked to discover how cold it was inside. He looked for ice and snow, but there was no trace of it. The variety of containers inside the box was likewise astonishing. So many colors! There were good smells and bad. He tried to separate the things which smelled good from those that didn't. He couldn't imagine why Tori would want to keep anything that didn't smell good. She could become ill if she ate some of the bad things.

He dragged several of the spoiled items to the fireplace and threw them in. The fire had long since died, but there was wood stacked beside the fire pit, and Mato had been making fire since he was a child. *That* was magic he already controlled. He hoped Tori would be pleased when she returned.

~*~

"Come outta there, you slimy bastard," Tori said, her voice low and growly. "I'll make you a deal. You come out peacefully, and I'll let you live. You can just crawl away into the sunset, and I'll go on my way. How's that sound?"

The cat stuck its head up from behind the

seat and looked at her as if she'd lost her mind.

"Oh, for cryin' out loud. What are *you* doin' there?"

The cat hooked four sets of claws in the Nissan's upholstery and dragged himself into the front seat.

"Are you trying to tell me you aren't keen on our houseguest?"

The cat curled itself into a ball on the passenger seat. It spoke not a word.

Tori re-entered the truck and put on her seat belt. "It's likely to be a rough ride," she said, "and I'm putting you on official notice. You might not be making the trip back with me. I've decided to upgrade my security, 'cause basically, you aren't cuttin' it. I'll admit you've bagged a mouse or two. Maybe more. But you also attacked Mato, and I'm just not down with that at all. You hear me, cat?"

The tip of the cat's tail moved in a short up and down path, but otherwise the animal remained stationary.

"I mean it," she said. "You better hope they have a nice animal shelter in Ten Sleep, or you could find yourself campin' out real soon."

~*~

Shawn figured he had two options: he could either return to the library or find a bookstore. He chose the library. Not only because he knew where it was, but because he didn't want to waste his money on Vicky Lynn's book.

He filled out an application for a library card, making up most of the information as he went. He used Emaline Pruett's address. What surprised him most was how eager they were to let him take books out of the library. His very first selection, of course, was Vicky Lynn's book about Uncle Bob. As soon as he got to the car he examined it more thoroughly than any publication he'd ever had his hands on, including some first rate girlie mags he'd stolen as a teenager.

Sadly, the book jacket said nothing about where she was living. The picture was pretty good, he had to admit. Obviously done by a professional. Even the short hair didn't bother him too much. That could always be fixed.

Maybe he could contact the publisher, he thought. Pretend to be a fan. He concentrated on the first few pages where he located not only the publisher's name and address, but the name of an editor, too. Bingo! Hello, Vicky Lynn. It wouldn't be long now.

~*~

Mato was hungry. Burning the bad foods had caused him to develop an appetite. Unfortunately, there wasn't much left in Tori's food storage box that interested him. He found some of the yellow stuff she had cooked with his egg and broke off a big handful. He chewed on it, but found it dry and unsatisfying. It definitely tasted better with the egg. Perhaps it shouldn't be eaten raw. The fire he'd started had already burned down to coals, perfect for cooking.

Using a metal tool consisting of a long, wide handle which flared at the business end into three points, Mato mounted two pieces of the yellow stuff. He then propped the makeshift skewer over the coals and waited. The yellow stuff soon lost its shape, the edges becoming soft and bubbly.

He pulled the food from the fire before it could dissolve completely, then gingerly touched the mass to see if it was too hot to eat. The stuff stuck to his fingers and stretched in long, gooey strings which sagged as he pulled away. He put one end of it in his mouth and started eating. Though hotter than he liked, it tasted just as good as it had when blended with the egg. He couldn't remember what she called it. But then, sometimes it was better not to know the true name of something magical. If this was something the she-giant had conjured from smoke and who-knew-what—perhaps bird droppings or something equally offensive—he would be better off not knowing its name. He wasn't too concerned, however, since anything that tasted so delicious had to come from something good.

He ate more of the yellow stuff, and followed that with an odd kind of bread he found in a cabinet. He knew it was wrapped in something, because light reflected off the surface. What puzzled him was the fact that he could see *through* the wrapping as if it wasn't there. Lightweight, but stiff, the stuff made a crackling noise when he put pressure on it. He found a knife small enough for him to wield and used it to cut through the mysterious wrapping. Inside were thin, flat pieces of a bread-like substance. With a little effort, he managed to break off a corner and chew on it. Dry, but flavorful. It went well with the yellow stuff.

At breakfast, the she-giant had produced water from a pipe which stuck out over a large square bowl built into her workspace. The pipe was flanked by a handle on each side, and he remembered she had pushed one or the other to release the water trapped in the pipe.

Stepping down into the great flat-bottomed, metal bowl, he put both hands on the lever to the right of the pipe and pushed. Nothing happened. He tried again, straining to force the metal handle away. It wouldn't budge. Until he pulled it.

Suddenly, water poured from the pipe, soaking him from the waist down.

He saw the container Tori had used to serve him when they broke their fast. Using his foot, he shoved it under the falling water and allowed it to fill, then turned the water off. There was no magic involved, he thought. Or at least, not a great deal of magic.

Having eaten his fill, he stood by the fire pit and removed his wet breechcloth. This he spread before the coals to dry, then lay on his back with his hands behind his head. He had much to consider. Not the least of which was his original mission.

The People had sent him to seek their future in a vision. This he must do in the cavern of dreams, the most holy of all sacred places. In the distant past, The People often sent young warriors there to battle with the demons who guarded the future. Many who went there never returned, and while it was tempting to make up stories of their bravery, no one really knew what happened to them. Sleeping Dove, Mato's grandmother many times past, had been the last of The People to go there and return. But she went on a second journey and never came back. The secret of how to reach the cavern died with her.

In the years since, The People had become desperate. Their numbers dwindled as animals and sickness caused more deaths than births. There was food aplenty if one knew where to look, but without new mouths to feed, what was the point of having it? He wanted very much to father children, and had always assumed that he and Reyna would be able to raise many. He was eager to get started, and had been for a long time. But her father, first among the elders, said no. No one who was unproven would discover Reyna's maidenly secrets. Nor was Mato the only one thus challenged.

But Mato had an edge. Winter Woman said he had a dreamer's blood running in his veins. "Go, and find the cavern of dreams," Reyna's father had said. "Sleep there and see the future, then return and bring the news for everyone to hear." Mato and two others left the same day. They traveled in different directions, for there were mountains on all sides. Each of them had visited Reyna and received her blessing, although Mato felt sure she wanted him to succeed the most.

He struggled with the thought that he cared more for Reyna than The People. He would find the cavern. He would conquer the demons. He would have the vision. He would take her for his mate. He would succeed in all these things, and more! If... If only he knew where to start looking.

Chapter Five
Trailheads

Tori's back, butt, and shoulders were sore from bouncing over the ruts in the road leading to civilization. It wasn't that the seat in her truck was lousy; it's that it wasn't designed for the nightmarish washboard her "driveway" had turned into. With every jarring lurch, the cat gave her a look of pure hatred, and more often than not added a short snarl for emphasis.

"If I paved it, people might drive on it," Tori said. She had become quite accustomed to having conversations with herself. "What would that prove? That I'm stupid, 'cause it would cost a freakin' fortune to pave this, and last time I checked the government wasn't handin' out grants for driveways." She snorted. "And that's with a *democrat* in the White House."

The oil pan made an audible clang as the

wheels thumped through another depression. Tori was feeling a little depressed herself when the paved county road finally appeared in the distance. "Yes!" she cried. *There is hope, after all.*

With a spray of dusty gravel, she swung the Nissan Frontier onto the paved road and jammed the accelerator to the floor. "Hang on, cat, we're goin' to town!"

A half hour later, Tori began to rethink her priorities. Ten Sleep was over an hour away, and while she was all but certain it had a library and some sort of store where she could find art supplies, she might be jumping the gun just a little bit. She wasn't made of money after all, and she didn't know beans about Mato. Not really. Plus, she had other priorities, not the least of which was making sure Shawn wouldn't come nosing around. His ten-year stretch as a guest of the Georgia Department of Corrections should be up. According to what the assistant DA had told her in a letter two years earlier, Shawn was most likely a free man, and had been for the better part of a month.

No, there was no need to drive all the way to Ten Sleep. Greater metropolitan Charm—population 13 at last count—was the better choice. She could pop in on Caleb Jones, buy some beer, and make a little small talk. She smiled. It'd be nice to chat with someone who could chat back.

~*~

"That's right," Shawn said, "Cassandra Woodall. She's an editor. Tori—"

"One moment, please," the woman on the other end of the line said. "I'll see if she's in."

The phone clicked twice before the elevator music kicked in. Shawn screwed up his lips in a snarl of exasperation. The music alone was enough to make him want to kill somebody. *What kind of moron would—*

"I'm sorry. Ms. Woodall is not available. Would you like to leave a message?"

"Where is she?"

"*Un*available," the woman repeated, a little more forcefully than Shawn expected.

"Well, tell her this is an emergency. The mother of one of her clients was badly injured in an automobile accident. She may not survive. She's been calling for her daughter, Tori Lanier, but nobody knows how to reach her." Shawn grinned at his own ingenuity, then forced himself to be serious. He couldn't afford for anyone to suspect he was playing them.

The woman sounded suddenly contrite. "Oh! I had no idea. I'm so sorry to hear that. I'm sure Ms. Woodall will return your call as soon as possible. May I have your name and number please?"

"This is detective uhm, Sutherland," Shawn said. "Pete Sutherland." He gave her the number of the disposable cell phone he'd purchased a scant hour before he placed the call to Vicky Lynn's publisher. "Please tell her it's urgent that she contact me."

"I certainly will," the woman said.

"Thanks." Shawn ended the call with the stab of his thumb to a little red button on a plastic package of wires and transistors. The world had changed a great deal during the ten years he'd wasted in prison. *Thank you, Vicky Lynn Donlevy.* The bitch had a lot to apologize for. A lot of makin' up to do. A whole lot.

He checked Peter Sutherland's wallet to see how much money he had left. At just over $200, he didn't have nearly enough. What if he had to buy an airline ticket? No, he told himself. Flying would be stupidly expensive, and from what he'd heard, security had gotten crazy. Bus fare was more like it. He had learned to sit quietly for long periods of time. Surely he could do it with a nice window to look out of. Still, $200 was way less than he needed. Suddenly, he had an inspiration. What if Sutherland had a safe in his house? Macon was only a couple hours' drive, and he knew the address. Best of all, there wouldn't be anybody home. If he couldn't find a safe or any more cash lyin' around, he could surely find something worth pawning. Ol' Pete had been pretty well fixed. The least he could do was make Shawn's life a little easier.

He climbed into the ugly, yellow Chevy. *Macon, here we come. Again!*

~*~

Caleb Jones had the weather-beaten face of a cowboy and the voice of a radio announcer. He smiled at Tori as she entered his store and plunked herself down in one of the four wooden chairs surrounding a pot-belly stove in the center of the building. "Well, look here now. What've we got in the store today?"

Tori stretched, clearly conscious of Caleb's eyes on her tight jeans. "I think I'm goin' nuts, Cal," she said. "Haven't had anyone to talk to in ages."

"I told you livin' alone wouldn't be easy."

"No shit." She shifted a bit, then grabbed a cushion from another chair and slipped it under her tender bottom. "That's better."

He chuckled. "Can I get ya anything? Coke? Beer?"

"I'll grab a couple things before I leave. Right now, I just want to rest my bones a bit."

Caleb stepped from behind the counter near the front door and joined her. His chair creaked slightly as he lowered his whipcord body into it. She had no idea how old he was. Somewhere between late 30s and early 50s. Hard to tell. He had thick eyebrows and deep wrinkles around his eyes and mouth—laugh lines. Caleb was good people. She knew that the day she met him.

"You know anybody with a good dog to sell?"

He laughed. "Who'd sell a good dog?" He rested his heels on the cold stove. "I thought you had a cat."

"I do. He's in the truck. It's just... He isn't workin' out."

Caleb nodded like an old sage. "Y'know, a good ratter can outwork a cat any day."

"A ratter?"

"Yeah. A dog that chases rats. Hell, they'll go after most anything that's smaller than they are. I knew a feller once—"

"I need a dog that's okay around... kids."

"Kids?" He gave her a puzzled look. "You got kids now?"

"No, no, 'course not. Someday, maybe. *Hopefully!* But not now."

Caleb shrugged. "I ain't the kind of guy to pry into a lady's business."

She punched him lightly. "I know that. It's just... There's a chance I may have to entertain someone. Someone... childlike. I'd like to have a dog; I really would, but I'd have to know it wouldn't cause trouble. Wouldn't go after a kid, f'rinstance. Know what I mean?"

"Sounds to me like you want a puppy."

The thought appealed to her instantly. "A puppy."

"Yep. Sure you don't want anything?" He walked to a coffee pot that occupied an ancient hot plate on a desk. The contents looked as dark as ink, and probably tasted like it.

"You gonna drink that or put it in your fountain pen?"

He looked at her with a straight face for a full five seconds, then broke into a broad smile that showed off his brilliant, white, artificial teeth.

"Okay then, do you know anyone with puppies they'd like to get rid of?"

Caleb rubbed his jaw and concentrated. "There's an animal shelter over in Buffalo."

"Swell. That's way on the other side of the Bighorn."

"Yeah. So? That's only an hour or two, three if you're pokey. You drivin' or ridin'?"

"I've got my truck," Tori said.

"Well then. There y'are. Go get a puppy. But be sure and bring him by. I'd like to see what you pick out."

She looked at him closely. "You're serious."

"Hell yes, I'm serious." He smiled. "Why wouldn't I be?"

"I was hopin' someone around here might have something. Buffalo? That's in the wrong direction. I'd planned to get home before dark. You know that road to my place is a real bi—"

He always looked surprised whenever she swore.

"The rain tore it up pretty bad."

He reached into his pocket and pulled out a cell phone. After a few thumb stabs, he put the device to his ear, then waited. Moments later, he perked up. "Maggie? Cal. You got a minute?"

~*~

Though he might never have thought it possible, Mato eventually tired of the she-giant's music. Those with voices used words he could not understand, though they were often exceedingly different from the words Tori used. He had never considered the possibility that there were more than two languages: that of The People, and that of the giants.

As a child he heard the stories the old ones told, about white giants and red giants, and about how they fought constantly. The red giants were more like The People they said. The white giants came from far away and brought terrible magic with them. They used that magic to drive the red giants away. Perhaps the red and white giants did not share the same language. The old ones did not say. Mato had always assumed they were telling the truth. They had no reason to lie, unlike the trickster, who *always* lied. At least with him, you knew what was right and good. One simply did the opposite of anything the trickster demanded, no matter how difficult that might be.

Sometimes he wondered if the trickster had made up the stories about the cavern of dreams. No one knew where it was. No one alive had ever seen it. And yet, everyone said it was a place of incomparable beauty, and that countless generations of The People had left their mark on it. If that was so, Mato thought, then there should be a trail. So many moccasins, even walking on rock, would leave a path. If only he could find it!

He left the music playing and went outside. The cat was nowhere in sight, though he checked his belt to be sure his knife was in place. The animal was stupid and slow. No match for Mato, unless it crept up and took him by surprise. He let that happen once. It wouldn't happen again.

Jumping down the steps to the ground, Mato strolled away from the cabin. He walked a short distance to the edge of a steep bluff that overlooked a valley. Rugged grey mountains graced the horizon on all sides. Vast swaths of green covered the valley, contrasting with the snow still remaining in the shadows of the distant peaks.

Mato had traveled much in his short life, but never as far as the most distant ridge. The cavern of dreams was out there, somewhere. Or it could be right under his feet! That's what made his mission so frustrating. He reached down and plucked a rock from the ground, pausing only momentarily before sighting a target, the trickster's favorite: a black bird with a bright yellow head and neck. According to the trickster, the bird was stuck midway between day and night as a punishment for not helping the trickster find food when he needed it. Mato heaved the rock, but the bird took flight before the stone came near.

No one ate the black and yellow bird, but whether that was because of its taste or because The People wished to twist the trickster's nose, Mato didn't know. There was far too much Mato didn't know, and he almost let himself be consumed by sorrow. But that wasn't the way of a warrior! All he really needed was a plan. Or maybe, just a place to start. And this place was as good as any. Better, in fact, for the she-giant would doubtless give him food and shelter. She might demand something in return, but he would worry about that later.

Breaking into a brisk run, he dashed back beneath the cabin and retrieved his spear. His favorite weapon, a blowgun, had been damaged, and he had not had time to make a new one. So, armed with the spear, he struck out for the base of the bluff on which the cabin stood. He would start in the middle and work his way to the outside. If there were an entrance to the cavern of dreams, he would find it. Mato struck the butt of his spear into the ground and shouted his challenge. "Mato will find the cavern. Mato will learn the fate of The People. Mato is bold! And Mato is coming." He took several quick steps, then hurled his spear as far as he could. He would begin his search wherever it landed. If the Spirits wished to help, they would direct his spear accordingly. If they sent the trickster instead, Mato was quite prepared to kill him, or die trying.

~*~

"Have you got a speaker on that thing?" Tori asked, after Caleb paused for the umpteenth time to relate something Maggie Scott had told him.

"Hang on a second, Maggie," Caleb said as he pulled the phone from his ear and inspected it.

"There's a button here somewhere," he muttered. He pushed one. "You there?"

"No, I'm somewhere else."

"Hey, Maggie," Tori said. She had met the feisty park ranger right here in Caleb's store on her very first visit to Charm. She suspected Maggie and Caleb had more than just a passing friendship, based on the similarity of their age and the fact that every time she spoke to one of them, the other popped up in conversation, if not in person.

"What's this I hear about you wantin' a dog?"

"Isn't that enough?"

Caleb started to laugh, but didn't say anything.

"Well, it might help if I knew what you wanted it *for*," Maggie said, her voice husky from too much time outdoors. "Ya gonna hunt with it? Or do you want it for protection? You're not gonna buy any sheep, are you? You know how I feel about sheep. And it takes forever to train one o' them dogs properly. They're too damn smart is why. Ain't that right, Cal?"

He nodded.

"Cal says yeah." Tori winked at the old cowboy, and he smiled back. "I mostly just need some company."

"So, you want somethin' that'll curl up in your lap? I'm so sick of folks with those silly, little-bitty dogs. Barkin' all the time. Nasty little brutes. Bite ya soon as look at you."

"I just want a plain old dog. Not big, not little, not scary, but not timid either."

"Right," Maggie said, exhaling heavily. "There's a shelter over in Buffalo."

"Just keep your ears open for me, okay? I don't want to drive all the way to Buffalo. I've got more important stuff to do."

"Like what?" Caleb asked.

Maggie remained strangely silent.

"Well, for starters, I need to learn some Indian words," Tori said.

"I can help you there," Caleb said.

"No, he can't," Maggie growled. "He wouldn't know Crow from Croatian."

"I've got some Indian friends," he protested. "They've taught me lotsa stuff."

"Right," Maggie said scornfully. "Cal can swear in Sioux *and* pig Latin."

"What words do you need to know?" Cal asked. "And in which dialect?"

The questions quickly proved just how little she knew. "I— I'm not sure."

Maggie cleared her throat, then dove in. "Do you need to learn some words used by Wyoming Indians? Or—"

"That's it," Tori said. "I just don't know which

tribe."

"Could be Crow, Sioux or Arapahoe," Maggie said. "They aren't all that different, from what I've heard, but they certainly aren't the same. Think of all the different countries in Europe, and all the different languages that evolved there. We've had a lot more Indian tribes than the Europeans have countries, and each of them has a dialect of its own."

"I was hoping it wouldn't be too difficult," Tori said.

"Who is it you want to talk to," Caleb asked. "Don't they know English?"

Tori swallowed. She wasn't ready to say anything to anyone about Mato, not even to people she could trust. "It's complicated."

"I've noticed that about you," Maggie said.

"Noticed what?"

"Nothing's ever simple where you're concerned."

Tori frowned. *What could be more simple than her life? Well, before Mato, anyway.* "I think I'm offended." She looked quickly at Caleb. "Should I be offended?"

"Don't drag me into this," he said. "I just wanted to help you find a dog; now you want a translator."

"I've got an idea," Maggie said. "There's a phrase book the BIA put together several years ago.

I've got a copy somewhere. I'll try to find it for you. Or, you could check the library over in Ten Sleep."

"BIA?" Tori asked.

"Bureau of Indian Affairs," Caleb said. "But from what I hear, those folks ain't real popular out on the reservation."

"Even so, a book like that would be very helpful," Tori said. "I spent a little time lookin' stuff up on the Internet, but I didn't find what I needed."

"Can't trust the Internet," Maggie said. "Gotta run. I'll drop the book off with Cal if I don't see you before then. Okay?"

"Wonderful."

"Good. Later. Bye, Cal. I'll see you... you know."

"Right," he said, then clicked the phone into silence.

Tori gave him a wicked smile and mimicked Magie's voice, "I'll see you... *you know?*" She poked him lightly in the chest. "What's that all about?"

"None of your bidness, lady," he said, showing off his new teeth again. "You need anything else, or are you just gonna keep me from gettin' any work done today?"

"Actually," Tori said, thinking back to the events of the morning. "I could use some art supplies. You got anything like that?"

"Like oil paints and stuff?"

"Yeah."

"Nah," he said. "Does this look like a dang WalMart?"

"How 'bout some crayons? Chalk?"

"I've got a paint-by-numbers kit," he said. "Thought they might sell big at Christmas time."

Tori hugged him. "I'll take two."

"Good," he said. "'Cause that's all I got."

~*~

Shawn found the garage door opener in the glove box. Sutherland was so thoughtful! He parked the car and entered the house as if he lived there, which he planned to do, for a while. He needed some time to figure his next move. And that depended on how cooperative Vicky Lynn's editor would be. He had expected an almost instant call back, but it didn't happen. He made the two hour drive down I-75 from Atlanta to Macon without interruption. Why hadn't she called? It just proved you couldn't trust a Yankee, especially a New Yorker. They didn't give a rat's ass about people. A Southerner would've already offered to meet him at the hospital, or bake a casserole or something.

He began a second search of Sutherland's house, a very thorough search. The first visit had yielded easy stuff: food, clothes, and booze. Now he needed to find the hidden stuff: cash and valuables, jewelry. Anything he could hock. He was tossing the last of the bedrooms when his phone rang.

"Yeah?"

"Detective Sutherland?"

He hesitated a moment, then responded. "Yes. Who's this?"

"Cassandra Woodall. You called and said there had been an emergency."

"That was a couple hours ago. I hope you're not too late," Shawn said.

"How is Mrs. Lanier?"

Shawn smiled. This lady thought she was smart. But she wasn't nearly smart enough to trick him. "Lanier? You mean Pruett, don't you? Emaline Pruett."

"Uh, right."

"She's probably not going to live much longer. She wants to talk to her daughter."

"How did you know to call me?"

He laughed. "I'm a detective, right? They pay me to figure this shit out."

"She asked for Tori?"

"No, she asked for Vicky Lynn, but she said you'd know how to reach her. What's the big deal? She needs to get over here right away."

"Which hospital?"

Crap, Shawn thought. "If you'll tell me where she is, I can have someone pick her up."

There was a strained silence from the other end.

"You're an *Atlanta* cop?" she asked.

"Yeah. Why?"

"Just curious. New York cops don't provide rides like they were some sort of taxi service."

Crap, crap, crap! "Well, we don't either, most times. But Miz Pruett has friends in high places."

"I see," said the woman. "But since Ms. Lanier no longer lives in Atlanta, you wouldn't be able to pick her up anyway. I'll be happy to give her a call and let her know what's going on. Now, what hospital is she in?"

"Grady," he said, trying to hide his anger.

"Room number?"

"I dunno. Last time I saw her she was in the ER. She's probably still in surgery if she isn't dead already." He winced. That was maybe too much.

"Is there anything else?" she asked.

"Miss Lanier's the next of kin," he said. "I need her contact information for my report."

"I'm sorry," Woodall said. "Company policy prohibits me from sharing the personal data of our clients. You'll have to get that somewhere else."

You'll pay for this, bitch. "Uh, right. Of course."

"You'll keep me posted if there's any change?"

"Yeah, sure. No problem."

"Thanks," she said, and hung up.

"Son of a *bitch!*" Shawn screamed, barely resisting the urge to throw his phone against the wall. *What was the world coming to? Where was the love? Where was the trust?*

Still fuming, he walked into the kitchen to continue his search. How he'd love to get his hands on the Yankee bitch's neck. He closed his eyes and imagined how she'd look while he choked her. He wondered if she was pretty. He couldn't tell from her voice on the phone. The image in his head changed from scheming faceless bitch, to scheming, faceless *naked* bitch. It made him smile.

He smiled even more when he found a credit card in a kitchen drawer. It bore Sutherland's name, and the issuing bank had been thoughtful enough to attach a sticker with a phone number in red. Activating the card was as easy as making a phone call.

He dialed the number and activated the card. The recorded voice asked him if he was interested in a special travel program available only to premier clients of the bank. Well, it certainly sounded good to him; he'd never been a premier client of anybody, so he signed up. After all, Sutherland could cancel at any time. That made him laugh.

Patience, he reminded himself. Good things came to those who waited, and Lord knows he had done plenty of that. Ol' Pete Sutherland had really come through. Not enough to pay off his debt, of course, but he made it possible for Shawn to keep moving toward his goal. So what if getting there meant a little side trip to New York? That might actually be fun. Thoughts of an alluring Ms. Woodall flitted in and out of his mind. And she looked hotter each time.

Concentrate! He'd need to pack a bag. Surely Sutherland kept one around here somewhere. And clothes. He'd have to check out the assistant DA's wardrobe. What did the well-dressed tourist wear to the Big Apple?

~*~

Mato found his spear after scrambling to the bottom of the bluff. The spearhead was completely buried, but the shaft was tilted slightly toward the sun, which was edging closer to the tops of the mountains in the distance. Not much daylight left for searching, he thought. Still, he needed to get started.

He'd only been gone from The People for a few days when he spotted the she-giant's cabin. He assumed it was some sort of omen at first, as he'd never been close to a giant before. Their music had lured him in. He had seen them from a distance, of course, everyone had, but he knew no one who had the courage to go near them. Their magic was simply too powerful.

Now he was beginning to rethink the magic issue. In the brief time he'd spent with the one called Tori, he realized that giants regarded their magic in much the same way as The People regarded their tools. A fine knife or a well-balanced spear in the hands of a skilled warrior usually meant The People would have game to eat and pelts to cure. Such weapons existed because someone *made* them— found the materials and worked them to perfection. Nor was there magic involved in hunting the animals the Spirits provided. Skill, yes, and luck, those were essential, but not magic.

In much the same way, the giants must have built their tools. Reyna could make a flute and play it. Mato could not. He could go through all the steps, and on several occasions had tried to fashion something as good as Reyna made, but he always failed. And yet, Reyna had no magic. He smiled, thinking of her. She had secrets, and he longed to discover them. *If he could find the cavern of dreams...* He let the thought drift away like the seeds of the white bark tree.

He looked along the base of the bluff. Rocks and boulders stretched as far as he could see, most too tall for him to see over. Shadows and rock could easily hide the entrance to a cavern, or the den of a bear, or a nest of snakes. Mato began his search by probing the shadows with his spear.

Chapter Six

There's always something....

"There's someone you should meet," Caleb said as he put two paint-by-numbers kits in a paper bag. "A guy I know up at the Community College."

Tori gave him her best suspicious look. "You're not trying to set me up with a date, I hope."

"Nah, nothin' like that." He grinned. "Watch out for Maggie, though. I wouldn't put it past her. No, the fella I'm thinkin' about teaches there. He's big on all that culture stuff. You know, like Indian rituals and which tribes came from where."

"He's an anthropologist?"

Caleb smiled. "Yeah, that's the word I was lookin' for. He studies that stuff. He can speak some Indian, too. I've heard him."

"Is he an Indian?"

"I don't think so. Seems like he told me he was from Illinois, or Indiana. Some place like that."

"They have Indians, too," Tori said. "But why should I talk to him?"

Caleb ran a hand through his thinning hair. "Well, you said you wanted to learn some Indian words, and he's an expert."

Tori tried not to look too dubious. "I dunno...."

"His name's Tom Purcell, and he seems like a decent sort. Plays a mean harmonica, too."

Tori laughed. "Well, that's certainly important."

Caleb paused. "I just had a thought. Have you got a tape recorder?"

"No, but I've got an MP3 player which can do the same thing. Why?"

"Well, if nothing else, maybe you could record your Indian friend's voice and play it over the phone for Tom. He could probably tell you what tribe speaks that way. Then you'd know what kind of translator you need."

Tori kissed him on the cheek. "Cal, you're a genius! That's exactly what I'll do. Have you got his number handy?"

Caleb whipped out his cell phone and started thumbing buttons, his eyes squinting but not leaving the tiny screen. "Got it right here." He read the number while Tori scribbled it on the paper bag.

"Tom Purcell?" she asked, pencil poised.

"Yep."

"And you swear he's a good guy?"

"He's the best dang harmonica player I ever heard," Caleb said, placing his hand over his heart.

Tori grinned. "And just how many harmonica players have you heard?"

"Three, I think," he said. "Countin' me."

"Amazing," she said, tapping her teeth with the nail of her index finger. "Could I interest you in a cat?"

~*~

Mato was quite comfortable moving through the tall grass and rocks at the base of the bluff. A startled bird or other small creature would occasionally break from cover, but usually not before Mato had spotted them. He heard the warning rattles of a couple snakes but backed away silently without drawing the ire of the rattle's owners.

A low growl emanated from a pile of boulders a few steps further on. Mato cursed himself for not being better prepared. Turning his spear upside down, he dipped the sharp stone tip into the pouch on his belt beside his knife. The pouch contained a gray paste that Reyna's grandmother had prepared. Very few of The People were entrusted with the knowledge since it represented some of their strongest magic. A tiny pinch of it in an open wound would put someone to sleep. It not only worked on people, but on animals large and small.

The hunters loved it, since it allowed them to tackle much bigger game, as long as there were enough members in the hunting party to haul out the meat and hide. Mato had failed to tip his spear with it in case he ran into something larger than a rabbit or a horned toad. The growl proved to be a handy reminder.

He carried his spear point forward, his grip firm. There was very little he was unprepared to meet. He suspected the growl had come from a coyote. Some of The People liked the taste of coyote, but not Mato. He preferred deer and rabbit. Or fish. Many of the mountain streams had plenty of fish in them, and Mato was an accomplished trapper. His fish baskets were highly regarded.

The growl came again. Louder. But Mato still couldn't see what it was. He gripped his spear tighter, in case something bolted toward him. Maybe it isn't a coyote, he thought. His heart began to beat a little faster, and his lips and throat went dry. He moved even more slowly than before, speaking in a low, even voice to calm the spirit of the animal. Sweat stood out on the backs of his hands. He wouldn't be able to see into the hidden opening without stepping out between the protective boulders, but that would leave him exposed to an attack. He took another step and heard an even deeper growl.

~*~

Shawn rummaged through every room on every floor of Sutherland's house, including the attic, basement, and a storage area above the garage. The search turned up nothing beyond the credit card (an expired version of which he discarded from Sutherland's wallet), some clothing, and a collection of suitcases in a variety of sizes and colors. Sutherland's taste in fashion left much to be desired, Shawn thought. The man had no sense of style at all. But he was neat. A neat freak, in fact. His shirts were arranged by color, though most were white; his shoes were lined up and shined; even his socks and underwear were folded neatly and stacked in orderly piles. No wonder his wife died when she found out he was going to retire. What an asshole!

Sutherland's sock drawer contained a surprise, however. At the back of the large drawer, Shawn found two dozen rolls of coins. Each of the red, white, and blue wrapped rolls contained twenty-five one-dollar coins, each baring the face of a U.S. president. Shawn opened one and dumped a quarter pound of James K. Polk coins into his palm.

James K. Polk? Who the Hell ever heard of James K. Polk? Peter Sutherland, evidently. Assistant district attorney, sock weirdo, and *coin collector.*

He'd seen silver dollars before, but these were different. Not only were they brass-colored, they were smaller than those with which he was familiar. Shawn divided the rolls of coins into four socks and hauled them out to the car. He had heard Yankees put tolls on damn near all their roads. Well, he'd be ready.

Thoughts of the goofy dollar coins stuck in his head. If Sutherland collected them, what other coins might he have hidden away? Not that he was looking forward to hauling great hulking bags of coins all over the place, but maybe the crazy bastard had some rare coins. Pieces of Eight, maybe, whatever they were. Maybe even real gold!

Redoubling his efforts to search the place, Shawn concentrated on furniture that looked like it might contain a false drawer or cover up a hidden safe. *Please, God, don't let it be a safe.* He kept digging, looking under beds, on top of kitchen cabinets, even behind and underneath the clothing in all the closets. He even revisited the storage areas in the basement and garage. He tore through boxes labeled "Christmas" and "Halloween," and a couple other holidays. All they contained were decorations. Were there any holidays the screwy lawyer *didn't* celebrate? Shawn's anger grew with each failed attempt to find the hidden goodies. There had to be something hidden somewhere!

Fearing he had overlooked the prize while ignoring the obvious, Shawn went back to the living room for one last search. On either side of the fireplace which anchored the central wall, cabinets and bookcases stretched from corner to corner with shelves above and storage below. The shelves bore an immense load of photos and what Vicky Lynn would have called "bric-a-brac." He called it crap. Souvenirs, mugs, kid's trophies, and other assorted bullshit that probably hadn't been dusted since Sutherland's wife croaked. Some neatnik he was!

He tore into the cabinets below. There was the usual collection of board games, blankets, and run-of-the-mill junk. Photo albums beyond count, too. He opened a few in case they were merely serving as cover for something really valuable. And then he hit the jackpot: thick 3-ring binders, each containing page after plastic page of coins in little cardboard holders. Sutherland's penchant for organization served him here, too. There were binders for every kind of coin he could think of, and then some. Not just pennies, nickels, dimes, quarters, half dollars and silver dollars, but 2-cent, 3-cent and 20-cent pieces. *Where had those come from?* Best of all, the final binder contained nothing but gold coins—page after beautiful page of gold pieces from all over the world. Each one housed in either plastic or cardboard with little notes attached, giving the pertinent details. Shawn had all the details he wanted, just looking at them. It was the mother of all mother loads.

Bless you, Pete Sutherland, you officious sonofabitch!

The binders joined the socks in the trunk of the yellow Chevy.

The only other thing Shawn found of interest was a personal computer, which he turned on while cooking a frozen pizza. The monitor was large and flat, and he had no trouble connecting to the internet. His introduction to Google at the library was enough to get him started, and within very little time he had a photo of Cassandra Woodall on the screen. A slightly overweight redhead, she probably wouldn't be starring in any of Shawn's fantasies, at least not based on *that* photo. She was attending some sort of writer's workshop, and the page included a short biography. He did a quick search on the name of the publishing house where she worked. Lo and behold, there was her business address. He printed her photo and the page with the publisher's address.

What a wonder the internet was!

He spent the next hour trying to find some useful information about Vicky Lynn, but all he came across were reviews of her stupid book, and screen after screen of stores willing to sell him a copy.

He toyed with the idea of flying to New York to have a little chat with Vicky Lynn's editor, but decided there was no need to deal with airport security if he could avoid it. Besides, it would only be a matter of time before someone either found Sutherland's body or reported him missing. Public transportation was definitely out, even if it meant a tedious drive or two. He had pretty much everything he needed for the trip; there was no reason to stick around here.

It occurred to him that when the cops found Sutherland, someone was sure to come nosing around his house. He'd seen enough police shows on

TV to know that cops could learn way too much about someone from the stuff they left behind. Not just fingerprints, but other stuff, like skin cells or blood or snot. He must've sneezed a dozen times while poking around in dusty storage spaces. Had to do something about that. Fortunately, the same TV shows which served to warn him also offered a host of ways to remedy the problem. He smiled just thinking about it. There was something totally cool about being smart.

After packing everything he thought he might need in the bright yellow Chevy, he rummaged in the garage for a couple of tools. He pulled the gas range away from the wall so he could get to the supply line. He very carefully cut a slice in the line and bent the metal hose to ensure the cut remained open, then pushed the stove back in place. He replaced the tools on the pegboard in the garage, taking care to put them in the spots Sutherland had outlined for them. All neat and tidy. He went back to the kitchen and sniffed to be sure he could smell the gas. *Oh yeah, this'll be great!*

He then drove around Macon until he found a place where he could buy a new disposable phone to replace the one he'd left in Sutherland's kitchen. Once back in the car, he debated with himself about driving back to the house to be sure the rest of his plan worked. Only a fool, he decided, would leave something so important to chance. So, he drove back down Ingleside Avenue to the subdivision where Sutherland had lived. He pulled in and stopped a few houses away from that of the former assistant DA.

He dialed the number of his old disposable phone. With any luck, there would be enough gas in the kitchen by now.

Nothing happened.

"Sutherland, you asshole! What are you doing?" Shawn couldn't resist pounding his palms on the steering wheel. In all the TV shows he'd seen, the disposable phones always made a tiny spark which detonated the gas. What had he done wrong? He dialed again, but got the same result.

Crap! Maybe he hadn't waited long enough. Maybe it took more time for the gas to build up to an explosive level. He turned on the radio, hoping to find some music to help him pass the time. There seemed to be plenty of country and the hip hop shit blacks liked so much. He didn't need any of that. Finally he found an oldies station on FM and settled down to wait. That was something he was definitely good at.

Thirty minutes later, he tried the number again. It still didn't work, so he left the car and walked back toward the house. He found a rock beside the driveway as he approached the exterior door to the kitchen. He heaved the rock at one of the window panes in the door, shattering it. He thought briefly about going back inside to retrieve the rock, then decided against it. Who'd notice a rock? He'd found an old Zippo lighter in Sutherland's garage, which he flicked into life, the flame bright and steady. He tossed it through the broken window and tried to turn away.

With a deafening roar, Sutherland's house went off like the ass end of a space shuttle.

Shawn found himself on his butt at the far side of the lawn, the smell of burnt hair thick in his nostrils. He gingerly touched his face, fearful that the explosion had caused permanent damage, but all he'd lost was an eyebrow.

~*~

It was late in the day when Tori got back to her cabin. She could hear the stereo playing from outside, and her phone started ringing as she walked in the door.

"Where have you been?" Cassy Woodall asked when Tori picked up the phone. Each word was pronounced slowly and distinctly, the way a frantic mother might question a guilty-looking five-year-old.

"I had to run into town. Such as it is." Tori held the phone in one hand while she deposited her purchases on her work table. *What was that awful smell?* She turned the stereo down. She liked "Sweet Home Alabama" as much as anyone, but why so loud? *Mato must have lead ears.*

"I've called at least a dozen times."

"Sorry," Tori said. "I forgot to take the phone with me. I don't get many calls these days."

"I sent you an E-mail and a ton of instant messages, too."

"I said I was sorry! Geez. I don't just sit in

front of the computer all day, y'know."

Cassy exhaled in exasperation. "I never thought I'd hear you say that. Listen, I got a really screwy call today. Some joker claiming to be an Atlanta cop said your mom was in an accident, and he needed to reach you."

"Oh, God. Is she all right?" Tori gripped the phone hard. How the hell was she going to get to Atlanta? And what was that damned smell? And where was Mato?

"Your mom's fine, as far as I could tell. I couldn't find a phone number for her; I think it's unlisted."

"It is, but if she's in the hospital—"

"That's what I'm trying to tell you," Cassy said. "She isn't. At least, I don't believe she is. I think it was your ex-husband trying to get me to tell him where you are."

A shiver worked its way up Tori's spine. "You didn't tell him—"

"No, of course not. But I tried to cover all the bases. He gave me a name, and I checked with the Atlanta police, but they'd never heard of him. I called the hospital, too, and they had no record of your mother."

Tori swore out loud. "It's Shawn all right. That's exactly the kinda crap he would pull. Thank you, thank you, thank you for not falling for it. He can be the world's sneakiest bastard."

"Yeah, well, I believe you," Cassy said. "I just thought you should know."

"I'll call Mom to be sure she's okay."

"Good idea."

"Uhm, Cassy?"

"Yeah?"

"Did you piss him off?"

Her editor laughed. "I'm sure I did. I could hear it in his voice, the creep."

Tori laughed, too, but it wasn't long-lived. "You need to be careful."

"Why? You don't think he'd try anything, do you?"

"He might. He's not only sneaky, he's vengeful."

"I can't imagine he'd come all the way to New York just to give me a hard time."

That was something Tori *could* imagine. All too easily. "I'm serious. You need to watch your back. Have you got a gun?"

"Are you serious? This is New York! Only cops and killers have guns."

Tori grunted. "You don't sound too happy about that. When did you become a poster child for the NRA?"

"When I started reading about home invasions," Cassy said. "But you're scaring me worse."

"Good. I meant to. You need to keep an eye out. Make sure you lock your doors."

Cassy laughed again. "You aren't listening. I live in New freakin' York. I have three locks on my door, and a can of mace in my purse. Besides, I don't have a clue what your— What's his name? Shawn? I don't have a clue what he looks like."

"He's actually not bad looking," Tori said, "if you dig self-centered, control freaks with massive personality disorders and no conscience. I've probably got a picture of him on my PC somewhere. I'll E-mail it to you."

"Thanks," Cassy said. "I promise to be careful. But only if you do, too."

"Why do you think I moved to Wyoming?"

"I thought it had something to do with Uncle Bob. Like a sequel?"

It felt good to relax and think about the book. "Well, yeah, there's that," Tori said. "There's been a new development, but I can't really talk about it just yet."

"A good development?" Cassy asked. "I mean, will it help you finish the book?"

The putrid smell in the room made it difficult to concentrate. "I dunno yet," Tori said. "I just— I don't know." *Where was Mato?*

"Call me when you do."

"Uh, right. See ya!" Tori clicked the phone off and stared into the fireplace. Several containers had been tossed in and burned. Parts of them stretched like the subjects of bad Dali paintings, while the rest were charred black and bubbly. Much of the burnt stuff was unidentifiable, but she could make out the remains of some bananas, a jar of guacamole, another containing pesto, a baggy full of blue cheese, and a steak she had been marinating overnight.

Mato, you little dweeb! What did I do to deserve this?

Rather than try to clean the mess, she raked the coals back to life and threw on a couple more logs. When that didn't generate the quick results she wanted, she squirted starter fluid directly on the hot coals and stepped back. A cloud of steam-like vapor arose, then whumped into flame. She began to wonder if she might regret leaving the cat with Caleb.

~*~

Mato forced himself to relax his grip on the spear. He flexed his muscles in sequence—hands, arms, shoulders, legs—all in an effort to stay loose for the inevitable attack. He still couldn't see the animal, but he was certain it was a coyote. The smell gave it away.

Staying behind the larger of the many boulders which hid the animal, Mato stretched his arms and scratched the soil in front of the opening with the butt of his spear, then quickly pulled the weapon back and reversed it. The growling continued, though deeper and more threatening.

Mato had no intention of advancing any further toward the coyote's lair. It might have offspring in there, in which case it would be even more dangerous. A mother coyote, like a mother of The People, will guard her little ones with her life. Nor did Mato wish the coyote any harm. The world was big; there was room enough for them both. Besides, the coyote could be a formidable challenge. It vastly outweighed him, and while Mato had the advantage of speed and the ability to out-think his adversary, the coyote brought sharp teeth, cunning, and agility to the game.

Reasoning that retreat made better sense than provocation, Mato stepped carefully backwards, away from the lair. He would climb high uphill and go around the coyote, leaving an encounter for another day. As he worked his way up and then crabwise across the steeply slanted, hardscrabble surface, he stepped on a loose pile of rock and slid downward.

Instantly, the coyote flashed into the open, a deep snarl in its throat, its eyes narrowed and ears laid back.

Mato continued to slide, straight toward the angry animal. He managed to turn just enough to get his backside on the hill and dug both his heels into the ground. It slowed his descent but left him open to attack. The coyote lunged at him, its speed shocking despite an uphill attack. Mato swung his spear around and hung on, his arms close to his sides in an awkward attempt to keep the stone point between himself and the advancing animal.

At the last moment, the coyote dodged to one side. Mato gained footing on an outcrop of rock that stopped his slide. He twisted to maintain his face-forward position and managed a two-handed stab in the coyote's direction. Still snarling, its brown-stained teeth sharp and threatening, the coyote spun away from the spear before losing its own footing.

Muscles and tendons stretched on Indian and animal alike, their lips drawn back in matching expressions of fear and effort. The coyote continued to slide, and Mato had just begun to feel momentary relief when his foothold gave out, and he, too, started skidding downhill.

The coyote reached the bottom first and danced in anticipation of his quarry coming into range. It crouched, mouth slightly open, a single strand of saliva swinging from a ragged black lip.

Now hurtling down the hillside, Mato gathered himself for his own attack. Once he managed to get his feet settled beneath him, he dove straight toward the coyote with the spear held at arms' length in a desperate full body lunge.

The tactic took the coyote by surprise, and it had almost no time to avoid Mato's stone-tipped weapon. Yet, it managed to flatten itself as it turned to bite Mato from the side, away from the spear.

Mato angled the point down and to the side, the tip of the stone blade just grazing the animal's hip. It howled in protest, growling and spinning, its feet a flurry of backpedaling motion as it scrambled to get away. Mato made no attempt to pursue. He still had no desire to maim or kill the coyote. He didn't need the meat, and had no time to cure the hide, which wasn't very desirable anyway. He just wanted to be left alone to look for the cavern.

As he watched, the coyote began to limp. It shifted its weight to one side and then the other, over-correcting for one faltering step after another until it finally dropped to the ground. Its head sagged. Eyelids drooping and chest heaving with each panted breath, the coyote finally put its head down and lay still.

Mato waited a few moments more. He had seen too many animals fight the magic and manage one last lunge or claw swipe. Eventually the coyote ceased to move except for shallow breaths. For the first time he noticed the scrawny teats, black and flaccid against the animal's chest.

"Forgive me, sister coyote," Mato said, "but you gave me no choice." He looked back toward the boulders from which the coyote had sprung. "And what are you guarding, hey? Is that the entrance to my cavern that you've claimed for yourself?"

He walked back to the disputed territory. As he expected, the sounds of coyote pups emanated from a dark recess at the back of the rocks. He squatted down and squinted into the blackness, waiting for his eyes to adjust to the reduced light. The coyote pups barely moved. Most slept or stretched or yawned, their bodies piled haphazardly. The dark space smelled of urine and blood, and now it smelled of him. He hoped the coyote wouldn't abandon her litter because of it.

Soon, the darkness lifted enough for him to see the back of the lair. Though deep enough for a family of The People to live in, the little hole in the hillside ended abruptly. There were no passages leading further back into the ground. The space belonged to the coyotes, not The People's dreams.

Disappointed, but still resolved to continue the search, Mato returned to the sleeping coyote. Leaving his spear on the ground, he grabbed the animal by its hind legs and dragged it back to its lair. It would awaken in the shade, if not during the night, and its pups would be close enough to plead their hungry case. He had lost some time, but perhaps he had pleased the Spirits in the process. For Mato was not only brave, but compassionate. Worthy.

And still eager to find the mysterious cavern.

The interstate highways were well lit where they wandered through cities, but not out in the boondocks. Shawn had put Atlanta behind him and was headed north on I-85 as the sun went down. Traffic had moved steadily as long as he had been south of town, but once he neared the Georgia State University stadium, it slowed to a crawl. He flipped on the radio and let himself drift along. There was no hurry. He knew what his quarry looked like, and where she worked. Catching up to her would be a simple matter of patience and observation. Then the fun would begin.

She owed him for making him drive all the way to New stinkin' York, home of the Mets and the Yankees. No, make that the *damn* Yankees. She'd pay for that. *Oh, yes indeed.*

He glanced at the dashboard. Plenty of gas, and plenty of time. He had money in his pocket and a plan in his head.

"Editor lady, I hope you look better than you do in your picture. If we're going to spend time together, I expect to enjoy myself, and I need a pretty woman for that." He chuckled. "Or at least, one that won't complain too much."

He suddenly felt a thrill of inspiration. Once he'd gotten the information he needed from the Woodall woman, maybe he could take her with him to find Vicky Lynn. He'd never had two women at the same time. The topic was a frequent one in the magazines he liked to read. The women were almost always hot, and the men.... He couldn't remember anything about them except that they always seemed to be enjoying themselves. Could he satisfy two women? The thought made him laugh. The proper question was: could they satisfy him?

The very least he could do was give them the chance. He glanced at a green and white interstate sign he cruised by. Charlotte, NC, was 200 miles away. He pointed the nose of the obnoxious yellow Chevy down the middle of the right-hand lane, set the cruise control for 70 miles per hour, and relaxed.

After a good night's sleep in Charlotte, he'd decide whether to try for New York on the second day.

Now that he'd given thought to the prospects of a threesome, he was more eager than ever to arrive at his destination. He reached for the glove box and popped it open. Nestled within was the boning knife he'd found in Sutherland's tackle box. The long, slender blade had a gentle curve, and the handle had a non-slip grip—a thing of beauty.

The ladies would undoubtedly hate it.

~*~

Caleb stood alone in his store. Business had been slow all week. In fact, if it hadn't been for Tori, he wouldn't have seen anyone all day. She seemed like such a nice gal; he couldn't understand why she hadn't connected with someone. If he'd been twenty years younger... Well, he wasn't. He had Maggie, sure, and she was a great gal, too. Just not as young or as pretty as Tori Lanier, Charm's reclusive author. He couldn't help but think of the way she filled those tight blue jeans. Man, oh man....

He went through the contact list on his phone until he came to the name he was looking for: Tom Purcell. He hit the dial button and waited for a response.

"H'lo?"

Caleb identified himself, then asked, "How's the academic world treatin' ya?"

"The kids' are driving me nuts, Cal, same as

116

always. You okay?"

"Me? Yeah. Like always. I just thought I'd give you a heads up. You may be gettin' a call from a friend of mine."

"'Bout what?"

"Indian dialects," Cal said. "She's tryin' to talk to some Indian she met somewhere, but she's not having much success."

Purcell mumbled something to someone on his end of the line, then spoke into the phone. "This friend of hers doesn't speak English?"

"Apparently not."

"That's odd," Purcell said. "How old is this Indian friend?"

"I don't know," Cal said. "Does it matter?"

"No, but it might explain why her friend doesn't speak English. There are still a few old timers who don't want anything to do with whites. Or, this alleged friend might just be making her work." He paused. "This woman friend of yours is white, right?"

"Yep. And she's a joy to look at, that's for sure."

Purcell laughed. "You old goat. I hope that ranger friend of yours never hears you say that. You'll be sleepin' alone for the rest of your life."

Caleb grunted in agreement. "Anyway, be nice to her if she calls."

"This hottie got a name?"

"Oh, yeah. Sorry 'bout that. Her name's Tori Lanier," Caleb said.

"Tori Lanier? The writer?"

"Yeah. You know her?"

"No, but I've seen her book. Civil War stuff. Interesting, but I suspect she's a one-hit wonder."

"I wouldn't know anything about that," Caleb said, "but she's a good kid. You be nice to her."

"What're you now, my father?"

"Treat her right," Caleb said, "or I'll be your worst nightmare."

Chapter Seven
Stirring the puddin'

Saddie Willets looked down at the preliminary report from the city's arson investigator. According to him, the home of former assistant district attorney Peter Sutherland was destroyed intentionally.

All Saddie could think was that it couldn't have happened to a more deserving person. Not that Saddie was vindictive. Her family and co-workers regarded her as a warm and loving parent and, generally speaking, a hard worker. A regular church-goer, she did charity work when she wasn't keeping the books for the bowling league, and maintaining a respectable 173 average.

But there had been a sorrowful incident in the life of Saddie's nephew, Terry. The boy had been accused of trafficking in child pornography. An unidentified tipster had assured local authorities that they would find plenty of damning evidence on young Terry's computer, which he kept in his freshman dorm room at Mercer University. Saddie had no doubt that someone had planted the pictures, just as Terry claimed, but there was no evidence to support his story.

Peter Sutherland had been assigned the case, and opted to prosecute, despite Terry's previously unblemished record, and testimony from several of his friends that many people in the dorm had access to his computer. Sutherland didn't care. It was an election year, and he was eager to help his boss retain his job. Stamping down hard on the exploitation of children made great press and scored political points. In Saddie's opinion, Sutherland was just as guilty of exploiting Terry, who wasn't much past childhood himself.

Terry got six months and a year's probation. The DA won re-election. Sutherland's name slipped out of the headlines, his job done and Terry's life ruined.

The file folder in her hands contained photos of Sutherland's home, or what was left of it. The building had been all but leveled by an explosion and the fire which followed. The arson investigator claimed to have found tool marks on a gas line, though he had yet to identify exactly what kind of tool had been used. Saddie toyed briefly with the idea of calling her sister to see if she knew anything about it, but she and her family had moved to South Carolina hoping to escape the stigma of the sex offender brand Sutherland had burned into Terry's record.

A yellow sticky note inside the folder directed her to contact Sutherland's family, since no one knew his whereabouts. Saddie crumpled the note in her fist, then dropped it in the trashcan beside her desk. She glanced at her watch. It's nearly 5 o'clock, she thought.

This can wait 'til tomorrow. No. Gosh, tomorrow is Saturday. Well, that's a shame, 'cause now it'll have to wait 'til Monday.

She glanced down at the wrinkled ball of yellow paper in her trashcan, a faint smile tugging at the corners of her mouth. "How does it feel to be screwed by the system, Mr. big-time, crime-fighting, assistant DA?" She followed that with an indignant sniff.

"Who're you talkin' to?" The voice belonged to Simon Andrews, the arson investigator in the neighboring office.

"Nobody," she said, sweetly. "Nobody at all."

Tori had poured herself a generous glass of wine and exited the cabin while the fire in her fireplace consumed the rest of the stuff Mato had piled in it. The smell hadn't gotten any better, so she raised both her windows and left the door standing open as well. She hoped it would air out fairly soon, since even in late spring, the nights could be chilly.

She walked to edge of the bluff that overlooked the deep green valley stretching to the rugged, gray mountains on the horizon. Sitting in the lawn chair she'd brought with her from Georgia, she took in yet another spectacular sunset. The western sky, in full riot colors of pink, purple, and coral, looked as if it had been painted by some madman— a madman with exquisite talent. She wondered if Mato had ever attempted to paint a sunset. He certainly had the skill, if not the tools.

Where was he, anyway? She stood and stepped closer to the edge. The valley floor was a good two hundred feet below. She took another long, slow sip of wine and scanned the panorama before her. He could be anywhere. She hoped he would come back, but had no real reason to believe he would. Maybe she made the whole thing up! She'd experimented with some weed in college, but nothing stronger. She couldn't be having some kind of weird delayed reaction, could she? Not likely. Or was it? She'd heard that some drug dealers laced their product with other drugs. What if....

No! That was ridiculous. She wasn't losing her mind. She knew what she'd seen: a two-foot tall Indian. But anyone she told would think she'd been smoking something way stronger than pot.

Surely he'd come back. After all, she'd bought him the paint set, and she wouldn't mind having an explanation about why he'd emptied the fridge.

"Ah, Tori."

She whirled around to locate the speaker.

Mato stood halfway between her and the cabin. "There you are!" she said. Though tempted to rush toward him, she thought it might be more prudent to take her time. Mato didn't seem intimidated. He merely stood looking at her with his hands on his hips. At least he was smiling.

"Hungry?" she asked, then pantomimed eating.

He nodded his head in a vigorous assent, then turned and preceded her into the cabin.

He was standing before the fire when she filed in a few moments later. "I hope you're happy," she said, then pointed at the smoldering garbage.

His eyebrows drew together in puzzlement.

"That!" she said, pointing again, and then holding her hands out, palms up, in what she assumed was a universal gesture meaning, "what the hell?"

Mato brightened, then walked to the fridge and opened it. He pretended to extract something, then held his nose with one hand while he carried the invisible yet malodorous object to the fireplace and tossed it in with a flourish. Smiling, he wiped his hands, as if to divest himself of any remaining trace.

"So, you elected yourself health inspector?"

He clearly failed to see the humor. She set her wine on the counter, then poured a tiny bit of it into the shot glass he'd used previously. She handed it to him. "I've heard all kinds of stories about Indians and 'fire water,' but I'll be damned if I'm going to let that turn me into a lousy host. Cheers!" She knocked hers back and finished the glass.

Mato sniffed the wine, then took a tiny sip. His face lit up with pleasure, and he erupted in a string of speech that left her utterly puzzled. But, since he had smiled throughout, she felt safe assuming he liked White Zin.

Thank God he's not a wine snob. Wouldn't that be a kick in the head?

Tori rummaged in the refrigerator until she found some ground beef. "Looks like burgers for dinner," she said.

Mato rewarded her with a blank look.

"I don't have any buns, so we'll have to use bread." She walked over to her pantry and found a can of refried beans. "But, we're in luck. Gourmet beans! South of the border hobo food. We spare no expense around here, my friend."

Mato was more interested in the can opener she used on the beans than on anything she said.

"I've got an idea. Why don't you go over there," she said, pointing to a spot near the fireplace, "while I fix dinner."

When she got the blank look again, she pulled out one of the paint-by-numbers kits and carried it to the designated art space. The paints were watercolor and came in a little plastic tray with 24 numbered colors. She also got a shallow cup of water and set it beside the paints. While he watched, she dipped one of the little brushes in the water, then rubbed the bristles in the dry paint until it came to life. *Blue number 7.* Had to be sky, she thought. She painted one of the spaces marked with a "7" then handed the brush to him.

Mato seemed to grasp the idea instantly, although he had a little trouble with the concept of cleaning the brush between colors. Beginner mistake, Tori told herself as she went back to the stove to finish preparing dinner.

The burgers were just about ready when she heard him muttering. *Was he complaining?* "What's the problem?" she asked, as she turned to look at him.

Mato was distinctly unhappy.

~*~

Shawn spent the night in a cheap hotel just outside of Charlotte, North Carolina. Though tempted to find a hooker, he figured it was way too late, and probably too expensive, although there were ways of keeping the price down. Then, too, it was a Friday night. The pretty ones were probably all taken by now. In the end, he opted just to drink a few beers, watch some TV, and get some sleep. It had been a busy day, and the next one would likely require that he keep his wits about him.

He'd thought about leaving early and trying to reach New York by Saturday night, but that didn't really make much sense. He'd have to catch up with the Woodall woman when she left her office, so he had the better part of three days to kill. Doing that in New York would undoubtedly be expensive. Better to take his time and plan on arriving Monday afternoon.

Drifting off to sleep proved more difficult than he anticipated. In retrospect, it probably wasn't such a good idea to torch Sutherland's house. Even if the cops didn't suspect that it had been burned down deliberately, they'd know who the place belonged to. It wouldn't be long before they tried to contact Sutherland. Someone would likely know that he had a place in the mountains, so they'd be alerting the cops up there to pay a visit to the fishing shack.

Yeah, that was pretty stupid, he thought. He'd have to think smarter, or they'd have his young ass back in the pen.

No. That won't happen. There was no way he'd be going back in.

No goddamn way.

~*~

"That's not a puppy," Caleb said when Maggie let herself into his house with a strange-looking mutt at her side.

"Well, hello to you, too," she said, dumping her hat and oversized bag on his kitchen table. She unhooked the leash from the choke chain on the dog and dropped into a straight-backed chair. "Yes, thank you. I'd love a drink. What're you having?"

Caleb stared at the huge dog. It had the big, broad head of a Rottweiler, but the coat and tail of a Labrador retriever. "Uh, I don't— I'll have a sour."

"That'll do." Maggie snapped her fingers, and the dog immediately looked up at her. "C'mere, you."

The dog lowered its head and walked the other way, into the living room.

"Mind's well, I see," Caleb said as he poured two heavy-duty whiskey sours. "Has it got a name?"

"It's a he, not an it, and his name needs to be changed."

"Why? Isn't he used to it already?"

Maggie shook her head. "I don't care."

"Well, what is it? Can't be that awful."

After a long pull of her drink, Maggie set her glass on the table. "His former owner, a guy I worked with I'm sorry to say, gave him his name."

"Which is?"

"Shit Head."

Caleb chuckled. "Is that one word or two?"

Maggie glared at him, obviously unwilling to answer.

"What's wrong with him?" Caleb asked. He seated himself in a twin of the chair Maggie occupied. When he whistled, the dog came straight to him, ears up and tail awag.

"There's nothin' wrong with him," Maggie

said. "That guy I mentioned? Got himself a desk job. He's moving to an apartment in Salt Lake City. Can't take the dog with him."

"You sure he isn't just trying to dump him for some other reason?" Caleb suddenly looked uncertain. "He's housebroken, isn't he?"

Maggie took another swallow, then smiled at Caleb. "He's a good dog with a bad name. Kinda like you."

"You're a hard woman, Mags." He let his head droop and feigned hurt.

Maggie got up and kissed his bald spot. "Forgive me? I'll make it up to you."

He grabbed her around the waist and pulled her into his lap. "Now?" he asked.

"With a guest in the house? Certainly not!"

"*Guest?* You mean Shit Head?"

"That's not his name anymore!" Maggie slipped out of his arms and got to her feet. "I don't even want you to mention it to Tori when she comes to get him."

"How can you be so sure she'll even want him? She said she was looking for a puppy, remember?"

Maggie finished her drink. "It's just a feeling I've got. Look at those eyes."

Caleb did as instructed and gazed into the dog's sad, dark eyes. "Okay. Now what?"

The dog lowered his head and pushed gently against the inside of Caleb's leg.

"What's he want?"

Maggie laughed. "Just a little love, m'dear. Just a little love. I think he and Tori will be perfect together."

Caleb nodded as he scratched the dog's head. "Does that mean we need to come up with a new name for him?"

"I don't know. I mean, he'll be her dog; she ought to be able to give him a name she likes."

"Well, that's real nice, but not very practical. I mean, what're we gonna call him in the meantime? I'm good with Shit Head, actually, but—"

"Absolutely not!" Maggie said. "I won't stand for it." She watched as he drained his glass. "You gonna have another?"

"I think I've earned it. You, too."

"Chili okay for dinner?" she asked.

"Yours or mine?"

"Mine, of course! Yours tastes like crap."

He laughed. "I was hoping you'd say that." He stood and went to the sink to make another round. "Y'know, we could always call him 'Shovel Head.' It might be close enough that he wouldn't get confused."

"Shovel Head?"

"Sure. Look at him." He made a clicking noise with his tongue, and the dog responded by swiveling his head like a radar array focusing on a distant signal. "Fits, doesn't it?"

Maggie grinned. "You're right, much as it pains me to admit it." She patted her leg. "C'mere Shovel Head."

The dog pranced directly to her and stopped when his nose bumped her navel.

"Shovel Head it is," she said.

~*~

Mato had his arms crossed and was frowning directly at Tori. Aw, Christ, she thought. *What'd I do now?* Hoping to find a clue, she scanned Mato's efforts with the paint-by-number kit, squinting as if by doing so she could force details to stand out like traffic lights.

The little Indian still held a tiny brush in one hand as he unfolded his arms and pointed at the poster paper he'd been painting on. Tori looked closer, still no wiser about Mato's agitation. Then he made a series of dramatic gestures, pointing at the painting, then at the paints. When she still didn't get the idea, he scowled and dipped his brush in Blue #8 and slathered it on top of the nearly dry Blue #7 she'd painted earlier by way of demonstration.

Damn. Did I use the wrong color? She knelt on the floor, picked up the artwork, and examined it carefully. The paint fully obscured the number beneath it, but she was quite sure she hadn't used the wrong color. So, what was his beef? Mato stood beside her, jabbering something in her ear while he pointed at the two different colors and made a wiping gesture with his free hand. Finally, she got it.

"You're an art critic!" she said, chuckling out loud. "You don't like the color selection."

Mato stared at her, still a little strung out over the whole color choice issue.

"Your first attempt at paints, and you're already a little prima donna." She laughed again. "Okay, sorry 'bout the 'little' crack. I didn't mean anything by that, honest." She smiled at him, hoping to cheer him, then she turned the paper over. The back side was the same color and texture as the front, except it was completely blank. She put the paper on the floor beside the uncovered sketch of the cat he had made earlier. She pointed to it, then at the paper, and gestured toward the plastic pallet of paints.

Then Mato smiled, too. He gave her a nod and stood over the paper, his face wrinkled in concentration. Tori stood up and observed as he cleaned his brush.

"Mato?"

He looked at her inquisitively.

Tori raised both index fingers and put them beside her forehead like the horns of a bull. She then lowered her shoulders and took a couple of steps around the cramped space in front of the fireplace.

Mato's face lit up. He immediately dipped his brush in Brown #1 and began to work.

Tori finished fixing their dinner, cutting one of the burgers into quarters to make it easier for him to handle. She dumped a blob of the mushy beans on his plate along with a small handful of potato chips. Nothing says lovin' like good nutrition, she thought, then called him to join her at the counter which doubled as dining table and work space. She had discovered a coffee stir spoon from a fast-food restaurant in the glove box of the truck which she'd placed beside his plate. She hated to think what might be on his hands. She hadn't quite figured out how to "talk" him into washing up before eating.

Mato put his brush in the rinse jar and reluctantly left his project behind. He bounded up into the chair across from her and fell to examining the provender.

Tori began to eat, content to let him take his time. He didn't, however. After sniffing the selections and observing how Tori held her burger in both hands while she attacked it, he did the same. He made sounds of approval, though he was chewing too hard to smile. He seemed to like the burger, and the chips, too, which he broke into manageable pieces. When he made to stick his hand into the beans, Tori called his name and demonstrated how she used her spoon. After a brief look of suspicion, he reached for the white plastic stirrer with its flat, shovel-like end, and followed her example.

They ate in silence until both sat back in their chairs, feeling bloated. "We really should eat three times a day," Tori said, "not just breakfast and dinner. It's healthier. All the experts say so."

Mato belched, then smiled.

"Well, I'm glad we agree," she said.

Mato slipped down off the chair and went back to his artwork. Tori wished she knew how to say something about sharing the clean-up duties, but decided just doing them would be easier. Besides, he was fully focused on his painting, and she was more than a little eager to see what he produced. She hummed to herself while she worked, only to pause when Mato stopped painting to dig through her CDs. He selected one and loaded it into the player.

Clever devil, she thought. *I wonder*—

The fast rhythmic lead in to "Sweet Home Alabama" roared from the speakers before she could complete the thought. She swayed happily to the music, one of her favorite tunes. "Good choice," she said, giving him a happy thumbs up. He gave her a similar sign of approval, then went back to his painting.

Tori finished the clean-up and thought about how she might give a copy of the music to him. The difficulties were all too obvious, until she recalled the portable MP3 player she'd been given as a gift by a company that wanted to do a recorded version of her book. She'd have to use her computer to rip the recordings from the CD and copy them to the memory chip in the MP3 player, but she was familiar with the task. Then she noted that the little machine had a record function, and her conversation with Caleb quickly returned.

What a great way to solve both problems, she thought. Now, if I can just figure out how to do this without scaring the bejesus outta Mato....

~*~

Shawn had spent the better part of the day driving through Virginia. The weather was decent, and he was content to plod along, doing the speed limit and playing the role of a garden variety good citizen. He even swore at a couple cars which passed him doing speeds well over the posted limits.

What a guy I am—what a grade A kinda guy!

Then he saw a sign for Washington, DC. It wasn't that he had any desire to visit the nation's capital. Rather, the idea of heading east instead of blindly plowing northward got him to thinking about what else besides DC lay in that direction. That's when he thought of Atlantic City, New Jersey. *Vegas East!*

He had time to kill anyway; why not lay up somewhere that guaranteed a good time? Clubs, gambling, babes... What more could he ask?

When the turn-off for I-66 loomed, he drifted into the appropriate lane and left I-81 and scenic rural Virginia behind. Screw the mountains, the valleys, and the cows. He wanted neon lights and jiggly flesh. He'd earned it.

~*~

Mato put a last dab of color on the flank of the bison he'd painted, tapered it to resemble the shadow of hard muscle, then stepped back to admire his work. *The great beast*, in all his glory! And all but ready to step into the room. The People had long acknowledged that Mato had the skill one needed to not only survive a night in the cavern of dreams, but to leave the tales of his people on the walls as well. He was pleased to have the additional tools the she-giant had given him, although he doubted the colors she provided would last as long as his own pigments. Still, the brush was far superior to anything he'd ever used and made it much easier to portray the images he had in his head.

Tori loomed over him, but not in any threatening way. She, too, admired his work: a magnificent animal standing with its head proudly raised. He had purposely made the animal's hump and forelegs bigger than they would appear on a normal animal. He wanted to show the greatness of the beast, and not just his own ability.

The she-giant spoke to him yet again. Could she not understand that her words made no sense to him? He doubted she was stupid; she had too much magic at her disposal for that, and yet it was obvious that the only way they could communicate was through gestures and play-acting. And he was tiring of that. Rapidly.

She had been sitting at the table while he worked, her hands busy with a short board bearing small, flat tiles, each marked with some magical symbol. She stared at another flat panel, larger than the one she touched and different in another significant way: the images on it changed almost constantly. Sometimes the changes were minor— tiny characters that appeared as her fingers tapped the marked tiles. At other times, images appeared. He had looked behind it in an effort to locate the source of these amazing displays, but there was little to be seen. There were several more of the tails, like the one at the back of the music machine, but he could not imagine what function they might have. It was all too much for him to comprehend, but at least it didn't seem to offer any threat, and so he ignored it.

Tori retrieved something from her work area and approached him with it. Small and colorful, the little box sported several small, flat circular bumps that reminded him of the tiles on her flat finger board. The she-giant pressed one of them, and music came out!

Mato stepped back in surprise. He had thought all her music was captured in the big box on the shelf. But here she had put some of it in a much smaller container, one he could easily carry. What a foolish giant! She was begging him to steal some of her magic!

And then she did something astonishing: *she handed the little box to him!*

He stood, dumbfounded, as she pointed to each of the flat, round tiles and recited their names:

"Volume, Forward, Back, Play, and Record."

He pronounced each in turn, doing his best to mimic her voice. When she went over them again, he had less difficulty repeating her words. Of course, he had no idea what the names meant, but he could work that out in time. She seemed to be urging him to test his luck. As she watched, he pressed one of the tiles until it made a clicking sound. The music stopped.

She smiled and urged him to do it again. He did, and the music returned. He pressed the others and gradually gained control. Eventually, she held out her hand for him to return the device, which he did. She pressed another of the tiles and began speaking into one end of it. Moments later she made the box repeat her sounds—*in her very own voice!*

He could barely believe his ears, yet he had watched her perform the magic without making any attempt to hide her movements. What came next surprised him even more, for she seemed to be asking him to speak. She wanted to imprison his voice, too!

If only one of the elders were here to guide him, but none of The People could hear him. None of them knew what great risks he had already taken. He called on the Spirits to watch over him, for he lacked the courage to anger the she-giant. Trapping her own voice in the box hadn't caused her to lose the ability to speak, so perhaps his voice would also survive.

He wished she had the kind of magic which

would allow them to understand each other, but that was not to be. He took a deep breath and looked at the box held so close to his head. He had been lucky in his risk-taking thus far. Dare he stretch it any farther?

Chapter Eight
New Guys

Shawn moved all his gear from the car to his hotel room. Not the cheapest place in Atlantic City, but close to it. He had no desire to waste a lot of money on a place to sleep, when he could spend it gambling or whoring. *Choices, choices.*

The money issue could have easily ruined his mood if it hadn't been for his good fortune in uncovering Sutherland's hoard of coins. He had no idea what the collection was worth, but it had to be considerable, just based on all the gold. His attitude had changed drastically since the day he'd gotten out of the state penitentiary in Reidsville. With any luck, he'd never see *that* place again. At least, not in this lifetime.

His thoughts of the future hadn't strayed much beyond getting even with the people who had put him away: Sutherland and Vicky Lynn. Everyone else was just following orders. Revenge might be sweet, but it wasn't free. Sutherland had been a good source of money, and damn timely, too. By the time he'd sent the top of the retired assistant DA's head into the treetops, he didn't have enough cash left to finance a cup of coffee, much less a hunt for Vicky Lynn.

Sutherland had certainly solved that problem, though Shawn remained low on actual spending money. The credit card was a death trap, unless he used it cleverly. As soon as the authorities suspected Sutherland's death wasn't a suicide—a conclusion they'd come to eventually—he needed to be rid of anything that could tie him to the crime. He might be able to sell the credit card, but whoever bought it could identify him. Bad idea. He could run up the charges for stuff he might need, but he'd have to avoid anything that would raise anyone's attention prematurely. That let out firearms and cars, and almost anything else really expensive.

He dumped out one of the socks containing some of Sutherland's presidential dollar collection. The feel of the heavy coins clinking together, almost like poker chips, brought a smile to his face. The government hadn't even used silver in the new coins. Instead, they'd used something that sorta looked like gold, but wasn't. Kinda like social security—a system that looked and smelled like a retirement plan, until you understood the details and realized it was all just a gigantic Ponzi scheme. That was government for ya. Didn't matter who ran the system.

He needed spendable cash, and quick. He didn't have to unload all of Sutherland's gold. Better to sell a little at a time to avoid raising suspicion. What he needed was a couple of profit-hungry coin dealers. He'd let the free market do the rest.

~*~

"Tori? It's Caleb. I've got a surprise for you."

Tori wedged her phone between her ear and her shoulder as she fixed breakfast for two. Well, one and a fraction, though she wasn't quite sure how large a fraction yet. Mato had a pretty good appetite, but still—

"Hey, Cal. What kinda surprise? Another paint-by-numbers kit? Actually, I could use some bourbon."

"Can't help you there," he said. "Don't have the right kinda license for that."

"Figured as much." She slid a delicately thin pancake onto a plate for Mato, then set the skillet aside. She dusted the pancake with confectioner's sugar and a smear of butter, then rolled it up with a fork. She poured a dollop of maple syrup on top and set the plate in front of the little Indian with a tiny cheese knife and an *hors d'oeuvre* fork.

She had already fixed a pancake for herself and dug in without another word. Mato watched her and quickly got the hang of eating the way she did, though not without getting a generous amount of the syrup on both hands. He didn't seem to mind, however, and devoured the pancakes as if he hadn't eaten in weeks.

"You were saying?" she said to Caleb, around a mouthful of pancake.

"Oh, yeah. The surprise. Maggie dropped it off last night."

Tori snickered. "Maggie spent the night?"

Caleb stuttered. "Uh—"

"Again?" she added quickly.

"Hey, we're grown-ups—it's legal!"

"I know, I know," Tori said. "I just think it's cute how you two act like such teenagers."

"Just 'cause there's snow on the roof—"

"Please don't go there, Cal. Okay?" She added a spoonful of brown sugar to her pancake and offered some to Mato. From the way he piled it on, the boy obviously had a sweet tooth. *Boy? No, he was definitely all grown up.* Then she wondered what kind of shape his teeth were in.

"I got your dog here waitin' for ya," Caleb said, a note of impatience creeping into his usually imperturbable voice.

Tori responded with a gleeful shout, "Maggie found me a puppy? Why didn't you say so?"

"Well," Caleb began, then let his voice trail off.

"Well, *what?* Is it sick or something?"

"No, no. He's fine. I took him for a walk this

morning, and his plumbing works better than mine."

"So, what's the problem?"

"Well, he's a little past puppyhood," Caleb said. "You didn't really have your heart set on a pup, did ya? Those little guys can be a lot of trouble. I'm speaking from experience. You'd have to housebreak him and all that. It's messy, and time-consuming."

"Just how far beyond puppyhood is he?" She could imagine Cal scratching his head, squinting and going through a half dozen other facial contortions while he figured out how to answer her question.

"I don't rightly know. Maggie didn't say."

"Good grief, Caleb. I don't want some feeble, old, broken-down mutt!"

"Careful now, you'll hurt his feelings."

"The *dog's* feelings?" she asked.

"Yeah. He's what ya might call 'sensitive.' I noticed that last night." He paused to say something, presumably to the dog, then came back on the line. "He's a charmer though, I swear. You'll love him the minute you set eyes on him. I'd keep him for myself 'cept I've already got that damned cat you didn't want. Don't ask me to keep the dog, too."

She watched as Mato sat back in his chair and looked at her, his eyes just barely visible above the edge of the table. "Well, I guess I can drop by and take a look at him, but I won't make any promises. You sure you don't have any bourbon?"

"Never said I didn't have any. I just can't sell it, legally."

"Oh. Right. Sorry."

Caleb sighed. "So, you want me to bribe you with booze to take the dog? You're the one said you wanted one."

"I said I wanted a puppy. It's a long drive to your place, Cal. I wanna be sure to take *something* home with me."

"I'll see what I can do. You probably oughta give me an autographed copy of your book, though, seein' as how I've gone to so much trouble on your behalf."

Tori smiled. "I'd be happy to give you one, Cal. D'ya think you might actually read it?"

"Sure," he said. "I've got canned goods up the gum stump. It ain't like I can't find a decent doorstop."

"And the dog's there with you? At the store?"

"He is indeed."

"Then I'll be by later this morning," she said.

"Maybe we can get some lunch over at Lu's place?"

"Consider it a date! See ya." Tori punched her phone off and began to clear the table. Somewhere during the last bit of her conversation with Caleb, Mato disappeared. She wondered if, when home, he ever helped out around the teepee. It didn't seem likely.

By the time she'd finished with the dishes a new thought occupied her mind: whether to follow up on Caleb's suggestion that she play her recording of Mato's voice for the guy at the community college. She wasn't sure what she'd tell him if he asked her where she met Mato, or any other question about him, for that matter.

On the other hand, she was dying to know what Mato had said into the recorder. Was it about her? What if he claimed she was holding him prisoner or something? She quickly let that thought die the rapid death it deserved.

She found the scrap of paper bag she'd saved with Tom Purcell's phone number on it, but before she dialed, she poured herself another cup of coffee. Adding cream and sweetener pushed the inevitable off for another few seconds, as did finding a paper napkin and the MP3 player.

Not content with that, she pulled up her E-mail and glanced through it, too. It didn't take long, and that left her looking around the cabin for some other chore that simply couldn't be delayed any longer. There wasn't too great an accumulation of trash yet, so she had no real reason to haul it out to the 55-gallon drum she used for general burning. A couple hands of solitaire might help me settle down, she thought. The ploy didn't work. Along with her growing discomfort about calling Purcell, she had a growing sense of guilt for not doing it.

"It's not like I owe it to Caleb, for cryin' out

loud." she told herself. "Damn it."

She dialed the number and waited for an answer, but it never came. Finally, it dawned on her. "It's Sunday!" The realization came as a relief—a valid excuse to put off the call, and not just for a few minutes, but for a whole day.

Whistling, she rounded up some clean clothes and headed for the shower. Lunch with Caleb ought to be pleasant, and the good Lord knew she had little enough reason to get dolled up. Mato certainly didn't care.

~*~

Shawn was exuberant at having found a coin shop open on Sunday. Of course, it was in Atlantic City, and mall stores didn't seem to honor the Sabbath the way stores did in Dublin, Georgia, where he grew up. The shop owner, an abbreviated, olive-skinned, little man with thinning hair and an expanding waistline, seemed eager to be rid of him once their transaction was completed. Shawn was eager to leave, too, except the idiot expected him to take a check!

"You *sell* money, for Christ's sake," Shawn said. "Use some! I don't want a check. I want cash."

"I don't have much here," the old fart said. "I need—"

Shawn reached across the counter and grabbed him by his necktie. "You've given me nothing but crap since I walked in. I offered you good stuff, and you tried to cheat me. Give me one good reason why I shouldn't kick your ass through that plate glass window."

The man looked like he was about to soil himself. "I— It was an honest mistake! You can't expect me to know what every coin in the world is worth."

"Which is why I asked you to look 'em up."

The little man was trying to pull away, but the effort was pathetic. "I wasn't trying to cheat you. I promise!"

"Right. Just get the cash, and I'll be on my way. There's a blackjack dealer waitin' for me."

"It's in my— It's in the back," he said. "I don't keep that much cash here, out front. Too dangerous."

Shawn released him. *He'd show him dangerous.* "Go."

The man returned in less than a minute with a thick wad of bills in hand. He counted out three grand in crisp new twenties. Shawn collected the binders containing his remaining nickels and dimes and headed for the door.

"It's a pleasure doing business with you," the man said.

Shawn stared at him for a moment, unsure if he should respond verbally. He settled for a gesture made with one hand and one finger. The coin dealer's expression didn't change.

~*~

Mato had hoped to take the magic music player with him when he left the she-giant's cabin, but Tori had put it somewhere out of sight. It had troubled him greatly when she started talking to another little box, which she held next to her head. He could have sworn there was a man's voice coming out of it, but of course he couldn't understand anything either of them said. It was all very frustrating.

Spear in hand, he chose a direct route toward the edge of the bluff, walking directly under the cabin. He intended to search along the base of the bluff, moving toward the rising sun. He would have enjoyed having the music with him as he walked. It was not only good company, but would likely scare away any animals that heard it. That was fine with him; he wasn't hunting. At least, nothing alive.

While still under the she-giant's home, he noticed that of all the flat stones piled up to support the cabin, the central pile was, by far, the largest. It required many paces just to walk around it, while he could circle the others with very few. Then he realized that Tori's fire pit stood directly above it. She couldn't have used a wooden floor under that, for obvious reasons. The giants were very clever, he thought.

But, so was Mato. And the more time he spent with Tori, the more clever he became.

~*~

Caleb was sitting in a rocking chair just outside the entrance to Lu's Place when Tori pulled in and parked her truck. She was eager to see the mysterious mutt, but it wasn't anywhere in sight. "Hey, Cal. Where's the pooch?"

"In the store," he said. "Thought we might grab a bite first. Lu's is the best place in town."

"Lu's is the *only* place in town."

"Well, yeah," he said. "You hungry?"

"Not really." She couldn't help but look at Caleb's building across the street. "C'mon, Cal! Please don't make me wait!"

He rocked forward and got to his feet, a huge smile on his face. "Kids just don't have any patience anymore."

"You wouldn't be happy if I wasn't eager to see this hound of yours." She gave him a hug.

"It ain't mine," he said, leading the way toward his store. "Maggie got him from some guy she works with."

"What's his name?"

"The guy's?"

"The dog's, Cal. What's the dog's name?"

He coughed and mumbled something in reply.

Tori squinted at him. "I didn't catch that."

"It's uh...."

"Cal?"

"Shovel Head," he said.

"What?"

Caleb opened the door and ushered Tori inside. It took a moment for her eyes to adjust to the reduced light level. "Where is he?"

"Shovel Head!" Caleb called.

Tori looked at him in disbelief. "*Shovel Head? What kind of name is that?* No wonder the dog doesn't want to come out. He's probably embarrassed."

"He is a little shy," Caleb said, hesitantly. "Although he wasn't all that shy when Maggie brought him 'round yesterday." He gestured toward one of the straight-backed chairs circling the iron stove in the center of the store. "Have a seat. I'll go look for him."

"Could he have gotten out?"

He shook his head. "I don't see how." He walked toward the back of the store while Tori settled into a chair. She could hear Caleb knocking about and was taken by surprise when something cold and wet pressed into her hand. She jerked her hand away and looked down into the saddest brown eyes she'd ever seen.

Shovel Head was wagging his tail furiously, his great head held low. Tori lowered her hand to the wide space between his ears at the top of his head, and the big, black dog pressed against her leg.

While she watched, her heart began pumping a little faster than before. Shovel Head rested his chin on the top of her thigh and exhaled with a gentle woof that puffed out his lips like a burst of air under a curtain. His soft sigh and utter surrender touched her more deeply and completely than she'd thought possible.

"Oh, Cal. He's adorable," she whispered, not wanting the dog to move, so thoroughly had he captured her heart.

"What's that?" Cal asked, returning to the front of the store. "Did ya find him?"

"Oh yeah," she said, feeling her smile push her cheeks ever higher.

"What d'ya think?"

She put a hand on either side of the dog's face, his warmth working its way through her palms, up her forearms, and into her heart. "I think he's perfect." It came out as a whisper, as if speaking any louder might cause the strange-looking dog to disappear. For some reason, his immense size didn't bother her at all, though he likely weighed nearly as much as she did.

"C'mere," Caleb said, patting his leg. The dog didn't move. "Shovel Head," he said, his voice dropping into the command register. "Come!" The dog closed his eyes and stayed where he was, glued to the top of Tori's leg.

"I don't think he's goin' anywhere," Caleb said.

"Yeah, he is," Tori answered, the smile still on her face. "He's goin' home with me."

~*~

The strip club had a name, but Shawn couldn't for the life of him remember what it was. The interior featured all the things he looked for in a high-class titty bar: loud music, garish lights, expensive drinks, and naked women, or at least women in the process of getting naked. Either condition worked for him. Best of all, he was putting it all on the credit card. God bless Pete Sutherland, formerly the architect of his incarceration, but now his greatest friend, to say nothing of being his supreme benefactor. He almost wished the old asshole wasn't dead, so he could thank him in person.

Shawn knew his future depended on his ability to maintain his wits, even though cops were genetically disposed to stupidity. Given two clues and a doughnut, they'd jump to whatever conclusion a clever con could dream up. Still, there were a few smart ones in the system, and those were the ones he had to plan for.

"Can I charge a lap dance?" he'd asked of a blonde whose chest measurement and IQ were in the same neighborhood.

"'Course you can, honey," she said, rubbing her hips against the inside of his thighs. "You can charge anything you want."

Was that a southern accent? "Anything?" he

asked, feigning innocence.

"Almost anything," she corrected.

It was going to be a long, long night, he hoped, sliding his hand down to her soft hip. All he had to accomplish was one fairly simple thing.

"I'd love to dance for you," she said. "Gimme your card, and I'll set it up, okay?"

Shawn tried to look coy, but he wasn't sure if he'd pulled it off. "It's a company card," he said, testing his imagination. "Is there some way you can make it look like the charges were for something uh... Y'know. Legit?"

"You're entertaining clients, right honey?"

"No, it's just me," he said.

She plucked the card from his fingers. "Pay attention, darlin'. Remember, you're entertaining *potential* clients, y'hear?"

"Oh, right," he said.

"Don't go 'way," she said.

He watched her saunter off with Sutherland's charge card in her red-nailed hand. The view from behind was every bit as wonderful as it was from the front.

Though it took a great deal of willpower, Shawn forced himself to glance around the interior of the joint for just the right players. He'd been there for over two hours, and had made the scan every fifteen or twenty minutes, but hadn't found exactly who he was looking for. Until now.

Staring back at him from across the room were a pair of young, black men, nursing beers. They had no interest in the flesh wiggling on the three, well-lit stages surrounding them. Instead, they were focused on him. He couldn't have asked for more.

The blonde reappeared as if squeezed from a tube of personal lubricant.

"You ready, hon?" she asked.

Shawn smiled as he took her hand and followed her to a more private area of the lounge.

~*~

Luanne Franconi's place was, indeed, the only restaurant in Charm. It could seat twelve people, eight of them comfortably, and often did. Lu only opened for business three days a week, and then only if the weather was good and the fishing wasn't. She never opened Monday through Thursday. Her schedule on the weekends she worked, however, was solid. Sundays meant a breakfast buffet. She did a lunch buffet on Saturdays, and a dinner buffet on Fridays. Lu had been in business for over twenty years. She'd never had a menu.

The breakfast buffet consisted of scrambled eggs, bacon, toast, waffles, and "seasonal" fruit, the season depending entirely on what Caleb had in stock. A simple woman, with simple tastes, Lu offered her three weekly feasts during limited hours. Folks knew what she had and were generally pleased to get it.

Caleb waved Tori to a chair and walked over to the coffee pot where he poured two cups of the dark brew into heavy, ceramic mugs. He brought them back and parked one in front of her. "It's not as good as mine," he said, keeping his voice low.

"You mean you can't lube a diesel engine with it?"

Caleb looked hurt for nearly a full second, then flashed his newly acquired pearlies at her.

"I wish I could've brought Shov—" She stopped. "I can't call him that, y'know."

"Why not?"

"'Cause it's stupid, that's why! And besides, it sounds like something my ex would have thought of." I wish that weren't the truth, she thought to herself.

"Then change it." Caleb's eyes sparkled. "He'll come to you no matter what you call him."

"Well, tell Maggie I can't thank her enough."

They chatted about nothing in particular as they picked at Lu's luncheon buffet. Caleb ate a bit more recklessly than Tori, but she was still full from the pancakes she'd shared with Mato.

"What'd Tom say when you played your Indian friend's voice for him?"

"I haven't talked to him yet. I'll call tomorrow."

Caleb didn't press the point. "I've got dog

food in the store, but no collars or leashes or anything like that."

"I've never owned a dog before," she said. "Do I need to get a book or something?"

"Feed him dry food, and give him lots of love," Caleb said. "The rest should work itself out."

She suddenly had a vision of Mato standing with his spear, trying to hold the big dog at bay. "You're sure he's okay with, uh, children?"

Caleb's lips twisted. "To be honest, I have no idea. But you don't have any kids."

"Technically, no—"

"*Technically?*"

She laughed. "Okay, no. I don't have any children. But ya never know when someone might drop by...."

"Do you even *know* anyone with kids?"

"Well, no."

"Then, there you are. Don't worry about it."

Tori looked at him, wondering what he'd think if she told him she was playing host to a two-foot tall native American with a taste for Southern rock music. "I guess you're right," she said.

I sure as hell hope so.

~*~

Mato had spent the day searching along the base of the bluff for an opening into the cliff. He'd found nothing, but wasn't overly disappointed. He had always assumed the journey of discovery would be a long one, although he'd gladly accept a token of the good nature of the Spirits. If They wanted to point Mato in the right direction, who was he to object?

Sadly, he'd seen nothing he could interpret as a sign from the heavens. The ground remained rugged; the bluff remained closed. He merely had to choose another mountain wall and begin his search again. Thankfully, that could wait for the next morning. He wondered what miracles Tori would present for him to eat. Thus far, everything she prepared had been rich and filling. Tasty, too! If he stayed with her much longer, he would grow fat and slow. The very thought made him shudder. Slow, fat warriors usually died young.

~*~

Shawn's head rolled on his neck as if filled with helium and connected to his shoulders by guide wires. The blonde with the chest designed by Boeing was gone. *What was her name?* He couldn't remember. It didn't matter. A brunette took her place, though she didn't have a Southern accent. He missed that. There was some other thing he meant to remember.

The brunette slid another glass in front of him. "Wanna buy me a drink?"

"Shure," he said, or tried to. "Wha' d'ya want?"

"Champaign, okay?"

He waved the credit card at the bartender. "S'okay by me," he said, "but not the real expensive stuff, 'kay?"

The bartender nodded and took the credit card.

Shawn looked across the room. The two black punks he'd seen before were still there, and still staring at him.

"You know those guys?" he asked the girl.

"I've seen 'em before. You probably shouldn't get involved with 'em. Know what I mean?"

He laughed. "I think I can figure it out." He struggled to his feet and gripped the edge of the bar for stability. "Gotta go."

She put her hand on his shoulder. "You sure, honey? The night's young."

"I'm sure," he said, "I've gotta go to bed."

"Want me to call you a cab?" the bartender asked. "You don't look so good."

"I'm fine," he said.

"You can put the fare on your card," the bartender said. "We've got a deal with the cab company. Your hotel can't be that far away."

Shawn relaxed against the bar. "Couple blocks is all." He belched. "A ride'd be good."

"Stay there," the barkeep said. "I'll let ya

know when the cab's here."

"Good," Shawn said. "Thas ex'lent." He looked again across the room. The two guys who'd been watching him made a show of ignoring him. "Be right back," he said, and launched himself in their direction.

They watched him approach, their faces impassive. When he arrived, he perked up a little. The booze hadn't fogged him into utter and complete incompetence. "You guys wanna have some fun?" he asked.

After exchanging looks of suspicion, they once again focused on him.

"What d'you want?" the bolder of the two asked.

Shawn pushed Sutherland's credit card across the top of the table toward them. They looked at it as if it were radioactive.

"What's that for?"

"It's my treat," Shawn said. "Y'all have fun with it."

The two stared at him. "You crazy, bro?"

Shawn nodded happily. "Outta my fuckin' mind."

They quickly exited the club with the card. Shawn left a few minutes later and allowed the bartender to pour him into a cab. All in all, it had been a perfect evening.

Josh Langston

Chapter Nine

Meanwhile, back at the ranch....

Caleb watched as Tori held the truck door open for the dog, which climbed onto the seat as easily as if he had been doing it all his life. Tori was clearly pleased, though Caleb was a bit puzzled. Dogs, especially big ones, belonged in the truck bed.

"Why not let him ride in the back?" he asked.

Tori gave him her "Are You Nuts?" look, but didn't say a word.

"Right," he said.

"Oh, about that bourbon. I—"

"It's in with the dog food," he said. "What about my book?"

"I left it next to your cash register," Tori said. "It was as close as I could get to your heart."

Caleb laughed.

The girl climbed into her truck and started the engine.

"Thanks for lunch," Caleb said.

She waved and pulled away in a cloud of Wyoming dust, the dog's head protruding from the passenger window. If I had a daughter, he thought, I'd want her to be just like Tori. He was certain Maggie would feel the same way.

~*~

During the ride home, Tori's thoughts drifted back to the new book. She'd been struggling with it, but hadn't wanted to admit that to Cassy. Once she'd figured out the code her great-times-many uncle had used in his memoirs, turning it into a novel was fairly easy. The man had lived an extraordinary life. Though a confidant of the great confederate general, Robert E. Lee, Bob Lanier had maintained an extraordinarily low profile. Just what one would expect from a spy. That made his exploits all the more interesting, and fueled her book. He had escaped death and capture so many times that all she had to do to make it a novel was change a few names and invent a romance. Uncle Bob's fictional lover turned out to be a great deal like Tori. Or rather, like Tori wished she could be.

But the new book wasn't going to be that easy. The second half of Robert Lanier's life was spent in virtual solitude, as far as she could tell. He had used at least three different codes when recording his life notes. One of them was the same code Tori had deciphered when working on her first novel. The other two were much harder. She was certain he had used one or both when sending coded messages to General Lee. As far as she knew, the Yankees had never figured it out. Of course, she was fairly certain they never intercepted any of his messages either.

Uncle Bob had written of his fascination with codes and cyphers to which he had been introduced by none other than Edgar Allen Poe. Poe's story, "The Gold Bug," about hidden treasure and the code-breaking which led to its discovery, had brought the topic of cryptology to the public's awareness. Treated as a new form of puzzle, codes and code-breaking enjoyed wide popularity beginning in the 1840s. Much of that interest had faded by the time the Civil War began, but not for Robert Lanier. Poe had bragged that he could break any cypher, and invited people to send him their inventions so he could prove his skill. Uncle Bob had followed the challenge closely.

Poe died long before the civil war began, but his influence had proven to Lanier that no simple letter substitution code could survive unbroken for very long, yet the confederacy insisted upon using them. The north used a word substitution code, and Lanier took his hint from them. His messages consisted of a single, three-number reference—page/line/position—and referred to words printed in a book that both sender and receiver had in their possession. Writing out such references was a long and laborious process, but paid off in security. If intercepted, the code was safe from anyone who didn't have the exact reference work on which the message was based. Changing the reference works made decrypting even more unlikely.

The trick for Tori was simply locating a copy of Uncle Bob's reference book. That turned out to be a copy of the King James version of the Bible printed by a long defunct publisher in Richmond, Virginia. She had located the book in a trunk left behind by a deceased relative. The lavishly illustrated book also contained pages for recording important events: births, deaths and marriages. It was there that she recognized Uncle Bob's bold yet precise handwriting.

Shawn had insisted they haul the trunk to the nearest antique dealer to see if they could squeeze a few dollars out of it. Tori managed to save the Bible and a handful of other books. Shawn had been enraged over her "treachery" in holding the books out, but he got over it somehow. The beating he'd given her probably helped. It had certainly gotten her attention. In fact, it was at the heart of the "disrespect" she'd shown him that led to a second beating and his arrest.

Beat me once, shame on you; beat me twice, and I'll see your sorry ass in jail.

The thought made her laugh. Ten years, he'd gotten. She was lucky the judge was sympathetic to abused wives. Especially lucky, considering what a lousy lawyer the assistant DA had been. She couldn't even remember his name.

Though the whole chapter had been dark and

depressing compared to her life now, it had contributed a great deal to the person she had become. Smart. Self-reliant. Confidant. She reached over and patted the huge, mostly black dog sitting next to her. *And no longer alone.*

~*~

Mato ended the day much as he had begun it: optimistic but unsatisfied. The cavern had to be somewhere nearby. He couldn't say for sure why he felt that way, but he did. Perhaps it was the Spirits working some subtle magic on him, or perhaps it was merely wishful thinking, though he doubted it. The cavern *was* nearby. It had to be! Could the power of the place be calling him? If so, it had pulled him far from home, far from Reyna.

What else could have driven him to reveal himself to the she-giant? She had rewarded him, repeatedly; feeding him and attempting to care for his wounds, though he knew they would heal promptly without her intervention. Still, she had demonstrated that he was more than some simple animal. She shared his love of image-making though he doubted she had any such skill of her own. Few of The People did either, and that made it easier to understand.

Tori was nearly as much a puzzle to him as was the location of the cavern. She had so much magic at her disposal, but she treated it as casually as Mato treated his blowgun or his bow and arrows. Such musing often occupied his mind as he probed amid the rocks at the base of the bluff, hoping to stumble across the hidden access to the cavern of dreams.

Forcing his way between a huge boulder and a sheer rock face jutting up from the valley floor, he noticed something peculiar. The light from the sun, just ducking behind the tops of the distant mountains, hit the rock face in such a way that shadows appeared on what should have been a flat surface. He squinted, then moved from one side to the other to see if the shadows revealed something natural, or something left behind by a distant relative.

Crudely incised into the rock was the figure of a woman, another of a great face, and an arrow. The cuts were shallow, but distinct. The eyes of the large face were closed, the face of a dreamer. He looked in the direction the arrow pointed and let his eye pick out a landmark he would not forget.

He thanked the Spirits for coming to his aid, then turned his steps back toward the lair of the she-giant.

~*~

Shawn woke up late and lay abed cursing the garbage truck which had roused him. Whoever had dreamed up the insane requirement that trucks must blare a hideous noise whenever in reverse gear should be forced to listen to the damned sound for days at a time. Who could sleep with that wall-penetrating racket?

He eased to a sitting position, but the

pounding in his head matched the ringing in his ears. He held his head in his hands, pressing his fingertips into his temples as if to manually erase the pain. It helped a little. Shuffling to the bathroom, he observed the usual morning rituals and took a shower. Though the tub was old and stained and ugly, the spray from the shower head was vastly superior to the water-saving dribble he'd endured in Sutherland's "master" bath. What a crock that was. The showers were better in the Reidsville pen. The only thing his present shower lacked was company. Either the blonde or the brunette from the previous evening would have fit the bill nicely, although it had been his experience that any ladies he met under such circumstances often looked less enchanting in the daylight than in the neon lights of their workplace. No surprise there, one usually got what one paid for.

As his headache gradually subsided, he recalled the other significant event from the previous evening. Just thinking about how the two blacks had reacted to his gift raised his spirits. It wouldn't be long before they were charging their asses off, if they hadn't already done so. When the cops eventually tracked them down, they'd demand to know how the two idiots had gotten their hands on the stolen card. He wished there were some way he could be there to see the expressions on the cops' faces when told that the card had been given to them by some friendly white guy they'd met in a strip bar. Wouldn't that be rich!

He checked out of the hotel, having prepaid

for his stay with Sutherland's card. From now on it'd be cash for everything, starting with breakfast. With any luck, he'd have his next meal in New York. Dinner with the Woodall woman? Perhaps. Perhaps not.

~*~

Tori arrived home without incident and let the dog out of the car. He sniffed around briefly, but rejoined her before she reached the door to the cabin. Mato was nowhere in sight, which was fine with her. She wanted to orchestrate the eventual meeting between them, and wanted to let the dog get used to the cabin first. He stuck to her side, entering the building only when she did, and then stopping as soon as they crossed the threshold.

"Go on," Tori said, but Shovel Head sat down instead and merely looked up at her. When she took a few steps inside, the dog followed suit, again stopping when she did.

Tori set the bourbon on the counter and knelt down to pet him. He leaned into her, burrowing the top of his head into her hands. When she stood and put the bourbon in the cabinet, the dog stayed by her side.

"You know," she said, staring at him, "you're going to need to find something else to occupy your time. You can't just hang around me forever."

He yawned, then lay down at her feet. When she sat down in front of her computer, he rolled over and came to rest beside her.

She looked up "Rottweiler" on the internet and compared the photos she found with the dog at her feet. His wide head was unmistakably that of a Rottweiler, but his coat appeared slightly longer. His ears were long and floppy, his feet broad. There was a patch of white on his chest, and some reddish brown on his cheeks and feet. Beyond that, he was black.

"How 'bout a name change?" she said.

The dog looked at her, his ears perked.

"You haven't left my side since we met. I oughta call you... Shadow." She leaned down and rubbed him behind the ears. "How's that grab ya?"

He stood up and shook himself.

"Well, I like it," she said.

Shadow nudged her leg one last time, then began to sniff his way around the cabin, carefully acquainting himself with the various aromas he found. The thick bed of towels she'd left for Mato in front of the fireplace definitely interested him, and he seemed to follow that scent all around the room.

When the door hinges creaked to announce the presence of someone new, Shadow growled deep in his throat.

Tori looked up in alarm.

~*~

"Well, what'd she say?" Maggie asked when she let Caleb into her house on the outskirts of Ten

Sleep.

"She said she was out of bourbon."

Maggie pinched him. "What'd she say about the dog?"

"Oh, him. He seemed to be hiding at first, then came out and turned on the charm." He walked to the cabinet where Maggie kept the Scotch. "What did you do to make him so attached to her?"

"Not a thing," she said. "In fact, Dawson, the guy I got him from, said I should be careful 'cause he sometimes got a little ornery, especially around folks he didn't know."

"He acted fine around me," Caleb said.

"Me, too. But Dawson's convinced the dog has an evil streak."

"Well, I never saw it, and I doubt Tori will ever be on the receiving end of it either."

"I'm guessing the dog knows the difference between good folks and bad. Dawson's a total butthead; maybe that's why the dog didn't like him."

~*~

Shawn had listened to the radio throughout his drive to New York. The trip had been uneventful, though the closer he got to the city the more convinced he became that Yankees just didn't know how to drive. They wandered all over the road. Nobody used turn signals, and anytime there was a decent space between him and the car ahead, some idiot came flying from behind him to fill it. Just driving defensively proved tiring, and he didn't enjoy doing anything defensively. By the time he reached the outskirts of the city, he'd worked himself into a terrible mood. If the Woodall woman gave him the tiniest bit of shit, he'd slice her open and leave her hanging like a field dressed hog.

The heavier the traffic got, the more he cursed her for forcing him to drive all this way. If she'd just come clean over the phone when he called, he'd probably have caught up with Vicky Lynn by now. Every such thought caused him to grip the wheel tighter.

He pulled into a gas station to fill up and get his head straight. A road map and coffee set him back ten bucks, and he soon began cursing at the sheer size of the city. A kidnapping might be trickier than he first thought. He pulled out the photo of Woodall he'd saved from the internet, and the address of the publishing house where she worked. There wasn't a great deal of time left if he wanted to be there when she called it a day. That was a laugh. Her day wouldn't be over until he said it was.

Now, if he could just find the right friggin' address.

~*~

Mato heard the growl the instant he pushed the cabin door open. He froze, instinctively ready to dodge for cover under the house, though hiding places there were limited at best.

The growl grew louder, and he heard Tori shout something. There was a brief scrambling of heavy, clawed feet on the wooden floor, and then a huge dark shape came streaking toward him. Mato dropped flat on the stoop as the gigantic beast flew over him. He heard Tori lurch up from her chair and follow, still yelling. *Was it a name?*

The animal turned, and he recognized it as a dog rather than a bear, though the differences appeared minor. He slipped into the cabin and crouched with his spear pointed toward the exterior. He wanted desperately to dip the stone blade into the sleeping paste in the pouch on his belt, but the animal was so fast he couldn't take the chance of leaving himself open when it turned and came to finish him off.

Tori was still yelling when she yanked him off the floor. The dog tore through the opening, its teeth clamping on air a few inches beneath him. He tried to tell her he was all right, but she couldn't understand him. Instead, she held him near her head while the dog stood on its hind legs, pawing her and sniffing at him.

He tried to twist around and get his spear into a position that might do him some good. Tori merely yanked it from his hands and tossed it on the counter. She then held him upright, over her head, and talked to the dog. *The dog!*

Somehow, her efforts began to have an effect on the animal. It sat at her feet, wagging its tail, but with both eyes focused directly on him. The last time he'd seen teeth that big, they were in the mouth of a wolf slain by the combined efforts of an entire hunting party. He would have no chance against this beast by himself.

Tori hung on to him as she lowered herself into a chair. The dog would soon be eye-to-eye with him! What was she thinking? Had she lured him into her confidence all this time just so she could feed him to this monster? The idea would have seemed inconceivable mere moments ago, but now... The dog looked hungry. Starved.

Mato twisted to see Tori's face. Surely she wasn't about to abandon him.

She was still talking to the dog, which appeared slightly less threatening than before. She kept one hand wrapped around his waist and extended the other to pet the dog. He held his breath while the animal came close and sniffed him. Moving slowly, he let his hand drift toward the knife at his belt. The she-giant might give him up, but he had no plans to volunteer as a sacrifice.

Suddenly, the dog moved his head to the side and rested his chin on Tori's leg. He no longer seemed interested in making Mato into a meal.

Tori was *still* talking.

Mato spoke to the dog as well. He kept his voice low, and a moment later the animal turned his head to face him. He sniffed Mato again, then licked him from his toes upward. Mato closed his eyes as the sloppy tongue rolled over him, but there was no damage done. Tori eased him gently to the floor and released him.

"Shadow," she said in her own low voice.

Mato copied her. "Sha-do," he said, reaching out to stroke the dog's nose.

The dog pricked up its ears but made no threatening moves. Mato's heart slowed to a regular, steady beat. He looked up at Tori, who had finally begun to pay some attention to him. It was about time.

She smiled at him. And winked.

It didn't take Shawn long to realize why so many New Yorkers traveled by taxi, bus or subway: automobile traffic in the city was clearly insane. After an hour of dealing with it, all Shawn wanted was to find a place to park. Alas, New Yorkers didn't seem to believe in parking. They only believed in taxis, and they drove them with their horns. Shawn's nerves neared the breaking point. One-way streets, blue-clad cops with no interest in the wetbacks at the heart of the madness, and an absence of parking options pushed him ever closer to the edge.

At last, he found a parking lot. He didn't care about the outrageous rate they charged. His only desire was to get out of the yellow Chevy and pursue his quarry on foot. No easy task, even if he had been able to park near her office, which he hadn't. He stopped for directions three times and got two answers, one of which was delivered in a voice he could almost understand. Tired, pissed, and devoid of anything like patience, he somehow arrived at Cassy Woodall's workplace.

Palming her photo, he took up a position in the lobby of the building and waited for her to appear. The place was old, and not very well kept. The buildings in downtown Atlanta had seemed more modern. This one just seemed busy. Very busy. It didn't surprise him at all that folks wanted to get away from it.

There were four elevators in all, lined up in opposing pairs, and he managed to keep them all in view from his spot near the building's entrance. If Woodall showed up, he'd see her. It was nearing five o'clock, and he figured she'd appear soon. He had no idea what her hours were, but five o'clock seemed a reasonable time to go home.

By six o'clock, she still hadn't shown up. He checked the building register and verified that he had the correct address. Woodall's name didn't appear anywhere, but the name of the publishing house was prominent.

Seven o'clock rolled around. Still no sign of her. Had she left early? What if her day ended at four? Would he have to go through this shit again tomorrow? Maybe he could get there early and catch her when she arrived. The thought occupied him for a long time. How would that work? If he waited 'til morning, could he drag her all the way to his car eight blocks away? Could he do that if she showed up now?

He'd been holding the long-bladed boning knife he'd taken from Sutherland's tackle box for hours. He kept it hidden just inside the cuff of his long-sleeve shirt, another gift from the retired Bibb county, assistant DA. *Where the hell was Woodall?*

He wouldn't try to grab her when she came out, he decided. It would be much easier to just follow her to wherever she lived. He could decide how to deal with her once he knew her home address.

Suddenly she appeared, carrying a light blue sweater over one shoulder and a purse with a long strap over the other. She looked much thinner than she had in the photo. So much so that he checked it again to be sure he had the right woman. It was her, no mistake. Her hair was shorter, too. Deep in conversation with some guy, she paid no attention to Shawn, though the three of them were the only people left in the lobby. Shawn turned away and pretended to talk on his cell phone. It didn't matter. The Woodall woman ignored him as if he had been a piece of furniture instead of a person. The bitch. He watched her leave the building, still chatting up her companion.

He wondered if he'd have to do something about the guy, too. He didn't offer much of a threat. Shawn had a few years on him, but the guy had a slight build, long hair, and walked like he had something up his ass. Definitely queer, Shawn thought. He could cut his nuts off, and the guy would probably thank him. The couple left the building, and Shawn hurried to catch up. They walked two blocks *away* from his car and then went down a broad set of stairs beneath a sign which announced a subway entrance.

Great, now I'll never be able to find the damned car. But he had no choice. He hurried down the concrete steps, using care whenever he came to a twist or turn. He caught sight of them walking briskly through a turnstile, each of them holding up some kind of card and waving it near a sensor. A uniformed subway cop leaned against a tile wall, watching him, *daring* him to try and jump the turnstile. He had no time for that! Scrambling to a ticket machine, he crammed money into the slot and waited for a response. While the Woodall woman and her gay pal were getting into a train, he was playing pat-a-cake with a friggin' machine!

When the box finally disgorged his prize, Shawn grabbed it and hurried through the gate toward the trains. The signs didn't make much sense to him since he didn't know where in hell he was. He picked a direction and raced down a brightly lit, tiled hallway until he came out on a broad platform. His target stood on the far side of the tracks which ran between them.

Shawn cursed to himself, and then backtracked. He could hear a train pulling in somewhere, probably right in front of Vicky Lynn's editor. He ran harder, up a set of stairs and then down, dodging faceless people as he went. The platform hove into sight, and Shawn darted through the opening. The Woodall woman was still there, but her boy toy wasn't. Shawn tried to get closer without appearing too obvious. There weren't many people on the platform, which made the task more difficult. Luckily, she seemed distracted, content to hug her sweater and her purse and focus on something inside her head while he got closer.

A growing roar signaled the arrival of the train. When it stopped, Shawn waited for her to get on first, then casually followed her. The rest wouldn't be too difficult, he thought. And after what she had put him through, maybe he could even make it fun.

Chapter Ten
Reaping and sowing

Tori grilled a steak on a hibachi, which she had perched on a conveniently flat boulder a few feet from the door of her cabin. She had once considered having a deck built around the huge stone, because it seemed like an aesthetic thing to do, but the best view of the valley was from the other side of the house. The boulder overlooked the dirt drive where she parked her truck and the big barrel where she burned her trash. Still, it worked great for the hibachi and meant that she didn't have to lean over it to tend the meat. It also made it difficult for big, black dogs to stick their noses into it.

Mato and Shadow seemed to have resolved whatever issues they initially had. Mato sat on the rock watching her cook, while Shadow did the same from the ground. The arrangement clearly pleased the Indian. Shadow couldn't have cared less.

"This is sirloin," Tori said, tapping the thick red slab of meat with a barbecue fork. "Sir. Loin. Steak," she said, then added, "Moo." Mato said something she assumed meant "meat," but it could just as easily have meant something clever like "man food" or "fuckin' A." It had been her experience that men had a limited vocabulary when it came to almost anything important, except maybe cars and football. She gave Mato a quick look. "You like football, Kemosabe?"

When he ignored her, she assumed he was a 'Bama fan. Shawn claimed to be a 'Bama fan, and that merely provided another reason for her to despise him. An Auburn girl through and through, she disdained anything that reminded her of the University of Alabama.

She took the steak off the grill, carried it inside and divided it, very unevenly, between herself and Mato. She had bread and veggies to go with it and started on her second bourbon and Coke. As long as the dog and the Indian didn't attack each other, there was an excellent chance she'd enjoy a pleasant evening.

Mato turned on the CD player and found a Lynyrd Skynyrd album she liked. Not too difficult a task considering that all the music was hers to begin with, but why Mato seemed to get off on "Sweet Home Alabama" remained a mystery. She poured him a shot glass of Coke just to see how he would react. He accepted the challenge and drained his glass several times during the meal.

Only when it ended did Tori call Shadow over. He got up from a blanket she'd spread for him and sat patiently at her feet while she fed him a few scraps. Mato observed all this with interest and eventually offered some of his own leftovers to the big dog. He laughed like a little boy when the massive canine with teeth like spear points gently eased the scraps from his hand.

She was a little concerned about the sleeping arrangements, but decided not to worry about them until she had to. It would give her time to observe her cabin mates, to see if the friction between them was truly gone. By the time she finished the dishes, however, Shadow was asleep with his head on Tori's slippers, and Mato was on the floor beside him, leaning back against Shadow's tummy.

Concerned such moments might be rare, Tori quietly slipped her digital camera from its usual spot above the fridge and got a splendid shot of her two companions. Neither moved a muscle.

Shawn entered the same subway car as the Woodall woman. He fretted that she might remember him from the lobby of her building, but she didn't seem to notice him at all. He might as well have been invisible. They went through six stops before she got off, and he made a mental note of it, much as he would have preferred to jot something down he could look at later.

She sauntered off the train, and he followed. He still hadn't settled on a plan, although if no better opportunity presented itself, he would simply grab her just before she entered her apartment and invite himself in. The boning knife was the only key he'd need, provided there weren't any nosy doormen around. He figured those odds at better than 50-50 and decided if he had to kill her, he could just as easily take out a doorman, too.

The woman turned directly into a corner deli after surfacing from the subway, and Shawn followed her inside. She poked around for a while, cruising up one aisle and down the next, tossing items into a canvas carrying bag she had pulled from her purse. The last item she selected was a bottle of wine. It seemed as if she knew she'd have company, Shawn thought with a grin. He let the knife handle fall partially into his waiting hand. The suspense was building, for him anyway. He bought a package of Juicy Fruit gum and left the store before she did, then settled in around a corner to wait.

She came out a few minutes later, whistling. He remained in the shadows until she crossed the street, then nonchalantly followed suit. None of the buildings in the area had doormen, he was sure. The word "brownstone" came to mind, but he wasn't sure why. If the buildings were brown, it was because they were nasty-dirty, not because that was the natural shade of the building material. Mostly what they were was tall and ugly, with wide cement stairways that led to locked foyers. Once she got inside hers, it would be difficult to take her down. She was almost at the top of the steps when he broke into a trot and called to her, "Mizz Woodall?"

She turned, frowning, her arms loaded with groceries.

He vaulted up the stairs while she squinted down at him. "Can I help you with those?"

Narrowing her eyes to slits, she focused on him until recognition dawned.

"You're—"

"Dead," he said, "if you say another word." He pressed the point of the long, wicked boning knife against her throat.

"Easy," she said, trembling. "I'm—"

"Quit screwin' around and go inside, or I'll take your tonsils out right here."

She obeyed, though between her fear and the groceries, it wasn't easy. Shawn relieved her of some of the load, and she managed to get the door open. He followed her in, past a bank of mailboxes and up a wide stairway to the second floor. There were two doors off the landing, and the stairs continued up.

Rattling her key in the lock, she spent a few harried moments getting into her apartment. Finally the door swung open, and they entered in single file.

"What do you want?" she asked, breathlessly, holding her purse to her chest as if it might ward him away.

He handed her the groceries. "Why don't you get started on dinner? While you're busy, I can explain." He extracted the bottle of wine. "I'll go ahead and open this. There's no reason we can't be civilized."

She stumbled away from him and into a tiny room some idiot decided would serve as a kitchen. It would have been cozy for one; two represented a crowd. The tiny space was made even smaller by a wide counter that serviced two stools. He sat on one and watched while she attempted to gather herself and put the groceries away.

"Take your time," he said. "I'm in no hurry."

She stared at him for a moment before she spoke. "A friend of mine's coming over," she said. "You don't want to be here when—"

"Why not?" he asked cheerfully. "I'm a people person! We can have a party."

Her argument fell far short of convincing, but she persisted. "I mean it. This is not someone you want to screw around with."

"Do you?"

She looked puzzled.

"Do you screw around with him?"

"Oh. Well—"

"I'll bet he's a cop, too, right? And a black belt?"

"Trust me, this—"

"Just cook something, okay? Quietly? You think I'm a moron? Christ, lady." He put the boning knife on the counter top in front of him while he removed the foil from the top of the wine bottle. "Where's your opener?"

She rummaged in a drawer and extracted a corkscrew, which she placed on the counter top.

Shawn used it to open the wine, pulling the cork with a gentle pop. There were wine glasses in a little rack on one side of the counter, and he poured two generous helpings.

"Might as well pour a third," she said.

"Might as well give it a fucking rest," Shawn responded. "Or do you just like to hear the sound of your own voice?"

"I'll bet you got a lot of that in prison."

He glared at her.

"Hearing yourself talk, I mean. Tori says—"

"Her name is *Vic*-toria," he said, "or Vicky Lynn."

"Not according to her book jacket," the woman said. "She's a respected writer. A woman with a wonderful future. Why can't you just leave her alone?"

"Why can't you just shut up and cook?"

This wasn't going the way he had planned. For one thing, the woman wasn't nearly as rattled as he figured she would be. Not that it mattered a whole lot; he'd make sure she was thoroughly frightened before he was through. Still, the mental image he'd been working on hadn't come to pass at all, and that bothered him.

"Why don't you get into something more comfortable," he said.

"I'm comfortable just like this."

He slammed his hand on the counter. "Well, I'm not! Now go in the other room and change into something sexy. Do it now, goddammit, or I'll be fixing dinner for one."

That put a little fear into her, he thought, a growing sense of satisfaction bringing a bit of warmth to his cheeks. Come to think of it, her cheeks were showing a bit of color, too. Maybe it was the wine. He didn't really care.

He followed her into her bedroom and watched while she tried to simultaneously hide and change into a nightgown. He flipped the boning knife end over end while he watched. The blade wasn't wasted on her.

"That's better," he said, when she finally stepped away from the closet. It wasn't a very revealing gown, nothing like what he had in mind, but it was better than the frumpy skirt and blouse she'd gotten out of. She wore a light robe-like thing on top. What had Vicky Lynn called it? A peignoir. Yeah. That was it. "Lose the peignoir," he said.

"I'll get cold," she protested.

"Tough shit."

"Really, I—"

"*Your* comfort doesn't matter. You haven't figured that out yet?"

A light knock on the door tore his attention away from her. "Who's that?"

"My friend," she said. "I told you—"

"Shut up," he hissed, waving her toward the door with the point of the knife. He motioned to a spot a few feet to one side. "Go. Stand over there."

She complied, and he went to the door expecting to find a peephole, but there wasn't one.

No peephole? In New York? What the hell was wrong with these people?

"Find out who it is," he whispered.

"I know who it is," she shot back.

"Ask anyway!" He punctuated his demand with quick jabs of the knife. "Now!"

"Who is it?" she asked.

There was only a brief pause before a woman's voice answered. "It's me, Rachel. Who did you expect?"

Shawn yanked the door open, and a balled fist crashed into his nose. The force drove him backwards, and his feet seemed to get tangled through no fault of his own. He couldn't remember a time he'd ever felt such sharp pain. He clutched his face with both hands as his butt hit the floor, all thoughts of the knife gone. He wasn't sure if the dimming lights were caused by blood leaking into his eyes or if he was losing consciousness. He hoped like hell he wasn't passing out.

Passing out? That would really suck.

~*~

Tori eased back in her chair with her research materials spread in front of her. These consisted of Uncle Bob's memoirs, a lengthy but unbound, handwritten manuscript in a legible though fading hand, the old Bible which she'd used to break his first code, and her own notes. She had made several photocopies of the manuscript pages, but preferred the originals when merely musing. Nor did she bother with her own published text; that contained nothing which would assist her in solving the remaining riddles. And those solutions seemed utterly out of reach. Without knowing exactly what printed text the old spy had used as the basis for his latter two codes, she had no hope of reading what he had written.

Why had he changed? Why needlessly complicate things? He had no immediate family—no one he could count on to work out whatever it was he had to say. She understood he may have wanted to shield some of the people who helped him during the war, and so coding his remarks about his espionage activities made sense. Didn't the U.S. government keep things secret for decades after the people involved were dead?

But the rest? Why? What could have driven his need for such secrecy? The only clue she had was the mention he made of treasure. The word was scrawled in the margin of the Bible on the page which fronted a copy of the deed to the Wyoming land. What little else she knew about his activities in the west was based on a pair of old family letters she'd found in the trunk with the Bible. Those had provided the impetus for her search to find his old cabin, which she bought and modernized, since it had stood vacant, literally in the middle of nowhere, for years. There had to be a reason he felt compelled to spend the rest of his life in isolation. The very fact that he made so many coded notes proved it! Or so she fervently believed. The idea that he may have just been a crazy old man, lost in the romance of his past, was one she resisted with all her being. There had to be something more. Something *here!*

She had spent more hours than she could count searching the Bible page on which he had written the trigger word. "Treasure" could be anything, and yet nothing in any of the passages on that page or the one facing it offered any clues. It was as if the word were written during a moment of idle doodling.

If it weren't for her success in breaking the first code, she'd have been tempted to think the second code was little more than some kind of obsessive-compulsive scribble. Why devise a code unless you needed to convey information to a second party? But Robert Lanier didn't *have* a second party. The only woman he'd ever been serious about had died of typhoid fever during the war. So, as far as she knew, he was writing to himself.

She turned to the section of the manuscript that contained his coded notes. They appeared to have been written at different times, possibly using different ink. The writing had faded with time, and she forced back a smile of relief that he hadn't used invisible ink on top of everything else. Nor was such a thought all that far-fetched. Poe's celebrated short story contained the idea that clues could be hidden in a document using heat-reactive ink. Tori had paid for several chemical and spectral scans on the paper Lanier left behind. Other than common watermarks, it contained no other hidden, or even partially hidden notations.

What if he had only been writing to or for himself, she wondered. What would that suggest? Certainly he would only need one reference book— one source of page/line/word number combinations. How many books were in print by the time he began coding his thoughts? A million? Ten million?

"He could have just as easily used his own journal," she muttered, her voice breaking the silence of the cabin. Shadow lifted his head and grunted. Mato seemed to be out cold.

His own journal? No way. But, just to be sure she had covered all the bases, Tori retrieved a photocopy of the manuscript and thumbed to the page where the second coded section began. Her eye moved immediately to the first column of numbers: 2/13/8. She flipped to the second page of the memoir, counted to the thirteenth line, and the eighth word, which read "Welcome."

Though confident a word of greeting was purely coincidental, she looked up the word from the second set of numbers in the column: "friend." With a growing sense of disbelief, she continued looking up the words referenced in the memoir and listed them on a separate sheet of paper. Within a few minutes, she had what appeared to be the first sentence, and it was far from the random collection of words such exercises usually produced. She inserted punctuation where warranted.

Welcome friend, whoever you are. You must be clever to have solved this puzzle. I pray that you are not merely clever but wise, too, for the treasure I have discovered cannot be entrusted to just anyone.

Tori's heart beat faster as the words unfolded. The feeling grew even more intense than the one she experienced when decoding Uncle Bob's original notes. This time there was an extra degree of urgency, despite its generic greeting. The message felt as if it had been directed to her specifically—a message which awaited delivery for over a century.

The idea that there might actually be a treasure was something she hadn't allowed herself to consider. And yet, now....

She pressed on with the transcription,

revealing words almost without reading them, striving to get as much of the message done as she could. She promised herself she would stop when she ran out of room on the page, and would only then insert periods, commas and anything else Uncle Bob had ignored.

Faster than she might have imagined, she reached the designated stopping point and began reading more carefully. When she finished the first scan, her eyes were drawn to the fireplace. Shadow and Mato were still parked in front of it, quite comfortably, even without any fire in the hearth. And that was a good thing, because in the opening lines of Robert Lanier's communiqué, he had given specific instructions on how to dismantle it.

~*~

"I say we stomp his head into the floor."

Shawn couldn't place the voice. *Was he back in the joint?*

"We can't do that! Just call the police."

That voice he knew. The Woodall woman. Jesus! How his nose hurt. He opened one eye a fraction and saw Vicky Lynn's editor standing next to a heavy, short-haired woman wearing masculine clothing but arguing just like any other broad. She looked like someone who moved furniture all day.

They were still arguing when he jammed his heel into the side of the heavy woman's knee. There was a satisfying crunch, and she went down in a howling pile. The look on Woodall's face was priceless and only got more so as he lifted an end table by its spindly-assed legs and brought it down with all his strength on the big woman's head.

The dyke on the floor went quiet, but Woodall began to scream.

Shawn rolled to his feet. "Will you shut the hell up?" He yanked a table leg free of the wreckage and threatened her with it, even though she was holding his knife.

He backhanded her knuckles with the table leg and sent the knife flying.

"We didn't mean to hurt you, I swear," she said, a stutter suddenly insinuating itself in her speech.

"Then you're even more stupid than I thought," he said, kneeling over the fallen woman.

"Please," Woodall said, "don't hurt her anymore. Let me take care of her."

He shook his head. "Nah. I can handle it." He could see a bubble of air, snot, and blood rising just under her nose. He popped it with the tip of his knife, and that brought a sharp cry from Woodall.

"Please," she begged. "She won't—"

"Back off!"

Using the index finger of his left hand, Shawn located the fallen woman's ribs, the task made difficult by her clothing and a layer of fat. He probed until he could feel the space between the ribs roughly over her heart. That's where he inserted the tip of the hideously sharp boning knife. He looked up at Woodall to see her reaction as he jammed the blade into the inert form on the floor and yanked it back and forth to ensure plenty of internal damage.

Woodall's face drained. He thought she might faint, but she merely made a high, keening sound and staggered backwards, almost as if he'd stabbed her instead of the woman on the floor. *Definitely a case of screwed up priorities.* He hoped her editing skills were more reliable.

"What have you done," she asked at length, her voice a harsh whisper.

Shawn pulled the knife free and wiped it on the dead woman's stomach. "Just making sure she doesn't lay another sucker punch on me." He pointed the knife toward the kitchen. "I left my wine in there. And you haven't finished fixin' dinner."

"Are you out of your bloody mind?" Woodall screamed.

"I'm tired, and I'm hungry. And my nose hurts like hell. So, unless you wanna join your little gal pal on the floor over there, you'll get your ass in gear."

She gave him a look that might have withered a lesser man, but Shawn was anything but a lesser man. He put the knife down and pulled a box of tissues closer. He alternated between sips of wine and dabs of soft, white Kleenex on his damaged nose. The bleeding seemed to go on forever but actually tapered off about the time Woodall put salad and a loaf of French bread on the table.

Shawn had watched carefully while his captive prepared the meal to be sure she didn't slip anything nasty into his portion. Even so, he had no intention of trusting her, so when she put the plates on the table, he switched them.

"Dig in," he said.

Her eyes no longer held any fire as she went through the motions of feeding herself.

Once he'd seen her eat, Shawn dug in. Not surprisingly, the food wasn't very good. One couldn't expect much in the way of TLC when the chef was being directed at knife point. Besides, it was some sort of gourmet crap and did nothing to satisfy either of his hungers.

They ate in silence, except for an occasional sniffle from the woman.

"I 'spect you know what I came for," Shawn said at last.

Woodall turned glassy eyes at him, but remained silent.

"I need to find Vicky Lynn."

She didn't respond.

"I figured you'd give me an argument," he said. "Not that it will matter in the long run. You'll tell me everything I want to know."

"Why should I tell you anything? You're just going to kill me anyway."

He feigned a look of surprise. "Why would I do that? You're Vicky Lynn's editor. If I killed you, who'd help her with her books?"

"Asshole."

He smiled. "Good! We're talking. Now let's see if we can push it a step further." He stood up and stepped behind her chair at the little kitchen counter. He put his hands on her narrow shoulders, pleased by her surprisingly smooth skin. "This is the part where you offer to tell me what I want to know in exchange for me letting you go."

"That'll never happen."

He squeezed her shoulders as if he intended to give her a massage. "You won't tell me what I want to know, or I won't let you go?"

"Either one."

He slipped the blade of the boning knife under the thin strap of her nightgown and lifted, slowly. The material stretched upward under the strain and then parted without a sound. Woodall made no move to keep the fabric from falling away from her body.

He did the same with the other strap, and when it parted, the front of her gown fell forward to reveal small, pale breasts. Shawn reached down and palmed one.

Woodall gave no response.

Shawn set the knife on the counter top behind him, then leaned forward and cupped one of her breasts in each hand, squeezing gently. Within moments, Woodall voiced a low moan and pressed herself forward into his hands. Shawn squeezed a bit harder, and Woodall's voice dropped an octave, her head drifting slowly forward as if to bare her neck for his kiss.

"You like that?" he murmured.

"Oh, yeah," she said, her voice a sensuous purr. She lifted her own hands and rested them gently on top of his.

"I—"

Suddenly grabbing his fingers, she pulled his arms forward while ramming her head back, smashing his face with the crown of her head. Once again, a debilitating pain exploded out from his nose. The blow was slightly off target, hitting his cheek as much as his nose, else he would have dropped like a hammered steer.

He lurched away, his hands once again drawn to his face. The pain left him stunned; he could focus on nothing besides avoiding another attack.

How could I have been so stupid? And where is—

"Looking for this?" Woodall asked, waving the boning knife from the other side of the counter.

"Yeah," Shawn said through clenched teeth, his nose once again gushing blood. "You'll pay for that."

"We'll see. Meanwhile, you're bleeding on my

carpet. Move back into the kitchen."

Chapter Eleven
Westward ho, ho, ho....

Tom Purcell sat in front of his computer with his head propped between his palms. A chart detailing his most recent spate of investments looked like some bizarre form of abstract art where shit had been thrown at a graph and then had slid sideways and down. His early foray into the options game had been marked by phenomenal success, but which only lasted for three months. His gainers outnumbered his losers four-to-one. Though a rank amateur, he had taken to the investment format quickly. By buying stock *options* rather than stock, he could invest in thousands of "shares" at a fraction of the share's actual price. If the stock went up, the value of the options usually went up, too. If he guessed wrong, and the stock price dropped, so did the value of the options. But the biggest difference was that options expired, shares didn't. An option had to be exercised before its expiration date, meaning shares had to be purchased for the amount specified in the original option contract, regardless of the market price at the time of the sale. If the option price was up, life was good. If the option price went down... Well, for the first three months, the price almost never went down.

Tom rewarded himself handsomely for his brilliant picks at the start of his investment career. The cherry red BMW convertible in his driveway stood as a testament to his early success.

In the options world, good guesses are rewarded handsomely; bad guesses are punished. Shortly after buying his car, and continuing for the last several months, the market had been kicking Tom Purcell's ass. And despite the fact his losses kept piling up, he felt certain his luck would soon change. It had to. He had spent the better part of his savings covering bad bets and had no intention of selling the car, too.

The depth of his due diligence—the background study successful investors conducted before putting money into a stock—was limited, and in many cases non-existent. That his early hunches had paid off, handsomely, was the worst thing that could have happened to him. It gave him a confidence he hadn't earned and a bravado his net worth couldn't support.

Rather than put time into studying stocks, Purcell preferred to rub elbows with other options traders in chat rooms and online, options-oriented message areas. The back and forth in these forums ranged from name-calling and a playground maturity level to in-depth analyses by people who seemed to know the most intimate details of companies he'd never heard of. He couldn't get enough of it.

An inheritance had allowed him to keep investing, hoping for the elusive 10-bagger that would reverse his recent failures. But it hadn't happened yet. The inheritance hadn't lasted long; he needed something else to shore up his investment accounts.

I need a rich widow, he mused, staring at the red ink in his financials. *I wonder if Cal's writer friend is single.*

~*~

Shawn's ruined nose delivered a non-stop torrent of blood that ran down his chin. The first bashing had thoroughly soaked his T-shirt. The outrage Woodall had perpetrated only made it worse. He held a dish towel to his face to staunch the blood flow. Woodall, meanwhile, held him at bay with the boning knife as she pawed through her purse with her free hand.

When she retrieved a cell phone, Shawn knew he had to act. He threw the blood-soaked dish towel at her, then grabbed the chair she had been sitting on when she attacked him. Holding it at arm's length, he rushed her, trapping her against a wall with her knife arm pinned to her chest.

Woodall dropped her phone to give her a free hand for the knife. She made the switch, then tried to stab him wrong-handed, but her efforts were clumsy. Shawn grinned despite the pain in his face; blood made his grip on the furniture tenuous. He used still more muscle to compensate.

"Tell me where Vicky Lynn is, and I'll back off," he said, his teeth clenched in anger.

Woodall ignored him and continued to struggle.

"You asked for it," he said, ramming the chair at her flailing arm, then bringing his knee up into her stomach. She folded forward, but didn't release the weapon, though her efforts to reach him with it grew weaker.

He grabbed her wrist with his right hand and punched her face with his left. She tried to duck and dodge, but he kept hammering her, the skin of his knuckles shredding on her teeth.

"Stop, please," she blubbered, dropping the knife. Her face barely resembled a human's.

Shawn grabbed her hair and dragged her into the living room, where he tossed her on the floor next to her dead friend. "Where's Vicky Lynn?"

Woodall wept hysterically. She had one hand on her face and the other on the corpse beside her.

"Tell me, dammit," Shawn yelled. When she still couldn't compose herself enough to talk, he kicked her. She tried curling up in a ball to protect herself, but he went on kicking her. Head, back, kidneys—any area she left uncovered became a target. Before long, she stopped whimpering. She also stopped protecting herself. Her arms fell loose at her sides, and her fetal position appeared more accidental than intended.

Well, just shit. She's dead.

Shawn thought briefly of feeling for a pulse, but he wasn't exactly sure how. He'd seen it done, of course, in movies and on TV. But really, who cared? It wasn't like he was going to call 911 and order up an ambulance. If she wasn't dead now, she would be soon enough.

What bothered him more was that she hadn't told him where to find Vicky Lynn. He realized he'd let his anger get the best of him. That was something the shrink in the prison at Reidsville had warned him about, too. Had to get that pesky temper of his under control. *Yeah, well, one day.*

He had few options other than to search the house. Perhaps he'd find a clue. He figured his best bet would be the woman's computer, if he could find it. Everybody had one, it seemed like, and they weren't that hard to use.

But Woodall didn't have one. At least, not in her apartment, and Shawn had been quite thorough in his search. Surely, she had one in her office. He thought about going there; he knew where the building was, but breaking in wouldn't be worth the risk. New Yorkers were a suspicious lot. They almost certainly had rent-a-cops patrolling the hallways. He'd avoid it if he could.

Moving on, he stepped into the bathroom to

inspect his nose. It had already started to swell, and he'd almost certainly have one black eye, if not two. The explosion at ADA Sutherland's house had left him with a missing eyebrow that gave him an odd look, and his newly disfigured nose didn't help that at all. *Thanks, bitch.* While cursing Woodall and her dyke pal, he washed his face, hands, and arms. His shirt was a mess, but there was no way he could wear anything of Woodall's; she was half his size.

Shawn went back into the kitchen and helped himself to the rest of the wine. It wasn't very good, way too dry, but Woodall didn't stock any booze. That discovery made him so angry he was tempted to go back into the living room and kick her some more, not that it would do any good.

Instead, he poked around in her refrigerator until he found a small rib eye and a bottle of white wine. Having finished the first bottle, he opened the second while he fried the steak. The dinner he'd eaten earlier hardly even qualified as food. He couldn't help but think back to Woodall's treachery, pretending to enjoy his attentions. *He'd* certainly been enjoying it. Then she had to go and ruin it. Up to that point, he'd planned on having a little fun with her, whether she told him where to find Vicky Lynn or not. But then the bitch reverted to form. He should've seen it coming.

He overcooked the steak. And the second bottle of wine was even worse than the first. What a crap evening, he thought. Returning to the living room, he walked straight to Woodall's bookcase to see if he could find Vicky Lynn's book. It didn't take much effort; the book lay face up in the middle of a shelf. Shawn opened it and read the inscription:

Thanks for everything, Cassy—
your support, your counsel, and your
friendship. I could never have done this
without you. How can I ever repay you?
Love, Tori.

Well, isn't that just fucking swell, Shawn thought. I'll bet she never thought Cassy would be paid off by having someone kick the shit out of her. That thought lightened his mood, but not nearly as much as when two glossy photos fell out of the back of the book.

He swept them up and carried them to a floor lamp for closer examination. In the first, Vicky Lynn stood outside a rustic building sporting a big red-on-white sign telling how the town of Ten Sleep, Wyoming, got its name. The other photo was of an old broken-down log cabin. He flipped them over to look for inscriptions, but only the one of the cabin bore any writing. It said: "Here's a 'Before' picture of Uncle Bob's cabin. I'll send you the 'After' when it's finished."

A quick search of the shelves failed to turn up the promised 'After' picture, which began to put a damper on his recently elevated mood. He slipped the photos into his pants pocket and put the book back on the shelf. As he contemplated what to do with the bodies, or if he should cover up his visit as he had at Sutherland's house, he noticed that Woodall's body wasn't where he'd left it. In fact, it wasn't anywhere to be seen.

Hurrying to the front door, he found an unmistakable blood trail leading out into the hallway. It crossed the hall to the neighboring apartment, then continued on up the stairs to the next level. *The bitch crawled out while I was screwing around in the kitchen!* That's when he heard the distant howl of sirens.

~*~

Tori went to bed early, as was her habit. She wasn't much of a TV watcher, though she had invested in a dish antenna and occasionally tuned in a movie. She was much more likely to spend her time reading or pouring over the endless supply of fascinating material available on the internet, two pursuits she'd learned to appreciate only after Shawn's timely ejection from her life.

Sleep eluded her, and she found herself thinking of Uncle Bob. In her mind, the man was every bit as dashing and romantic as she'd painted him in her book. Athletic, clever, imaginative, and well-educated, Robert Lanier was a regular 19th century James Bond, only without the gadgetry.

Like Tori herself, he had grown up in the South. Born to a minister and a seamstress in the tiny, south Alabama town of Camp Hill, Lanier had excelled in the country schoolhouse provided by the bigger planters in the area, and eventually moved to Arlington, Virginia, where he courted Miss Anne Carter Lee, known as Annie, the second daughter of the man who would one day command the Confederacy's Army of Northern Virginia.

Though a romance with Annie never fully blossomed, Lanier's relationship with her father, Robert E. Lee, grew strong. Lee's sons were all determined to have military careers, but Lee felt Lanier's talents were better suited to a life in the shadows. His keen mind allowed him to accurately deduce fact from observation, and the coded messages containing his deductions had saved many lives. Sadly, the very nature of his efforts meant that he would enjoy no wide acclaim during his lifetime.

Tori understood the need to maintain the secrets that defined his life during the war. Too many lives could have been ruined if those secrets were revealed too soon. That she was finally able to shine some light on them, and tell at least a part of Lanier's story, gave her great satisfaction. But it was his continued secrecy that had puzzled her for years.

Nearly all of his post-war life had been lived under another layer of shadow—dark curtains of his own design. When she began the task of restoring his old cabin, she half expected to find hidden panels in the walls or a stash of secret documents buried on the grounds. Neither had come to pass. At least, not until now.

She eyed the fireplace for the thousandth time since finally breaking the second code. The temptation was strong to grab some sharp tool—any pointed piece of steel—and use it to attack the mortar and stone. But she resisted the urge. Tomorrow would be soon enough. And those were the thoughts that carried her off to sleep.

~*~

Shawn raced down the stairs two at a time, his mind nearing the ragged edge of panic. Gotta pull it together, he told himself. *Gotta look like anybody else on the street. Gotta look normal, whatever the hell that is in New York city.*

When he reached the front door, he took a deep breath and forced himself to calm down. The sounds of the sirens had grown louder; the cops would arrive at any moment. Looking across the street, he spotted his best option: the deli. Lose himself in there and no one would suspect he had anything to do with the mayhem across the street. They'll be looking for someone on the run, he thought. Well, that won't be me.

He strolled as casually across the street as he could, and when he reached the midpoint glanced down at the blood stains that covered the front of his shirt.

Shit, shit, shit!

The cops were almost there! He grabbed the hem of the shirt and quickly yanked it over his head. As he wadded it into a red and white ball, he checked the front of his pants for more telltale stains. Fortunately, his slacks were free of gore. He crammed the shirt into his armpit and kept walking, as if enjoying a warm, late spring evening, though it was actually growing a bit chilly. New Yorkers are idiots, he told himself, they won't think anything of it. He stuffed the bloody shirt into a trashcan outside the deli, then went in.

His first order of business was a new shirt. No matter how stupid the locals might be, he didn't want to take unnecessary chances. Grabbing the first thing that looked like it might fit, he ripped the tags free and pulled the shirt over his head. When it slipped over his nose, he received a sharp reminder that the condition of his face wouldn't make for a great prom photo. He wandered around the store until he located an aisle containing cold remedies, laxatives, tampons and Band-Aids, among other health care supplies. He helped himself to aspirin and bandages, two of which he gently stretched over his nose.

"Rough night?" asked a bored clerk at the sales register.

"Yeah," Shawn said. "Some asshole sucker-punched me. I got 'im back though."

"Gotta be careful in the city," opined the clerk as he rang up the sale.

After counting his change, Shawn perused the magazine rack by the front window, which gave him a convenient view of the street and Woodall's apartment.

He still couldn't believe the bitch had

survived. What a complete pisser! But at least he had what he'd come for. The photos in his pocket would surely lead him to Vicky Lynn's door. He smiled as he watched an ambulance join the three patrol cars parked helter-skelter outside the apartment.

A half dozen uniformed men milled around, trying to look important while two guys raced up the wide front stairs with their stretcher/bed gizmo. As soon as they went inside, Shawn wandered by the candy counter, helped himself to a candy bar and returned to the sales counter. He pointed out the cigarettes he wanted, grabbed a book of matches from a glass bowl, and fished a nice, crisp twenty out of his pocket to pay for it.

The new T-shirt itched. Ignoring it, he paused outside the store to admire his reflected finery: a white shirt with a big red heart and bold black letters that announced to the world: "I♡New York."

And some people buy these shirts 'cause they like 'em.

~*~

Tori awoke to find an enormous, black dog sleeping beside her. His broad head lay even with her pillow and his body occupied a portion of bedroom real estate she rarely shared with anyone since Shawn had been dragged away a decade ago. That episode had certainly taught her the joys of sleeping alone. To be sure, there had been the occasional fling: a friend of Cassy's, a couple guys she met in bars, and even a female she'd met at a writer's conference, though that had turned out to be mutually embarrassing and caused her to swear off Cosmos forever and switch from vodka to bourbon. Other than that, she'd been largely celibate. Her history with Shawn had left her with what her therapist in Atlanta had called "trust issues." She preferred to think of it as just being aware that most males were assholes. Caleb, and hopefully Mato, were exceptions.

She looked at Shadow. "Are you an exception, too?"

He made a whuffling sound, his big, black lips rippling slightly.

"Out?" she asked.

He stood on the bed, stretching, and she marveled at just how big he really was. At five foot nine, she was on the tall side herself, and she felt sure the dog could look her in the eye if he stood up on his hind legs. His appetite was likely to be enormous, too. "Are you going to gobble up all my royalties?"

Shadow jumped down and padded over to the door, then sat and waited for her to let him out. Mato stood by the fireplace with his paper and paints, an outline of the big dog already completed in his unique minimalist style. Tori stopped to admire his work, then rewarded him with a smile and went to fix them all a bite of breakfast.

The day promised to be busy, starting with a

call to Purcell—*ugh*—then off to find tools so she could start work on the fireplace, although she had no idea what Uncle Bob might have hidden there. She just hoped that whatever damage she was about to inflict on her home could be repaired without forcing her into even more debt. After all, her royalty checks weren't *that* large.

~*~

"Tom!" said Warren Noblewski, President of North Central Community College. "I've been looking for you."

Great, muttered Purcell under his breath. Noblewski was legendary for finding endless ways to waste an associate professor's time. He meant well, but if there was a gene intended to help someone determine the difference between valuable effort and running in circles, Noblewski didn't have it. "What's up, Warren?" Purcell asked.

Noblewski looked as if he'd just won a lottery and was about to share his winnings. "I've got some good news!"

I could sure as Hell use some.

"You knew Dr. Devlin was planning on retiring," Noblewski began, "but she hadn't given us a date."

Awesome, Purcell thought. He wants me to organize the old biddy's retirement bash. *Woohoo. Punch and cookies in the library.* "And now she has?" he asked.

"Oh, yes, indeed. As department chair, she opted to maintain the school's collection of native American artifacts. Dr. Nelson, the new chair, advised me this morning that he would rather not assume those duties on top of everything else he has on his plate. Naturally, I thought of you."

Purcell was stunned. "You want *me* to take over the collection?"

Noblewski grinned like the Cheshire cat. "Actually, I do. You're nearly as knowledgeable as Denise, er... Dr. Devlin, and I'm sure you'll have some fresh ideas about how the collection can best be displayed." He rocked back on his heels, thumbs hooked under his overworked suspenders. "Are you interested?"

Possibilities raced through Purcell's mind. While far from being the largest assemblage of native artifacts in North America, the collection was indeed impressive, and far larger than the space available in which to display it. In fact, the bulk of the collection had to be kept in storage, with pieces rotated in and out as time and interest permitted. But what really intrigued him was the opportunity to bargain for other artifacts—buying, selling and trading what they had for whatever they needed to fill out the collection. And therein lay the seeds for many, many opportunities. Lucrative opportunities. Everyone knew the museum's board of trustees was almost an illusion. It met annually to rubber stamp whatever the supervisor of the collection wanted, then re-elected its members and went back to eating the chicken dinner that was their annual reward.

"I'd be honored," Purcell stammered. "I—"

"Excellent! I'll see that an addendum is added to your contract." Noblewski nudged the younger man conspiratorially. "We can't expect you to do it all out of the goodness of your heart, eh?"

It was Purcell's turn to beam. "I don't know what to say," he began.

"Let's keep it between us for now," Noblewski said. "I'll make an announcement at the next general faculty meeting. But, as of the first of the month, you're in charge of the collection."

"Thank you, sir," Purcell said. "I'll do my best to justify your faith in me."

"I'm sure you will, Tom." The older man paused briefly before continuing. "You know, of course, that our goal is to keep the community involved. That means good press. You'll need to work with our public relations staff to make the most of any opportunities."

"Of course," he said, trying to recall if he even knew who was responsible for the school's public relations, most of which involved a remarkably unsuccessful basketball team.

"Great!" the school president said, his deep voice booming down the hall. "Keep me posted."

"Absolutely," Purcell said. "Every step of the way."

~*~

Tori was feeling quite satisfied with herself, having called Tom Purcell first thing after breakfast, without attempting even the most obvious delaying tactics. She suspected it may have had something to do with her wanting to clear the decks before she tackled the fireplace.

A man answered the phone on the first ring. "Humanities."

"May I speak to Dr. Purcell?" she asked.

"I'm Tom Purcell," said the voice, "but I don't have a doctorate."

"Oh, sorry."

"Don't be," he said with a chuckle, "they're overrated."

"I meant..." She let the explanation fade. "My friend, Caleb Jones, suggested I give you a call."

"Yes, of course. You're Tori Lanier. I've read your book."

His remark left her momentarily flustered, though she couldn't be sure why. Many people had read her book. "I hope you enjoyed it."

"Absolutely. I hope you'll do another."

"That's the plan."

"I look forward to it," he said. "So, how's Cal? I haven't seen him in ages. Is he still chasing that hot little forest ranger?"

"Oh yeah. They're quite an item, the talk of downtown Charm."

"I can imagine. Do you know them well?"

"Well enough. They were a great help to me when I was getting settled."

"I'm not surprised. Cal has a nose for good people. So, how can I help you?"

Tori felt a flush of warmth despite her natural inclination to distrust men. This one, however, carried Cal's seal of approval. "I've made a recording," she said. "It's of an uh... an acquaintance of mine."

"And you need someone to translate for you, correct?"

He was making things too easy, she thought. But then, she figured she deserved to have things go her way once in a while. "Yes." She fumbled briefly with the MP3 player, then got it oriented properly toward the phone. "Are you ready?"

"Certainly," he said.

She wondered if he was smiling. There seemed to be a hint of amusement in his voice. "Did I say something funny?" she asked.

"No," he said. "It just seems all so mysterious. Who is this acquaintance of yours? Where did you meet him? In Charm?"

"I— Well, yes, sort of. Near there. We weren't actually in town." She didn't like having to play

Twenty Questions. "It's not like we're close or anything, 'cause we're not."

"Okay."

"He's an artist," she said, feeling the need to offer something that felt like an insight. Her confidence that Mato hadn't said anything embarrassing in the recording had begun to slip. "I'd like to ask him to do some work for me—a mural, actually."

Where the hell had that come from? Although, she thought, staring at the unadorned walls of her cabin, a mural might look pretty cool. And Mato certainly had mad skills.

"How did you come to have a recording of his voice?"

"Cal suggested it."

"I see. You need to understand, I'm an anthropologist, not a linguist," Purcell said. "I can't guarantee anything."

"Cal said you could speak several Indian languages."

His voice continued to carry a smile. "I'm familiar with some of the plains dialects, but I'm no expert. I just don't want you to get your hopes up, even though I'll do my best. Okay?"

"Sure."

"Why don't you go ahead and play the recording for me?"

Tori pushed the PLAY button and held the little machine near the phone. The recording lasted only a few seconds; Mato was anything but verbose. She set the MP3 player down and listened for Purcell's' response. When he didn't say anything, she prompted him with a simple, "Well?"

"Would you play it again, please?"

"Sure," she said, and played it again. At his request, she played it two more times after that.

"Hmm," was all he said.

"Is that a good hmm or a bad hmm?" *What had Mato said?*

Purcell remained oddly silent, which only fed Tori's discomfort. Finally, he said, "Can you E-mail the audio file to me?"

"I suppose," she said, allowing a bit of testiness to creep into her voice. "What did he say?"

"I'm not sure, exactly. The dialect sounds a little like Arapaho, but it's not."

"Could you make out anything?"

"Not much. His name, Mato, means 'bear' in Arapaho. There's also a modifier—draws, or sketches, something like that. I got a few words here and there, but I couldn't put anything in context. That's going to take some time. I need to do some research to identify the exact language. There's a lot of overlap, common roots, that sort of thing."

Tori began to relax. It seemed unlikely that

Mato had portrayed her as something or someone horrible. Big maybe, but not unkind.

"I'm puzzled by the voice," Purcell said. "It has an odd timber to it, high-pitched and yet mature. Almost female."

"Oh, he's definitely male," Tori said, recalling her little friend's ultra-compact, but well-chiseled physique.

"Indeed. Well, I have no reason to doubt it," Purcell said, "but I'd really like to hear more. Is there a chance you could make another recording?"

Tori looked toward Mato's empty sleeping pallet, which he'd left right after breakfast. No surprise there. "I'm not sure when I'll have a chance," she said, "but I'll try to remember the next time I see him."

"That'd be great. Meanwhile, if you'll shoot that file my way, I'll get started on it. I'll send you a transcript as soon as I've got one. Fair enough?"

"Yes, thank you. Oh, and perhaps you could make a recording for me."

Purcell's voice lost some of its warmth. "I don't understand."

"I still need to ask him about that mural. If you can't ask him for me, perhaps you can teach me how to ask him myself."

"Oh, of course," he said, friendly once again. "And just how did you plan to reward me?"

"*Excuse* me?" she said, feeling her eyes widen in surprise.

"If I'm going to be doing all this work for you, I'd like to know what's in it for me."

He'd caught her completely by surprise. "Well, I— Uh—"

"Why not let me buy you dinner?"

Chapter Twelve
Living with secrets

Shawn feared that making his way through the New York subway, and then through the streets to the parking lot where he'd left the look-at-me yellow Chevy, would be a nightmare. But it wasn't bad at all. After a moment of indecision when he surfaced after the subway ride, he ambled straight to the parking lot. Fear of losing his way had only been part of the problem. Anyone with half a brain knew the Big Apple was the promised land for gangbangers and hoods. The Mafia ran the place, after all. The last thing he wanted was to accidentally piss off some greaser with a Jones for snuffing rednecks.

He unlocked the car, then checked the trunk to be sure no one had ripped him off while he was dealing with Vicky Lynn's editor. What a cluster fuck that had been. All he wanted was a little information.

Was that so much to ask? He'd ended up killing some broad he didn't even know, while the one he really meant to punish was probably working with a police sketch artist at that very moment. No, he thought, there's no point in that; *she knew exactly who he was,* so the cops probably had his picture and were already looking for him.

Woodall couldn't know that he found the snapshots and now had some ideas about where to find Vicky Lynn. Woodall would surely warn her about him, and there wasn't a damned thing he could about it. Could he try to track her down in one of the city's hospitals and finish the job? The thought appealed to him, but ultimately would require too much time, and even if he was successful, it was a dead certainty she'd have made the phone calls before he got to her.

Aw, screw it.

Besides, he had other problems. It wouldn't be long before some smart-ass cracker cop tied him to Sutherland, and when they did, they'd start looking for the stupid yellow car. They might even put the New York incident together with those in Georgia, and that would be enough to get the friggin' FBI involved. *Wouldn't that just be goddamn wonderful?*

While rooting around in the trunk, he discovered a compact tool box Sutherland had thoughtfully provided. Inside, he found a Phillips screwdriver amid the usual hardware. Shawn picked it up and turned to see what other vehicles were parked nearby. A Ford SUV was the closest, so he removed the Ford's plates and installed them on the Chevy. He tossed the Georgia plates back in the trunk with the screwdriver and drove out of the lot. He wondered briefly what the driver of the Ford would think when the cops pulled him over. Another good citizen gone bad, he guessed, laughing.

He recalled something some old fart had once said, though he never understood why anyone would make a big deal about it. Now, though, it seemed like an excellent idea to him, too. "Go west, young man," he told himself. "And step on it."

Mato was troubled by the actions of the she-giant. Though she often said and did things he didn't understand, she had never tried to harm him. Still, he was suspicious. Once again she had pressed one of her magic boxes against her head and spoken to it. The previous evening, while he pretended to sleep, she ignored him, which made it easy to observe what she was doing, even if he had no idea what it meant or where it might lead. She didn't disguise her use of magic, so she probably didn't care if he saw her. He had begun to relax when she put the box containing his voice next to the box she spoke to, *and then let his voice out!* Not just once, but several times.

He wanted desperately to say something and confirm that he still owned his voice, but that would have given him away. So he waited until she was speaking again, then coughed and pretended to mumble in his sleep. His voice felt normal; she hadn't taken it from him after all. It occurred to him that she probably used the same magic on his voice that she used to capture the music in the silvery discs. It was not so different from his drawings. He didn't take anything away from the animals he portrayed; he merely imitated their shapes. He reasoned that Tori's sound magic operated in a similar fashion. The realization came as a great relief and allowed him to focus his thoughts on his earlier discovery, the carvings in the rock wall.

The arrow was certainly a sign left by one of The People, and obviously pointed to something of great importance. He couldn't help but wonder if the arrow had been carved in the stone before or after Tori's cabin had been built. Perhaps the arrow pointed to something beyond the cabin. He closed his eyes and built a picture in his mind of the arrow on the rock. He recalled how he had to twist his body to align himself and sight down the shallow channel cut in the stone, possibly by an ancestor.

The image in his mind was clear, consisting of only those details which interested him. He saw the colors of the cabin, the darks and lights, the texture of the rock, and the tiny bend in the shaft of the arrow. The carving had not been done by a steady hand, but it didn't matter. The message was clear. Only the vast blue sky stood behind the cabin. The arrow pointed to the ground on which it stood.

Such markers were exceedingly rare. None were needed to point the way to the best hunting grounds, or the places where edibles grew in abundance. The People knew where these things were, and the knowledge was shared by all. The path to a place like the cavern of dreams, however, would never have been known by many. At best, no more than two or three would ever know how to find it. And if something happened to them before they passed the secret along, the knowledge could be lost forever. Which is exactly what had driven Mato to his current circumstances.

The arrow pointed the way to the entrance, and the she-giant's cabin stood right on top of it.

~*~

Tom Purcell stirred his coffee and mused about the recording he'd listened to the previous evening. He hoped Tori had already E-mailed a copy of it to him, though she hadn't sounded too eager about doing it. Had he over-played his hand when he asked her to dinner? It was hard to tell with some women. She seemed okay with the give and take of their conversation, but had maintained a certain reserve. Of course, he knew very little about her. She was single, a writer, and obviously something of a recluse. And, of course, she was a friend of Caleb's. That was good and bad. The old cowboy was certainly a straight arrow—a regular boy scout when it came to the business of day-to-day living. But what made him such a good person also made him something of a bore. Purcell couldn't imagine spending more than an occasional evening with him.

They had met by chance in the cafe of a

backwater Wyoming town which featured Saturday morning country jam sessions. He and Caleb had each brought harmonicas and managed a lively duet with banjo and guitar accompaniment. They weren't fast friends, and never would be, but their meeting proved the value of having a wide circle of acquaintances. After all, without Caleb, he would never have been introduced to Tori Lanier. He had even gone back to the library to have another look at her book. The photo of her on the jacket had been most encouraging.

Her recording, however, would be a challenge. His comments to her about the speaker's language having Arapaho roots may have been accurate, though the evidence to back up the conclusion was extremely thin. What had particularly gotten his attention was a possible reference to a cave of some kind. While he told himself he was merely trying to reduce premature conjecture, the real reason he'd said nothing was because he had no intention of sharing a possible source of valuable artifacts with someone who merely wanted to have one of her walls painted.

Still, the full meaning of the message eluded him. There were simply too many words he didn't recognize, and without that knowledge, syntax and grammar were pointless. His best bet, of course, was to find her friend, Mato, and have a little talk with him. Indians tended to be guarded, and he respected their reasoning, for it seemed any and all non-tribal authority figures were simply out to screw them. It hadn't ended with the 19th century, either. Federal, state, and local governments had a long and well-documented history of ripping off the native population. Not that Purcell was any great champion of Indian rights, but he figured he was smart enough to get what he wanted without landing on any tribal shit lists.

It was all about options: the opportunity kind, which could make him some serious money, and the investment kind, which would allow him to multiply it. And just then, he was way behind in both.

~*~

Billie Johansson looked at the poor woman lying on the hospital bed. She had arrived the previous evening via the Emergency Room and had spent several hours in surgery. Her dressings would have to be changed soon, and it would be Billie's job to do it. That would be no great challenge for the skilled nurse, and with any luck, her patient would remain asleep during the procedure and thereby avoid the pain. Billie glanced at the woman's chart: Cassandra Woodall, 34, beating victim.

Billie was nearing the end of a double shift, otherwise, she wouldn't have been able to talk to the EMTs who brought her patient in. Apparently, she had escaped her attacker and crawled up a flight of stairs before she found someone at home and willing to help. The 911 call had gone out immediately, but the woman lost consciousness before the ambulance arrived. From what Billie could tell, she was extremely lucky to be alive, although she'd carry scars from the beating for a long time.

Staying alive was obviously the most important concern now, but if her luck held and she made it, she was going to need some serious cosmetic surgery. Billie checked the woman's pulse and blood pressure, then updated her chart. The nurse pushed a strand of hair back from her patient's forehead. "Poor baby," she said. "We'll take care of you. We need you to get well so we can find out who did this to you." She pursed her lips, then added, "And put his sick, demented ass away forever."

~*~

Once again Tori read over the decoded instructions from Uncle Bob's journal. She'd lost count of how many times she'd done it. The coffee helped refresh her, but it didn't relieve the kink in her back, a nagging little bonus from her work on the hearth. She had spent a couple hours giving the fireplace a thorough cleaning. Not only did she haul away the ashes and carbonized remains of Mato's cookout, she vacuumed the accumulation of ash from the seams between the rocks lining the fireplace. What she discovered was a metal plate that formed the base.

She had always assumed the floor of the fireplace was cement or stone, but once she cleaned off the thick layer of congealed crud that covered it, she found cast iron. Sitting on the floor by the hearth, she massaged her lower back as she inspected the rocks that topped the iron plate. No metal edge was visible since the outer side of the plate was obscured by stones of varying size and color.

According to Uncle Bob's notes, the stones around the hearth were interlocked and could be pushed one way and another, like a Chinese puzzle box, to allow the floor to be pulled out of the way. That may have been the original design, but whoever worked on the fireplace during the cabin's restoration had been unaware of it. She couldn't resist a little gasp at the realization of just how close some nameless worker had come to discovering Robert Lanier's great secret—without benefit of codes, persistent study, or sleepless nights.

The bastard!

But she shook off such thoughts as completely unreasonable. She'd been on-site during most of the work, assisting where she could, hauling materials, making decisions, running errands, and seeing to a thousand details that never occurred to her in what she laughingly looked back on as the "planning stage."

Retrospect provided the unassailable fact that there had been painfully little planning involved in bringing the cabin back to life. It would have been easier, and likely cheaper, to have built something from scratch. A mobile home would certainly have offered more amenities than Uncle Bob's Lincolnesque digs. *Ah, but it wouldn't have had nearly as much character.* That had to count for something.

Yeah, right.

Of course, if she *had* hauled in a trailer or just pitched a tent, she'd have saved herself the trouble of wrecking the damned fireplace. She poured herself another mug of coffee and gave the hearth stones one last inspection before she began to blast away at them with a sledge hammer. Carefully moving from stone to stone—since Uncle Bob hadn't bothered to say which one went first, or in what direction, for that matter—Tori gave each a push and a pull. She'd worked her way through two-thirds of the stones when she paused to examine the lower tiers of rock. Those bore the unmistakable signs of new mortar and reflected the efforts of one of the laborers she'd hired. The stones in the top tier, however, were much tighter. So tight, in fact, there was no room for mortar.

Tori tested the next stone and detected a slight movement. Using both hands, she attempted to wiggle it back and forth, but like a loose tooth in the early stages, it only moved a tiny fraction. None of the rest of the stones moved at all. She couldn't see any mortar, but it certainly *felt* as if they were locked in a solid, and permanent, bond.

Sitting back on her heels, Tori contemplated writing a new book in which she cast Uncle Bob in the role of depraved villain—a man whose devious mind designed tricks and traps that lured young women into wasting their lives solving riddles about nonexistent treasure. "Could you spare me one, tiny, little break? Just one?"

Shadow wandered over and pressed his nose to her cheek. Rubbing him behind the ears acted precisely like a switch, which caused his butt to hit the floor and his mouth to open, bathing her in the hot exhaust of dog breath.

"Bleah!" she said, turning aside.

When Shadow licked the side of her face, she pulled further back, her elbow striking the slightly loose stone with an upward, glancing blow. The stone rose a half inch, then fell back into place. *Up? The son of a bitch moved up?*

Tori grabbed it with both hands and lifted. With barely a sound, the rock came free, and she rolled away from the fireplace, clutching it to her chest. Shadow padded to her, focused on her burden. When she set it aside, the dog stuck with it, his olfactory senses clearly working overtime. Tori could only imagine what had been dripped on the stone in the hundred-plus years it occupied that spot. She smiled at the big dog. "Go for it, tough guy. I've got work to do."

The front edge of the hearth had a decidedly gap-toothed look, but the rocks to either side of the vacant spot now responded when she pulled on them. They traveled roughly an inch, then came to rest with an audible click. Tori moved her hand to the next rock in the series and pulled on it, only to have the rest of the row swing out and away from the fire pit. Connected to a hinge hidden under masonry in the side of the fireplace, the row of stones moved with only a short squeal of rusty protest. The left side operated the same way, leaving two straight arms of stone projecting into the room.

A hole in the cast iron slab had been revealed when she removed the locking stone. Slightly wider than her hand, she imagined the spot was fashioned for Uncle Bob's larger paw. She tried to lift it, but it didn't budge.

She examined the arms more closely and discovered that the stones were mounted on lengths of iron, and that a channel ran through the back side of each. When the arms were extended, the channels were parallel. She pulled on the base, and it slid toward her, the weight carried in the channels of the arms. There had once been a layer of grease which served to lubricate the action, but time had not treated it kindly. The plate squealed as Tori pulled on it. Shadow backed across the cabin, nose to the floor and tail tucked, his eyes never leaving the hearth and its banshee wail.

When the back edge of the plate neared the front edge of the hearth, it stopped. Holding her breath, Tori slowly got to her knees and looked into the big hole she had just revealed.

~*~

Mato had taken his leave immediately after breakfast. How the she-giant decided what foods to prepare was yet another mystery. If it had been up to him, he'd have been happy to eat the eggs and yellowish-orange stuff every day. That morning, however, she mixed milk with some sort of dried grains and topped it with bits of a soft, cream-colored fruit he'd never tasted before. It had a distinctive flavor but a paste-like texture. It went oddly well with the crunchy grains. He wondered if he'd ever be able to obtain these things for Reyna, and possibly the rest of The People, to sample.

Such possibilities would have to wait, however, until he completed his mission. Knowing that he was on the right path gave him a surge of confidence. He began his search at the flat-topped boulder on which Tori had cooked meat over a clever box which contained fire. It seemed as though the giants put all their magic in boxes of one kind or another. It was difficult not to envy them for it. In his experience, boxes were almost impossible to construct from the materials The People had readily at hand. Their tools simply weren't up to the challenge. He would have to examine the she-giant's tools more closely. Perhaps there were some he could barter for, or simply steal. She seemed to enjoy the foolish images he created with the brush and paints she had given him. There might come a time when he could trade them for tools or other things of real value.

The boulder contained nothing out of the ordinary. Mato traversed the area around the cabin and examined several similar outcrops of stone, any one of which could have hidden a secret passageway into the bluff. The cavern was in there somewhere; it had to be! All he lacked was an entrance. He would dig one if he had to, but that was a task he would undertake only as a last resort.

When he had exhausted all the other possibilities, he turned his attention to the stacks of stone which supported the cabin. Those in the corners were exactly what they appeared to be: piles of flat stone, stacked and chinked in an orderly fashion. Solid and unyielding, they held no secrets. He had suspected as much and wasn't disappointed. The larger stack supporting the fire pit, however, retained an element of mystery.

He circled it slowly, carefully examining each stone. They were held in place by some sort of hard, white substance that looked like clay, but was much more dense. He scraped at it with his knife, but barely managed to leave a mark. He found a spot where some of the white material had cracked, and shoved the tip of his obsidian blade into it, working it back and forth, grinding the white stuff to powder. It was slow work, and it pained him to abuse his knife that way.

Tori had many knives, all made from the shiny metal the giants used so much. Mato stopped working, mentally kicking himself. The she-giant had so many knives she wouldn't miss one if he borrowed it to do his work. Moving silently, he hurried out from underneath the cabin and ran up the steps to the door and through it.

The she-giant sat on the floor doing something to the rocks surrounding the fire pit. He still had no idea why she had gotten so upset with him for burning her spoiled food. He supposed there were some things about giants he'd never understand, and that was likely one of them.

Walking silently, he made his way to the work area where she kept her food preparation tools. The great black dog watched him, but did not betray him. Who would have thought that such an animal would be willing to share living space, and yet this one treated him the same way it treated the she-giant. Even more surprising, Mato found himself enjoying the dog's company. He doubted that he would ever get any of The People to believe his stories about the monstrous animal who was as tame as the rabbits Mato kept as a boy. He shrugged himself back into the present.

A set of six identical knives occupied a wooden rack on the counter. Mato helped himself to one of them and carried it back out of the cabin. Tori never looked up from whatever she was doing. He sympathized with her frustration, noting how she often spoke to the empty room while she worked, as if she expected the walls to answer.

Once back under the cabin, he renewed his efforts to scrape away the hard, white material which held the stones in place. The work was not particularly difficult, but it went slowly. When he finished scraping away most of the clay-stuff from one side of the stone, he started in on another.

He had begun to make progress on the second side when he heard an anguished shriek from above. The sound left him immobile, tensed for action, but content to wait for some audible clue as to what he should do. Eventually, he heard another squealing noise, very similar to the first. Moments later, he heard a third such noise, only much louder. *What was the she-giant doing up there?*

Leaving Tori's knife in the crack between the stones, Mato raced back to the house. What kind of magic could the she-giant use to make stones scream like tormented souls?

~*~

Purcell's broker reached him by phone between classes and the conversation lasted just long enough to ruin his day completely. Normally, notice of a margin call would be made via email, except that Purcell's margin account had been tapped out the last time he guessed wrong. He had 48 hours to come up with enough cash to cover his most recent option investment, a tiny pharmaceutical company whose backers claimed they were only months away from a sure cure for psoriasis. The data from their field trials had been turned over to the Food and Drug Administration, and they were waiting for approval to forge ahead with their product.

Purcell bought heavily when shares were trading at $20, and the word in the chat rooms was that the stock couldn't miss; it was a moon rocket, and the fuse had been lit. He'd watched the option price scream up, and he borrowed against the BMW for more options when the share price hit $30. Life was good, or at least potentially good. *Potentially awesome!* He had been coasting along with a song in his heart for three weeks.

That morning the FDA announced they had problems with the trials; the numbers didn't justify the company's claims. By the time Purcell caught up with the news, the share price had dropped below $10, and the broker wanted $15,300—plus fees—to cover the shortfall in his margin account. 48 hours. Fifteen grand. He didn't have fifteen *hundred*. Suddenly, life was not good. Life was not even certain.

As soon as the next class was over, Purcell decided, it would be time to give the school's Indian artifact collection a serious appraisal.

~*~

Shawn's new destination was Ten Sleep, Wyoming—the name on the sign in the photo Vicky Lynn had sent to Cassy Woodall. *Ten Sleep*, what a stupid name for a town. Since his knowledge of geography was limited to good deer hunting areas in Georgia, Alabama, and northern Florida, Shawn invested in a map of the United States.

He knew Wyoming was somewhere out west, but for him, "out west" was largely a function of Hollywood. "Out west" meant cowboy hats and shoot-outs, and cemeteries on barren hillsides with wooden crosses for grave markers. It also meant forts made from big logs stuck in the ground. And Indians. And buffalo—lots and lots of shaggy-ass buffalo. But according to his new map, "out west" meant I-80, at least halfway through the center of the country.

Knowing the cops in New York, and maybe

the FBI, were looking for him, he took care to stay under their radar. No speeding, no game-playing with moron motorists (though there were gracious plenty to mess with), and no giving in to the temptations promoted on billboards along the route. Shawn would go back to being a solid citizen while he traveled through the heartland of America. He had the time and resources to take the trip slow and easy.

"Keep yo' eye on the prize," he said. The prize was Vicky Lynn. The more he thought about it, however, the more he realized she was only part of the prize. A big-time author now, she probably had lots of money. *His money.* And he was dead set on claiming his share.

Chapter Thirteen
Hi ho, hi ho....

Tori put her hands on the iron plate that formerly served as the floor of her fireplace and leaned out to peer into the darkness beyond. Some ambient light spilled down into the void, but not enough to illuminate it clearly. She grabbed a lamp from the end table beside her easy chair. The lamp, table, and chair comprised the bulk of her "living room" furniture; a modest TV sitting on a bookshelf rounded out the suite. Fortunately, the cord was long enough and allowed her to park the lamp near the opening.

Gingerly testing the strength of the platform jutting into the room from the fireplace, she slowly added her weight until she was crawling across it on hands and knees. Thus far, the process was managed in silence, but something—a sixth sense perhaps—caused her to look over her shoulder at the cabin door. Mato stood there, clearly surprised by what he saw. There was no point in trying to hide anything, so Tori motioned for him to join her. Mato bolted across the room and leapt up beside her on the iron plate. Together, they looked over the edge at a short drop to the ground.

Stone walls surrounded the opening and revealed four things: a roughly two-foot diameter hole leading further underground, a metal door with some sort of locking mechanism, a rack holding several short lengths of wood, presumably torches, and on the floor, a package wrapped in oilcloth.

Mato dropped into the opening without a word. He plucked a torch from the rack and with a flurry of hand-to-belt pouch moves, produced a flint and striker. Within seconds he had the torch burning. A cloud of dark, acrid smoke curled up into Tori's face, making her eyes water. She closed them as she backed away, but moments later, when she eased forward and looked again into the opening, Mato was gone. She called after him. But instead of hearing from the little Indian, Shadow barked back at her. She turned in his direction and saw that the big dog was already in motion. His nails clicked and scrabbled on the iron plate, but only long enough for him to cross it. He jumped into the opening and followed Mato down the rabbit hole, crawling faster than she thought possible.

Tori sat for a moment, bewildered. She was the only one who hadn't plunged headlong into the passage. What did Mato and Shadow know that she didn't? *Who in their right mind crawled into a hole in the ground, for cryin' out loud?*

Not, by Gawd, Tori Lanier!

She eased forward and slid over the edge. The iron plate hit her roughly at the lower edge of her ribcage. Definitely not a huge drop. She bent down and retrieved the package. The oilskin wrapper was held in place by common twine. The knots were tight and would not yield to her efforts to untie them, so she placed the package on the iron plate until she was ready to examine it. Squatting, she bent forward and peered into the opening, which slanted sharply downward. The darkness was absolute; no hint of Mato's passage remained, and the prospect of following him on her hands and knees left her trembling.

"I'm not Alice," she said, "and this sure ain't Wonderland. It'll be a cold, cold day in hell before I crawl in there."

That said, she turned her attention to the little door. The latch was stiff, but after working it back and forth a few times, she had it operational. A spot of oil was in order, she thought; she'd take care of that soon enough. Throwing the latch to its opposite extreme, she unlocked the door and pushed against it. Squealing like its counterparts in the fireplace, the door swung outward, revealing the crawlspace under the cabin. She wasn't sure where or how an exterior latch was hidden, but it seemed logical that there was one. It was also obvious the door wasn't designed for someone her size. She closed and latched it.

Half expecting a white rabbit and a mad hatter to appear, Tori turned her back to the plate, put her palms on it, and hoisted herself out of the hole. Swinging her legs around, she scooted back into the cabin, grabbed the oilskin-wrapped package, and carried it to her worktable. Mato and Shadow, she reasoned, would resurface in their own good time. If they couldn't jump up on the iron plate, they could exit through the side door. She, meanwhile, had a package to investigate.

~*~

"Dr. Devlin?" Purcell asked.

"Yes?" The voice on the phone sounded old, as if the speaker's larynx were made of parchment.

"It's Tom Purcell. I wonder if I might have a moment of your time?"

"Of course," the woman said. "I'm still trying to get the hang of this retirement thing. Time is what I have the most of."

She seemed at ease, a good way to start. "I don't know if Dr. Noblewski mentioned it or not, but he's asked me to take over the schools' native American artifact collection."

"Yes," she said, "he did mention it." She paused for a moment. "You should consider yourself lucky. That's quite an honor for an associate professor."

"And quite a responsibility," Purcell added.

"It's going to be difficult to maintain anything like your track record."

"Probably," she said. "Where are you working on your doctorate?"

"Ah, well, that's on hold just now."

"Really? Then I'm doubly surprised at Dr. Noblewski's decision. The curator position requires an expert. Protecting our native American heritage is terribly important, far too important to leave in the hands of someone..." She paused a moment before going on. "Well, let's be honest here. It's too important to leave in the hands of someone with less than stellar credentials."

Purcell coughed. "Evidently, Dr. Noblewski has faith in me."

"Evidently. Hold on."

He heard Devlin put the phone down and blow her nose. He used the time to get his temper under control.

"So," she said when she returned to the line, "What do you need from me?"

"Some advice," he said, trying to sound both sincere and concerned. "I feel reasonably confident about appraising the value of most artifacts that would be appropriate for our collection. Where I lack expertise is in the area of which buyers and sellers to trust."

"Hmm," she said. "Assuming, for the sake of argument, that you can make accurate appraisals, you are wise to seek my counsel when it comes to dealers and collectors. Those, after all, are the people who make up the market."

"Of course."

"Your safest bet is to trade only with those people or organizations with whom I traded."

He clenched his fists, but managed to keep the tension out of his voice. "That will certainly be my primary guide, but new dealers and new opportunities are bound to crop up. Do you know of anyone I should specifically avoid?" He looked at the ledger in which she had painstakingly recorded every transaction involving the collection during her tenure as curator. "There are quite a few names listed in your records. Can they all be trusted?"

She was less than eager to respond, so he waited, allowing the void in the conversation to become uncomfortable.

"I'm not in the habit of speaking ill of anyone," Devlin said.

Except me. "Nor am I," Purcell said. "Still, if you have reason to doubt the honesty of one or more of our acquisition partners..." He let the idea float.

"There is one man: Simon Gibbs. I never trusted him. He's got shifty eyes, like Nixon."

"The former president? *That* Nixon?"

"Yes, of course, that Nixon." When she exhaled, it sounded like she had opened a valve on a steam engine.

Purcell jotted down the name: Simon Gibbs. "Anyone else?"

"There may be one or two more, but I'm loathe to—"

"Perhaps if I read a few names, would that make it easier?"

"I think, *Mr.* Purcell, that you should concentrate on acquisitions. Don't sell anything, and for goodness sake, don't trade anything. Acquire the absolute best artifacts available. That way, you'll have a positive impact on the collection while you're obtaining your doctorate. You'll find ample opportunities to write articles and develop some standing in the field. I will, of course, be watching you. I'm a great believer in peer review."

"I see," he said. "Well, thank you. I—"

"Will there be anything else?"

"No, I think that's everything."

"Then, good day, Mr. Purcell. I look forward to your first exhibition." With that, she rang off.

Purcell shook his head, thankful he wouldn't have to work with Devlin. That would have been more than he could bear. At least he'd gotten something out of the call besides a mild irritation. He had a name: Simon Gibbs. *And all I need to do is track down old "Shifty Eyes."*

~*~

The hole in the ground beneath the she-giant's fire pit slanted quite steeply, and Mato was forced to slow his steps lest he pitch forward into the darkness. The light from his torch was barely adequate, and he wished very early on that he had taken the time to fashion a new one. Not only did it give off a feeble light, it did so amid thick smoke which made his eyes water and left a bitter taste in his mouth.

With his left hand on a side wall and the torch in his right, Mato followed the path as it continued down, curving gently before it began to level out. He was very near a larger chamber, as light from the torch occasionally shone through irregular openings in the right-hand wall. When he stopped to peer through one of the larger such openings, Tori's huge pet bumped into him from behind, almost causing him to drop the torch.

"Dog!" he cried. "Are you trying to kill me?"

The animal tilted his great head to one side and looked at him intensely, then licked his face.

Mato spat and pressed his arm to his head to wipe away some of the dog slobber. "Be careful you do not put out my torch," he muttered, though in truth he was delighted to have the enormous animal along for company. He patted him on the head. "Come," he said.

The dog paced slowly beside him, and Mato kept the torch in his right hand, near the wall with the openings so he could look through them. Had there been anything to see on his left, the dog's great body blocked any view of it. There was plenty to see on his right, however. When the path eventually leveled out almost completely, the partition ended, and he stood at the threshold of an enormous cavern.

He cursed the torch for not illuminating everything at once so that he could take in his surroundings in great gulps, like a swimmer coming up from a prolonged dive. The dog stepped away, his nose to the ground, and followed scent trails known only to animals. Mato felt a pang of jealousy, but quickly recovered when he approached the nearest wall and held the torch high over his head.

As the light hit the wall, a vivid painting became visible. Mato gasped at the size of it. How had the artist managed to work so high up on the wall? How had he kept everything in scale when the images were so large? Then it struck him that the images might have been rendered by giants.

No! That couldn't be! This had to be the cavern of dreams—it belonged to The People, not the giants. He doubted they could even crawl through the opening he had just traversed. The dog managed, but Mato was sure he had to hunker down and slink through a good portion of it. He thought about Tori. She could make it, he thought, if she crawled through the opening and nearly half way to the cavern. At that point, the ceiling leveled while the path continued to slope downward. An adult, male giant might have trouble getting his shoulders through the hole. That, ultimately, was the element which convinced Mato that the artwork had *not* been done by anyone but The People. The cavern was *their* secret.

Their place.

Their *sacred* place.

At least, it had been. Now the she-giant, Tori, knew of it as well. That concerned him greatly. How could he allow such knowledge to be shared outside the rightful owners? He had no way of making her un-learn it. There seemed to be but one way to restore the secret, and he doubted that he could bring himself to do it. Tori had been good to him. Almost loving.

How could he bring himself to kill her, even if it was to protect the most sacred secret of The People?

~*~

Shawn was all too happy to put Pennsylvania behind him. He'd never seen interstate highways in such terrible condition. Obviously, the politicians had managed to screw up the roads right along with the economy. It was most likely a plan to ensure that everyone suffered equally. Well, maybe not the highway workers; they seemed reasonably happy, but then, they were working. Union guys, he figured, or guys who knew somebody. That's always the way it worked, and ultimately the blame lay with the politicians. He wasn't sure if old Sutherland had been elected or appointed. But, if he'd been one of the elected big shots, then Shawn had done his civic duty by shooting him.

He patted the front of his "I♡New York" T-shirt. *They could pin the medal right there.*

It had been a long day, especially with the roads the way they were. And driving like he gave a damn was tiring, too. Just east of Cleveland, he saw a truck stop that seemed to have everything he might need in one convenient place, and there was a cheap motel right beside it. He pulled in and parked.

He bought a T-bone that tasted much better than the steak he ate in Woodall's apartment, and got a double order of fries to go with it. He squirted ketchup liberally over the meat and potatoes, then dug in. Three cans of Budweiser helped to wash it down, and he chased the meal with coffee and a slice of apple pie. The waitress looked like she might have been a hottie twenty years earlier, but she'd let herself go. Too bad, he thought; he had a whole night to kill.

Wandering through the gift shop, he walked past racks of chrome-covered truck accessories, CB radios, and assorted NASCAR crap. He by-passed a rack of Jesus memorabilia but stopped when he got to a section that offered clothing promoting various colleges. A dark red sweatshirt caught his eye. It not only had a big University of Alabama emblem on the front, but the distinctive elephant head on the back, over the words "Roll Tide!"

He'd always wanted something like that.

Shawn didn't care that it was a little large for

him, it was the only one of its kind on the rack. Nearby he found a white ball cap with the stylized letter "A" on it in dark red. The hat was adjustable, and he quickly fit it to his head. He would have liked to buy new shoes, too, since the running shoes he had on were dotted with blood, most likely a mixture of his own and Woodall's. Sadly, the store didn't sell shoes. That would have to wait.

After paying for his new finery, he drove to the motel and got a room. Though sorely tempted to look for some female company, or at least a decent bar where he could throw back a few, Shawn decided he needed rest more than beer or sex. It was a rare concession, but he felt it was a sign of maturity.

He turned on the TV and watched wrestling for a while, but it looked even more phony than usual. Further down the dial he located something called the Ultimate Fighting Championship, and was instantly captivated. There weren't any pretty boys in the UFC, although some amazing babes appeared on the screen from time to time. Most significant to him was the reality of the fights. These guys were really hurting each other. The blood didn't come from some stupid little Hollywood prop. He wished the fighters didn't bother with mouth guards. Then he might see some teeth flyin' around along with the blood and sweat.

Looking down at his own lacerated knuckles, he recalled how he'd torn them up on Cassy Woodall's mouth. He was still amazed that she'd survived. *Vicky Lynn wasn't that tough.* He fell asleep before the UFC broadcast ended, with thoughts of Vicky Lynn and Cassy doing the nasty while he watched.

~*~

The first thing that went through Tori's mind after she removed the oilskin wrapping from the package, was that Uncle Bob had left behind another coded diary. She recognized his handwriting instantly and closed her eyes tight as she prayed that, this time, he'd just written out whatever was on his mind. She let out a long and heart-felt sigh of relief when she discovered that's precisely what he'd done. On the first few pages, anyway.

Most of the thick, unbound stack of papers contained what appeared to be a hand-written dictionary; only the words were utterly foreign to her. On closer examination, she realized that what she held was a translation dictionary—from a language she didn't know, to English.

The first section was explanatory and told how Robert Lanier had moved to the Wyoming territory in search of gold and silver. What he'd found instead, was an Indian woman. She had been attacked by some animal and lay, near death, not far from where he eventually built his cabin. Yet, it wasn't her injury which gripped his attention. Rather, it was her size. Though perfectly proportioned, and obviously full-grown, the Indian was no bigger than a newborn baby.

Tori's heart began to race. Could this thick

stack of paper be what she hoped it might be? She read on.

Lanier sheltered the tiny woman and put a tourniquet on her leg, the lower portion of which had been horribly mangled. The tooth marks suggested her attacker had been a small animal, like a fox or a weasel. A larger one would have simply eaten her whole.

When she eventually regained consciousness, Lanier tried unsuccessfully to talk with her. She was obviously terrified of him, and he suspected he was as much a mystery to her as she was to him. After a time, however, his reassurances seemed to work, and she surrendered herself to his care. Unfortunately, her lower leg already displayed the dreaded symptoms of gangrene: discoloration and a vile-smelling discharge that he'd encountered all too often among the Confederate wounded who survived the battlefields. The smell was a clear harbinger of death.

The woman was certainly no fool, and her size had nothing to do with her intellect. She knew the leg would have to come off, or she would die. She even gave Lanier her own crude knife and went through the motions of hacking it off.

When he reluctantly agreed to do it, she held him off until she had dipped her stone blade into a little pouch on her belt and administered a tiny cut to herself. Within moments she passed out, and Lanier was relieved to conduct his impromptu surgery without seeing her experience the kind of pain so many wounded had faced in the war. He recalled an encounter with a certain Dr. Tichenor, a surgeon and staunch Confederate, who championed the concept of antiseptic surgery, except for Yankees. Though he used alcohol on wounds sustained in battle—and met with significant success—he later developed a patent medicine which Lanier purchased the moment he found it available.

He used it liberally on the Indian woman's leg—before, during, and after he removed everything below her left knee.

Her name was Leokah Nah, which he learned later meant Sleeping Dove. Oddly, she also called herself *mato*, meaning dreamer or seer.

~*~

Simon Gibbs wasn't hard to find. He maintained a website that specialized in Indian artifacts and was well-known among collectors. Fortunately for Purcell, he lived in Billings, Montana, which wasn't all that far, even without an interstate highway. When Purcell called, the man seemed eager enough to talk about the artifact world, and insisted that he had one of—if not the most—varied collections anywhere on Earth. And every item in it was available, for the right price.

When Purcell asked if Gibbs was interested in *buying* quality pieces, the man instantly became less open. "Where'd you say you worked?"

"North Central Community College," Purcell

said. "I teach anthropology."

"And *you* wanna sell *me* some artifacts?"

"Yes sir, I do."

There was a moment of silence before Gibbs spoke again. "I can't do this over the phone. Bring me what you've got, and we'll see if it's worth my time."

Purcell got directions from the website then drove to the storage area where the excess from the school's collection was housed. He selected a Haida ceremonial mask from the Pacific Northwest, a Lakota Sioux *chanunpa,* often mistakenly called a "peace pipe," and a doll whose tribal origin was unknown. It was made of straw and wore a tunic fashioned from prairie dog hide. None of the pieces was particularly rare, but all were certifiably authentic. Most importantly, Purcell felt certain their collective value would more than cover his margin call.

The drive to Billings was uneventful, if boring, and Purcell arrived late in the day. The building was located in an office park which had seen better days, but not in any recent decade. Purcell entered the foyer of Gibbs' building, which had all the charm and authenticity of a concrete *wikiup*. The walls were decorated with what appeared to be Indian artifacts, but which probably came from somewhere in China and were as rare as groupies at a rock concert.

"You Purcell?" asked a heavyset man with a

deeply pock-marked face, and Tom had to admit, shifty eyes.

"I am."

"You got the items?"

"I do."

"Then, c'mon in. Let's have a look," the older man said, turning away.

Purcell followed with the unmarked box containing the artifacts tucked under his arm. They travelled down a short hallway, which opened into an office roughly three times the size of the foyer. This time the room was decorated more lavishly, if not with an Indian theme.

Gibbs' desk took up most of one side of the room and supported a huge, flat screen monitor. His computer was out of view. The desk was uncluttered, although a bank of shelves bore an abundance of catalogs, magazines, guide books, and other literature pertinent to the field of American Indian artifacts.

"So," Gibbs said, "let's see the goods."

Purcell produced them one at a time, allowing Gibbs plenty of time to examine them as carefully as required to authenticate them. He muttered to himself during most of the examination and never asked a single question. He consulted a number of catalogs and checked something on his computer before he finally said anything to Purcell.

"So, what d'ya think they're worth?"

"Individually?"

"The whole shootin' match," Gibbs said. "I wanna see if I'm dealing with someone who knows his business."

As opposed to someone you can rip off with ease? He smiled. "Considering their excellent condition, and the documentation that proves their authenticity, I suspect they'd sell for something like thirty thousand on the open market."

Gibbs started laughing.

Purcell felt embarrassed. Surely, he hadn't been *that* far off in his valuation. "You disagree?"

"Well, of course I disagree! The whole idea of an open market is silly. Yes, there are buyers and sellers, but this isn't anything like a stock exchange. It's more like investing in fine art, except there's a whole lot more fraud involved. You saw all that crap in the waiting room? Junk. All of it. But people buy it off the internet every damn day. I know. 'Cause I sell it!"

Purcell gestured at the three items on the desk. "I guarantee this isn't junk."

"You're absolutely right; it's not. But how many so-called collectors know that?" He picked up the doll. "I can get one of these for around twenty bucks. 'Course, it's not as old as this, but making it look old isn't hard. Straw is straw, and there's no shortage of prairie dogs, in case you hadn't noticed. I could have these mass-produced if I wanted to, 'cept there's no market for 'em."

"But that one's genuine! It's got real value."

"It's worth what a collector will pay for it, nothing more." Gibbs held the mask to his face.

The multi-colored god of something-or-other stared out at Purcell with fixed eyeballs. Gibbs was humming a tune he recognized, but couldn't name. That proved annoying, as did just about everything Gibbs did. "What about the pipe?"

"It's a beaut," Gibbs said. "In perfect shape, too. Even has a bowl. Most of mine just have the stem. God only knows what happens to the bowls. It's not like the two pieces are good for anything separately."

"What do *you* think they're worth?" Purcell asked.

"You'd be insulted if I gave you a figure," the heavyset man said.

"Try me."

"Five thousand for the lot."

Purcell's legs suddenly felt weak. "You're joking."

"Nope." He waved a hand at the three pieces. "This is nice stuff. Museum grade, even. But hey, times are tough. There aren't as many buyers as there used to be. Lots of folks are tryin' to cash their shit in so they can eat and pay the mortgage."

"This has got to be worth more."

"A high end collector might pay more, but

let's face it, they've already got stuff like this. More than they need. What people want—and what still has value—is the stuff nobody can get."

"Like what?" Purcell asked. He had a very good idea what was in the school's collection. If Gibbs would name an item, there was a strong chance the school had one.

"We're talking unique here, right?"

"Obviously."

"How 'bout a scalp? A genuine, trophy-grade, scalp." Gibbs sat at his desk with a broad smile on his moonscape face.

"How 'bout Buffalo Bill's bones?"

"I'm serious."

Purcell picked up the doll and carefully covered it in protective bubble wrap, the way he had prepared it for delivery. He put it in the cardboard box and reached for the mask.

"You look like a decent guy," Gibbs said. "I'll give you seven grand. That's the best I can do."

Purcell paused. "I need fifteen. Overnight."

"Outta the question. For this stuff, anyway."

"There's gotta be something you want."

Gibbs nodded. "There is, certainly. My problem is, I don't really know what it is. I won't recognize it 'til I see it. Know what I mean?"

"I think so," Purcell said. "You want

something so freakin' rare nobody has one."

The older man smiled. "That's exactly what I'm talking about."

Swell, thought the curator of the North Central Community College American Indian Artifact Collection. *Just fucking swell.*

Chapter Fourteen
Candle, candle, burning bright....

Mato found himself drawing ever closer to the walls in order to view the paintings. Examining them became his sole focus, and considerable time went by before he realized that his torch had burned down so much that it might not last long enough to allow him to make it out of the cavern. Turning away from the images on the walls, he tried to orient himself and locate the path which would take him back to the surface.

There it is, he thought, striking out across the center of the chamber. Despite the diminished light, he spotted a wide and jagged gap in the floor which angled through the cavern. There wasn't time to investigate, with his torch sputtering low, but he vowed to look at it more closely on a future visit.

Calling to the dog as he hurried forward, Mato reached what he thought was the exit route. By then his torch had nearly burnt out and gave off just enough light to help him avoid gaps in the ground and the sharp points of rock that stabbed up and down like demon's teeth.

The dog reached him just as the torch sputtered its last. A few tiny red sparks arced through the instant night as the glow from the torch dimmed to nothing.

The darkness was absolute. And terrifying. Mato had never been wrapped in such complete blackness. He reached out to touch the dog for reassurance, and he responded with a gentle nudge.

Mato felt certain he had been facing the right way when the torch died. If he kept his right hand on the wall, he should be able to follow it and walk out. Unfortunately, the dog had other ideas, and wandered away in the dark. Mato called to him, trying to form the word the she-giant had used, though it felt foreign. "Sha-do!" he called. Then again.

He heard a sound from somewhere nearby and turned to face it. Such a movement proved foolish in the extreme, since he had not yet put his hand on the wall, which would guide him out. Stretching his arms to both sides, he shifted in the direction he thought would bring him to the wall, yet he felt nothing. He moved two steps without touching the wall, and he was certain he had been at least that close. Reversing his steps, he returned to his starting point, or at least, what he *thought* was his starting point. Without any light at all, it was impossible to tell where he'd moved, or what direction he faced. Growing desperate, he held the dead torch at arm's length and pivoted in a complete circle, hoping to touch the wall somewhere in the process. He didn't.

Where was the dog? He called to him again and heard something in the distance, though he had no way of judging how far away the sounds were. The cavern distorted all the senses, and the dog was just as blind as Mato. What if he fell into the great crack in the floor?

"Sha-do!" he cried again, unable to keep the sound of fear from his voice.

The dog barked in response, so Mato called him again, and kept calling until the great beast lumbered up next to him. Mato reached out and felt the big wet nose, the long, lolling tongue, and the creature's hot, damp breath. His relief was intense, and far greater than he'd imagined possible. That breath which had once been sour enough to turn his head now seemed sweet. It was certainly welcome.

"We must get out," he said as he slipped his hand under the leather strap around the big dog's neck. The animal began walking, and Mato had no choice but to go with him. He could hear the dog sniffing the cavern floor, and the sound comforted him. The big animal knew where he was going and how to get there, even if Mato didn't.

Mato let the dog take charge, though self-reliance was something he'd been taught from childhood. He doubted he could have done it if there'd been some other choice, but the dog didn't hesitate. He moved with certainty, and much faster than Mato liked. What if another crevice loomed ahead? But he'd seen nothing like that when they walked in, so the route back should be safe. Assuming, of course, that they were leaving on the same trail that brought them there. Mato had no idea if that was so.

~*~

Tori poured over the pages her distant uncle had left as a preface to his dictionary. At times his remarks were formal and businesslike, but just as often they suggested he had profound feelings for his tiny companion. She wanted to believe there was some hint of romance between them, and as long as she kept herself from thinking of Sleeping Dove in terms of her stature, those thoughts succeeded. But when she thought the same things in terms of herself and Mato, the scenario broke down completely. Yes, she cared about Mato, but her feelings were utterly platonic. Her leg weighed more than he did!

What helped to explain it, she felt, was the obvious amount of time Lanier and Sleeping Dove spent together. Travel would have been extremely difficult for her, unless Uncle Bob carried her. That didn't seem likely, as she refused to divulge any clues about where her people lived. Both of them, it seemed, had been content to concentrate on the dictionary, and while communication between them came slowly, it did eventually happen.

Tori used the dictionary to fashion a few questions for Mato. She paused, wondering if Mato was really his name. Lanier had indicated it was a title, though she had little credibility to spare for seers and fortune-tellers. She was comfortable with history, not fantasy.

Having the word list forced her to think about what she wanted to know, and how she might ask her questions. The easiest way to understand how he might respond was to translate the words for "Yes" and "No." That would necessitate a real game of Twenty Questions, albeit a more interesting version than she'd ever played before.

The first question was easy, though it violated the yes/no limitation. On a clean sheet of printer paper she wrote, "What is your name?" using the same pronunciation key Uncle Bob had devised. *Is it possible Uncle Bob invented phonetics?* That was a question for another day. She had very different questions to ask, and it was going to take some time to figure out how to ask them.

She glanced toward the fireplace, wondering when Mato would return. He seemed to have put a great deal of faith in the old torches racked on the wall. She wished he had taken a gas lantern or a flashlight. Looking around the cabin, she saw both. The lantern, though ancient, was a typical kerosene-burning model and stood nearly as tall as Mato himself. Beyond cumbersome, and clearly, not an option. There were two flashlights, however, one of which worked. It required six D-size batteries and provided not only a large beam of light, but a red distress flasher and an AM radio. It, too, was a bit bulky and would be like her carrying around a microwave, or maybe a dishwasher. She wondered if Caleb had any of the newer LED flashlights in stock. Wouldn't *one of those make a fabulous gift!*

She tried to go back to drafting her questions, but another thought intervened, bearing the voice of Tom Purcell. She didn't know anything about the man, except that he knew Caleb and played the harmonica. But *he* knew about as much and had asked her out to dinner! How had that happened? He couldn't know what she looked like, could he? Well, possibly. Her picture was on the jacket of the book, and she had to admit, it was a pretty good one.

Was he going solely on *that* photo? The one Cassy had fussed over and sent out for retouching? And what did he look like? Sure, he *sounded* okay, but then, there were some dead girls in London who might've said the same thing about Jack the Ripper. She was glad she had put him off. *Where would they go, anyway? To a buffet at Lou's? That'd be romantic.* She sighed. It would also be pretty safe. She could drive to Charm and meet him there. Maybe leave Shadow and the shotgun in the truck. Maybe Mato, too.

No! That was stupid. She couldn't risk letting anyone know about Mato. Unless, of course, it was something Mato himself wanted. She felt a great circular argument swell inside her head. The world could handle Mato all too easily. She doubted, however, that Mato could handle the world. He had much to learn before he could even make an informed choice about revealing his existence, and that of his tribe, assuming he had one. And if he didn't, where the hell had he come from?

When had her life taken on such a science fiction flavor? There were far more important questions to be answered. Like, what was Mato up to? And where was Shadow? And was Tom Purcell any good in bed?

"Geez, girl!" Tori chided herself, then smiled. "Just sayin'...."

~*~

Purcell drove straight home. The sun went down before he got there, and he stopped for a burger at some mom 'n pop-style fast food place. If it had a name, that nugget of information failed to filter into his brain. His mind was occupied with the weighty task of finding approximately 8,500 more dollars before the close of business tomorrow. And that, of course, was assuming the check Simon Gibbs had given him was worth more than the paper it was written on.

Throughout the drive, he had been telling himself that selling the school's artifacts was okay. His financial survival was more important than the school's possession of a couple common examples of 19th century Indian life. Selling them was no big deal. Making a valuable contact, like Simon Gibbs, was far more important, and would undoubtedly lead to future deals. He was just paving the way, making Gibbs receptive to doing business with him. No foul, no harm done.

Deep down, however, he knew he wasn't fooling anyone, least of all himself. Grease from his burger dribbled down his chin, and he wiped it off with a paper napkin. What am I eating, he wondered, staring at the red meat oozing hot juices from between a cushion of white bun. But then, he knew, he didn't care. Eating had become automatic. Like breathing. Like... like investing.

I'm losing it. I'm really, really losing it!

He forced himself to think of something else: Tori. Now *there* was a pleasant topic—an attractive woman who just might be able to point him in the direction of salvation. Of course, she wouldn't know that, as long as he was careful. Some wining and dining were in order. Perhaps a bit of romancing. That could have multiple benefits. The world had become increasingly more stressful. He needed relief. A little TLC. He also needed to probe in such a way that Tori would give up access to her Indian pal. After that, he'd work the old Purcell magic on him and see what there was to see.

So, how is that going to generate eight and a half large in the next 24 hours?

He wished he knew. Had things worked out the way he originally planned, the BMW would have already been paid off, and he could take out a loan against it. Unfortunately, he was already upside down in the car loan department, and he didn't have much of anything else he could hock. Tori Lanier's status as his way out began to loom ever larger. At the very least, he was going to have to pay her a visit.

And soon.

~*~

Is that light?

Mato strained to see into the distance, but the darkness all around made it impossible to judge how far away anything was. Except for the dog, of course. He was right beside him, and Mato had left his hand locked on to the leather strap around the dog's neck. His faith had been rewarded, it seemed, for what he thought *might* have been light, was definitely turning into exactly that. They were going to reach the surface after all.

Mato heaved a massive sigh of relief. His trial wasn't over. Obviously, he still had much to do, not the least of which was a trip back into the cavern for his dream journey. He wondered how late in the day it was. How much time had he spent in the cavern? Given a better source of light, he'd still be there. He had so much to see, so much to learn! Suddenly his mission was not only possible, but partly complete.

Somewhere, from the back of his mind, he knew he would have to deal with the she-giant. He wished he hadn't learned her name; that would have made killing her much easier. But when you knew someone's name—their true name, not just what they did, or who birthed them—then your *souls* were connected. The Old Ones had spoken of it, according to legend, and that meant powerful magics were at work: far more powerful than anything the giants had at their command; far more powerful than anything Mato would ever command.

The very idea of killing Tori made him sad. But he could see no way around it. The existence of the cavern of dreams had to remain something which only a very few among The People could know. Such knowledge was not, *could not,* be available to giants—white, red, or any other color.

He let go of the dog as they neared the opening through which they had passed earlier in the day. Mato could not see Tori from the spot where he stood at the bottom of the opening under the fire pit. Reaching up and gripping the edge of the moving floor, he pulled himself up and over. His weapons were on the ground at the entrance to the cavern, just where he'd left them.

Tori turned to him and smiled.

Don't do that, he thought. *How can I kill someone who's smiling at me?*

"What is your name?" she said.

It took him a moment to realize that she had queried him in his own tongue. *What new magic was this? What had happened?*

"What?" It was the only thing he could manage in response.

Tori looked confused for a moment, and turned away to look through some papers on her table. Then she smiled and repeated her question.

"I am Mato," he said. "You may call me Black Otter."

His response seemed to be more than she could handle. He tried to simplify it, as if he were talking to a child. "Black Otter," he said.

Once again, she consulted her papers, then spoke. "No Mato?"

Did the giants not have names as well as duties? "Yes, Mato," he said, then stood tall and proud. "Name Black Otter."

Understanding made her face glow with happiness. "Black Otter!" she cried, as if she had made some great discovery.

He nodded.

"*And* mato," she said, smiling even more.

He nodded again. Perhaps there was hope for her, after all. If they could speak to each other, maybe he could swear her to secrecy. Maybe he wouldn't have to kill her.

She worked through another question, her voice stumbling over the words of his people, The People. When she finished, he shrugged. Had he misunderstood? "Again," he said.

After consulting her papers, she repeated the question. It came more easily the second time, and he understood completely. She wanted to know if there were others like him. Did she really expect him to betray The People? He frowned at first, then scowled. "Are there more giants like you?"

Her hand flew to the table, and she made marks feverishly on the paper in front of her. "Again?" she asked.

"Are there more giants?" he asked, shortening his question for the sake of simplicity.

She consulted her papers yet again, made a few more marks, then looked at him. "Yes," she said. "Many."

"Do they know of me?" he asked.

Again, she studied her papers; her magic obviously resided there.

"No," she said after a long pause.

That set his mind at ease. If she was the only one who knew of The People, then the secret would die with her.

The last thing Tori wanted to do was talk on the phone, but life rarely honored one's preferences. She stared at the little screen on her cell phone. The number was plain, but there was no name to go with it. She picked it up and answered with a brusque, "H'lo?"

"Tori! It's Tom Purcell."

She glanced quickly at her watch, relieved to see it was well past the dinner hour. There would be no meals out that evening, which meant she and

Mato—No, *Black Otter*, she corrected herself—could have a long overdue conversation, as slow and awkward as that might be.

"Right, Tom. How are you?"

"Fine, fine. I wanted to apologize for coming on a little strong the last time we spoke."

"It's no problem," she said. *I've dealt with pushy types before, and compared to my ex, you aren't even in the running.*

"Well, it's been bothering me, and I wanted to make it up to you."

"There's no need, really."

"I insist. I thought we might get together for breakfast, rather than dinner. It'd be more relaxed, for both of us."

There was something of a strain in his voice, she thought. Nothing definite or sinister, just *something*. An edge? Maybe. "When did you have in mind?"

"How 'bout tomorrow?"

That might work, she mused. But did she even want to have breakfast with him? After all, she could now speak directly to Mato, or Black Otter, or whatever he called himself. She certainly didn't need an interpreter.

"I guess," she said, instantly reversing herself. It'd give her a chance to tell him she didn't need his help any more, and doing it over breakfast would be easier.

"There's a great little restaurant over in Ten Sleep—"

"I thought you had morning classes to teach."

"Oh." He paused. "Not tomorrow. There's uh, an assembly or something. I'm not involved, so I don't really know what it's all about, but morning classes have been cancelled."

That sounded more like high school than college. They certainly never did anything like that at Auburn. At least, not during either of her two years there. "And you don't have to attend the program?"

"Nope," he said. "It's administrative, not academic. There are some perks to being a faculty member."

"I see. Unfortunately, Ten Sleep is a bit of a haul for me," Tori said, then added, "actually, anywhere is a bit of a haul for me. Charm is much closer."

"Charm it is, then."

"Oh, wait. What day is tomorrow?" she asked.

"Tuesday. Why?"

"Lu's Place isn't open tomorrow."

"Then we'll go somewhere else."

"There is no somewhere else, in Charm," she said, unable to resist a smile.

"Then we're back to Ten Sleep. I'd offer to meet you in Buffalo or even up here, near the campus, but I've got stuff I need to do in the afternoon."

"Yeah. Me, too," Tori said.

"Then it's Ten Sleep or nothing, if you're willing to give me a chance."

"Well—"

"It's only breakfast."

What could it hurt? "Okay."

He gave her the name of a restaurant which she recognized from previous visits, and they settled on a time. After they hung up, Tori began to feel better about the date. She hadn't had one in ages, other than her lunch with Cal, and that was like lunch with an uncle; it didn't really count.

~*~

Shawn had a tough night. His nose had swollen somewhat between the time he went to bed and the time he got up to investigate it. Looking in the mirror, he thought his reflection resembled something like a raccoon wearing nose strips. He remembered the Disney comics he'd seen as a kid. The bad guys were always burly animals, dogs maybe, who wore black masks and looked stupid. That's what he got from the mirror. *Nice.* And the missing eyebrow didn't help. He thought about drawing it in with a pen, then discarded the notion, figuring it would only make him look like a fag.

His left eye wasn't as black as the right, but his nose looked like hell. He'd been taking aspirin every couple of hours since he left New York, hoping to avoid some of what he was looking at. Maybe he should have stuffed the aspirin up his nose. It hadn't done shit to stop the swelling.

The bandages, he realized, were causing some of the problem. As his nose expanded, the adhesive pulled tighter, pressing on the damaged tissue. The pressure couldn't have amounted to much, but he wasn't in any kind of mood to consider discomfort by degree. He cautiously lifted a corner of a bandage, then pulled it off ever so slowly. As the adhesive pealed back, he vented his anger at Vicky Lynn and the Woodall woman. Both were responsible. And while Woodall had certainly gotten hers, Vicky Lynn has thus far gotten off way too easy.

He yanked off the last bit of tape with a vehement curse, then tackled the remaining strip.

Once he had the bandages off, and had rinsed his face carefully with warm water, he looked out the motel room window. Lights from the truck stop cut through the darkness, but bore a misty tinge. The clock on top of the TV said 4:14. He must've gotten up to turn it off during the night, but he couldn't remember doing it. Had he only had three beers? They hadn't helped his throbbing honker much, he thought. Punching Vicky Lynn's lights out would probably do more for that than all the aspirin in the world.

How the hell far away was Ten Sleep, Wy-goddamn-oming from Cleveland? He'd looked it up at the truck stop just before dinner. 1,500 miles, give or take. "But, Vicky Lynn, you're gonna make it all worthwhile."

He pulled on his Roll Tide sweatshirt and slipped back into his jeans. His socks smelled so bad he left them on the floor, and put his bare feet into his running shoes. The truck stop sold boots and underwear, and he'd likely be able to get socks there, too, but he was eager to get back on the road. Shopping, he could do damn near anywhere. Unlike Vicky Lynn and her fancy New York editor friend, he didn't need designer clothes. He didn't need gourmet food, either. Steak and eggs would be just fine. And fries. With ketchup.

Lots and lots of ketchup.

~*~

Tori read the rest of Robert Lanier's dictionary preface. Between the faded ink and the natural flourish of his penmanship, the task had been difficult. His usual style was somewhat flamboyant, but in these private notes, the size of his characters shrank, almost as if in some sort of sympathetic attempt to balance the size difference between himself and his companion.

Sleeping Dove's recovery had surprised him completely, since he hadn't expected her to survive at all. Yet, within two weeks of losing her leg, she was up and busy. Mostly, at first, trying to get away from him.

Those had been trying times, for Lanier had invested significant emotional capital in the tiny woman. He had listened to her feverish speech while she slept, hoping to learn something of her language. The most he managed, however, was an approximation of some of her words. These he wrote down in his journal while stretched beside her near a campfire.

Much of what she said was lost in moans and sighs, even in occasional screams. But he applied himself to the task and wrote down as much as he could. Later, when she was awake, he read those words back to her. The results of this exercise were mixed. More often than not, she looked at him like a man possessed, but at other times she seemed clearly shocked, as if he knew secrets about her that she shared with no one else. Less often, but more memorably, she smiled, as if comforted.

At some point, they formed a bond. Lanier fed her, kept her warm, and offered what comforts he could. In return, she shared her words, pointing to anything and everything, giving names or making gestures of explanation. These games continued long after she healed.

He made crutches for her and eventually fashioned an artificial limb as well, complete with a spring-tensioned ankle of his own design. His notes included sketches of the wooden leg, including dimensions.

She would often leave his camp, disappearing while he slept only to return later, weary and smelling of creosote smoke, but happy. From time to time he attempted to follow her, but she invariably disappeared like a wraith.

At first, when he questioned her about these nocturnal journeys, she pretended not to understand his questions, but as their ability to communicate improved, such fictions grew too thin to sustain. After many months she showed him where she had been going: a hole in the ground concealed by a handful of boulders. She had fashioned torches from branches of the creosote bush. These she bore underground and tossed in his campfire when she returned.

Eventually she allowed him to go with her, and he discovered his *second* treasure: the cavern.

Chapter Fifteen
"To sleep, perchance to dream...."

Mato was gripped by indecision. He had much to do, both in the cavern and later when his mission had been accomplished, and he could return home. The prospect of actually finishing what he started would have made him feel profoundly happy if not for the problem of the she-giant. He did not want to think of her as Tori, his friend and benefactor. A nameless she-giant could be dispatched without remorse, like any large animal. But a friend... That would be hard. Rather than dwell on it, he decided to gather what he needed for his next foray into the cavern.

Tori watched him as he gathered his weapons and the thick cloth he slept on.

"Hungry?" she asked in his language, looking up from her papers.

When he nodded assent, she went to her big,

white food box and opened it. She poked about for a few moments, then brought out bread, sliced meat, and the dark yellow stuff she cooked in his eggs. These things she cut into pieces of a convenient size for him. She also gave him something to drink, pouring the liquid into a small glass for him, and a large one for herself.

The beverage was unlike those she had given him before. It was dark red in color and had a strong, dry taste that stayed in his mouth and complemented the flavors of his food. He liked it, but decided it was not something he could drink much of. It didn't refresh like water, or the dark brown stuff which sent bubbles up his nose.

When finished, he thanked her for the food, an act which set her to marking on one paper while she studied another. Such cumbersome magic! He much preferred the ease of the magic he practiced, for that only occurred while he slept.

"I go now," he said and hopped casually up on the opened hearth.

She spoke in her tortured way, each word dragged from the papers before she forced it through her mouth. She wanted to talk, to learn more about him, to tell him about her own people. He was tempted to stay, for there was much he wished to learn as well. But he had a mission, and the Spirits would not be pleased if he put it off now that he knew how to achieve it.

Ignoring her protests, he dropped down into the hole beneath the fire pit. The dog jumped up on the metal plate, too, and made to drop down beside him.

"No," Mato said, and held up his hand, palm outward. "Stay."

The dog twisted his head one way and another, but obeyed. Tori approached, too, sitting beside the dog and rubbing the space behind his ears. They both watched as he helped himself to three torches. He tucked two of them, unlit, under his arm with the sleeping mat. He draped his bow and quiver over opposite shoulders and lit the third torch.

When he had it burning, he picked up both the torch and his spear and marched down the steep slope into the hole.

~*~

Tori watched the little Indian preparing to leave. At first, she feared his departure would be permanent, but when he jumped down into the opening beneath the hearth, she knew he was only venturing into the cavern Uncle Bob had mentioned. She knew that at some point, she would also have to make that journey, though the mere thought of crawling into a dark hole in the Earth left her shaking.

One of the things she liked about Wyoming was the openness of it. Air. Space. Room. All things which wouldn't be there for her if/when she followed in Mato's footsteps. Even the word, "underground" conjured a frightening set of mental images. Caves. Bats. Crawling things. Things that didn't crawl, probably because they were dead, feeding other crawling things which....

Geez, girl—you're gonna flip yourself out!

"Hey, Shadow! Want some cheese?"

She pulled her knees up and pivoted on her behind, spinning until she had her back to the fireplace. Shadow bounded down into the room and danced around her feet until she reached the table where she and Mato had eaten. She flipped a cheese cube into the air. The dog locked onto it and snatched it cleanly when it approached his nose, the effort smooth and efficient, the morsel gone in an instant. Shadow licked his chops and watched her, not begging, but making it abundantly clear that he wanted another. As many, in fact, as she'd care to toss his way.

"Two more," she said. "I don't want you getting constipated." She tossed him a few scraps of luncheon meat, too. A glance at his bowl showed a handful of dry dog food waiting for him. "That doesn't make you human, y'know." He pressed his big, triangular head into her leg and wagged his tail, then walked back to the hearth and lay down where Mato's blanket had been.

"You miss him, don't you?" she asked.

Shadow lowered his head to the floor and closed his eyes.

"Yeah," she said. "Me, too."

~*~

Purcell arrived at the restaurant in Ten Sleep before Tori. He bought a paper and ordered coffee, then ignored both while he waited for her to show. He hadn't slept well, thanks to the wisdom of Simon Gibbs. What had once seemed such an obvious way out of his financial bind had evaporated. He might be able to get enough cash out of the fat, pock-marked, junk merchant to pay off his margin call, but it'd likely take a sizeable portion of the school's collection to do it.

He briefly contemplated asking Tori for a loan, but then realized the idiocy of such a thought. He might be able to con her out of a few bucks somewhere down the road, but he doubted she would be an easy touch. There was something about her that gave off an aura of caution, as if she'd been burned once before and wasn't about to let it happen again. It reminded him of the show he'd been talked into attending a few weeks earlier: the drama club's production of "The Music Man." Now he had a tune from it stuck in his head: "A Sadder But Wiser Girl For Me."

Fortunately, he was able to shake it off. The last thing he needed to complicate his life was a female—*any* female. And that went even for the woman who had just walked through the door.

There was no doubt in his mind that it was Tori Lanier, though she turned many more heads than his own. Cowgirl chic in a western shirt, boyish hairstyle, and jeans that left no doubt she was all girl, Tori owned the room. He smiled automatically and stood up to greet her.

~*~

Tori's misgivings about meeting Tom Purcell for breakfast hadn't diminished during the drive to Ten Sleep. Long before she even reached Charm, she had convinced herself that it was a complete folly. In order not to be late, she left fairly early, and she was disappointed, if not surprised, to see that Mato had not returned. Shadow was camped out where he'd parked himself the night before, and only reluctantly abandoned the spot when she bribed him with a treat. Who knew dogs had such a great love for cheese cubes? Before leaving, she fed Shadow and left a sandwich in a plastic bag on the table for Mato.

She used the drive time to play a game she'd once enjoyed, back when she was still attending writing conferences and doing book signings. If she knew she'd be meeting someone for the first time, she tried to construct a mental image of them, based solely on their voice, if she'd heard it, and any other non-visual clues she had about them. Purcell, she figured, probably looked like a movie star or the Marlboro Man, the images in her head being pretty much the same. If pressed, she would have conceded that the idea came to her during the night, and even prompted her wardrobe choices.

She removed her sunglasses and carried them into the restaurant. The place was just as she remembered it, pleasant and a little campy. A bit heavy on the frontier motif, but otherwise comfortable, despite having a sizable crowd for a weekday morning. It seemed like every man in the place had just ridden in from a ranch. Everyone except the man who stood and greeted her by name. He resembled the Marlboro man about as much as Popeye's girlfriend, Olive Oil, resembled the Statue of Liberty.

"Mr. Purcell?"

He hurried to her, his hand extended. "I'm delighted to meet you," he said, steering her toward a table for two in a corner. "Coffee?" Rather than wait for her response, he snapped his fingers for a waitress and gestured for another mug. Tori caught the look of venom on the server's face, though Purcell missed it completely.

Tori took a seat, pleased to find herself feeling much less intimidated than she'd been on the phone. They exchanged pleasantries while ordering and waiting for their food. Finally, Tori decided it was time to tell Purcell she'd solved her translation problem.

"I hope you won't think badly of me," she began.

"That's not possible."

She smiled. "But after I put you to all the trouble of working on that recording, I've found a book that allows me to work out my own translations. So, you won't have to worry about it after all."

The news left him thunderstruck, but he

recovered quickly. "Have *you* translated the recording you sent me?"

She wondered why she hadn't thought of doing just that. "No, actually. I went straight to translating uh, live. You know, while we talked."

"Fascinating," he said. "And a little difficult, I would imagine."

"No kidding." She chuckled. "Try writing things down phonetically, then looking them up, and then reversing the process to respond. It's tiring."

"What language is it?" he asked, his eyes peering just over the rim of his coffee mug.

Tori had no idea what to tell him. He'd already heard the recording, so he would know it wasn't one of the languages he spoke. If she made something up, he'd likely know that was bullshit, too. What could she say? She opted for honesty. "I don't really know."

"It's not in the title of the book?"

Sometimes, however, honesty sucked. "The book is hand-written. It hasn't been published."

He looked at her with renewed interest. "That's truly remarkable. I've seen notes from 18th and 19th century scholars—I suppose we'd call them ethnographers today—who wrote down the words of the Indians they encountered. Some of them were remarkably accurate, some were... Well, let's be charitable, and just say they meant well. I presume your translation guide isn't one of those."

"I don't think so," she said, feeling defensive. *Uncle Bob didn't do shoddy work. Complicated? Oh, hell yes, but he got his facts straight.*

"Well, that's a relief." Purcell chewed some toast while he pondered his response. "Would you mind terribly if I looked at it?"

"The dictionary?"

"Yes." He stared directly into her eyes. "It's my profession. All my life I've been fascinated with the study of native cultures. It's extremely rare when one has the opportunity to observe the fruits of field work first hand."

"Well, I don't know," she said, groping for some reason to deny his request.

"Is there a chance I could meet the author?"

She laughed. "Not without a Ouija board, or a spiritualist. He's been dead a long time."

"Was it the man you wrote about? The Confederate spy?"

"He was my great-great uncle. And yes, it is his work. It's fragile, as you can imagine. I couldn't let it out of my possession."

Purcell was as unctuous as a discount funeral director. "Of course, of course. I completely understand. How amazing that your Indian friend happens to speak the very language your uncle studied so long ago."

"It's quite a coincidence," she said.

"I'd say it's an *amazing* coincidence." Purcell looked smug. "There aren't that many Indian dialects spoken in Wyoming, and I've got a pretty good handle on all of them."

Tori drained her coffee mug and set it gently on the table. "Evidently not, else you'd have had no trouble with the recording I gave you."

He wasn't to be denied. "I apologize if I sound argumentative. It's just that notes like those are exceedingly rare, and having a chance to look over originals such as you've described would be a once-in-a-lifetime opportunity."

She pushed back from the table. "I'll have to think about it."

"Please. Is there anything—"

"And I'd prefer to talk it over with my friend before I made a decision."

"But, why?"

"Because it impacts him, that's why."

"It's not like he owns the language," Purcell argued. "You don't understand. I've looked through the available language samples in the school's collection, and it's extensive. But I couldn't find anything that matched the recording you sent me. It's unique."

Tori smiled as she stood. It pleased her that Purcell had to look up to her, even when they were both standing. "I'll let you know."

He placed his hand on her arm, just above her wrist. "How can I impress upon you how important this is?"

"You already have," she said, gently removing his hand. "As I said, I'll let you know."

"And what do you expect me to do in the meantime?"

She shook her head at his little quandary. "Wait, Mr. Purcell. I expect you to wait."

~*~

When Mato woke from his dream, the memory of it remained vivid. Though it took a moment for him to orient himself to his surroundings, as utterly and completely black as they were, he remembered where he was, and more importantly, why he'd come. His flint and striker were in a pouch on his belt. He felt around in the dark until he came across the two spare torches he'd brought with him. In a matter of moments he had one lit, and he quickly restored his bearings.

He wasn't surprised in the least that the true meaning of his dream was obscured. He recalled a recent vision. The details were as clear and certain in his mind as if he'd lived through the experience during the night, which, in a way, he had. His task now was to record as many of those details as he could. But that meant finding something with which to mark the cavern walls. He needed a clean space— an area which didn't already bear the illustrative efforts of some previous dreamer—and the paints to do the work. Why hadn't he prepared properly? Why had he been so rash as to enter the cavern without first preparing the pigments he would need?

Though not quite willing to declare himself a failure, he spared himself no end of self-criticism. He hurried back to the surface, running most of the way until he burst into the antechamber in Tori's cabin. Dropping the torch, he leapt up onto the hearth plate and into the cabin.

The dog greeted him like a long-lost relative, licking his face, arms and hands, until Mato shoved him away. There was important work to be done; he couldn't waste his time frolicking with an animal. Although, he thought, as his stomach rumbled, I could use something to eat.

Oddly enough, there was food waiting for him on the table, wrapped in a thin, slippery fabric *that he could see through!* He had seen Tori use it before, but this was the closest he had ever come to it. Fortunately, the material had an opening, so he didn't have to tear it. The bread was unremarkable, and she had given him two slabs of it. What intrigued him was what she put *between* the pieces of bread. Two substances: one very thick, the color of sand with a strong but pleasant odor, the other was thinner and purple. It too had a pleasant odor, if milder. He tasted the combination and smiled. The wonders of the giant's world were not limited to magic. They had amazing food, too. Perhaps that was how they grew so large. He ate half and put the rest back in the marvelous wrapper to take with him.

He gathered up the paints Tori had given him and bolted back down the hole to the cavern. The dog followed, which was fine with Mato. It would allow him to work until the third torch burned down to nothing. The dog would lead him back to the cabin. Yet none of that mattered. He had to record his dream. He had to include every detail, and he had to do it fast before his memory faded and the dream joined the bulk of such things, which dissipated like mist on the wind. He refused to fail in his mission. He would record it all. He would get it exactly right. It didn't matter in the least whether he understood it or not; that was something for the elders to decide. And now, for the first time in generations, he would be the one to bring the elders back to the cavern of dreams. He would be the object of their songs. Mato Black Otter would be remembered!

~*~

Shawn made good time, despite having to deal with all the toll booths. Who's idea was that, he wondered. *Weren't the interstates paid for with tax money? Why should he have to pay twice? It wasn't right.*

Traffic got completely crazy as he neared Chicago, so he stopped for breakfast, still fuming about the tolls. A trucker on a nearby stool at the counter suggested he quit complaining and ignore them. "Just drive on through. They'll get a photo of your license plate and they send you a bill, but they can't make you pay. They might throw your butt in jail, but hey, if you've got principles, that shouldn't bother you."

Shawn examined the expression on the wise-ass's face. The guy was twice his age. Probably twice his weight, too, but it wasn't muscle. It was too many years behind the wheel of some great hulking 18-wheeler. Shawn decided the asshole wasn't worth the time it'd take to teach him manners. Besides, there were way too many other truckers around who seemed interested in their conversation. He imagined they'd likely side with the long-haul lard ass.

"Yeah," he said at length. "I'll do that. They can just mail me the damn bill."

His pronouncement brought a round of smiles. They're all assholes, Shawn thought. But in light of the bogus license plate on his stolen car, the chances of anyone mailing him a ticket were pretty slim. All those tolls he'd already paid? A waste of money, and a thing of the past.

After paying for breakfast, he examined a rack of sunglasses. The swelling in his nose had gone down a bit, but the bruises were worse. He bought a pair of aviator-style shades that mostly hid the purple flesh around his eyes, gassed up the hideous yellow Chevy, and rejoined the heavy traffic heading west. Somewhere along the way, I-80 had morphed into I-90, and Shawn resolved to reach Wyoming by the end of the day. 1200 miles was a lot of road, but he figured he could goose it through South Dakota, and he sure as Hell wouldn't be stopping to sightsee along the way.

~*~

The breakfast had been good and bad, Purcell concluded. He'd waved goodbye to Tori and watched her glide through the restaurant to the exit. She probably stopped to admire his BMW, he thought, wishing he'd somehow worked a mention of the car into their conversation. Some females were swayed by cars. But the more he thought about it, most of those he knew who might be impressed that way were fresh out of high school. Tori Lanier was no school girl.

So, even though he'd failed to impress her, he'd discovered she had something even more valuable than an Indian friend who spoke a dialect he hadn't heard before. She had a hand-written dictionary from the 19th century. What would Simon, the souvenir monger, think of that? And how much would the notoriety of its author jack up its value?

Of course, there was the issue of ownership. Tori wasn't even willing to let him look at it, but if he stole it, who was she going to complain to? There were no cops in Charm, and the Sheriff in Ten Sleep wasn't exactly a world-class detective. If the manuscript had just come into her possession, as she claimed, she probably wouldn't be able to prove she ever had it in the first place. Simon Gibbs wouldn't be able to resist something like that, even if the market for it was restricted to the most exclusive set of ultra-private collectors. Neither he nor Gibbs could take a chance on having it surface in any legitimate venue; Tori Lanier would jump on that in a heartbeat.

Nothing was going to happen, however, unless he got his hands on the dictionary. What he needed to do, and do quickly, was find out where she lived. It was somewhere in the boondocks, but that description fit most of the state. Then he remembered Caleb, their mutual friend. The old cowboy was bound to know where she lived. All he had to do was charm the information out of him. Without raising any suspicions, of course. And he'd need an alibi—something to prove he wasn't anywhere near Tori's cabin when the "alleged" manuscript went missing. He figured Gibbs could handle that. He dialed Caleb's number from his cell phone.

"Hey, Cal? It's Tom," he said, casually examining the sunglasses Tori had left behind in the restaurant. "You won't believe who I just had breakfast with."

"Tori?"

"Yep. What a doll. She's even prettier than I imagined."

Caleb's voice went a little gruff. "I 'spect you treated her properly?"

"C'mon, Cal. I was the perfect gentleman. In fact, I'm hoping to prove just how gentlemanly I can be. But I need your help."

"How's that?" Caleb asked.

"Well, she left her glasses here in the diner, and I'd like to return them to her. It'd be a great excuse to see her again."

"But?"

"But I don't know where she lives."

Caleb laughed. "It's not hard to find, but it's smack in the middle of nowhere."

"Can you give me directions?"

"Yeah," Caleb said. "No problem." He paused briefly, then added. "Promise me one thing?"

"What's that?"

"You'll call her first? Tell her you're on the way?"

"Of course. I'm a gentleman, remember?"

~*~

It wouldn't be long before Mato once again ran out of light. The torches didn't last nearly long enough for him to finish his work. There was a fairly large, cleared space near the center of the chamber, and it had been the site of previous bonfires. The ashes had been pushed over the edge of the nearby crevice, and there were countless footprints left behind. Most of them were similar in size to his own, but a few showed that at least one giant had roamed the sacred cave. That was troubling, but he refused to let it get in the way of his work.

He wasn't eager to take on the task of hauling firewood into the cavern, but if that's what was required, he would do it. But maybe there was another way. Would the Spirits be offended if he borrowed some of the she-giant's magic to illuminate the chamber? A giant had already been there, after all, and no great calamity had resulted from that. Or had it? How long had it been since anyone of The People had last visited this place? Perhaps *that* was the calamity. He gave a groan of frustration. These were not the sorts of things he should have to deal with. Where were the elders when he needed them?

Looking up on the wall where he'd been working, he inspected the outline he had completed. The paints the she-giant gave him were of poor quality, and would rinse away if they got wet. Water trails were evident on many of the walls, but he had found a space relatively free of them. Still, he couldn't risk having his work disappear simply because he used inferior materials. The outlines he had drawn with the she-giant's paints would have to suffice until he made the proper pigments and filled them in. The amazing brushes she had given him would be a great help. Good brushes, poor paint. It made no sense, but then, the giants rarely did. The Spirits honored him when they made him one of The People rather than a giant.

Mato had looked carefully at many of the other paintings, surprised by the great variation in the rendering skills displayed. Some were painstakingly detailed, though the scale was often distorted. In others, the lines and colors flowed as naturally as the subjects they imitated, but their realism sometimes masked the meaning of the dream which inspired them. Fortunately for him, interpreting the dreams would be left for someone else.

The paintings beckoned. There were animals, large and small. Some he recognized, like elk, bear, and wolf. Some were strange: great shaggy beasts with horns, and long, long noses—so long that they had to be creatures from the dream world, for he had never seen their like. There were men and women, too. And children. And Spirits. And there was his own work: one solitary figure. So simple, and yet so puzzling.

The mystery of how his predecessors had painted high up on the walls had been solved when he located a stash of flat stones and roughhewn planks. These he stacked in order to make a steady surface on which he stood to do his own work. The planks were quite heavy, and it had taken all his strength just to lift an end of one. He couldn't imagine how they had gotten into the cavern in the first place. He doubted that the dog would even be able to drag one of them very far.

As his last torch burned low, Mato prepared to return to the surface. There was still much to do. He called the dog, and they left the cavern together.

Chapter Sixteen
Thieves in the night

"I think I've found what you're looking for," Purcell said into his cell phone. He tried to imagine the look on the artifact dealer's face.

"Do tell," Gibbs said.

"How about an authentic, 19th century, hand-written, native American Indian-to-English translation dictionary?"

"Oh? My, my. Hmm." There was an extended pause, and Purcell assumed Gibbs was pouring over his reference materials to find something similar. "That would be extraordinary," he finally said. "I'm impressed. It certainly didn't take you long to come up with something after our little talk."

Purcell felt justifiably smug. "I'm not in the habit of screwing around. And, as I mentioned before, I'm in a bind, cash-wise. I can't afford to waste time."

"No need to explain," Gibbs said. "We've all been there at one time or another."

"Then you won't mind extending me a little credit against the value of the manuscript?"

"Ah. There it is. I wondered when you'd hit me up for cash."

He's smiling, the fat bastard. He thinks he's got me over a barrel. "It's a cost of doing business. I have some expenses I need to settle before I can get my hands on the artifact."

"You don't have it already?"

"No," Purcell said. "I just found out about it."

"It's not part of the school's collection?"

"I never said it was."

"Then, where is it?" Gibbs asked, innocently.

Purcell smiled. *Yeah, like I'd tell you!* "I'm not quite ready to divulge that information."

"Well, no, I don't suppose you are." There was another lengthy pause. "I'll need to know a great deal more about this document before I can even begin to estimate it's value."

"Oh, come now," Purcell said. "I think we can both agree that whatever it ultimately sells for, the figure will be significant."

"If the artifact actually exists."

"Of course."

It exists. It has to exist.

Purcell wondered if his margin call nightmare was truly about to be over. "I need ten grand. In cash. Today."

Gibbs started to laugh, but Purcell cut him off. "I know of at least two other dealers who would jump at the chance to get their hands on this. I only called you as a courtesy. If you're not interested..." He let his voice trail off, praying Gibbs wouldn't call his bluff.

"You know I'm interested," Gibbs said. "But ten thousand dollars is a lot of money for something I haven't seen."

"What makes this manuscript even more interesting is the name of the person who wrote it," Purcell said. "Just the fact that his name is on it will jack up the value significantly. I'm sure of it."

"But you're not going to tell me who it is, are you?"

"Nope."

Gotcha, asshole!

"However, once I have the manuscript, I'll send you a copy of the front page, and maybe a few from the middle, so you'll have something to share with your customers—a little something to get their attention. I presume with an artifact like this you'll want to conduct an auction?"

"Probably," said Gibbs. "It depends on how much interest there is."

"When can I collect my advance?" It pleased him immensely to hear Gibbs muttering to himself on the other end of the line.

"After lunch. I need some time to get it all in cash. Can you meet me here?"

That would work out well, he thought. His broker had a branch office in Billings. "Sure. I'll see you then."

It would mean an awful lot of driving, but the effort would be worth it. He'd have to figure out how he was going to get the manuscript away from Tori. Maybe wait until she went to sleep? No way; too dangerous. Living alone out in the wilderness, she'd almost certainly have a gun of some kind. He had no intention of providing her with a target. If there were only some way he could lure her out of her house long enough for him to get in. That would do the trick, but she wasn't likely to do anything for him, even if he was willing to call attention to himself, which he wasn't.

Damn! How was he going to get her out of the way?

He aimed his beautiful BMW toward Charm. There was always Caleb. Maybe he could figure out a way to get Caleb to invite her into town. How hard could that be?

~*~

Shawn had driven just over 700 miles, and felt like he'd been sitting in the stupid yellow Chevy for a month. His butt hurt, his legs were stiff, and he'd developed an almost homicidal hatred for Minnesota drivers. That he'd resisted the urge to run dozens of Land O' Lakers off the road was a testament to his vast willpower and dedication to the job of finding Vicky Lynn. He pulled into a truck stop outside the South Dakota town of Kimball, loaded up on gas, and stretched his legs. He'd earned himself a meal, by God! Leaving the car parked in the immense shadow of a red Freightliner, he entered the cafe and took a seat in a booth.

The place was far from packed, but it seemed like forever before anyone waited on him. Eventually, a girl in her early twenties cruised up to his table. She was attractive in a down-home sort of way, and he figured she'd probably lived her whole life somewhere close by. With a little make-up and the right clothes, she'd be a knock-out. The boredom in her eyes told him everything he needed to know.

"You need a menu?" she asked.

"That depends," he said, staring at the name tag on her blouse, "Ellen."

She coaxed one last pop out of her gum. "Depends on what?"

"Whether or not you're on it."

"I'm not," she said, without a hint of emotion. "You gonna order, or do you just want to try to talk your way into my pants?"

Whoa! "Damn girl, you've been doin' this a while, haven't you?"

"I deal with horny truckers all day long. You think you're the first one to come up with that lame shit?"

"Sorry," he said. "I'm just not used to seeing someone as pretty as you in a place like this."

She looked at him through squinted eyes, then smiled. "That's okay. No harm done. But look, I'm really, really tired. My feet are killin' me, and I've got another two hours before my shift is over. So, if you're gonna order, do me a favor. Do it now, so I don't have to make an extra trip back here, okay?"

He chuckled. "Fair enough. I want a steak, rare."

"You want a good steak or a cheap one?"

"I want the best," he said. "And fries. And a beer."

"We don't have beer."

"Damn. Okay then, coffee. With cream."

"Anything else?"

"You already said you weren't available."

She leaned close and whispered in his ear. "I know what you're thinking. You're wondering if there's any chance you might spend some time with me when I get off work. And normally, you'd be right, 'cause you're kinda cute with your hard guy glasses, and your nose all messed up. And that's exactly the kinda thing that usually turns me on."

"But?"

"But I've got a raging case of the clap, and unless you'd like to share it, I suggest you just eat your steak, drink your coffee, and hit the road." She pushed his ball cap toward the front of his head. "Thinkin' about it is as close as you're gonna get."

He watched her walk away, enchanted by the mechanics of female architecture. Ah, but she was intrigued; he sensed it. When she returned with his coffee, he tried again. "You go to school around here? You could be a cheerleader."

"I bet that'd pay well." She tapped the letter 'A' on the front of his sweatshirt. "Is that what they teach down there at Arkansas? Aren't they the pigs?"

"Hogs," he said. "Razorbacks." He pointed to the letter 'A.' "But this is for Alabama. Whole different animal."

"Yeah? What kind?"

"Elephant." He turned so she could see the emblem on the back of his sweatshirt.

"Well, that certainly makes sense." She glanced briefly up toward the ceiling. "You a graduate?"

"Nah. I just like the football. Never thought I needed a college education."

"I got my degree right here," she said. "Proctology."

He frowned.

"The study of assholes. I see 'em all day long."

She dropped a handful of little paper containers full of cream on the table and left.

Shawn grinned. The girl was sharp in more ways than one, though she probably told the same jokes over and over. He glanced at a wall clock provided by a local farm supply company. It was later than he thought, even though he was gaining a little time headed west. Ten Sleep was still a long way off. So much for his vow to get there in one day. He'd have to find a place to spend the night.

Ellen stood near the cash register talking to a cop. His tan uniform was trimmed in dark brown, the creases sharp. His shoes, gun belt, and other leather gear were polished, and anything metal shined like he'd just prepped for inspection. The two hugged, and she kissed him on the mouth like she meant him to remember it. Vicky Lynn used to kiss him like that, a long time ago.

When Ellen delivered his meal, he couldn't resist asking her about the cop. "That your boyfriend?"

"Not anymore. He's my fiancé."

Shawn sat up straighter. "Is he the one who gave you the clap?"

"He *shot* the guy who gave me the clap. Thirty-seven times."

"He must've been pretty pissed."

"Not really." She kept a perfectly straight face. "He ran out of bullets."

"Next you're gonna tell me he pleaded self-defense, right?"

She shook her head. "Resisting arrest." She placed the check beside his plate. "Enjoy your meal."

He did. And afterwards he drove to the first motel he could find, where he spent the night.

Alone.

~*~

Tori wasn't going to arrive home until much later than she'd originally planned. While in Ten Sleep, she'd done some shopping. Caleb was a dear, but he didn't have everything, and she took advantage of the opportunity to stock up on essentials, mostly wine and consumables, and an LED flashlight for Mato. Anything she knew she could buy from Cal she intentionally left out of her shopping cart. She even picked up a new swim suit, since summer was right around the corner.

She looked forward to seeing Caleb as she drove to Charm. He was as close to family as she had, and that was something she missed. If her mother weren't so dead set against leaving Georgia, she'd have relocated her to Wyoming, too.

Caleb was mildly surprised when she wandered into his store. They chatted as she picked up odds and ends—cheese cubes and dog food, bottled water, eggs. "You say you were just in Ten Sleep?" he asked.

She nodded.

"Then why didn't you get this stuff there? Woulda cost less, I'm sure."

"'Cause then I wouldn't have had an excuse to drop by and see you."

He smiled. "You tryin' to get yourself a discount?"

"Nah." She parked in front of his wood stove. "I had breakfast with your friend, Tom."

"So I hear."

"Really?"

"Yeah. He said he thought you were a real cutie." He gave her a stern look. "He didn't... You know. Try anything, did he?"

She chuckled. "No. Nothing like that. He seemed more interested in what I'm doing than what I look like."

"What you're doing? You mean writing?"

"Sort of. It's all related."

"Was he able to help you with the translation?" He walked from his register to the coffee pot. "Want a cup?"

"Haven't gotten over the last one," she said with a wink.

"It's your loss." He refilled his mug, the coffee almost invisible against the dark stains. "So, did you send him a recording?"

"Yes, but he couldn't get much out of it. I've

since found another way to get it done."

Caleb sat beside her, careful not to spill his steaming brew. "The internet, right?"

She shrugged, not quite ready to reveal her secrets. "The thing is...."

"What?"

"Well, I'm probably just being silly, but he seemed a bit pushy, like I owed it to him to share my research material. I don't intend to do that, with him or anyone else."

"And you told him as much?"

"I think I made it pretty clear," she said. "But I've got this nagging suspicion. I dunno. Like I said, I'm probably just being silly."

Cal blew on his coffee and remained silent for a while. "He asked me how to get to your place."

"He did? When?"

"Oh, hours ago. Late this morning. He called and said you'd left your sunglasses at the restaurant, and he wanted to bring them by. Said it'd give him an excuse to see you again."

She frowned, then noticed the reaction on Caleb's face and forced a smile.

"You want me to call him back? Say the word, and I'll straighten him out. Pronto."

"I think I can handle him," she said. "But if you see him, tell him I've already got a boyfriend."

He looked surprised. "You do?"

She stood and kissed him on the cheek. "Why do you think I come by here so often?"

He laughed. "You don't come in often enough. That's for damn sure."

"That's 'cause you're a luxury, Cal. I can't afford to come in here very often."

~*~

Mato was hardly a beginner when it came to making the paints he would use on his rendering in the cavern of dreams. But he usually made them at home, where there was an abundance of the materials he needed. He mentally reviewed the colors he required and the clays, soils, and stones he had to find. Reds, browns, yellows, and black presented little problem. For white he would have to settle for scraping the stone walls on which he worked. He had never found a way to make blue, however, and had been astonished to find several shades of it in the paints the she-giant had given him. He had tried to point this out to her, but she did not seem to understand. How frustrating giants were! If he could have used her paints, he would have. But they would never last, and he had no idea how long it might be before an elder saw his work.

So, blue was out. He had no desire to alter his dream and possibly cause an elder to misinterpret it, but in this case he had to make an exception. He would substitute shades of gray, and that would have to do. In addition to the various minerals, he also needed animal fat and blood. Tori had some strips of extremely fatty meat in the box where she stored her food. Some of that would do. Blood wouldn't prove difficult either, he thought, automatically checking the stone tips on his arrows. He would need something to grind the stones to powder, which would allow him to produce the various shades he needed. None of this was difficult, but it was time-consuming—rather like making a new blowgun from scratch. Laborious.

It would likely be the following day before he could re-enter the cavern and actually begin his real work. He hated delays, but then he remembered he had found the cavern, and that had ended the longest delay of all. What was one more day?

~*~

Tom Purcell congratulated himself on having nothing to do until dark, when he would aim his shiny, red BMW south and drive to Tori's cabin. With the money left over from paying his margin call, he intended to treat himself to a very nice dinner, alone. When his phone rang, he was tempted to ignore it, but associate professors did that at their peril when school presidents called. He clicked the answer button. "Dr. Noblewski! What can I do for you?"

"Tom," he said, "I'm so glad I reached you. When they told me you had cancelled your classes this morning, I thought perhaps you were ill. Then I went by your office, and the staff said they hadn't heard from you all day. We were getting worried."

"I'm perfectly fine," he said, though he dreaded whatever it was the old man had in mind. It was doubtless some sort of "little project." They were always "little projects," and they always required vastly more time than they were worth. "I just had some family business to deal with. I've got almost all of it under control now."

"Excellent," Noblewski said. "Listen, I know this is terribly short notice, but I'm in a bit of a jam, and I need your help."

Damn it!

"Sure," he said, trying to put a smile in his voice.

"We're having a retirement get-together this evening for Dr. Devlin. I had arranged for a friend of hers from one of the big Montana schools to come and reminisce about their work together in building competing artifact collections."

"Sounds interesting," Purcell said, though forcing himself to use those exact words was a challenge.

Noblewski roared on. "It would have been, I'm sure, but at the last minute, Dr. Devlin's friend backed out. Something came up. Don't recall what he said, actually, but it doesn't matter. He can't come, and now I have no speaker."

Please don't do this to me!

"So, I need you to fill in. You can handle that, can't you? I understand you've spent a good bit of time lately working with the collection. I think it would be appropriate for you to share some of your expertise, perhaps point out some of the more important acquisitions. You could then prompt Dr. Devlin to explain what went into the process, especially since you'll be following in her footsteps."

"Well," Purcell began, "I—"

"It's rare for an educator at the beginning of his career to have such a responsible position, but I'm sure you already know that."

"Of course. You're absolutely correct."

"Dr. Devlin mentioned that she thought the position required someone with a doctorate."

Purcell winced. "She said something similar to me."

"I think this would be a splendid way for the two of you to demonstrate that the collection is in capable hands. And Tom, it would be an especially good opportunity for you to show how much you appreciate the work Dr. Devlin has done."

"I hadn't thought of that," Purcell said. *Truer words had never been spoken.*

"Well, there you are then. What do they call it? A win-win. Yes, I like that. Win-win."

"When does it start?"

"8 PM. The Godwin Room. We're having dinner off campus. Would you care to join us?"

"No, thank you," Purcell said. "Unfortunately,

I already have plans for dinner. Besides, I need some time to prepare my remarks."

"Certainly. Well, I look forward to hearing them. And I'm sure Dr. Devlin does, too."

"I'll do my best, sir."

"That's the spirit!" Noblewski sounded inspired. "If only we could manage a little of that win-win business with the basketball program."

"My thoughts exactly, sir."

~*~

Tori hadn't seen Mato or Shadow since early that morning. She had fixed food for both of them before she left to meet Purcell in Ten Sleep, and it was nearly dark when she finally got home. That had been an hour and two glasses of chardonnay earlier. Neither Mato's weapons nor his paints were where he normally left them, and Shadow's water dish was still full. The sandwich, however, was gone. She doubted they had spent any more time in the cabin than she had. But she wasn't worried. They would take care of each other. There was something fascinating about their relationship. She felt sure Mato was new to the whole dog-as-friend concept, as opposed to the dog-as-food model. He was probably all too familiar with that.

After their initial encounter, Shadow had treated Mato with incredible gentleness, almost as if he thought of the little Indian as a child. If that was a result of his Labrador retriever genes, she didn't know. Her own knowledge of dogs was pretty thin.

Her knowledge of love and loyalty, however, were well-developed, and there was no doubt in her mind that Shadow and Mato were simpatico. Extremely so.

The concept left her thinking of Cassy. They often went weeks without talking, but ever since Cassy called to warn her that Shawn was up to his old tricks, she'd felt that checking in with her editor on a regular basis was probably a good idea. And, in fact, she was overdue.

She refilled her wine glass and tossed a log on the fire. She and Mato had worked their way through the issue of using the side door in the rock wall under the house. Though Tori would have struggled to squeeze through it, Mato and Shadow managed with relative ease. Uncle Bob's penchant for spy-stuff worked pretty well, even if a good century had passed since he'd put it in place.

Not too shabby for an old-timer.

Cassy's phone number was one of two she had set up on speed dial. She punched the code and waited. Eventually, Cassy's answering machine kicked in, and Tori left a message. Though Cassy often worked late, Tori knew she wouldn't be in her office at this hour. It had to be nearly 10 PM in New York.

Probably out with Rachel. Though she didn't share Cassy's preference in partners, she nevertheless felt a twinge of jealousy. At least Cassy had *some* romance in her life. Tori had a dog, sort of, and a very short Indian. She also had an associate professor of anthropology who would rather jump her dictionary than her bones. All in all, her love life sucked.

Of course, there was always Shawn. Thoughts of him invariably made her check to see if her shotgun was still loaded and parked where she expected it. If Shawn ever did walk through her door, there was a better than even chance he'd go back out in a bag. Maybe a body bag, maybe a garbage bag. It was all the same to her.

She forced her mind back to the present. The discovery of the hidden hole in the ground presented some issues she would eventually have to resolve. Uncle Bob's notes made it quite clear there was something of tremendous value at the other end of the hole. He had made the trip and returned to write about it, so there was no reason to believe that she'd have any trouble doing the same thing. Except for Mato. She seriously doubted he'd like the idea. The way he marched down into the tunnel made it obvious he felt entitled to enter. He certainly hadn't motioned for her to follow.

According to Uncle Bob's notes, it had taken quite a long time before Sleeping Dove let him explore it. Tori would have to talk it over with Mato, and that would be quite an undertaking. It wouldn't hurt to do a little prep work, maybe write out some of the history between Uncle Bob and Sleeping Dove. If she could simply demonstrate that she meant no harm, and in fact, wanted to protect whatever was down there, then surely Mato would go along.

Surely.

But then, it would be much easier if she actually knew what was down there. She looked over at the hearth and the cheery fire burning there. She already had a lamp. Would she need ropes and climbing gear? How did one dress to crawl underground? There would certainly be information about it on the internet, but she knew the answer to the real question *wouldn't* be there. It was a simple question. But profound.

Do I have the guts to crawl into a hole in the ground?

~*~

For Tom Purcell, the gathering in honor of retiring anthropologist and artifact collection curator, Denise Devlin, was torture—the rack, the iron maiden, and the death of a thousand cuts, all inflicted at the same time. Until then, "brutal" was just a word, a mere concept. Denise Devlin and Warren Noblewski brought it to reality. Up until the moment he discovered the open bar.

Never a heavy drinker, Purcell allowed himself considerable latitude that evening. He'd earned it. Having completed his remarks, he exchanged a volley of platitudes with the demon doctor Devlin, then surrendered the podium to her so that she could regale the crowd with her vast knowledge of Indian collectibles.

What a monstrous, crushing bore the old biddy was! He desperately needed the semblance of escape promised by repeated servings of adult beverages.

Having left the front of the modest crowd, he intended to find a quiet corner where he could wait out the proceedings before driving to Tori Lanier's cabin. At just about that moment Dr. Noblewski stood up and introduced a surprise guest, a full professor and long-time pal of Dr. Devlin. Purcell stared at Noblewski with what he knew was intense puzzlement, but the school president only shrugged.

The guest took center stage to announce that he was working on a deal to secure an extremely rare, hand-written, 19th century translation dictionary. He hadn't been able to determine yet which Indian dialect it was, but he felt certain it would add immeasurably to the prestige of his school's collection. He apologized to Dr. Devlin, in the spirit of one-up-manship, and announced how relieved he was that he wouldn't have to compete with her in the bidding for the manuscript.

Purcell somehow managed to find the bar, despite the haze that his future had become. *Had Gibbs lost his mind? How could he share details of the dictionary with some idiot who intended to show it to the world?* He suddenly needed a drink even more than before.

Given his modest familiarity with alcohol, he would have been hard pressed to identify good booze from bad, so he relied on names he'd heard while growing up: Southern Comfort, Jack Daniels, and Smirnoff. He tried them all. An accommodating bartender made helpful suggestions about what to mix with the various spirits. The barman, an aeronautical engineering major named Erik, taking advantage of the GI bill, saw to it that Purcell's glass never remained empty. It wasn't long before Purcell forgot his troubles.

During the latter stages of the evening, he tipped lavishly, smiled widely, and when he got home, puked violently.

He also postponed the midnight mission to Tori's cabin for 24 hours.

Chapter Seventeen
D-Day

Shawn woke up feeling much better than he had the day before. His face looked better, too. The bruising under his eyes had gone from black to a mottled combination of blue, green, and purple. Colorful, but slightly less grim-looking than before, and it all still fit conveniently under his dark aviator glasses. Sadly, his missing eyebrow wasn't similarly disguised, but then, one couldn't have everything. At least the swelling in his nose had subsided. It remained a far cry from normal, but that would come in good time. He could be patient when he had to.

He showered and dressed, but resolved to find a place where he could pick up some clean underwear, socks, and a new T-shirt.

The "I♡New York" garment had served its purpose and needed to be retired. Quickly. Shawn sniffed it, then dropped it in the motel room trash can. The sweatshirt would have to suffice in the meantime.

Breakfast came from a fast-food restaurant. He bought a large coffee and a carton of cigarettes and figured he wouldn't need to stop until he reached Wyoming. He still had most of South Dakota to cross, but he was rested. More importantly, he was motivated. With any kind of luck, he'd be back in Vicky Lynn's life by dinner time.

While walking to the car, he briefly pondered the wisdom of dumping the Chevy with its DOT yellow paint job. Whatever possessed Sutherland to buy such an ugly color car? He shrugged. *There really was no accounting for taste.*

He turned his ball cap around backwards and got in the car. Later, when all this crap was behind him, he'd get a real muscle car, tricked out with fancy rims, a big ass engine and straight pipes. He'd have it painted red. With flames. And maybe a confederate flag.

If he saw Ellen's state trooper boyfriend while he was drivin' that, he'd blow his damn doors off. Shawn gunned the engine as he pulled out of the motel parking lot. He got the tires to squeal as he accelerated, fishtailing slightly as he maneuvered into traffic.

And spilled his coffee.

~*~

Tori was surprised to discover that Mato had

returned during the night. He and Shadow were asleep when she got up, and didn't stir while she showered, dressed, and made breakfast. The meal consisted of toast and eggs; her bacon had mysteriously disappeared.

She noticed the Indian had left a small pile of stones and a baggie full of dirt on the floor. She recognized a container that had once been in her refrigerator. It sat on the floor with the plastic lid in place, and she decided that was probably the best way to leave it.

Shadow got up first and wandered to her, where she could offer him a bit of morning worship before he went outdoors to perform his ablutions. He seemed happy, and that fit nicely with her own mood. She reminded herself to call Cassy sometime during the day, and her mother, too. There was no telling what crazy Shawn might be up to.

Mato finally woke. He stepped outside briefly and came back in with Shadow. The little Indian stretched and yawned, then climbed up on the chair beside the table and helped himself to the food.

"It's customary to say a greeting," Tori said pleasantly in English.

He merely stared at her.

"Good morning," she said, then gestured for him to say something.

When he didn't get it, she scraped the eggs off his plate and back into the bowl, then set it aside. "Good morning," she said again, pronouncing each syllable with care, then repeating her previous gesture.

"Gud mawrning," he said, although it sounded more like a question than a declaration.

It was good enough, however, so she restored his eggs, making sure he got an extra gob of cheese, too. He smiled at that, and then said something to her which she felt sure she hadn't heard before. She had left the dictionary pages on the counter by the sink and quickly referenced them. Smiling, she repeated the greeting he had extended to her. *Gotta remember that one.*

While they ate, she stumbled through their odd version of a chat. She noticed, however, that Mato seemed to be making an effort to repeat her words just as she repeated his. He also seemed to be re-using sentences such that new words were given a common context, so Tori did the same thing. "This is called paint," she said, gesturing to the watercolor tray. "This is called a brush. This is called a cup. This is called a rock."

Between them, they built a vocabulary. Mato's memory was clearly better than hers, but then it had to be. He wasn't taking notes. Tori often checked the dictionary to see if Uncle Bob had already recorded a word, and if he hadn't, which was surprisingly rare, she listed it in her own handwritten addendum.

Clearly a natural multi-tasker, Mato left the table and began working with his rocks and dirt and—she sniffed, yep—bacon fat. At first, Tori couldn't imagine what he was doing, but when he began to poke around in her cabinets for small containers, she thought she might have figured it out. She then volunteered a selection of empty jars and butter tubs. Anything fairly small that had a good lid went into the effort. Mato was clearly pleased.

She worked out the primary question inspired by his efforts. "What are you going to paint?"

When he gave her a suspicious look, she waved her hand at his growing collection of colors and repeated the question.

His answer was short, and curious. "I dream. Must draw." She looked up the words and guessed at the meaning.

"In cave?" she asked, wondering if this was how the Lone Ranger and Tonto got started.

"Yes," he said, in English.

"Tori see?" she asked.

Mato's face registered shock. "Go cave?"

"Yes," she said, feeling a bit offended.

He seemed to be considering his words before he responded, and she took care to record them. The translation did nothing for her feelings, and she responded with what she felt was an appropriate degree of vehemence: "Tori *not* too fat!"

He got up and walked to the hearth, which

Tori had closed, and looked at it in obvious frustration. Tori marched up next to him and opened it, sliding the metal plate into the room. Makes it easier to clean, she thought as Mato climbed up on it and pointed at the hole in the ground. He repeated his earlier opinion.

Gently pushing him to one side, Tori climbed past him and dropped down to the ground. Her intention had been to prove that she wasn't too big for the hole, but the idea of crawling in headfirst had zero appeal. Undaunted, she dropped to all fours and *backed* into the opening. It wasn't comfortable, and required that she jettison her dignity, but she managed to do it. She kept wiggling, in reverse, until her head dropped below ground level.

"See?" she yelled, "Tori not too fat!" In fact, once she got moving, it wasn't too hard to maintain a decent pace. The light from above dimmed quickly, however, and she crawled back to the surface. When she was finally ready to make the trip, she'd do it facing forward, and she'd damn sure bring a lamp. Maybe two.

Mato was laughing, and she couldn't help but join him. She climbed up on the iron plate, brushing dirt from her shirt where she'd scraped the top and sides of the tunnel. He pointed to her stomach, where an even larger smudge appeared.

"Too fat?" she asked, with a dash of dramatic indignance.

"No, no," he said, pretending to cover his head from imaginary blows.

Later she asked him if he wanted her to get more paint. That conversation seemed to take forever, until she realized he was trying not to insult the water colors she had given him. He had no concept of the kind and quality of paint she could buy off the shelf. There had been a time when she'd looked at paint chips, thinking that she might eventually put drywall up over some or all of the log walls. That had been in the early stages of reconstruction, when she still had some money. *Where had she put the darn things?*

She left Mato crushing rocks into powder while she searched for the chips. What she found was a pamphlet she'd picked up at a hardware store in Ten Sleep that unfolded to reveal dozens of colors from all across the spectrum. Feeling triumphant, she presented it to Mato with the declaration she'd already worked out in his language. "Good paint. Not wash away. Mato want?"

He stared at the colors, running his fingers over the different shades, but acting almost reverently when examining the blue hues. "Tori have?" he asked.

She shook her head, and the resulting look of disappointment on his face nearly made her cry. "Tori get," she said, emphatically, then spent the next half hour explaining that she couldn't get them all; he had to pick a few, and she would get those. Eventually, he got the idea and made a mark on the sheet beside each one he wanted. Of the six colors, three were shades of blue.

He watched, but didn't interfere as she gathered her purse and keys. Her sunglasses were nowhere to be found, however, and then she remembered she'd left them in Ten Sleep, and Caleb's friend was going to return them. Wyoming was littered with her lost shades. *I should buy them by the case,* she thought.

She left the dog and the Indian behind. Ten Sleep wasn't quite ready for either one.

~*~

Tom Purcell survived his morning classes somehow. He couldn't recall that as a student he'd ever been so callous to an instructor who was clearly suffering. But his charges seemed to revel in his discomfort, speaking loudly, dropping books, and making incessant demands. By the time he retreated to his office to absorb some of the cool, dark silence, the phone rang. He eyed it with loathing. A mosquito would have been more welcome.

"Purcell," he grumbled into the receiver.

"Got it?" Gibbs asked.

Much as he wanted to hang up the phone, since Gibbs wasn't standing close enough for him to shove it where it belonged, Purcell merely said, "No."

"Why not?"

Because, you fat, syphilitic blister, you spilled the goddamn beans! What he said was, "Because last night, one of *your* customers announced that it was on the fucking market. It's a wonder my source wasn't in the audience or there'd really be hell to pay."

"I can't control what my customers do," Gibbs said.

"Then I'll sell it to someone who can."

"The hell you will."

"The hell I won't," Purcell roared into the phone, then instantly regretted it.

"You owe me ten grand."

Purcell would have laughed if his head wasn't still throbbing from his last rant. "And you've got some paperwork to prove that?" He could imagine Gibb's face turning purple. It was only fair; there was plenty of anger to go around.

"Listen," Purcell said. "Nothing has changed, except the timeline. I've already made the arrangements, and I should be able to get the manuscript tonight. What I need from you is an alibi. I don't care what it is, but it has to be solid, because my source is going to suspect me, and I need to be able to prove that it couldn't have been me. Understand?"

"Of course," Gibbs said. "You'll be my houseguest. We'll have dinner someplace where people can see us, then we'll leave together. You can go collect the artifact then come back to my house. I have a housekeeper. She'll see you with me in the morning."

"Can't you come up with someone who'd claim I spent the evening with them? I've got to be completely covered or the deal's off."

Gibbs muttered to himself. "Well, I do know a woman...."

Purcell frowned. "What kind of woman? I don't—"

"The kind who'll agree to cover your ass, for the right amount of money."

"A hooker?"

"Of course not! Do you think I associate with people like that?"

"How would I know?" Purcell said. "Not that I care. Is she reliable?"

"Yeah."

"Then set it up."

"I'll bring her to dinner with us," Gibbs said. "Six PM. My office. Don't be late."

Purcell hung up without saying goodbye.

~*~

It was late afternoon when Shawn rolled into Ten Sleep. The town appeared to be even smaller than the one he grew up in. But rural Georgia seemed vastly different than this place. Maybe it was due to the openness. Once you got outside the cities, Georgia was all trees. And farmland. Wyoming seemed to be mostly sky. And farmland. What Shawn needed was a realtor.

He drove down the main drag looking for real estate firms. It didn't take long to find one. He wandered in and was greeted by an older woman with dark hair and a thick German accent. She had a smoker's cough and looked about as sturdy as a praying mantis. In fact, she resembled a praying mantis in several other ways, too. He hoped it wasn't something in the air or water.

"I'm lookin' for a piece of property that sold in the last couple years," he said. "I'm tryin' to find my sister. We got separated when we were kids."

"Vhat happen?" the woman asked.

"Our parents were killed in a car wreck," he said, improvising.

"How terrible," she replied, though it sounded like she'd said "tar-e-bull."

"I don't remember much about it. We were awfully young. Anyway, they stuck us in foster care, and I've been trying to find her ever since."

"You poor t'ing," she said. "You vant some coffee?"

"No, thank you. I'm okay. I'm just eager to find her. She goes by the name Tori Lanier." He paused. "Make that, Victoria Lanier. Like I said, she moved here a couple years ago."

"Here?" the woman said. "To Ten Sleep?"

"This area," he said. "I've got a picture of the place."

The woman brightened. "Is goot! Show me."

Shawn resisted the urge to say, "Ya-vol" or whatever it was the Nazis always said in the movies. Instead, he pulled the slightly mangled photo of Vicky Lynn's cabin from his pocket and placed it on the woman's desk. He put the picture of Vicky Lynn standing in front of the Ten Sleep sign beside it. "That's what she looks like."

The woman clucked over the photos, concentrating more on the one of the cabin. "I remember this vun," she said. "It vas on ze market for ages."

"Really?"

"Oh ya. Nobody vanted it. Too far out. Tar-e-bull condishon. Falling down it vas."

"But she bought it?"

"I don't know. Ve didn't handle ze sale. Vas someone else. Chet Andrews, I tink."

"Chet Andrews?"

"Ya." She gave him a conspiratorial look. "He's not so sharp, dat von. You need to buy sometink, you come to me, ya liebshen?"

"Ya," he said. When had Wyoming become part of the Reich, he wondered. "Any idea where I can find this Andrews guy?"

She snapped her fingers. "Natürlich! Come."

Shawn followed her to the front door, and she pointed across the street and down the block.

"There," she said. "On ze right. You can't miss. But, you need nice house, you come see me, ya?"

"Oh, hell ya," he said, never letting his eyes move from his next target. He checked his watch and smiled. He had all day.

~*~

Mato killed the time waiting for Tori by constructing new torches. He'd used up all the old ones, and was frankly glad to see them gone. They were so old and dry they didn't last long. He spent the better part of the day foraging for material, then hauled it all back to the cabin.

Shadow stretched out beside him while he worked. Music from Tori's magic discs helped relieve the tedium. One piece in particular had become so dear to him that he hummed along with the music even though he had no idea what "Sweet Home Alabama" meant. He would miss Tori's music when he returned to The People.

No thoughts of his home went through his head without thoughts of Reyna as well. He wondered how she fared. He had been gone for so long, she probably thought him dead. If only there was some way to send her a message! She would be so proud knowing he had not only found the cavern of dreams, but had already spent the night there and received a vision from beyond.

Reyna was such a clever woman. It would not surprise him if one day she were responsible for interpreting dreams sent by the Spirits. He wished she were here now. He would lead her into the great cavern and show her the wonders he'd discovered. She would reward him passionately. Perhaps they could form a permanent bond. He prayed that might be so. But if she thought him dead, she might have already accepted someone else's bed. That brought a scowl to his face. He called the dog.

"Will you join me in battle if someone else has claimed Reyna?" he asked.

The dog wagged his tail.

"I will need your teeth and claws and cunning," he said. "There could be a battle. But if you stand by my side, no one can stop me!"

The dog licked his face.

"You will need to be much more fierce," Mato said, wagging his finger at the animal's nose. "You must promise me you will not lick the other warriors."

The dog stretched out beside him and closed his eyes. It was not a good omen.

~*~

Chet Andrews seemed to be waiting for him when Shawn walked through his door. The man stood half a head taller than Shawn and wore a cowboy hat. That seemed amazing. Shawn had never seen an adult wearing a cowboy hat. Out in the open.

The man approached him with his hand outstretched, and Shawn had no choice but to grab it and hang on. The handshake damn near lifted him off his feet.

"How kin I hep you today?" Andrews asked.

Can you lose the stupid cowboy accent? "I'm looking for someone," Shawn said, and spread the two photos on the realtor's desk. "She look familiar?"

"Oh yeah," he said, picking up the snapshot of Vicky Lynn. "Who could forget a hot number like her?"

"That's my wife yer talkin' about," Shawn said.

"Oh?" Andrews looked instantly contrite. "Sorry. Didn't mean any harm. She's a fine-lookin' filly, she is."

Who the hell are you—Yoda the Kid? "No problem. It's a long story, and I don't want to get into it. I'm just tryin' to reconnect is all. Do you know where she's livin'?"

"Absolutely," he said. "She's a few miles outside Charm."

Shawn looked at him, wondering if there was an insult in there somewhere. "Charm?"

"Yeah. It's a town. Sort of. Very small." He started typing furiously on his computer. "I had the listing. It's been a couple years. I've got it somewhere. Stand by." He went on typing, driving his mouse all over his desk, and muttering. After several minutes of frantic activity, he stopped. "Crap."

"What's the problem?"

"I can't find the records, but I'd know that cabin in my sleep."

"Then tell me how to get there."

"Well, I only actually went out there a couple times," he said. "It's way out in the sticks."

Shawn resisted the urge to tell him the entire state of Wy-goddam-oming was in the sticks. "So, how do I get there?"

"That's the thing," Andrews said. "I can't remember."

"You've gotta be shittin' me."

Andrews shook his head. "Wish I was. It's northwest of here. Go to Charm. There's only one intersection. Head north. Somewhere along the way there's a side road that leads right to the cabin. Ya can't miss it."

"The cabin?"

"The road."

"Would anyone in— What was the name of the little town again?"

"Charm."

"Would anyone in Charm know where the place is?"

He nodded. "Absolutely. Ask anybody there. Provided...."

"Provided what?"

"Provided there's anybody there."

Shawn shook his head. It just kept gettin' better and better.

~*~

There was absolutely no doubt in Tom Purcell's mind that Simon Gibbs' friend was a hooker. She not only looked and dressed like a hooker, she acted like a hooker. In fact, though he'd never actually met a hooker, if he had, the woman on Gibbs' arms was exactly what he would have expected. She was somewhere in her thirties, he thought, though exactly where was hard to determine considering the volume of makeup she wore. She appeared fairly slender without being in the least bit athletic. Her hair was limp despite the sparkles she had sprayed into it, and her clothing looked like it could use a good cleaning. At least she smelled pleasant. He'd been worried about that.

"Tom," Gibbs said, "this is Wanda."

She stretched her hand at him but didn't respond to his grip. At all. He maneuvered the limp collection of digits up and down, then followed Gibbs to a table near the front of the restaurant. He prayed none of his fellow faculty members had reservations.

"So," he asked her, "what do you do?"

She squinted at him. "You for real?"

He laughed. "Never mind. Hungry?"

"Starved," she said.

"Well, order whatever you want," he said. "It's on Simon."

The artifact dealer scowled at him, then patted Wanda's arm. "Yeah. Go ahead. Get whatever you want."

They discussed timing. They discussed possible problems. They discussed the ether Purcell had liberated from a chemistry lab. The labeling on the container was a bit dodgy, but he felt reasonably confident it would keep the Lanier woman unconscious while he searched her cabin. They discussed dinner. They discussed Wanda. They discussed Purcell's alibi. In fact, they discussed everything but where he would be going to "collect" the artifact. Wanda remained oblivious to their discussion. She was far too busy eating.

Purcell reached under the table and put his hand on her thigh. It was warm, smooth, and surprisingly soft. She responded by asking Gibbs to pass the ketchup, which she dumped on her steak.

It was nearly eight o'clock when the dinner plates were cleared away, and Gibbs suggested that they retire to his house. He collected the check, grumbled over the amount, paid, and led his companions out.

Though it had taken hours, Purcell was finally free of his headache. He looked at Gibbs and Wanda; they made an interesting couple. If all went well, he'd only see them one more time. All he had to do was wait until Tori Lanier went to bed. The rest should be easy.

~*~

Tori arrived back at the cabin after dark. Why a trip to the hardware store always required a half day astonished her, but it seemed to be a law of nature. She had Mato's paint. She had extra brushes. She even brought a drop cloth, although it seemed somewhat less than likely that anyone would give a shit if Mato spilled his paint in a freakin' cave. It wasn't as if the place would show up on the Charm Tour of Homes.

She also brought back a bucket of chicken. True, it was cold by the time she got home, but then cold fried chicken had been a staple of her diet the whole time she grew up in middle Georgia. It would, by Gawd, be just dandy for Mato. And Shadow certainly wouldn't complain. It was a serious shame, however, that no one in Wyoming knew how to make good cole slaw. *What was up with that?*

Mato was excited by the quart cans of paint. Tori would have bought smaller quantities, but that was the smallest size they had. He also marveled at the new brushes. She had tried to find a variety of sizes since she had no idea how large an area Mato intended to paint. Most eventualities were covered, she thought. Unless he wanted a roller. *That*, she hadn't bought. She figured he had managed pretty well to this point using his fingers; a set of genuine, camel hair brushes—Ace hardware's finest—should really set him free. And, in truth, she was eager to see his work. There was no denying his talent.

She glanced at her watch. Cassy should be

home by now, she thought. She used the speed dial again, hoping to catch her friend and editor while she ate, and before she curled up with a pile of manuscripts, or Rachel.

Once again, the phone switched to voice mail, and Tori left yet another message. She made a mental note to call Cassy's office in the morning. She was more than a little worried about her.

Mato finished a second drumstick and looked at her with an expression she found hard to catalog. He was sated, for sure, and his eyelids threatened to close for the duration. Tori glanced through her notes. It had become slightly easier to form conversational sentences, as more and more of his words felt familiar.

"You go cavern?"

Mato mumbled something. It may have been a belch; she wasn't entirely sure.

"You draw now?"

That seemed to motivate him. She walked to the hearth and opened it. Along with the paint and the food, she had picked up a high intensity camping lantern and a pair of rubber knee pads. If she was going to crawl after him, she might as well crawl comfortably.

She put the pads on, grabbed the lantern, and sat down on the iron plate. "Go now?" she asked.

Mato didn't look too thrilled with the idea. Shadow couldn't make up his mind who he wanted to side with.

"Wait a sec," she said. "I need to hide the dictionary."

The dog twisted his head at her, as if to say, "What the hell?"

She had carried the manuscript with her in the truck when she went into town, but now that she was home, she felt she needed a hiding place for it. If the loser from the community college came by, she didn't want to leave it spread out in the open where he might be tempted to "borrow" it.

Instead, she slipped the oilcloth-wrapped package into a plastic bag that formerly housed some wool sweaters she'd purchased in Cheyenne. Using her brand-new camp light, she walked out to her truck and slipped the package into the shelf formed by her spare tire, which was bolted in place beneath the truck bed. Let him look for it there, she thought. Then she grabbed a package that she'd left on the front seat and went back inside.

Mato looked ready to go. He had a quart of paint in each hand. Having anticipated this moment, Tori unveiled her most brilliant purchase: a plastic kiddie wagon. While Mato watched, she placed the six quart-size cans of paint, plus rags, plus a can opener, in the wagon, then carried it to the iron plate. She donned her rubber knee pads, grabbed her camping lantern, and set the wagon on the ground.

"Ready?" she asked. The question was in

English, but Mato must have figured it out. He nodded in the affirmative and dropped into the opening beside her and put the rest of his gear in the wagon.

"C'mon, Shadow," Tori called, and the dog joined them, too. It made for a very crowded antechamber.

Mato grabbed the handle of the wagon, flipped the switch on the LED flashlight Tori had given him earlier, and went straight into the tunnel. Shadow was right behind him.

Tori took a very deep breath. Her companions were already out of sight. "Oh, what the hell," she muttered. "What could possibly go wrong?"

With that she got down on her hands and knees and followed them into the Earth.

For some reason, cursing seemed to help.

Chapter Eighteen
What goes on underground, stays underground.

"This is Charm?" Shawn said as he pulled into the intersection with its three commercial buildings. A few homes were scattered back from the roads, but none of them were close enough to contribute to the image. As far as he could tell, there wasn't much point in anything being there at all. Unless, of course, it was to point him toward Vicky Lynn.

When his stomach rumbled, he evaluated the options available: a closed restaurant, an unoccupied building that may have done car repairs once upon a time, and an antiquated country store. It, however, was open, and Shawn went inside.

The sole occupant was an old geezer who might have been an extra in a John Wayne movie: tall and whip slender with weathered features and teeth a good many years younger than the rest of him.

"Howdy," the man said.

Christ, he even talks like somebody in a bad western. "I'm hoping you can help me find somebody who lives around here," Shawn said. He eyed the offerings on a candy counter and noticed there was nothing chewy.

"I live around here," the man said, helpfully.

"Nah. I mean, somebody I know. An old friend." Shawn gathered up several peanut butter cups.

"Good choice for this time of year," the man said. "They get a little soft in the summer. I don't have the best air conditioning."

Shawn looked down at the brightly colored wrappers on the candy. "This shit's been here since last summer?"

"Probably not," the old timer said. He reached for one from the display and gave it a little squeeze. "Feels okay to me."

Shawn put the candy back. "Is there anything in here that's safe to eat?"

The man stopped smiling. "If it looks like food, son, it is. And if it's safe enough for me, it's safe enough for you. Now, who's this you're lookin' for?"

"Her." Shawn dropped the photo of Vicky Lynn on the counter. "Calls herself Tori Lanier. You know her?"

The old guy stared at the picture for a while

before picking it up and carrying it to a window, where he examined it further. "I might," he said, momentarily distracted by something. "Aw, hell. You hear that?" he asked.

"What?"

"Sounded like something in the storeroom. Goddam kids," he muttered as he walked toward the back of the store. "Always stirrin' up trouble. Can ya give me a minute? I'll be right back."

"Kids?" Shawn asked, but the old guy evidently didn't hear him. When he was alone, Shawn unwrapped a peanut butter cup and ate it. Then another. They tasted fine. He tossed the empty wrappers in the wood stove sitting in the middle of the room.

Within minutes, the old guy returned, still muttering.

"What about kids?" Shawn asked. "I didn't think there were enough people livin' around here to even have kids."

"Oh, we got 'em all right. There's nothin' around here for 'em to do, see. They're always causin' trouble. It's one of the reasons Charm will never amount to much. Innocent folks stop by and before ya know it, bad things happen to 'em."

"C'mon. Out here in the middle of nowhere?"

The old guy shook his head. "Happens all the time. We don't have a lawman around here; the town's not incorporated or anything. We have to call over to Ten Sleep and get the sheriff involved, but it's always small-time stuff. Y'know. Kid stuff."

Shawn bought a sandwich wrapped in cellophane and a six pack of beer. "So, you think you know where my friend lives?"

"I believe so." He pointed north. "You head up that way about seven or eight miles. There's a dirt road on the left. Her house is at the end of it."

"That's it? One turn?"

"Yep. How did you say you knew her?"

"We go way back," Shawn said, heading for the door. "Thanks. You've been a big help."

The old guy just waved and went back to whatever he had been doing before. Shawn put his beer and sandwich on the passenger seat and then walked around to the driver's side. That's when he noticed both tires on the side away from the store were flat.

"Son of a bitch!" He looked more closely and discovered that each had a cut in the sidewall. One spare wasn't going to get him anywhere. He continued to swear as he walked back into the store.

"Whatsa matter?" the old guy asked.

Shawn glowered at him. "Somebody slashed my damn tires."

The old codger's eyebrows dipped down in consternation. "You're kiddin'! You haven't been here but ten minutes and..." He paused and shook his head. "It's those kids. I tell ya, they're gonna ruin this town."

"You got anything I can use to patch 'em?"

"Depends on how badly they're cut."

"Looks like just one puncture in each, but they got the sidewalls."

The old man shook his head. "That's what I was afraid of. I've got some stuff you can squirt into 'em. It'll seal something small, like a nail hole, but not something like that."

"What the hell am I gonna do?"

"Well," the old guy said, "I could run you over to Ten Sleep, and you could buy a couple new tires."

"Can't they send a wrecker?"

"You can call 'em and ask," he said. "But they don't like to drive out this far, at least, not this late in the day."

"And what's to keep the little bastards from comin' back to flatten my other tires while I'm gone?"

"Faith?" The old guy shrugged. "I doubt they'll be back. They don't hang around after one of their stupid pranks. You got a phone?"

Shawn had long since discarded the phone he bought in Macon. "No."

"You can use mine," the old guy said. He retrieved a thin phone book from beneath his cash register and handed that over as well. "I usually close up shop around six, but if I drive you, they may not be open by the time we get to Ten Sleep."

Shawn placed the call and agreed to an extra service charge for the wrecker to come all the way to Charm. From the way the guy on the phone sounded, it wouldn't be cheap, but short of stealing a car from the old fart minding the store, he didn't have any choice.

"I really feel terrible about this," the old guy said. "Here you are, your first time in Charm, and this happens. It's awful."

"And you think you know who did this?"

He nodded. "Oh, I know exactly who did it."

Shawn grinned and cracked his knuckles. "Looks like I've got some time to kill. Can you tell me where I might find 'em?" He was perfectly willing to perform a public service for the town by beating the little pricks into pulp.

"They're long gone by now," the old man said. "You'd never catch 'em."

~*~

"You *slashed* his tires?" Maggie said, her voice registering a level of shock Caleb rarely heard from her.

"You're darn right I did. That fella's scary. There's no way he intended Tori anything but harm."

"How do you know that?" Maggie asked. "Did

you bother to call her and ask?"

"I tried, right after he left, but there was no answer."

"Where are you now?"

"I'm halfway to your house. You said you were cookin' a pot roast."

"I am, but... Geez, Cal. That's vandalism."

"No, it's not," he said, wincing. "Okay, maybe it is, but I don't regret it. You shoulda seen that guy. He had 'crazy' written all over him. I'm just lookin' out for Tori. You'd have done the same thing under the circumstances."

Cal waited for her response, but it didn't come. "Maggie?"

"I'm thinkin'."

"'Bout what?"

"About what the hell I'm gonna tell Tori when she finds out what you did. You don't know anything about that guy."

"I knew enough," he said, confident he'd done the right thing. "The only thing that concerns me now, is what he'll do once he gets those tires fixed."

"What d'ya mean?"

"Well, I told him how to get to her place."

"You *what?*"

Caleb wished he could take his words back, either to the guy in his store or to Maggie. "He was almost there already. In Charm. He'd have found her place sooner or later. I figured slashing his tires was enough; I didn't need to give him any other reasons to come back lookin' for me. Still...."

"What?" Maggie asked. "Still, what? What aren't you saying?"

"That fella's bad news, Maggie. Real bad. I'm worried about Tori."

"C'mon by the house. We'll talk about it over dinner," Maggie said.

"You still got your gun?"

"My shotgun? Yeah. Why?"

"I may need to borrow it."

~*~

Mato's head was full of conflicting notions. He had some painting to do, and he wanted to see for himself what Tori would think when she saw it. He also felt an obligation to keep his work—and all the other work in the cavern—secret. Giants shouldn't see it. But then, at least one already had. And now Tori was right behind him in the tunnel. She would be in the heart of the cavern in a matter of minutes, and he would be faced with the challenge he'd been dreading.

Could he really kill her? His weapons were already in the cavern where he'd left them earlier. She wouldn't suspect anything, wouldn't even suffer if he used the sleeping paste in his belt pouch.

Rather than think about her murder, he thought about what he would do with the body. She was far too big for him to move. The ideal thing would be to push the body into the crevice. He had no idea how deep it was. He had dropped stones into it, but he never heard them hit the bottom. Of course, once she was dead, he could cut her up and throw the pieces into the pit. The Earth would swallow her up as if she'd never lived.

That thought shook his resolve. *She did live!* He knew her. She had cared for him and tended his wounds. She had fed him and given him a place to stay. She provided the means for him to travel to and from the cavern at will. She had even given him the tools to accomplish his mission. How then could he take her life, when she had given so much—and given it freely—to enhance his life?

The dog squeezed ahead of him and ran down the path into the cavern, fearless and faithful. If he called to him, the dog would come. If he called to Tori, she would do the same, and all she said she wanted was to know him better. How could that be wrong? How could that justify her death? And yet, the cavern was a sacred place, and the presence of a giant, any giant, was a sacrilege.

Suddenly, she rounded the curve behind him and her light eased into the chamber, filling the dark corners. The cavern was even more magnificent than he realized. There were colors he had never seen, some painted by The People, others by the hands of the Spirits. All the varied shapes and shades and textures impressed upon him how important it was that he finish his own work.

Resolving his dilemma about taking Tori's life would have to wait. For a little while, at least.

~*~

"You're tellin' me I won't be able to buy tires until tomorrow morning?"

The driver of the tow truck turned his head to the open window and spat out a long stream of brown tobacco juice. He wiped his chin on his shirt sleeve and pushed his straw cowboy hat to the back of his head. "It ain't up to me, pard. If it was, I'd sell 'em to ya tonight. But the station'll be closed before we get there."

Shawn couldn't believe it. "Where the hell am I 'sposed to spend the night? In the car?"

"There's a couple motels to choose from, and one of em's pretty close by the station. I can drop you off."

"That'd be just peachy." Several times during the drive to Ten Sleep, the drive *away* from Vicky Lynn, he had contemplated just stealing the tow truck. The driver couldn't stop him; he was barely big enough to see over the steering wheel. But in the back of Shawn's mind was the thought that maybe, just maybe, Vicky Lynn had mellowed in the years they'd been apart. Yes, he was still angry at her, and yes, she'd still have to face some punishment for betraying him, but when that was all done, maybe they could make a fresh start.

345

If there was any chance at all for that to happen, he certainly couldn't go around beating people up and stealing their trucks.

"You don't understand," Shawn said. "I've been on the road for days. I can't stand bein' away from my girl for a minute longer than I have to."

"Oh, I understand love all right," the driver said. He changed radio stations and was rewarded with a classic Hank Williams tune. "Why don't you just call her up and ask her to come get you?"

Shaking his head, Shawn responded, "It's a surprise. She thinks I'm still in Georgia. Besides, I don't want her to think I couldn't make it all the way on my own. What kinda message would that send?"

"Well, under the circumstances—"

"A man does what he has to," Shawn said. "I told her I'd find her, and by Gawd, that's what I'm gonna do. I can't be callin' her to come bail me out. Not when I've come this far. Hell, I'm tempted to get out of this truck and walk back to her place."

The driver glanced at him and pursed his lips. "You know what? If you'd be willin' to come up with a little tip money, I'll bet my friend Tucker would come back to the station. He can sell you the tires, and I'll help him mount 'em."

Shawn was genuinely surprised. "You'd do that for a total stranger?"

After nodding, the driver launched another stream of brown saliva through his window. He turned up the radio as Hank Williams lumbered into the final chorus, then chimed in for the finale, "I'm so lonesome, I could cry."

"Sounds like you've got me pegged," Shawn said.

The driver smiled. "I'm a pretty fair judge of character."

~*~

Tori realized very quickly during her crawl through the tunnel, that her purchase of rubber knee pads had been a stroke of pure genius. Her only regret was that she hadn't also bought a matching pair of gloves. Those thoughts faded, however, when the tunnel expanded enough for her to stand. The downward slope remained about the same, and she stared in awe at the paintings on the surrounding walls. No wonder Uncle Bob had called it a treasure. Though not a great connoisseur of art, she had seen her share of galleries and museums, but she'd never seen anything like this.

Mato's light was in the distance, since he walked while she crawled, but she would catch up quickly enough. Hurrying, however, was nowhere in her mind. She tried to imagine how long it had taken to paint so many images on these walls. When she found the unmistakable rendering of a woolly mammoth, an answer began to form. Mato was merely the latest in a line of artists that snaked back so far in time that dates were calculated geologically.

She watched from a distance as he organized

his materials and scrutinized the rock which would be his canvas. He had drawn some lines in his typically sparse fashion, but he seemed unhappy with them. Using a wet rag, he wiped the lines off, then used a sharp piece of stone to scratch the surface. He would incise a line or two, then pound away at the surface until he achieved the texture he wanted. The process was fascinating to watch, though she worried he might hurt his eyes from flying stone chips. Those were a real consideration, and reinforced her decision to give him plenty of space, even if it compromised her view of his work. There was plenty else to look at, after all.

Shadow wandered through the cavern from time to time, his nose operating in doggy overdrive. She hoped he wouldn't relieve himself somewhere inappropriate, but he didn't seem interested in marking territory. He came terribly close to the edge of a great crack which bisected the cavern floor. The jagged edges were fashioned in a lightning bolt pattern. But no human was responsible for that massive tear in the Earth. She approached it gingerly and held her lamp over the side for a look.

The steep walls fell away into a darkness her light couldn't penetrate. She kicked a pebble over the side of the chasm and watched it disappear in silence. That was as close to eternity as she cared to go, and she backed away to safety.

Mato kept working, though she could not make out what he was trying to accomplish. *Is he going to do a carving rather than a painting?* There were several of those in the cavern, so he wouldn't be breaking new ground. She smiled at her own pun. They were both artists, after all; she felt entitled to enjoy their crafts on a variety of levels.

She dearly wished she could have been present when Uncle Bob followed Sleeping Dove into the cavern. What marvelous conversations they must have had! Surely the Indian woman knew some of the chamber's history: the legends that were captured on its walls, and the stories of the people who recorded them.

Did Mato know them? And would he share them with her if he did?

A new thought intruded. If Mato trusted her enough to share his secrets, would she betray him by including those tales in her book?

Uncle Bob knew that revealing the existence of the cavern was the quickest way to kill its use as a functioning part of Sleeping Dove's religion. Whether it was exploited like some tourist attraction, or locked up for study solely by people like Tom Purcell, the result would be the same— tragedy for Mato and those who raised him. This cathedral of stone, which rightly belonged to Sleeping Dove, Mato, and the rest of their clan, had to be protected. Their claim to this treasure went back for untold millennia, and nobody was going to take it from them as long as she had anything to say about it.

She sat down to watch Mato work, and ponder how in hell she was going to do what she had just vowed to accomplish.

~*~

Purcell found the turn-off Caleb had told him went to Tori's cabin. He slowed the cherry red BMW when he ventured onto the dirt track because he had no intention of scraping off the oil pan, or any other valuable engine part, while he traversed the hideous washboard Caleb called a driveway. If he'd been thinking, he would have rented a Jeep, or a Humvee. *Or maybe a friggin' tank.* God only knew what kind of animals roamed out here. How did Tori survive in this wilderness? She was obviously a lunatic and had no business keeping valuable artifacts.

Well, he would soon fix that.

At some point, he realized he would have to get out of the car and proceed on foot. It certainly wouldn't do to alert Tori by roaring up to the cabin with his radio blaring and his lights on high-beam. At least he had taken the time to find a decent flashlight, so with any luck he'd be able to avoid stepping on a rattlesnake or disturbing a mountain lion while sneaking up on the house.

Caleb had said it was a very long driveway, so he wasn't too concerned when he didn't see anything after driving for half an hour, especially since he was driving slowly. Eventually, however, he saw lights in the distance and shut his own headlamps off. He got out of the car for a better look.

The cabin sat on the top of a bluff overlooking a broad valley. The drive twisted up and around until it reached the top of the bluff. Stars littered the sky as if spray-painted on a moonless, black velvet blanket overhead. A tiny streak of celestial fire caught his eye. What an incredible view she has, he thought. But who in their right mind would want to live out here?

He got back in the car and put the top down, determined to drive closer without using his lights. If he hit a deer, or a jack rabbit, or a migrant worker, that would just be tough. The mission came first.

Parking at the base of the bluff, he put the top back up, even though there was no hint of rain. He didn't care to share his ride with the great outdoors. With the flashlight in one hand and the ether in the other, he crept up the long, rugged slope to the top of the bluff. The cabin stood well off center, and he puzzled over its placement. The view would have been the same either way, but centering the building would have been much more aesthetically pleasing. That, in his mind, lent credence to his belief she should not be allowed to keep the artifact. At least, not one as significant as the dictionary.

He crept closer to the cabin, painfully aware of each footstep. Though he tried to avoid tromping on anything that might make noise, he wasn't very successful. He didn't have any scouting days in his childhood, and neither woodcraft nor outdoor living skills were a part of his college studies. Somehow, he managed to reach the building without alerting its occupant.

Sniffing the air, he caught the pungent aroma

of dog crap. Shuffling as quietly as he could to a wall without windows, he aimed his flashlight at the upturned bottom of his running shoe. There, pressed into the swirls and grooves of his Nike knock-off, was a turd the size of his fist. *Tori has a dog!* The thought raced through his brain like a jolt of electricity. And, judging from the size of the evidence, the animal was huge. No wonder she wasn't afraid of the wildlife out here. If anything attacked her out here, the damn dog could just eat it!

Slow, deep breaths helped him get his pulse down to a more normal level. His hands were sweating despite his resolve. He needed to do this. It wasn't like he had a choice. He could browbeat Gibbs to a certain extent, but eventually the man would force him to produce. At the very least, he'd want his ten thousand dollars back, and it would be a cold day in Hell before Purcell got his hands on that kind of money. Unless, of course, he stole the manuscript. Dog or no dog.

At least the creature hadn't barked. Yet. Maybe he could use the ether on both of them. No, he told himself with an involuntary shake of the head. No dog was going to hold still while he farted around with ether and a mask.

Maybe it wasn't dog shit. The thought lightened his mood instantly. Maybe it was coyote scat, or the calling card of a friendly neighborhood wolf. They wouldn't mess with him. They were afraid of people. That's what everybody said, wasn't it?

He crept back to a window and looked in, expecting a scene of quiet, domestic boredom. Instead, he saw a small cabin, full of furniture but nothing else. No dog. No Tori. When her cell phone started ringing, he nearly wet himself as he ducked down below the window sill. When no one answered, he straightened and looked back in.

Something bizarre was going on with the fireplace, but he wasn't sure what. That would require a much closer look. But where was Tori? Had she gone for a late-night walk and left the lights on? And her phone behind? That didn't make much sense unless— He froze. Had that smarmy asshole, Simon Gibbs, gotten there ahead of him? It didn't seem likely, but....

Damn it. He'd run out of other options.

He was going in.

~*~

Caleb sat at Maggie's kitchen table with an empty plate in front of him, and Maggie's dog, Pretzel, beside him. The little brown mutt had her chin on Cal's lap as she looked up into his eyes and willed him to let her lick his plate.

"Don't you give that dog any scraps," Maggie said. "She'll get fat."

Cal rubbed her head. "If she does, I'll just bring her to my place and she can work it off chasing that useless cat Tori left me."

"Speaking of Tori," Maggie said, clearing the

table, "what are we gonna do? Did you get through to her yet?"

"Nah. Left another message. It's gettin' kinda late. I'm worried about her."

"She might have a boyfriend," Maggie said. "Maybe she's spending the night somewhere else."

Cal shook his head, chuckling.

"What's so funny?"

"She told me I was her boyfriend."

"You're right," Maggie said. "That is funny."

He stopped laughing. "Hey now...."

"Give it another hour, then call again. If she doesn't answer, we can talk about what to do next, but there's no sense gettin' all worked up over nothing. Tori's a big girl; she can take care of herself. She's used to livin' alone, and besides, she's got that big old dog lookin' out for her."

"Shit Head?"

"It's Shadow."

"Right. But he licks; he doesn't bite."

"That's not what I heard. The guy I got him from said he had a serious problem with strangers."

"Yeah? Well, the guy's an asshole, and he obviously doesn't know anything about dogs."

Maggie ignored him and let a bit of left-over pot roast roll off her plate and onto the floor. Pretzel was on it and gone before Cal had time to make a smart remark. "Thought you said not to give her scraps."

Maggie fixed him with a curious stare. "What in the world are you talkin' about?"

"Never mind." Just because Maggie wasn't worried didn't mean she was right. Besides, he didn't think he could wait an entire hour before trying to call Tori again. After that, the next call he'd make would be to the sheriff.

Chapter Nineteen
So, what was okay about the OK corral?

Two new tires, plus tax, plus the ransom the two cowboy wannabes robbed him of, and Shawn was once again on his way. He'd go right through Charm, only he wasn't stopping this time. Later, when he had more time, he'd go back and hunt down the little butt wipes who slashed his tires. He'd see how much they laughed when he did it to their cars. Or maybe he'd just slash them. That made him smile. It also made him think of the boning knife he'd left in New York. That was too bad. He liked that knife. Very handy, to say nothing of sharp.

He checked the clock on the dash and shook his head. Good thing he wasn't on any kind of schedule, otherwise he'd be *way* behind.

There wasn't a single light on in any of the buildings in or near the completely misnamed "town" of Charm. He'd seen roadkill with more appeal. He wouldn't have bothered to slow down when he went through, except that it marked the place where he needed to turn. That bit of intel had come from the ancient storekeeper. What a waste of space he was! Someone should just put him out of his misery, like an old, sick dog. One shot. Pop! Done.

He'd been running with his bright lights on since he'd left Ten Sleep and could count on one hand the number of vehicles he'd encountered. He'd checked the odometer to make sure he didn't go too far, but missed her driveway in the dark, anyway. A little backtracking solved that problem, and he pointed the ugly yellow Chevy down the dirt road that would take him to Tori. He drummed his fingers on the steering wheel in anticipation.

Wondering what she'd say when he walked through the door, Shawn slowed down to avoid the worst of the ruts in the dirt track. He found it hard to believe she drove on this section very often. The bumps and twists were enough to loosen your teeth. As a result, he kept his clenched.

About the time he'd convinced himself he'd taken the wrong "road," he spotted lights far in the distance. "'Bout damn time," he muttered, braking to avoid a particularly deep pair of gashes which cut diagonally across his path. If he hung around, he'd have to do something about the driveway. This was nuts.

Plodding on, he eventually came to the base of the bluff on which Tori's cabin stood. It certainly wasn't much to look at. He couldn't imagine why she'd want to live out here. Gazing all the way around, he took in the star-littered sky and the shadowy mountains in the distance. *The place is empty.* If they were going to get back together, they'd surely have to move somewhere else. This place gave him the creeps.

~*~

Purcell had searched the cabin as thoroughly as he knew how. He'd looked under the bed, beneath dresser drawers, in the freezer and through all the books on the shelves. He'd examined every inch of the desk and its drawers. There was nothing hidden there. Tori had boxes under her bed, and he went through those, too. But it was all the same: clothing, a few pictures, and mementos. No ancient manuscript.

The only truly old thing he found appeared to be a diary, though it contained little more than page after page of number sequences. He remembered reading something about a code book in Tori's novel, but he had skimmed a lot and hadn't paid much attention to the background material. The book in his hand probably had something to do with what she'd already written, but it certainly wasn't something that interested him now.

He turned on her computer, hoping to find out if she had scanned the document. If she had, he'd have to erase any traces of it once he found the original.

Where the hell could it be?

He looked at the fireplace, knowing all too well that would be the next place to check, but crawling underground wasn't something that appealed to him. He would be more than happy to wait for her to come to him. And she had to be down there! Her truck was outside, and her purse was inside. He didn't need any more evidence than that.

Tired and frustrated, he went to her refrigerator and helped himself to some wine. There was also a bag of cheese cubes in assorted flavors. He brought those out, too, and popped a few in his mouth, chewing contentedly.

He checked his watch. It was late, sure, but not too late. She'd have to come up sooner or later, and when she did, he'd find the manuscript. More than likely, she had taken it with her, though why that made sense he didn't know, and he had no intention of asking her. The best way to handle this would be to hide out until she resurfaced and went to bed. He could use the ether on her while she slept, grab the manuscript, and go. If she didn't have it with her, he'd have to crawl down into the hole to retrieve it. He didn't like that idea. At all. But if that's what it took, then he'd do it.

As soon as he finished his wine, he'd go find a hiding place. He had exercised considerable caution while conducting his search so that he didn't leave her place a mess. In fact, viewing the cabin as dispassionately as he could, it didn't look like he'd done anything to it at all.

Am I good, or what?

The cheese is decent, he thought. *The wine isn't bad, either.* He was tempted to turn on her stereo, just to break up the silence and disguise the occasional howl of a coyote from outside. That, of course, would be stupid, since it would alert Tori as she crawled up from below. He wished he could figure out where the hole in the ground actually went and the elaborate steps she—or someone— had taken to hide it. Maybe he should have read her novel more carefully. Perhaps there'd been a clue he missed. *Yeah, well, if pigs could fly....*

He drained the last of his wine and was about to rinse the glass when he heard something outside.

~*~

"Are you sure this is an emergency?" asked the woman on the phone at the sheriff's office. "It doesn't sound like much of one to me."

Cal grimaced. He'd been afraid this would happen. "No, I can't prove this is an emergency. I'm just worried. That young woman is living out there all alone, and there's some strange guy tryin' to find her. I saw him, and he wasn't the kind of guy any parent would want their daughter bringing home."

"I'm sorry sir, but that still doesn't sound like an emergency."

"So, you're not going to send anyone out there?"

"Not without a better reason. That's a long haul."

Cal exhaled fiercely. "You'd rather send a coroner?"

"If you're so concerned," she said, "why don't *you* drive out there and check on her? If there's something fishy goin' on, call me back."

"That could take hours."

"It beats wakin' up the sheriff for no reason," she said. "You don't have to work with him."

Caleb rang off and looked at Maggie. She was wearing the racy, pink pajamas he'd given her for Valentine's Day. They weren't really pajamas so much as they were long johns, without the trap door in the back, but she looked pretty darn good in them. Thanks, no doubt, to the thousands of miles she'd hiked as a nature walk tour guide.

She gave him her best come hither look and crooked a finger at him. "You wanna go chasin' after shadows, or would you rather stay here and keep me warm?"

"Dammit, Maggie," he groaned. "You aren't playin' fair!"

She looked crestfallen, and then concerned. "You really are worried about Tori, aren't you?"

He nodded. "Yes, I am."

"Some romantic you are!" She sighed and crossed her arms.

He smiled. "Rain check?"

"Yeah, okay."

"Is your shotgun still in the closet?"

"Yes, but you're not takin' it without me." She donned her official, government-issued, Smoky the Bear ranger hat, and walked away.

"Then you'd better get dressed," he said, admiring the view as she went back into the bedroom to change. "And don't dawdle!"

She popped her head back through the opening and batted her eyelids at him. "I love it when you talk dirty."

~*~

It finally dawned on Tori what Mato was up to. The scraping and smoothing were only meant to enhance features already present on the stone surface. By the time he refreshed the outline, she recognized the technique. When finished, he would have a combination of paint and texture, plus a hint of depth supplied by the surface he was painting on. Part painting, part bas relief. Each would complement the other.

He's brilliant!

She enjoyed watching him work and tried to do so as unobtrusively as possible. He, on the other hand, would often look over his shoulder to see if she was still interested. They would exchange smiles, and then he'd go back to work. At one point he began whistling a tune from one of her CDs, and she tapped her foot in time to the rhythm. He probably has a decent voice, she thought.

The temperature in the cave was slightly cool, but not uncomfortable, and she suspected they were far enough underground that it remained steady year-round. Slipping her hands in her pockets, she found the MP3 player she'd used to record his voice. The tune he was whistling was on it, along with about two dozen more. The built-in speaker wasn't large enough to fill the chamber with sound, but it was good enough to hear if you stood close.

She turned it on and selected the song Mato played constantly when in the cabin. As the strains of "Sweet Home Alabama" came out, he stopped and looked at her in surprise. With a gentle arm motion, she offered to throw the MP3 player to him. When he put his brush down, she did. He slipped the cord around an outcrop of rock so that it hung down just out of his way. When he went back to work, he was whistling along with the music.

It wouldn't be long before she could make out what the figure in his drawing was doing. She yawned and wondered if Mato would give it up for the night, but he just kept working. Even Shadow was tired. He curled up and went to sleep. She was glad she'd brought extra batteries for the lamp.

~*~

Shawn found two vehicles parked near the cabin: an older truck, and a newer sports car. A BMW.

Whoa! Looks like little Miss Vicky's done pretty well for herself.

He had driven as close as he dared without alerting whoever might be inside. He stepped past the car and the truck and approached the cabin. The lights were on inside, but he couldn't hear anything.

Was there someone else in there? Were they in bed? He clenched his fists and his jaws, but then relaxed. *With the lights on?*

That never used to be Vicky Lynn's style. Maybe leaving the lights on was just what folks did when they lived out on the edge of nowhere. He shrugged it off and walked through the door.

"Don't move," said a slightly built man standing by the sink in the one-room cabin. He held a shotgun in his hands, but not with any evident skill.

"Who're you?" Shawn asked.

"I'm the one with the gun, asshole. Why don't you tell me who you are?"

Shawn laughed. "You must be Vicky Lynn's boyfriend." He shook his head and walked two steps closer. "She sure has lowered her standards."

"I told you not to move," the man said. "And I meant it."

"Right," agreed Shawn. "That's why you shot me two or three steps ago." He continued moving forward. The guy was sweating so much Shawn was surprised he could hang onto the shotgun at all. He half expected it to squirt out of his hands at any moment.

"I swear I'll shoot!" he said, his voice rising. He tried stepping away, but only backed into the stove.

Shawn reached down to the table and grabbed a cheese cube. Moving very slowly, he brought the cheese to his mouth and ate it.

"Now, turn around, and face the door."

"So you can shoot me in the back?" Shawn shook his head. "I don't think so. In fact, I don't think you could fire that thing if you had a manual and a coach whispering in your ear."

The man raised the gun to his shoulder. "I'm close enough, I wouldn't even have to aim."

"That's true," Shawn said, taking another step closer.

"You had your chance," the man said as he squeezed the trigger.

~*~

Mato didn't know if the work he was doing would be the first of many, or his last. The Spirits might choose to reveal that, or they might not. Such was the mystery of the dreams, and the world from which they came. But whether this was to be his first or last, Mato wanted it to represent the very best work he could do. Everything about it, therefore, had to be perfect.

When he re-entered the cavern with Tori behind him, he knew that whatever he created, it would serve as his offering to the Spirits. If they chose to honor him with sufficient passion, he would finish the rendering in a single night. If they were pleased, they would direct him in whatever followed; they would determine whether the she-giant lived or died. He prayed that their sign would be clearer than his dream, for that featured only a man. A tormented man, to be sure, and while Mato knew the source of his torment, he had no idea why he deserved it, or how it had come about. If it even had, yet.

He sincerely hoped the Spirits smiled on Tori, for she had found a place in his heart. Though they came from different worlds, she wanted nothing more than to befriend him, talk to him, share with him. Indeed, her gifts represented a value he could not begin to calculate. How would he ever repay her? With a knife? The very thought angered him. Did the Spirits even know who she was? Could the Spirits see the giants the way The People did? What if the giants had their own Spirits? Which were stronger? What if by following The People's Spirits he angered those of the giants?

Squeezing his eyes shut, he forced the swirl of questions and arguments from his mind. He had too much work to do to waste precious energy on issues he would never be able to resolve. Let the old ones agonize over these things. When they had the answers, they could share them. Until then, such thoughts were banished from his brain.

Looking back over his shoulder, he saw Tori leaning against a rock. She smiled at him, but her eyelids were drooping. The dog lay beside her with his head in her lap, asleep. It would not be long before he was alone.

~*~

Purcell squeezed the trigger, despite the voice in his brain which screamed: *No! Stop! You can't just kill a man!*

But nothing happened. He expected the weapon to buck in his hands while it exacted the ultimate price from the redneck facing him. The man's chest should have been ripped out of his body, and he should have flown backwards as if yanked by an angry god. But he didn't. Instead of dissolving in a haze of red gore, he stepped even closer and ripped the gun from Purcell's hands.

"You're s'posed to take the safety off, dumb ass," the man said. Then he gripped the weapon by the barrel and swung it at him. The stock connected with Purcell's jaw.

The shock of the blow was stunning and completely eclipsed the feeling of pain. Briefly. Then the pain reasserted itself with a vengeance. He felt himself dropping, as if the shot to his chin had turned off his knees. Something behind him jabbed into his back, propped him up, and kept him from getting away. The something forced him to remain in range of the madman swinging the shotgun that had so recently been in his hands.

"Stop! Please!" he screamed, as the blows continued to come. They hit at random—shoulder, arm, neck, side of head, front of head, hand. He couldn't get up, couldn't get away, couldn't get it to stop. In a final lunge of desperation, Purcell managed to crawl under the table. There, he was able to curl up, tight, while the invader jabbed him again and again.

Purcell pleaded with him the entire time. "Stop! Please? I give up! I'll do anything! Please stop!"

And eventually, his attacker did stop.

Purcell couldn't move without feeling stabs of tooth-grinding pain. He couldn't *not* move without feeling the same thing. *Why couldn't the bastard have knocked me out? Why couldn't he just kill me?*

"Come out from under there," the maniac said.

"No," Purcell whimpered. "You'll hurt me."

"I'll hurt you worse if you don't come out."

"You'll kill me."

The maniac shook his head. "Nah. I'm tired. And you aren't worth killin'."

Purcell looked up at him as he slowly uncurled. Every movement registered pain. Every part of him throbbed. "May I go?"

"Maybe. Tell me why you're here and Vicky Lynn isn't."

"Who's Vicky Lynn?"

The man snarled and raised the shotgun for

another swing. He still held it by the barrel, and Purcell couldn't help but notice how much blood—his blood—was on the stock. "Okay then, *Victoria*," the madman said, pronouncing the name as if it were contaminated.

"Tori?"

"Yeah. You her boyfriend or something?"

Purcell had no idea how to respond, though he was willing to plead anything. Lover? Sure. Thief? Yep. Reporter? Census taker? "I'm a teacher," he said. "Anthropology. She has some material I need. That's all."

"You're not bangin' her?"

"What? No! God no."

"She's not good enough for you? Vicky Lynn's hot. Any guy who's ever seen her knows that." He paused and frowned. "You queer?"

"No!" Purcell said.

"Get up." The madman reached for another cube of Monterrey Jack from the bowl on the table. He ate that one, then reached for a bite of cheddar.

Purcell stood waiting, unsure if motion might set his crazed attacker on another rampage, when suddenly the red-shirted man unleashed a flurry of slaps to his already battered face.

Stumbling sideways to escape, Purcell threw his arms up for protection. Fortunately, his attacker didn't follow him. "What was that for?" he wheezed.

"What'd I do?"

"Nuthin'. I just couldn't resist one of my favorites." He gobbled down another bite of Monterrey Jack and started laughing. "I call it 'smack and cheese.' Want some more?"

Purcell shielded his face with his arms. "Hell no! I just want to get out of here. You're... Never mind."

"I'm what? Jealous? Bothered by some pansy who doesn't think my wife's pretty?"

"I never said that! She is pretty. She's beautiful!"

"Are you driving the car or the truck?"

Purcell struggled to keep the topics straight. "Huh? I drive a BMW."

"Gimme the keys."

"Why?"

The madman tapped the shotgun in the palm of his free hand. "Do I really have to answer that? *Professor?*"

After they swapped car keys, Purcell asked, "May I go now? Please?"

"As soon as you tell me where Vicky Lynn is."

"Down there," Purcell said, pointing to the hearth. "There's a hole in the ground."

The madman's eyes flared open wide as if he'd sat on a burner. "You *buried* her?" He raised the shotgun over his head.

"No! No. She crawled down there. At least, I think she did."

"Why? Where does it go?"

Purcell shrugged. "This is the first time I've ever seen it. Seriously! I've never been here before, and I swear to God, I'll never come back."

The madman seemed to be mulling something over, and Purcell was afraid to press him, so he waited. Finally, his attacker told him he could go, and Purcell shuffled toward the door.

"You see that ugly, yellow, piece of shit Chevy out there?"

Purcell squinted into the dark. There was a car parked a good distance beyond his BMW. "Yeah, I see it."

"That's your new ride," the madman said and shoved him through the door from behind.

Violently propelled into the darkness, Purcell flew over the steps with his arms windmilling. In a shockingly brief instant of clarity, he realized he was hurtling directly toward a waist-high boulder with what looked like a cast iron hibachi grill on top. His forehead connected with the rock approximately half way between the ground and the grill. It was the last thing he felt before he lost consciousness.

~*~

"This is totally insane," Maggie said,

examining the wrecked windshield and crumpled hood of her government-issued, four-door sedan.

Caleb stood on the other side of the car examining the dead deer which had raced out of the darkness and stopped, as if completely puzzled, in the middle of the highway. The misguided ruminant was thoroughly dead, but certainly no longer confused.

"Happens all the time," Caleb said. "Wasn't your fault."

"I shoulda swerved."

Caleb looked at the trees on one side of the road, and the boulders on the other. "I'm thinkin' no, not so much. Besides, you didn't have time to swerve."

"I had time to say, 'Oh, shit!'"

"True," he said, walking close enough to put his arm around her. "But I seriously doubt the deer felt a thing. Broken neck, far as I can tell."

"I just hate it," Maggie said. "I'm all the time complaining about tourists who drive too fast, hitting animals, causing havoc. I just never—"

"I know." He gave her a hug. "It sucks to be just like everybody else, doesn't it?"

She started crying, and he wrapped his arms around her, patting her back. He hated it when she cried. Hated it when *any* woman cried. What would someone think if a guy tried that nonsense? "C'mon, now. We've got to keep going. There's Tori to worry about, remember?"

Maggie stared at him. The beam from one of the headlamps went right over his shoulder, illuminating tree tops on the side of the road. The other headlight appeared to still be directed at the road. "The car's a wreck. We can't drive it. We've got to call the police, or something, don't we?"

Caleb glanced at the dead deer. "I don't think we'll get in too much trouble. The deer was clearly at fault, so even if her family decides to press charges, we should be okay."

"Do you not have any sympathy for that poor creature?"

"Not a whole lot, no," Caleb said. "It clearly lacked the good judgment gene, so we've probably done the local deer population a service."

"You're not being funny."

He shrugged. It wasn't the first time he'd heard the observation. "We've got to get to Tori's place. Can't do anything about the deer or the car, at night anyway. I'll look at the car in the daytime. Now, get in so we can go."

"I hate this, Cal. I really do. What if we get to Tori's house and everything's fine and dandy? We'll have killed that poor animal for no reason at all."

"The poor animal is dead because it stopped in front of a ton of steel moving 60 miles an hour."

"You're heartless."

"You're hysterical. It's one of the many reasons I fell in love with you."

Maggie sniffed and smiled, then wiped a tear from her cheek with the back of her hand. "You're just sayin' that to make me feel better."

"I'm saying it 'cause it's true. Now get in the car, woman. And don't worry about hitting anything else, 'cause I'm drivin'."

They both clamored into the vehicle, but the windshield was so badly fractured they could barely see through it. Having an errant headlight didn't help much either. Cal got out and opened the trunk. He removed a tire tool and used it to bash out the windshield completely. Tiny, square chips of safety glass littered the hood, seats and floorboard. He raked them out of the way and got back in the car.

"Ready?"

Maggie nodded. "You know the air is filled with bugs this time of year."

"Then we'd better keep our mouths shut." He started the engine, pleased that it still worked, and they resumed the drive to Tori's cabin. Between the bugs, the missing windshield and the wandering headlight, they cut their speed to half of what it was when they encountered the deer. Anything else they hit would almost certainly end up inside the car with them.

~*~

Shawn leaned out over the iron plate and

peered down beyond it. The queer professor had been right; there was a hole back there, and a bunch of footprints on the ground all around it. He couldn't imagine why Vicky Lynn might have wanted to crawl into it. There had to be something mighty tempting at the other end of wherever that tunnel went.

He was giving serious consideration to just closing up the hearth and taking a nap. She could pound on the tricky cover when she returned, which would wake him up and give him time to figure out what he needed to do. If anything.

On the other hand, maybe the tunnel went somewhere interesting, like to a hoard of buried Spanish treasure. His grasp of history was roughly equal to his knowledge of geography, so he couldn't be dead certain that the Spaniards ever got this far. He thought the French might have farted around in the area way back when, but he was pretty sure they did everything by canoe, and he didn't think there were any big rivers nearby. Indian gold? Maybe, but probably not. They were mostly into beads and shit. *Hadn't they traded New York City for some bling and a couple blankets? Idiots.*

More than likely, the tunnel led to a secret exit, a way out if someone she didn't want to deal with came around. Who wouldn't want a secret exit? Especially one that went— Where, exactly?

He looked back down at the hole, knowing full well he was going to have to crawl into it to find out where it went. And that really pissed him off.

Tori had left a bulky, kerosene-burning lantern on a high shelf. It looked to Shawn to be about as old as the cabin, which made it not just a piece of crap, but a genuine, antique piece of crap. He lit a cigarette and the lamp with the same match, then carried both to the tunnel's mouth. But something wasn't right. Then he figured it out. He *really* missed the boning knife; it just didn't seem reasonable to crawl into a hole in the ground without some sort of weapon. The shotgun would have been okay, except it meant both his hands would be full.

He went back to Tori's little kitchen and selected a nasty looking blade from a collection housed in a wooden block on the counter. Very handy. He stuck the knife in his belt and returned to the tunnel entrance. "The things I do for love," he muttered, and crawled into the opening.

Chapter Twenty

Once the dust settles, who has to vacuum?

Mato stepped down from the wooden platform he'd been working on all night. He had no idea how close to morning it might be. Tori was still asleep, and while the dog would occasionally grunt or kick his legs, he never opened his eyes.

Stepping away from the wall, the Indian gave his work a critical appraisal. The size was right, and the colors were close. The figure clearly represented the man Mato had dreamed of. He still didn't know if he was a giant or one of The People, though the latter didn't seem likely considering the clothing he wore. The meaning was still a mystery to him, though he had remembered one more detail that had eluded him previously. Sadly, it only added to the mystery, though it did clarify the location. When he returned with Reyna, she should be able to explain it to him. He looked forward to that.

It had been a long day, with much work accomplished. Feeling justifiably proud of himself, he gathered his brushes and paints and put them in the giant's clever wagon. How had they known to make it for someone his size? So many mysteries! It would have been nice if he could have carried his weapons in it, too, but there was no room for them. He chose to leave them where they were for now. In the morning he could retrieve them, as he knew he would want to visit the cavern one last time before he went home to report his success and bring Reyna, and the elders if they chose to come, back with him.

Tori's lamp had grown steadily less bright as he neared completion of the painting. Fortunately, it lasted long enough, and would still give off a bright enough glow to guide their way to the path and back to the surface.

He put a hand on Tori's shoulder and gave her a shake.

Slowly, she opened her eyes and gazed around the cavern, as if lost. Her confusion melted quickly away when she saw his smile and felt the dog resting comfortably beside her. She said something which he didn't understand, but he nodded his head as if he did. Slumber-tinted words rarely meant anything. She probably just had to pee.

After stretching, she roused the dog and stood up. It always seemed odd to him how tall she was, especially when they were side-by-side, and he had to stare almost straight up to see her face. She was good about sitting down near him when they talked so their eyes were more nearly level. There was a great deal to like about this— He thought "she-giant," but stopped himself. She was a woman. A big one, to be sure, but a woman. And she was his friend.

They had just turned to leave the cavern when the dog froze in place. Mato watched his head turn as his ears perked up. A low growl emanated from somewhere deep in his chest. Mato was quite glad the dog wasn't growling at him.

But who was he growling at?

~*~

Shawn had never liked the idea of crawling. It was fine for people who had to work on their hands and knees, like flooring guys and the people who sprayed for bugs, but it wasn't fine for him. Pushing the lantern ahead of him was a hassle, too. It gave off a constant hiss and probably leaked some kind of toxic gas. He could be sucking up some powerful chemical shit that would give him cancer or black lung.

Or make his willie shrivel up and fall off.

That thought not only caused his willie to shrivel up, but it prompted him to press on faster than before. The sooner he got his nose a healthy distance away from the lantern, the better.

Eventually, the trail began to level out, and the ceiling receded to the point where he could stand up. That came as a tremendous relief. He held the lantern at arm's length as he proceeded. The light it cast bounced off the creepy walls and threw shadows into places he knew he would never explore. He had heard of people who actually enjoyed mucking around in caves, crawling through bat shit, and squeezing into cracks and crevices where people just weren't meant to go. That's why God invented snakes and bugs and whatnot. Crawly stuff.

Shawn wasn't a big fan of the dark, either, and was pleased by the constant light level the ancient lantern provided. He'd gladly trade it for something with batteries, of course, but it didn't look like there were people exactly lining up to make an exchange.

While on his hands and knees, he had noticed a variety of footprints in the dirt floor: shoe prints from an adult, the smoother prints of a child, and many more from a dog. He hoped like hell it was a dog. A bear or a wolf would constitute the worst possible sort of surprise. He checked again to be sure the knife was still in his belt, though God only knew what he'd do with a stupid kitchen knife if a bear got pissy about him invading his space. That slowed him down. The path appeared to go around a corner up ahead, and the wall on his right had sprouted openings.

And was that light up ahead?

"Hey!" he yelled. "Anybody down here?"

~*~

"Look, I understand you're concerned about

Tori. I am, too," Maggie said. "But do you have to drive so fast?"

"I'm doing thirty-five miles an hour," Caleb said, trying not to sound too exasperated. "That's not exactly light speed."

"Well, it's too fast to drive without a windshield. My eyes are watering so much I can hardly see."

"Try squinting."

"Try slowing down."

Grudgingly, he complied. The needle sat just over the 30 MPH mark. "There," he said.

"There what?"

"There, I slowed down."

She leaned over and stared at the speedometer. "Did you ever consider being a union negotiator?"

"Nope. Think I should? Would I have to wear a tie?"

"Probably."

"Don't much care for ties," he said. "It's the slave collar of the modern world."

She looked at him like he'd just coughed up a tuna. "You never cease to amaze me."

He grinned. "That's good, isn't it?"

"I suppose."

They drove on in silence for a while until a moth the size of a golf ball slammed into Cal's forehead. It stung. "The hell was that?"

Maggie scraped moth guts away with her thumb, then wiped her thumb on his shirt. "Might've been a sparrow."

"In a previous life, maybe," Cal said, but he slowed down anyway. It wouldn't pay to push Maggie too far. Truth be told, nothing on Earth would tempt him to screw up their relationship, odd as it was. He loved everything about her, but honestly couldn't understand what she saw in him.

"Isn't that the turn off?" Maggie asked.

Caleb braked even further, though not enough to come to a complete stop. He carefully steered Maggie's shattered Ford onto the washboard Tori called her driveway. Twenty miles per hour was about all he could reasonably manage without throwing one or both of them out of the vehicle.

"Y'know," he said, "this old heap's got pretty good suspension."

She eyed him dubiously. "It won't by the time we get to Tori's place."

He chuckled, despite his concern for their young friend. Maggie was probably right.

~*~

Tori turned off the lamp as soon as she heard Shadow growl. *Who in hell could it be?*

She reached down and slipped her hand under the dog's collar. If he went after someone in the cavern, there was no telling where the chase might lead, and the crevice she had investigated earlier sat uncomfortably close by. Better to keep the dog at her side. She could always release him if there was nothing to worry about. Not that he'd do anything anyway, the big wimp.

When Shadow growled again, she shushed him, and they all three knelt down on the chamber floor. She didn't expect anyone to start shooting, but she truly had no inkling who might have followed them into the alimentary canal of the Earth. *Tom Purcell? Not a chance.* Assuming the man had any balls at all, he'd probably rented them.

Then she heard the voice. "Hey! Anybody down here?"

Tori's heart slammed into overdrive. She knew exactly who it was, though the voice had, blissfully, been out of her life for a decade. She wanted nothing more than to hide.

"Yo! Anybody home?" her ex-husband yelled.

Mato must have read the anxiety on her face, for he dropped the handle of the wagon and disappeared into the shadows. It didn't seem like he had taken more than a handful of steps, and he was gone. Like he'd never been there.

The light from the path at the edge of the chamber grew brighter and brighter. Tori looked around, trying to find a place to hide. There were many possibilities, but it was way too late to test any of them. Bravado, she figured, might be her best bet, not that she had many options to choose from.

"Shawn? What are you doing here?"

He blundered into the chamber with her old kerosene lantern held high. "Where the hell are you?" he asked. "I can't see shit."

Nice to know some things hadn't changed, she thought. "I'm over here." She straightened up.

He was dressed in a hideous, red, Alabama sweatshirt and blue jeans that may not have ever been washed. They were stained with a variety of things she didn't even want to think about.

"It's been a long damn time," he said.

"Not long enough for me."

He frowned and pushed his ball cap to the back of his head. "I missed you."

"I didn't miss you," she said. "In fact, I was kinda hoping somebody'd shoot your ass while you were in prison."

"Only the guards have guns, y'know."

"Really? Who knew?" She let go of Shadow's collar. "I've got a dog."

"I can see that," he said. "I've got a knife."

Oh, crap!

"Where's the kid?" he asked.

That pushed her brain sideways. *"What?"*

"Where's the kid? I know there's one down here, somewhere. I saw his footprints. Am I a daddy?"

That really made her brain spin. "*What?*"

"You had my damn kid! And you didn't have the decency to even tell me? What the hell kind of woman are you, anyway?"

Tori was stunned. The idiot actually thought she would have brought a child of his into the world—while he was still in it! "Get a life, Shawn. If I thought you had knocked me up, I'd have had the little monster ripped out before the end of month two."

"I don't believe you!"

"They have meds for that, y'know. The pills are called, 'If Shawn Knocks You Up, Just Take This.' Works like an enema. You know what an enema is, right?"

The look on his face told her everything she needed to know. Shawn was very close to imploding. At some point, he'd become a mindless train wreck looking for a place. Her only hope was to get away while he was blinded by his own hate.

Instead, he produced the knife. "I thought we might have a chance. Maybe make a new start."

"I'd rather die."

"No problem," he said. "In fact, I'm going to enjoy cutting you up."

Just then, Shadow leaped out of the darkness and sank his teeth into Shawn's leg.

~*~

"Geez," Cal said when they pulled up beside Tori's cabin, "looks like she's having a party."

Finally, Maggie mirrored his concern. "Let's go inside."

They parked the Ford behind a Chevy in a bizarre shade of yellow. Thankfully, the car took on the general gray cast of everything else when Cal cut his headlight off.

A brand-new BMW was parked behind Tori's truck, and they walked past it after a quick inspection.

Just outside the cabin they came across the unconscious form of Tom Purcell. At first, Caleb was worried that he may have broken his neck, but as they looked down on him, he moved.

Cal kneeled beside him and leaned close. "Tom?" he asked, his voice low. "You okay?"

Maggie knelt beside him. "He looks worse than that deer I killed," she said. "He's definitely not okay. No way. No how."

"Call the sheriff," Cal said.

She pulled out her cell phone and made the call. Afterward, she announced, "They said there's an ambulance on its way. But Lord only knows how long it'll take to get way out here."

Caleb looked at Purcell with undisguised loathing. "If Tori was pissed enough to toss him out on his ear, I don't really care how long it takes the meat wagon to get here."

"Meat wagon?"

"Rodeo talk," he said, straightening his shoulders. "We need to look inside."

"What about him?" Maggie asked, with a stab of her thumb in the associate professor's direction.

"What's the worst that could happen?"

Maggie frowned. "Well, for openers, he might die."

Cal shrugged. "Can't say that'd choke me up too much."

"I never did really care for him," she said. "You're a better harmonica player."

Cal smiled, then gestured toward the old cabin. "Onward, darlin'."

~*~

Mato reached for his weapons a short time before the dog went after the intruder's leg. Moving quietly through the demon's teeth spread throughout the chamber had taken a good deal of concentration. It wasn't until he reached his bow, arrows, and spear that he allowed himself to consider anything else. Like the clothing the man wore. He'd seen it before—in his dream.

He shook off the familiarity and slipped the

quiver over his shoulder. If he could move quietly enough, he might reach the deeper shadows where he could string his bow without being seen. He had no hope of successfully attacking a giant unless he took him completely by surprise. One blow from the huge man would send him to the shadow world. No, he had to maintain some distance, and not simply because he didn't have his best offensive tool: the blowgun. He hadn't had time to make a new one. He had to make do with what he had.

His spear would therefore be his second weapon of choice, the bow and arrow, his first. Only as a last possible resort would he even consider attacking the giant with his knife, with or without the sleeping salve.

Tori seemed to be taunting the man, though he couldn't understand what she was saying. A few words drifted through—familiar by virtue of repetition—but not enough of them made sense such that he could follow the conversation. He doubted what they said mattered very much. It was obvious, to him, that Tori intended to enrage the man, though the tactic seemed fraught with danger. But then, they were giants. Who knew how best to deal with them? Perhaps if she made him angry enough, his head would pop right off his shoulders and save Mato the trouble of stabbing him in the heart.

While they argued, he worked his way into the shadows. At one point the dog looked in his direction, but the intruder didn't seem to notice.

Mato, on the other hand, had gestured wildly for the dog to look the other way. In retrospect, that had been plainly stupid. *Why distract the dog?*

Once he had successfully slipped behind a large rock formation, he quickly strung his bow. Unfortunately, Tori and the dog were in the way, and he had no clear shot. He took the time to dip the points of his arrows in the sleeping paste. Tori and the man continued to talk, each taunting the other, as far as he could tell. If only he could get a shot!

He peeked around the upward pointed demon's tooth. The man had grown visibly more angry. Tori remained outwardly calm, but he suspected she was fully atremble inside. When the dog latched onto the intruder's leg, Mato slipped into the open and drew his bow.

Tori, who hadn't seen him, and almost certainly didn't know where he was, bolted from her spot and ran straight toward the intruder, completely blocking his aim. If only they could talk!

While the man kicked and screamed at the animal on his leg, Tori grabbed the wrist of his knife arm before he could use it on the dog. The three of them went down in a pile of limbs and lantern. Tori's lamp had been out for several minutes, and except for the fiery fingers that erupted from the spilled lantern of the intruder, the cavern was rapidly growing darker.

Mato still had no clear shot.

~*~

Tori's cabin, though well lighted, stood empty. Obviously, a struggle had taken place, but Caleb saw relatively little blood. And, aside from Tom Purcell, he hadn't found any more bodies.

He and Maggie walked around the tiny cabin in a matter of moments and deduced that the answer to the riddle was almost certainly to be found at the end of the narrow tunnel in the dirt beneath the hearth.

"My guess is, Tori crawled in there to get away from that asshole outside," Maggie said.

Caleb gave his jaw a worried rub. "Except there's three cars out there. And the ugly yellow one? That crazy joker I was tellin' you about drives it. I'm guessing Tori tried to get away from him."

"And he went in after her?"

Caleb nodded. He didn't like the scenario, but he couldn't think of a happy one that made any sense.

"What're we gonna do?" Maggie asked.

Though he wanted to volunteer to crawl into the hole and play hero, he knew his old bones weren't up to it. "I think we'll just have to wait here and see who comes out."

Maggie eyed the opening. "I could crawl in there. I've got a flashlight in the car."

"And what if that jerk shoots you, or cuts you up so badly you can't get out? Much as I'd want to crawl in after you, I wouldn't be much good in there."

"We don't know that!"

"Yeah," he said. "We do."

Maggie spotted the shotgun lying on the table. The stock was covered in blood. "Oh my God, Cal. Look at that!"

"Has it been fired?"

She sniffed the barrels. "No."

Caleb nodded. "That's probably Purcell's blood."

Maggie squinted at him. "How do you figure that?"

"You saw the poor bugger outside," Cal said. "Didn't he *look* like someone who'd been beat half to death with the butt of a long gun?"

"I see your point." She looked helpless. "So, what do we do now?"

"Hand me the gun, please?"

She held it by the barrel and passed it to him. He wiped off the worst of the blood with a kitchen towel and sat down on the hearth to wait.

"I'd say it all boils down to who comes outta that hole first," he said, checking to be sure the shotgun was loaded. It was, and he clicked the safety off. "And if it's who I think it'll be, may God have mercy on him. 'Cause I sure as hell won't."

~*~

Tori knew she'd be no match for Shawn's strength, but she had hoped that between Shadow's teeth on his leg, and her efforts on his knife arm, she had a chance.

She was wrong.

Though she managed to get him off his feet, it didn't serve any real purpose. Her hope was that she could sink her own teeth into him and make him let go of the knife. Instead, he just shifted the weapon to his other hand.

She heard a terrible yelp from Shadow and hoped it was nothing more than Shawn landing a lucky kick. Then she felt the sharp kiss of the knife in her stomach and let go, her mind screaming at her to stop the bleeding.

Shawn was laughing at her, and that only gave her strength. She reached for the remains of the kerosene lantern and swung it with both hands as hard as she could. It connected with his shin, and he doubled over with a howl. When he stood upright, she saw a tiny arrow go straight into his chest, roughly where his heart would have been, if he had one.

Once again, Shawn responded with an animal-like snarl. He spun around, peering into the growing gloom, trying to spot whoever had pricked him with the annoying little arrow. The thin shaft came away easily in his hand, and he snapped it in two as an afterthought. Suddenly, two more shafts followed the first. One landed in his neck, the other in his upper arm.

Shawn screamed even louder as he tore the barbed sticks from his flesh. That's when he spotted Mato less than ten paces away. The little Indian was armed with nothing more than a spear, but he stood his ground as if the entire Sioux nation had his back.

Tori began to feel faint, but she was so terribly proud of Mato, she couldn't let anything distract her. She swung the lantern at Shawn's leg once again, not caring that the effort bore more symbolism than substance.

Shawn lurched toward Mato, the blade held loosely in his hand. Evidently, the jerk had learned something about knife fights while in prison. How would Mato deal with that? And yet he didn't give an inch. He crouched, making himself an even tinier target than before. Shawn bent down to reach for him, and Mato stabbed his hand with his spear.

Tori grinned while her ex-husband cursed. He leapt around wildly, screaming about how he would stomp the little Indian into the ground. But as she watched, his movements became spastic. He slurred his words and grew sluggish. Mato had already turned away, no longer concerned that his massive opponent might somehow recover and fulfill his threats. Instead, Mato retrieved Tori's battery-operated lamp and lugged it, two-handed, across the chamber to where she now lay.

Shawn toppled to the floor. Shadow limped toward him and sniffed, but Shawn didn't move. Shadow then lifted his leg and sent a thick stream of urine all across the fallen man's chest. Tori grinned from ear to ear, but Mato burst into a howl of laughter. Slapstick, she thought.

How fitting.

Tori could feel herself growing weaker by the moment. Mato looked as if he wanted to drag her to the surface, but they both knew that wouldn't work. Shadow finished his editorial remarks and gave her face a concerned lick.

I refuse to die down here! I won't give that asshole the satisfaction.

Drawing on a reserve of strength she didn't know she had, Tori replaced two of the batteries in the lamp, then got to her feet. Mato had dumped out the contents of the little wagon and had placed the lamp in it instead. The light was dim, but it was enough to show them the way out. Shadow took the lead.

Tori followed as quickly as she could, though the reality was that she made the kind of headway rush hour drivers are used to. Way the hell out here, she thought. *Where's the justice?*

Soon, the ceiling had dropped to a level that prevented her from standing upright. Shadow barked at her, though she couldn't see him in the dark. Still, it comforted her to know he was there. Mato would occasionally tap her on the leg, and that reassurance proved equally valuable. Tori pressed on, though moving on her hands and knees resulted in even slower progress.

She felt... drained. Her energy was leaking

out. She refused to think about the blood, which really was dribbling away. A parting gift from a man she hated. And that made her angry. He had no right to come back into her life! No right to hurt her, or keep her from living the way she wanted to live.

Though her progress came in slow, painful stages, it came nevertheless. She thought she could detect light from somewhere ahead, although Shadow remained in the way. He wouldn't stray far, and that was heartwarming, but in doing so he blocked the light. She wanted to call out, but that was silly. There wasn't anyone there! She had to do this by herself. And so she pressed on. And on.

Until she couldn't go another inch. She just needed to rest for a moment. She just needed to close her eyes.

Just for a little while.

Just....

~*~

"I see the dog," Caleb shouted. "C'mere, Shit Head!"

Maggie punched him. "I thought it was Shovel Head."

"Nah. Tori changed it to something else, but damned if I can remember what it is." He whistled for the dog and slapped the top of his thigh. After a while, the canine burst out of the hole. When he saw them, he jumped up on them, barking and wagging his tail.

"Where's Tori?" Caleb asked, as if the dog would launch into a detailed explanation.

"Here," Maggie said, shoving her flashlight into his hand. "Shine that down in there."

Caleb complied, then jumped down into the antechamber and shoved the light deeper into the tunnel. "I see something!"

"Is it... Is it Tori?"

"Hell, I don't know. I see some hair, that's about it."

"Well, can you reach her?"

He stuck his arm in and stretched it as far as he could, though he knew before he tried that whatever lay in the tunnel was well beyond his reach. He came up shaking his head.

"We've got to do something, Cal. We can't just leave her stuck in there."

"We don't even know if it's her!"

Maggie frowned. "You'll know when you start draggin' her up here. Now get down in that hole and pull her out!"

"Yes ma'am," Cal said. All he really needed was a little inspiration.

Chapter Twenty-one
Oh, go ahead; curse the darkness.

Tom Purcell came awake slowly. He knew he was outdoors because his nose was pressed against dirt. That didn't concern him as much as the discomfort he felt. All over. He rolled onto his back in order to breathe more easily, and doing that hurt, too. He flexed his fingers and hands, then tested each limb in turn. If something was broken, it would surely hurt even worse than the general ache from everywhere else. Thankfully, nothing screamed "Broken Bone!" He managed to sit up.

A trillion stars lit the sky, but he cared more about the presence of another automobile behind Tori's cabin.

Oh, damn. Car! Keys!

He slapped his pants leg and felt the comforting presence of a key ring. He glared at the quiet building, knowing his attacker waited inside—with the shotgun. How he dearly wished *he* could go in and blow the redneck away. The man deserved it for what he'd put Purcell through.

But then, maybe he'd brought some of his crazy, killer friends with him. They could be ransacking Tori's house right now—maybe gang raping her, or worse.

What if they got their hands on him?

He couldn't take any more. He'd suffered enough. Tori might be in trouble, but if so, no one could blame him. She'd just have to tough it out. He needed to leave as quickly as he could hobble to a car, and just doing that would be a challenge.

The moment he stood up, he was overcome with dizziness and had to prop himself against the boulder until his head cleared. He'd have to contend with blurred vision *and* darkness. His numbed brain told him not to worry; there wasn't much to see, anyway. He staggered away from the cabin and somehow reached his beloved BMW. It wasn't locked. He opened the door and slid behind the wheel, then sat and waited for the fog to lift from his brain. When it did, he reached into his pocket for the keys. They felt odd, but he assumed it was simply the result of the beating. He switched on an inside light while he fumbled with the keys, then realized they weren't his.

The redneck. They had swapped keys. His escape lay behind the wheel of the ugly yellow car. Purcell couldn't even turn his head to look at it; the pain was simply too much. Still, he had to get away. The redneck and his friends, most likely outlaw bikers and escaped convicts, could come after him at any moment.

Stumbling out of the BMW, Purcell managed to stagger to the yellow car. It was parked a few yards away from an even uglier vehicle, one with a crushed hood and a missing windshield. Obviously, a victim of the bikers. They'd probably stolen it, beaten the owners to death, and driven it here to finish their bizarre blood ritual. Well, they sure as hell weren't going to include Thomas R. Purcell in their festivities!

He crawled into the Chevy and experimented with the keys until he found one that worked in the ignition. Giving it a vicious twist, he brought the engine roaring to life. The switch for the headlights was on the dashboard somewhere, but he couldn't find it. Couldn't, in fact, see much of anything clearly. His vision seemed to be deteriorating. He put a hand to his swollen forehead and felt blood from the cut where he'd slammed into the boulder.

I should be dead!

But he wasn't, unless he hung around Tori's deathtrap. Grabbing the gear lever, he shifted into what he thought was reverse and tromped down hard on the accelerator. The car shot backwards and crashed into a four-door parked behind him. Purcell slammed into the windshield as the engine continued to race, and dark, oily smoke poured out from somewhere.

Dazed and shaken, his vision blurred by blood, Purcell fumbled at the door for the handle, but he couldn't find it. He would have panicked, but he lacked the mental clarity. The smoke grew thicker. The world grew hazy.

Tom Purcell knew he was done.

He sat back, closed his eyes, and waited to die.

~*~

Caleb, on his elbows and knees with his butt in the air, expected Maggie to make some smart remark. But she didn't. He wouldn't have minded if she had; it might've given him something to smile about while he wiggled into the hole.

He had Maggie's flashlight in one hand as he pulled himself forward and down with the other. He could see Tori's head a bit further down the tunnel. At least, he thought it was Tori's head. The hair color seemed right.

Crawling forward until he was completely inside the dirt enclosure, he reached as far as he could and touched the side of her head. She was lying on her back. Pushing a little farther, he felt an earring and a soft, feminine cheek. He allowed himself a moment's rest, then called to her. "Tori! It's Cal. I'm going to get you out."

Other than a weak movement of her head, she didn't respond. It didn't matter. He'd felt her move and knew she was alive.

"I'm comin' out!" he yelled to Maggie, somewhere behind him.

"I'll grab your feet!" she yelled back.

"Good Christ, don't do that! I'll end up flat on my face. Just stand by, okay?"

He didn't bother to wait for her reply. Instead, he reached for the collar of Tori's blouse and pulled steadily, praying the fabric wouldn't rip apart and come away in his hand. Thankfully, it didn't, and Tori's body moved.

Cal backed up and pulled again. Tori moved a little more. He continued the process, moving backwards like some sort of mutant inchworm, dragging the unconscious woman toward the opening. He could tell when his feet were no longer in the tunnel, because he wasn't banging his ankles against the walls. He felt Maggie's hand on his lower leg.

"Mags, please don't pull just yet. Gimme another minute, okay?"

"Right, sorry. I'm just worried about—" She stopped in mid-sentence. "What was that?"

Cal had trouble understanding her. The sound was muffled. "What was what?"

"I'll be right back."

"Fine. Whatever," Cal said, and went back to hauling Tori's limp body out of the ground. When he had moved her a short distance more, he tossed the flashlight behind him and used both hands to pull. He had just managed to drag her upper torso clear of the tunnel when Maggie came running back into the cabin.

"My car's on fire!" she gasped.

"What? How?"

"Come on, I need you!"

"But, Tori—" Cal began.

"There's no time! That idiot, Purcell, tried to drive off, but smashed into my car instead. Both of them are on fire!"

"Let 'em burn," Cal said.

"But he's still inside one!"

Cal had no choice but to leave Tori where she was and follow Maggie, though he clearly didn't want to. Purcell didn't deserve his sympathy. He'd only go for Maggie's sake, and he wouldn't be gone long.

~*~

Mato prayed to all the Spirits he could think of, but none responded.

Once Tori stopped moving, there was nothing he could do. He couldn't get out with her body in the way, and there was only darkness and probable death behind him. Even the magic which powered Tori's lamp had abandoned them, and he stood in the blackness beside her. There had been hope as long as she kept moving, and she had made slow but steady progress, reaching the area of the tunnel where she had to crawl, so the surface wasn't that far. But then she had stopped, and he feared she was dead.

He knelt down in the darkness and felt for her feet and legs. Sliding his hands down her calf, he gingerly searched for the signs of life that pulsed through all creatures of the world. Blood was the essence of life, and it surged through the bodies of The People, carrying its magic from toes to fingers. Like all the matos, for as long as The People had lived, he had special blood. He had been called upon from time to time to share it, and did so willingly, knowing that the gift given him by the Spirits was meant for anyone who needed it. Without such sacrifice, The People would have died out long ago.

But could he share his blood with Tori? A giant? And if so, could he manage it in the dark? How could he see where to make the cuts—his and hers—that would allow their blood to mingle?

As he sat, brooding in the dark with his hand on Tori's foot, *her body moved!*

He had heard sounds in the tunnel earlier, but assumed it was merely the dog running back and forth, clearly concerned for his companions stuck in the ground. And then, Tori's body moved again! Mato tensed. Had the Spirits finally answered him? How many times had he sought their guidance— their help in troubles great and small—without receiving so much as a simple sign he could understand? Meanwhile, Tori's body was moving away from him by degrees. Someone, or something, must be pulling her from the other end, he decided. The Spirits would have simply made her disappear from one place and reappear in another.

Could the strange one in the cavern have brought more of his kind? Would Mato have to battle them as well? He no longer had any weapons other than the knife at his belt, and the sleeping paste was gone, too. He had used it all on the one who hurt Tori, the same man who had been in his dream.

He had no choice but to wait and see what trials awaited him. Tori's body continued to move, and he thought he heard her groan, but there were other voices, too. Yes, other giants were definitely pulling her out of the tunnel. Mato stayed back lest they see him.

In fairly short order, Tori's upper body had been pulled into the area beneath the fire pit. Someone sat over her, talking with another he couldn't see. He wished he could understand the giant tongue better. Tori had taught him much, but he had much more to learn. If she died, that knowledge would die with her, for surely no other giant would have time for him. Nor, he knew, would he be likely to trust any of them.

Suddenly, the one who had pulled Tori from the tunnel got to his feet and left. Mato raced out of the tunnel and put his head on her chest. Though weak, her heart continued to beat. There was still time!

Mato drew his knife and carefully cut into his wrist. He did the same for Tori and pressed their limbs together, tight. When he had performed the ritual in the past, the elders would gather around and chant, begging the Spirits to aid in the healing. More often than not, it worked. But he had never attempted it with a giant! How long should he maintain the contact? Would she need all of his blood? Was he prepared to die for her? What about Reyna?

Why did he always have so many questions? He wanted to shout his frustration to the heavens. But then someone else appeared. A giant.

No, two giants!

And one of them screamed at him.

~*~

When Caleb got outside, flames were already licking up around the edges of the car hood. Maggie had both hands on the door handle, pulling with all her strength. He ran up next to her and realized at a glance that the collision had jammed the car door. A buckled side panel kept it from opening.

Inside the vehicle, he could see Purcell, his face almost unrecognizable under the blood pouring down from a deep gash in his forehead. He appeared to be sleeping, or dead. At that point, Cal wished it were the latter.

"We'll have to go 'round to the other side," he said.

Maggie moved before he finished the sentence. That door, however, was locked. She pounded on the window, trying to get Purcell to do something for himself. He rolled his head to the side and looked at her, his face blank. She gestured frantically, trying to get him to understand that he had to unlock the door. He squinted at her, perplexed.

Caleb nudged Maggie to the side and smashed the car window with a rock, then reached inside and unlocked the door.

"Wish I'd thought of that," Maggie said as he yanked the door open and launched himself toward the helpless occupant.

"C'mon, asshole," Caleb muttered as he dragged Purcell from the burning car. He dragged him out into the open and laid him out on his back.

Purcell stared up into the sky, his head moving slightly from side to side.

"Do you think he'll stay where he is?" Maggie asked.

"Doubt it. When he gets his wits back, assuming he had any to begin with, he'll probably wander off somewhere." Caleb paused to consider the possibility. "That wouldn't be any great loss though, would it?"

"There's fifty feet of nylon line in the trunk of my car," Maggie said. "We could tie him up."

"Works for me," Cal said. "Call the sheriff again while I get the rope. Oh, and see if that ambulance is lost. Tori's going to need it."

While she busied herself on her cell phone, he retrieved the line and hogtied Purcell. Cal's cowboy friends from his old rodeo days would've been proud of him.

"I called the helicopter service we use in the park," she said as they headed back into the cabin to look after Tori. "They'll get here way faster than an ambulance, but we can toss Purcell into it whenever they get here."

The two hurried through the door and proceeded directly to the hearth. When they looked over the side, they spotted what appeared to be a tiny Indian doing something to Tori's hand. Maggie screamed.

Caleb merely frowned. He struggled to remember if Tori had ever told him the name of her Indian friend—the same one she wanted to talk to. This had to be the same guy, but why hadn't she bothered to mention he was also a leprechaun? Cal put his hand out to reassure Maggie, who finally settled down. She had obviously scared the hell out of the bantam redskin.

"What's he doing to her?" Maggie gasped as the Indian stood up and gave them a look of sheer exasperation—a look Cal knew had occupied his own face when confronted with certain forms of mystifying female logic.

"Whatever it is, he's finished," Cal said.

The Indian held his wrist tightly and gestured at Tori's. The message seemed clear: they needed to apply pressure. Then, instead of climbing out of the antechamber or waiting for them to join him, he went through a door in the rock wall and disappeared. Cal hadn't even noticed the door previously.

"Gimme a hand," he said. "We have to get her out of there."

"Why? Wouldn't it be easier to wait for the EMTs?"

"Sure," he said, "but then they'd get a look at this bizarre fireplace arrangement. Obviously, Tori went to a lot of trouble to make sure it was a secret. We owe it to her to help her keep it that way until she has a chance to explain."

"You mean about the little Indian, or whatever that was down there with her?"

"Yeah, and probably a whole lot more."

They tied a bandage around Tori's wrist, but didn't notice the wound in her stomach until they pulled her further from the tunnel. "Oh, my God, Cal. She's been stabbed!"

Cal tore off his shirt and applied it like a compress while Maggie searched for real dressings. She found some first aid supplies in Tori's bathroom, and the two of them did their best to clean the wound and cover it. Caleb lifted the limp woman off the ground and set her on the iron plate, then climbed out. Together, he and Maggie moved her to the bed.

At some point while they worked on Tori, the dog wandered back in. When they stepped aside, he jumped up on the bed and stood beside the unconscious woman.

"Hey!" Maggie said, ready to chase the dog away, but Cal stopped her.

"Give him a moment. It can't hurt."

The dog sniffed Tori's nose, the bandage on her stomach, and finally her wrist. He seemed satisfied with what he found and lay down beside her. Tori murmured something, then lifted her hand and rested it on the dog's back.

Maggie still looked worried, but Cal waved her off. He was more concerned with making the fireplace look normal. It turned out to be less difficult than he'd anticipated, and by the time he finished, they heard the chopper approaching.

"Wish they'd gotten here faster," Maggie said as she grabbed Tori's cell phone from the kitchen counter.

"What's that for?" Cal asked.

Maggie didn't look comfortable explaining her reasoning. "It's just in case we have to call her next of kin."

~*~

Unwilling to risk being seen by the giants, Mato waited under the cabin. His eyes adjusted rapidly to the dark, though sunrise would soon bring everyone into the light. Everyone except the giant still in the cavern. Mato contemplated what he might do about the man, if anything. He had seen him while visiting the land of dreams and visions, and there was no doubt in his mind that the man belonged where he lay. His clothing, while in some ways similar to Tori's, also bore a rendering of an animal Mato had only seen painted on the cavern walls. Though not as shaggy, the beast on the back of the man's shirt had the same large ears, and the same impossibly long nose.

In his dream, Mato had seen the man stumbling around in the dark, unable to find his way. Bruised and dirty, his face bore the unmistakable aspect of fear. When given the chance to come into the real world, the giant's first act was violent. The dog recognized him as evil; Mato could do no less. Just as he had in the dream, the giant would awaken in the dark. Alone. And afraid.

Of course, Mato had the option of returning to the cavern and finding him. But how was he supposed to lead the angry giant back to the land of dreams? That would require a great deal more magic than even Tori possessed, and she had more magic than anyone on Earth. No, it would be better to leave him alone. Let him find his own way.

While he pondered these great questions, new noises came from the sky. Bright lights, heavy winds, and a terrifying racket threatened the cabin, and all who stood near it. Mato hid behind the stacked stones under one corner of the building as a strange craft floated down from the sky amidst the loudest of noises and the most violent of winds.

Giants seemed to be running everywhere,

and there was much shouting. They were all consumed with activity, carrying things, rolling things, moving, talking, working their magic individually and in groups. Little of it made any sense, and Mato felt great relief when the strange flying machine suddenly grew nosier and lifted back off the ground!

The sound was so loud he almost missed the whimpering behind him. He whirled around to find the great black dog at his back. Mato reached up and patted his neck. "Would you like to come with me?" he asked. "It is time to find a new mato, and for Black Otter to return to his nest."

The dog swiveled his head from side to side, then licked the little Indian's face.

~*~

"Are you feeling up to visitors?" the nurse asked Tori.

"Sure," she said. "Who is it?"

The nurse gave her a conspiratorial smile. "It's a couple, and they claim to be your only living relatives. We hear that all the time from people who don't want to wait 'til normal visiting hours. I didn't have the heart to tell 'em we're already smack in the middle of visiting hours."

It had to be Cal and Maggie, Tori thought. Cassy was the only other one who even knew where she lived, and she hadn't been able to reach her in over a week. She needed to find a phone and call her, let her know she was okay. But she got sidetracked when the door to her room eased open, and two worried faces peered in.

"How're you feeling?" Maggie asked.

Cal held a little flower arrangement and looked fully out of his element. He put it on the windowsill.

"I'm doing okay," she said.

"Better than just okay," the nurse chimed in. She looked at Tori and smiled. "When they brought you into the emergency room, you were actually pale from loss of blood. Fortunately, whoever stabbed you didn't hit anything vital. A few stitches kept what blood you had left in your system." She looked up at her visitors. "But I've gotta tell you. If she had been brought in any later, she wouldn't have made it."

"I'm feeling pretty good now," Tori said. "When can I go home?"

The nurse shrugged. "That's up to the doctor." She looked straight at Cal and added, "She really does need more rest."

They watched her leave, then moved close to the bed.

"How's Shadow?" Tori asked, but they seemed confused by the question. "My dog?"

"Oh!" Cal laughed. "He's fine. He was worried about you, y'know. Wanted to get in the chopper with you."

"Chopper?" Tori asked. "I don't remember much from the time I was crawling around in the dark until I woke up here."

They brought her up to date as much as they could. They'd closed up the hearth and locked the cabin. Tom Purcell was in custody because the car he had been in when he wrecked Maggie's vehicle was stolen and had a cache of valuable coins in the trunk. Those had also been stolen. They didn't think Purcell was involved with either theft since everything had come from somewhere in Georgia. However, there was a homicide involved, and the police weren't about to let him walk away until they could prove his innocence.

"It wasn't him," Tori said. "It was Shawn, my ex-husband."

Cal and Maggie exchanged bewildered looks. "Okay," Cal said, "so where is he now?"

"He's probably still in the cavern," she said. "Last time I saw him, he was dealing with three arrows and a spear."

"The little Indian!" they said in unison.

Tori nodded.

"Are you going to tell us about him?" Maggie asked. The expression on her face turned to one of wonder as she pointed to the cut on Tori's wrist that she and Cal had bandaged. It had almost completely healed. Only a pale pink line remained where the Indian sliced her.

"I wondered about that little scar," Tori said. "I don't remember it."

"The Indian made it," Cal said. "It looked like he cut himself, too. I didn't understand what he was doing."

Tori recalled how quickly Mato had recovered from his own wounds when they first met. She also recalled how the Indian woman Uncle Bob had met managed to survive her own terrible injury in very little time. There had to be some details somewhere, and she finally had an idea where they might be. She needed to get her hands on Uncle Bob's journal and his notes in the dictionary. There had been a third section of code in his journal, and she felt certain she knew why he had been so secretive about all of it.

Cal touched her shoulder. "You still with us?" He smiled. "We're still waiting to hear about your little Indian friend. Oh, yeah, and about the hearth and the tunnel."

"In due time," Tori said. "I just can't talk about it here, or anywhere else that isn't private."

"But if this Shawn character is trapped underground, and the police are looking for him...."

"He won't be coming back. Not without my help, and that's not going to happen." Tori crossed her arms and shook her head. "Other than you, I can't let anyone else know about this. About any of it. Not now. Maybe not ever. You'll just have to trust me. I promise I'll explain it all to you, when the time is right."

"Well," Maggie said, "you do what you have to do. We can wait. And if it looks like you're making a mistake, we'll let you know." She handed Tori her cell phone. "I thought you might need this. I'm sure glad we didn't."

The gesture reminded Tori that she needed to touch base with Cassy. She excused herself and dialed the editor's office. Cassy's secretary answered.

"This is Tori Lanier," she said. "I need to speak to Cassy."

"I didn't realize you hadn't heard," the secretary said. "It's terrible! Cassy's in the hospital. Someone attacked her in her apartment last weekend. She was beaten badly." Tori heard the quiver in the young woman's voice as she added, "The doctors don't expect her to live."

Too shaken to say much more, Tori ended the call and explained the situation to Cal and Maggie. Shawn's signature lay all over the incident, and Tori felt responsible. "I've got to go see her," she said.

"You've got to get well yourself," Caleb said.

"I'll be fine," she said, drawing them closer. "But I need your help. Can you bring me a couple things from the cabin?"

~*~

Shawn kept waiting for the lights to come on. He knew his eyes were open, but it didn't seem to make any difference. Nor did blinking, yawning, or stretching. He sat up and rubbed a few spots that itched. His hand still hurt like hell from where the little guy stabbed him with a spear. The sharp bite of fear made him turn his head, but the darkness was complete. It didn't matter where he looked.

And the silence was rapidly becoming unbearable.

He felt around in his jeans for his matches. When he found them, he struck one and held it away from his face in an effort to make out his surroundings. The match quickly burned out, and he only had two more. He used one to light a cigarette, though the pack had been in his back pocket, and he'd pretty well mangled it when he fell.

His head still hurt, too. What had happened? He'd seen Vicky Lynn; he remembered that much, and she had sassed him. That had made him angry. He drew deeply on the cigarette. He had one match left. The weed didn't give off much light at all. Certainly not enough to guide him while he tried to find the way out. Weren't they supposed to post exit signs in these places? What the hell was he even doing here? He stood up and remained standing, though he felt dizzy. The little guy had drugged him, somehow.

When his cigarette burned down to the filter, he used it to light another. He didn't really want or need another, but he didn't want to waste his last match. He had no idea what time it was. He wasn't even sure what day it was. The more he dwelled on how little he knew, the more worried he became.

When would someone come looking for him? What would he do when he ran out of matches?

He began to move, slowly. Shuffling his feet with his hands extended in front of him, he bounced like a slow-motion pinball off stalagmites and stalactites or whatever the hell they were called. Pointy rocks. He went through the entire pack of cigarettes that way, but had no better idea of how to find the way out than he had when he started.

Though he had been growing more and more apprehensive, he didn't quite freak out until he'd smoked his last weed down to the nub. He felt it burn his mouth, and then it went out.

One match left.

And then, nothing but darkness.

He decided the thing to do would be to light the matchbook cover. Surely that would give him enough light to find the path he'd used to get here. He prayed it would, anyway. More carefully than he'd ever done it before, he tore out the last match, turned it in his fingers and dragged it across the striking surface. When it flared, he almost dropped it, and the sudden light seemed way too bright.

He held the match, trembling, as he went about lighting the cardboard cover. And then, success! The matchbook cover blazed, and he held it in front of him, determined not to waste a moment of precious light. But the flame tickled up and touched his thumb, eliciting a curse as he released the tiny torch and stepped backwards.

Only, there was nothing there.

He saw the matchbook cover on the ground, still burning, as he dropped past it. He screamed in the dark, flailing his arms and legs in the desperate hope that he might stop himself. The fall lasted too long; he fell too far. And then he stopped.

Forever.

Chapter Twenty-two
When in doubt, look it up!

Tori felt certain Caleb had been assigned as her guardian angel. Maggie may have been one, too, since they flew together. Whatever kind of heavenly creatures they were, she was damned glad to have them in her life. Neither had breathed a word about Mato to anyone, as far as she knew, and neither would without her permission. The subject of Shawn never came up.

She had been sitting in her hospital bed for most of the day, and it was a monumental relief when Cal and Maggie showed up with the dictionary and Uncle Bob's journal. They even brought pens and some paper to write on.

They sat quietly in her room while she decoded the last of Uncle Bob's secret journal entries. As she suspected, the code was linked to his dictionary, and the message was intended solely for those sympathetic to his way of thinking. The decoding went quickly, and she resisted the urge to read his remarks, word by word, as she deciphered it. Instead, she concentrated on the decoding; the words were merely words, their context ignored. Until she was done. Then she read it all with rapidly growing interest.

Uncle Bob recounted an injury he had suffered when building the cabin to disguise the entrance to the cavern. A log had fallen and knocked him unconscious. There had been significant bleeding. But when he later awoke, nearly cured, Sleeping Dove told him what she had done, describing the very same procedure Caleb said Mato had used on her.

The reality of his words sank in almost instantly. If the world knew of the healing power of Mato's blood, there would be no stopping the stampede of people looking for him. Whatever life he had previously enjoyed would be shattered irrevocably.

But there was more. Sleeping Dove had revealed another secret. According to her, anyone who received such a transfusion would be blessed—or cursed—with a similar ability for approximately five days. Tori looked up in shock.

I could heal Cassy!

She resisted the urge to shout for Cal and Maggie to help her leave the hospital. She explained what she'd just learned as she hunted around the room for her clothes.

"But you can't just up and leave without the doctor's permission," Caleb said.

Maggie agreed. "You've been through too much to race out of here and fly off to New York."

Tori looked at her with a big smile on her face. "Oh yeah? Watch me."

Cal put his hand on her arm, but it was merely a gesture, not an effort to stop her. "Are you sure?"

She slipped an arm around each of them. "I've never been more sure of anything in my life." She gave them a joint hug. "I hope you won't mind keeping an eye on Shadow for a while longer."

Cal frowned, and Maggie suddenly found the toes of her shoes very interesting.

"Cal?" Tori looked from him to his sweetheart. "Maggie? What aren't you telling me?"

After clearing his throat, Cal said, "We don't have him."

"Then, who does? Where is he?"

"We don't know. We didn't see him when we left the cabin the other night. I figured he was scared by all the noise and lights. That chopper made quite a racket."

"But?"

"But when I went back to the cabin to get your stuff, I still couldn't find him. I left food out for him, and water. And I drove around looking for him..." His voice trailed off.

Tori felt a stab of guilt. What if Shadow was in trouble? What if he needed her?

"I'm sorry," Cal said.

She gave him another hug. "It's been a crazy couple of days. I'm sure he'll come back when he's good and ready." She said it, but she didn't believe it. "I'll look for him when I get back."

"We'll help," Maggie said.

"I know you will. And we'll find him."

She hoped she wasn't kidding herself.

~*~

It had taken an entire month, but somehow Tori managed to arrange a long-overdue dinner party. She had cleaned her tiny cabin from top to bottom, and even bought a couple of folding chairs in order to seat her guests. Always reasonably neat and tidy, Tori had never felt her remote home would be the proper venue for entertaining. It was barely big enough for her, let alone a handful of guests.

But these guests were special, and at least one of them had traveled a great distance to be there.

As she looked around her crowded table, she saw the smiling faces of Cal, Maggie, and Cassy. They all held their wine glasses high and waited for Tori to make a toast.

She had considered this moment on several

occasions while preparing for the gathering, but had been unable to come up with anything meaningful that didn't also sound contrived. In the end, she simply trusted that she would come up with something appropriate.

"I love you all," she said at last. "Thank you for coming."

They clinked their glasses and dug in. Cassy had insisted on buying ribeye steaks, which they cooked on Tori's hibachi only because Cal came up with a system of rotating the meat so that the slabs hanging over the sides got equal time over the coals. Everyone claimed the final product was perfect, and would have even if Cal had burnt them to cinders. Maggie brought veggies and Tori baked bread.

They ate until they could barely move. Conversation drifted from one inconsequential topic to another until Cal brought up the unavoidable question.

"What're we gonna do about this Shawn character?"

Cassy's smile faded, as had some of her scars. Her miracle recovery did not include amnesia to blot out memories of the attack.

Tori patted her hand and smiled. "He's gone, and he'll never hurt anyone else again. Ever." She paused to take a sip of her wine. "I've only been back down in the cavern once since that night. And without Mato, I can't say I'm eager to go back, but I had to know what happened."

They all sat expectantly, for she was finally about to break her silence on the matter.

"The sheriff came by, as I knew he would. Shawn had a stolen car, and they were looking for him in relation to a murder back in Georgia. He was also implicated in an arson investigation, but they didn't give me any details. I confirmed that Shawn was the one who stabbed me."

She paused and took a sip of wine. Her audience didn't move.

"They asked me if I knew where he was."

"What'd you tell them?"

"The truth, sorta. I really don't know where he is... exactly. I'm guessing hell, but who really knows? Right?"

"Was the cop okay with that?"

"No, but I wasn't about to tell him about the cavern, or Mato. Knowing what happened to Shawn doesn't trump the importance of what happens to Mato and his people. As far as the police are concerned, Shawn is still at large." She gestured at a vague horizon. "He's out there, somewhere. Good luck finding him."

Cal eased back in his chair, the wine glass resting comfortably in his hand. "Okay, sure. But what'd you find down below? You obviously know more than you told the lawman."

"The only traces I found of Shawn were cigarette butts and footprints from his running shoes. I followed them right to the edge of a deep chasm that cuts across the big chamber. There weren't any footprints coming out."

She got up from the table and picked up a handful of photos she had printed from her digital camera. "I thought you might be interested in these," she said, handing the stack to Cassy.

She passed them to Cal and Maggie one by one until she came to the last. "This is painted on a wall down there?"

Tori nodded as Cassy put the photo on the table for a better look. Cal and Maggie craned their necks to see, too.

"That's the painting Mato did the night Shawn came," Tori said.

Cassy grimaced at the bent figure, his arms extended. "Looks like he's stumbling around blind."

"He was. There is absolutely no light down there. It's unnerving."

Cal tapped the lower portion of the photo. "And that's the drop-off? It looks like he's about to fall in."

"How could Mato have known?" Maggie asked. "I don't get it."

Tori explained again about the dreamers. She had pieced a few theories of her own together with conjecture from her Uncle Bob's writings, but in the long run, no one would ever know. Unless, of course, Mato came back, and they were able to learn enough of each other's languages to communicate. That didn't seem likely.

"And you don't really think he's an Indian?" Cassy asked.

"Well, not in the conventional sense, no. And it's not just because he's so small."

"You've lost me," Maggie said. "Either he is or he isn't." She refilled her wine glass and offered the bottle around. They were on their third, but there was plenty more for later.

"I believe he's a primitive," Tori said, "and it was convenient for me to catalog him as an Indian, because that's the first model I thought of. But I don't believe that's quite right. I think he represents a completely different branch on the evolutionary tree."

"The missing link?" Cal asked.

"No," Tori said. "First off, he's not missing. Secondly, he's fully evolved; he's not some half-human, half-ape hybrid like we were told about in school."

Cal looked at Cassy with mock surprise. "Were you told about them in school?"

She winked back. "I went to Catholic school. We never talked about stuff like that."

"I think we need to tell someone," Maggie said. "If Mato is a different species, then the world needs to know about him."

Tori shook her head. "Absolutely not. If word got out, there'd be no end of people looking for him, and not just those who'd want to study him. Don't forget that whole healing business. What if he lives in your park? Imagine what would happen. It'd be like a gold rush, only worse."

"There would be missionaries as well as people wanting to exploit them," Cassy said. "They need to be left alone. Untouched. They don't need to be contaminated by our society."

Caleb had been following the conversation, but he looked bothered by the direction it had taken. "And what do you suggest when one of them gets sick? Especially if it's something we can cure? What about allowing them to have warm clothing and good food? Clean water. Or a hot bath?"

"We shouldn't play god," Tori said. "We shouldn't force any of those things on them. We should let them know what the options are. They can decide if what we have to offer is appropriate for them."

"And in the meantime?" Maggie asked.

"We don't say anything to anyone."

The sound of music just outside the door had them all turning their heads to investigate. Tori got up from the table and opened the door. "Oh, my God!" she said, her voice barely audible above the strains of "Sweet Home Alabama."

The others scrambled up amid a flurry of wine glasses, napkins, and chairs. They all crowded around Tori at the door.

Mato stood outside, grinning. Beside him stood Shadow with the MP3 player hanging from his neck, and on his back rode a pretty young woman about Mato's size. She appeared only slightly apprehensive, though Tori imagined she could rightly be terrified. Tori knelt down and smiled, hoping to reassure her.

"Gud mawrning," Mato said.

And Tori realized how much work they still had to do.

~The End~

~Afterword~

While working on this story, my darling bride found an article about a race of humans dubbed "hobbits" which she thought would interest me. It did. And for a while, I felt as if some journalist had scooped my budding novel. Fortunately for me, rationality quickly returned. The article actually gave me a surge of inspiration, and I've included an excerpt. Follow the link (published with permission) to see the entire story. It's not terribly long, and I encourage you to read it.

http://www.eurekalert.org/pub_releases/2009-11/w-aa111709.php

"Hobbits" are a new human species— according to the statistical analysis of fossils

Homo floresiensis not diseased sub-population of healthy humans

Researchers from Stony Brook University Medical Center in New York have confirmed that *Homo floresiensis* is a genuine ancient human species and not a descendant of healthy humans dwarfed by disease. Using statistical analysis on skeletal remains of a well-preserved female specimen, researchers determined the "hobbit" to be a distinct species and not a genetically flawed version of modern humans. Details of the study appear in the December issue of *Significance*, the magazine of the Royal Statistical Society, published by Wiley-Blackwell.

In 2003 Australian and Indonesian scientists discovered small-bodied, small-brained, hominin (human-like) fossils on the remote island of Flores in the Indonesian archipelago. This discovery of a new human species called *Homo floresiensis* has spawned much debate with some researchers claiming that the small creatures are really modern humans whose tiny head and brain are the result of a medical condition called microcephaly.

As mentioned in the story, tales of "little people" appear in almost every culture in every corner of the world. The reference to miniature Indians in the notes of Lewis and Clark (1804) is true, as far as I can tell. Likewise, references to historical figures—Robert E. Lee, Edgar Allan Poe, Dr. George H. Tichenor, etc.—are based on available fact.

Finally, a word of explanation to my friends who happen to be Alabama fans. I wasn't picking on you, really! I needed an elephant design for the back of Shawn's shirt, and I couldn't think of a more rational explanation for an adult to wear one.

About the Author

Josh Langston writes books which amuse, anger, enlighten, and entertain. He regularly mines history for background material that's little known but reliably fascinating. His plots are complex, interconnected, and layered with humor and suspense; his characters are rarely predictable, and even his bad guys tend to be both engaging and diabolical.

When not writing, Josh can be found teaching and/or mentoring new writers. His students rely heavily on his four humorous textbooks. He currently has well over a dozen fiction titles on the market along with an historical fantasy trilogy set in the 1st century BC which he co-authored with his great Canadian friend, Barbara Galler-Smith.

Josh is happy to visit with book clubs online, or locally, where possible. Readers may connect with him through his website: **www.JoshLangston.com**.

And now, turn the page for a preview of Book
Two in the series:
A Little More Primitive

Book Two

A Little More Primitive

A Provocative Predator

He's Back
and He's
Not
Happy

JOSH LANGSTON

A Little More Primitive

Chapter One

It's always the little things....

Tori Lanier focused on the computer monitor in front of her. The wide, flat screen was a thank you gift from her friend and editor, Cassy Woodall, whose life Tori had saved by providing a blood transfusion. Tori considered the gift extravagant, but Cassy insisted she keep it. Now, Tori couldn't imagine working without it. She didn't, however, feel quite the same way about the other new additions in her life, a pair of young lovers for whom the word "civilization" remained a mystery.

Tori had typed and retyped the same sentence several times, her concentration derailed by the intimate sounds coming from behind a makeshift screen on the other side of the one-room cabin.

Why the hell couldn't they do it when she wasn't around?

Though she couldn't see them, she easily imagined the two diminutive bodies writhing on the little mattress she'd picked up at a yard sale in Ten Sleep, the nearest town of any size. She had no idea how old the lovers actually were, but they had the stamina of teenagers on Viagra: steam-driven and drip fed. It made her so jealous she could spit, not that she'd ever admit it.

"I'm takin' the dog out," she said, mostly for her own benefit, then snapped her fingers to summon Shadow, a gigantic animal of questionable lineage and occasional loyalty. The gentle but immense, black Rottweiler/Lab/bison mix trotted over and rested his massive head on her thigh. She scratched him behind the ears as he turned his soulful brown eyes in her direction and wagged his tail. He was likely just as horny as she was, and neither would be getting lucky any time soon.

"Out," she said. The command sent the dog thundering toward the door. Tori opened it and followed him into the bright sunshine. "Don't eat anyone," she said as he took off across the top of the bluff on which her cabin stood.

She'd come to Wyoming primarily to avoid her ex-husband; she'd stayed primarily because of the view. As Shadow plunged through the brush chasing butterflies, prairie dogs or buffalo—anything in roaming range would do—she was content to just stare at the mountains.

In all too typical fashion, however, her reverie was trashed by the buzz of her cell phone.

She fished the tyrannical device from her pocket, stabbed the Answer button, and held it to her ear. "H'lo?"

"Mizz Lanier?" a male voice asked. The accent was thick as grits—heavy, with a touch of Cajun flavoring. *Nice, actually.* But then, she knew the man behind the voice, and whatever mystery there might have been, fled.

"Whatcha got, Dallas?"

Dallas drove the UPS delivery truck and had never worked up the courage to attempt the obstacle course Tori euphemistically termed a driveway. She wasn't entirely unsympathetic. One section in particular worried her as it ran alongside the base of a steep incline. Winter weather often loosened the grip of rocks and boulders on the hill, and the ground through which Tori's "drive" meandered was littered with huge stones that had broken loose. A wash on the opposite side of the narrow trail prevented her from making wide detours. She'd dealt single-handedly with most of the debris, although her friend Caleb, a retired rodeo cowboy turned grocery merchant, had helped her nudge a couple of the largest boulders out of the way.

Maintaining the route between her cabin and the highway was a pain, but she managed. It helped that she drove a little Nissan pickup with better-than- average ground clearance. Dallas drove one of the ubiquitous, boxy, brown UPS trucks, about as far from an off-road vehicle as one could get. As a result,

Dallas called when he reached the turn-off to tell her she had a package.

She'd made the mistake of driving out to accept a delivery she'd been anxiously awaiting, and he'd been smitten. *Who knew cupid wore cowboy boots?*

She'd noticed his name neatly embroidered on his brown UPS shirt and made small talk about it while he recovered enough to get her signature on his snazzy, computerized delivery gizmo.

Since then, he found something to discuss with her on every trip. She suspected he broke up multi-parcel deliveries so he'd have extra reasons to drop by, though God only knew how he could justify driving umpteen miles into the boondocks just to chat her up. Evidently, loneliness could drive a man to do extraordinary things. Too bad navigating her driveway wasn't one of them.

"It's pretty big," he said, "but not too heavy."

"Who's it from?" Tori hadn't ordered anything lately. She could only stretch her royalty checks so far. Living off the land was not an option. That sort of thing was fine for outdoor types, but not for Tori Lanier, novelist and unofficial guardian of two very small Indians. *And* a sacred hole in the ground.

"It's from New York," Dallas said. "Can't make out the name."

"Why don't you just leave it?" She glanced skyward. It didn't look like rain, but she knew from experience that could change with little warning. "I'll pick it up later."

"I dunno," he said. "I really hate to leave stuff out. Ya never know who might drive by."

"On that road?" She laughed. "Nobody."

He didn't say anything, but Tori could sense his disappointment. "Okay. Lemme grab my keys. I'll be there in a minute."

"No hurry," he said. "I've got time."

Shadow spotted her when she fired up her truck. She slowed to a stop so he could jump in the back. She doubted Shadow got out any more often than Dallas did.

The UPS man was sitting in the high seat of his huge vehicle when she bounced across the last set of ruts which marked the end of the driveway. He left his vehicle and approached hers with a large box in his arms.

"Told ya it was big," he said when he handed it to her.

She put it on the passenger seat where Shadow wouldn't attack it, or worse, then turned to conclude the transaction by signing his computer thingy.

"You ever been to the music festival in Ten Sleep?" he asked.

"The woodchuck thing?"

He took on a pained expression. "It's called

'NoWoodstock.' You know, like the big hippie concert in New York? 'Cept it's not like that at all."

"Right," she said, slowly. "I missed it last year."

"I was thinkin'... You know, maybe you and me—"

"It's mostly country music, right? I'm not much—"

"It's blues, too. And some rock. Lots of different stuff. Gospel."

Swell. "I dunno," she said, stalling until she came up with a plausible excuse for shooting him down. The last UPS delivery guy never called. In fact, she'd never met him. He'd just leave her stuff and drive away, even in the winter. Some deliveries sat for days. Since he was no longer around, she assumed he'd been canned for forging her signature on the delivery gadget. In any event, Tori had no desire to make her way onto the new guy's shit list.

"There's always a crowd," Dallas said. "Lotsa food and stuff. C'mon, it'll be fun. My treat."

She smiled. He wasn't unattractive. Get him out of those silly brown shorts and he might even look like an adult. *Hmm.* "How old are you?"

"Twenty-two," he said, a streak of uncertainty shading his answer.

"Wouldn't you rather go with someone uhm... a little younger? I'm—" she coughed, "almost thirty." She covered her mouth to keep from giving herself away. She'd been on the wrong side of thirty for a couple years. Okay, four years, but who was counting?

"No," he said, grinning like a medal-winner at the Special Olympics. "I like older women!"

She fixed him with a stare. "Do I look like an older woman?"

"No, ma'am," he said, quickly.

"*Ma'am?*"

"I mean, no. You're... You know. Kinda pretty."

"Well, there's a ringing endorsement." She walked around to the driver's side of her truck and got in. "I'll have to check my schedule. When's the big do?"

"Second weekend in August."

Surely, she could find some sort of commitment by then. "I'll let you know."

He tapped his phone. "I'll call ya, okay?"

"Right," she said, starting the truck's engine. She pulled out onto the county road to turn around, narrowly missing the bumper of the big brown truck. She waved as she drove back to the house.

"Kinda pretty," she said—out loud—then yanked down the sun visor and checked her reflection in the vanity mirror. Okay, she admitted to herself, she wasn't likely to end up in the Sports Illustrated swim suit edition, but she was still a damn sight better than "kinda pretty," and if Dallas the delivery dude didn't recognize it, he needed glasses. Big time. The more she thought about it, the more she looked forward to turning him down when he called back.

She made a rare shift of gears, higher speeds not being desirable on her private version of the Oregon Trail. That and a sharp turn while negotiating the cliff passage caused the package to lean, teeter briefly, and then fall toward her. She shoved it back in place, then stared at it in curiosity. From New York. Had to be Cassy. She didn't know anyone else who lived there.

The box appeared big enough to hold a lamp, assuming the shade was shipped separately. Which, if true, meant yet another encounter with the love-struck UPS driver. "Kinda pretty," she muttered, urging her subconscious to get over it and move on to the package. Her conscious mind made the effort, but there was interference.

Christmas in July!

Zzt... Date with Dallas.

Brown paper packages tied up with strings!

Party with Dallas.

Package!

Party.

Package!

Party? *With Dallas?*

Oy.

~*~

Jarred Carter, MD, sat in the fifth-floor nurses station reviewing a file on Brooklyn Memorial Hospital's patient database. Though merely a first-year resident, Carter had been working at the hospital long enough to recognize when something—like the recovery of a critically ill patient—went well beyond the ordinary.

There were plenty of staff members eager to chalk up such rare occurrences as the work of the divine. Carter wasn't so sure. A confirmed agnostic, he had no problem taking credit for any such cures which occurred on his watch, although to date, there had only been two. Still, it bothered him on several levels that he couldn't pinpoint what had triggered the reversals.

Turns for the worse were far more likely, especially given cost-conscious administrators, lowest bid contractors, and overworked staff. A hospital was a terrible place to be sick. But that's where the experts were, so what choice did anyone have?

The record he found so interesting concerned a patient named Cassandra Woodall: single, late thirties, no unusual medical history. Woodall had been delivered to the emergency room, barely alive. Whoever had administered the beating she'd suffered had surely intended her to die. That she survived at all was nothing short of a miracle. She had been consigned to intensive care, and while a number of surgeries had been discussed, she was in no condition to undergo any of them.

Carter, on call at the time of her admission, had been assigned to her care, though no one really expected her to live through the night, much less the week which followed. He had looked in on her as often as required, but when her condition varied at all, it was inevitably for the worse. She was, prognostically speaking, a loser.

And then, in the space of 24 hours, everything turned around. It happened so fast, he almost didn't notice. Cassy Woodall was going to live. And not just as a shell of the woman she'd once been. Cassy's injuries were healing in ways that defied medical experience.

Carter wanted to know why. He *needed* to know why. What made this woman different? What made it possible for her to survive a beat down on the order of the worst he'd seen in two-plus years as an intern on ER night shifts at one of New York's shittiest locales?

The pictures scrolling on the screen in front of him suggested but one possibility. Someone had entered Woodall's room and administered a treatment of some kind. The public wasn't supposed to know about the in-room video hospital administrators had installed in the wake of a much-publicized string of mercy killings the previous year. The resulting video database was enormous, and combing through it would take a lifetime, unless one knew what he was looking for. Carter did.

•

Though grainy, the picture on the screen in front of him revealed enough detail to satisfy him that Cassandra Woodall's miraculous recovery was linked to a visitor rather than to anything done by the staff at Brooklyn Memorial.

He needed to know who the visitor was, and what—*exactly*—she had done.

~*~

Mato rolled onto his back. A light sheen of sweat marked the passing of his lust. And not just his. Reyna shared it. She had the usual glassy-eyed look of the recently sated, her head resting on Mato's arm. She, too, looked up at the ceiling of the giant's cabin—their home the past several weeks.

"Do you think we have pleased the Spirits?" he asked.

She smiled. "I am pleased. Is that not enough?"

He rolled toward her and smoothed a long, dark hair from her forehead. "That is more than enough. I just hoped...."

"You want a child, of course. I am not stupid, Mato. But I wonder, is this the best place to have one? What would Winter Woman say?"

Winter Woman was Reyna's grandmother, a person of vast respect among The People. Mato could have no greater ally on Earth. Still, the woman could be unpredictable. He couldn't be sure she would welcome the news that Mato and Reyna had added yet another generation to her pedigree.

"She will be pleased," he said, though caution tempered his certainty. "And if not, she will get used to the idea. What choice does she have?"

Reyna curled toward him, her hand doing delightfully casual and deliberately carnal things. "What if she becomes angry? Do you think she is ready for a great-grandchild? The child of two dreamers?"

He smiled. *Two dreamers.* That would be the issue most on Winter Woman's mind. The tribe needed dreamers—those who glimpses of the future often meant continued life for the clan. The Old Ones sang of times when there were few such gifted members of The People, and those times had been difficult indeed. Still, there was no certainty that if Mato and Reyna produced a child, he or she would have the gift. Winter Woman would know, of course. She might wait until she held such a child in her withered arms before she even decided if she would welcome it, or not.

"I would rejoice at the chance to present a child to her," he said at length. "Nor would I care if our child knew the gift of dreams. I would be proud, and I would challenge any who dared find fault."

She hugged him. "You make *me* proud."

"I am Mato!" he said, as if he had just entered a room full of warriors who didn't already know him. "I am a hunter. I am a provider!"

She pinched a recently evolved roll of flab

around his middle. "I fear someone has been providing for you, too much."

He pulled away and took to his feet, embarrassed. The door to the cabin burst open and Tori, the she-giant, entered along with her dog. Mato and the dog had long ago achieved an understanding based on mutual admiration and respect. Shadow, while clearly the physically superior member, was also the junior member, intellectually. The great animal shuffled toward them, his nose busy with the scents their love-making had painted in the air, then collapsed beside their bower. Mato dug his hands into the thick fur of the dog's neck and rubbed him diligently. Both Shadow and Tori approved.

The she-giant placed a huge box on the table in the eating area of the cabin. She stepped back and contemplated it in silence.

"What is it?" Mato asked, concentrating on the words to get them right. The past several weeks had been spent in concentrated study of the giant's language. He was getting reasonably good at it, owing mostly to his superior memory. Tori still struggled with the speech of The People, and they both knew he needed her language more than she needed his. Still, he often had trouble finding the right words, especially for concepts outside the experience of The People.

She shook the box and shrugged. "It's from Cassy."

Mato and Reyna had met the woman. Another she-giant, Cassy had traveled an unimaginable distance to visit with Tori a few weeks ago. Tori had tried to explain, pointing to the sky and telling him how her friend had ridden in one of the giant's machines that traveled through the air. Reyna assured him it was all nonsense, a boast by the giants meant to demoralize them. Mato knew better. He had learned that much of what the giants took for granted, he mistook for great magic. Reyna had yet to make the logical leap needed to discern the difference. The giants were incredibly clever, but what they had at their disposal wasn't magic. They had something Tori called tek-nol-ogee. He had thought, at first, that it was just another word for magic. But it wasn't. It merely referred to cleverly designed machinery.

The revelation had brought him great solace, but he had yet to convince Reyna. She was still held in the grip of superstition, and a lifetime of teaching focused on the evils of giants. Such a background was not easily changed. But, in time, he knew she would recognize his superior wisdom.

Tori plucked a knife from a drawer and made several cuts through the thin, almost invisible membranes which held the box securely closed. They parted easily under her skillful hands, and she unfolded panels of the thin brown container.

She stepped back, clearly surprised. "What the hell?"

Mato and Reyna scrambled out of bed to get closer. Mato reached the giant-sized chair first and reached down to assist Reyna. They stood side-by-side gazing in wonder at the contents of the box.

~*~

Carter gripped his phone lightly as he spoke into it. "Ms. Woodall?"

"Yes?" She sounded less than thrilled.

"This is Dr. Carter, from Brooklyn Memorial."

She didn't respond immediately. "Is this about my bill? Because my insurance is supposed to cover everything. I—"

"No," he said. "It has nothing to do with that. In fact, I couldn't care less about your bill. I just wanted to check up on you."

"You *did?*"

"Yes. I try to follow up on all my patients."

"Oh. How nice. I didn't think doctors did that anymore."

"Well," he said, breathing a subtle sigh of relief, "my folks were old school. They thought it would be a good habit to get into, and I have to agree. Although—" he laughed "—you'd be surprised at how many think I'm trying to pull something over on them."

"I hate to hear that," she said. "There's so little trust in the world these days. How can I help you?"

"Actually, that's my question," he said. "How're you doing? Your recovery was nothing short of miraculous. I couldn't help but wonder about you."

"Why's that?"

"Well," he explained, "it's not every day one is presented with a miracle. Either as a patient or a physician."

Again, she didn't respond immediately, and he wondered if he'd overplayed his hand. "Uhm, Miss Woodall?"

"I'm still here," she said. "It's an unusual situation. Perhaps we could discuss it."

"Over dinner?" he asked.

"I... Uh, sure."

"Would you care to suggest a place?"

She mentioned a restaurant not too far from the hospital.

"That'll work," he said. "My schedule is crazy; I can't plan more than a day or two in advance. So, would tomorrow evening be too soon?"

They sealed the deal, and Carter hung up. Could it really be that easy, he wondered. Then he smiled. A little charm could go a long way.

~*~

Tori stared at the contents of the box. What had Cassy been thinking? Or, perhaps more *à propos*, what had she been smoking?

Mato and Reyna were equally transfixed by

the sight, standing shoulder-to-shoulder on a kitchen chair. "Nekkid as newborns," Tori's mother would have said, shortly after she'd run screaming from the room. Though still not at all comfortable with their casual attitude about clothing and hygiene, Tori refused to let them ruin her consternation over Cassy's gift.

Inside the box, cushioned with a more than generous supply of bubble wrap, stood a two-foot-tall doll. The fully clothed, more or less adult-looking male figure stared at her from a face so lifelike she half expected it to step forward and introduce itself. Thankfully, it didn't.

"Jesus, Mary, and Joseph," she muttered as she reached for the envelope taped to the doll's abdomen. Once she'd removed it, the libido twins advanced, poking the helpless figure and examining its stylish attire.

Tori removed a note from the envelope and scanned it quickly:

> Allow me to introduce Lance. He's a ball-jointed doll, custom-made for my friend Rachel, who was with me the night of the attack.

Tori remembered the chronology all too well. Cassy's friend had died trying to defend them from Tori's insane ex-husband.

> I've known about Lance for years. He was one of Rachel's prized possessions, and she claimed he was the only male she

ever loved. Rachel's mother insisted I take him, as if I wouldn't remember Rachel all on my own. Anyway, I thought about Mato and Reyna and how hard it must be for you to travel anywhere with them. I thought if people grew accustomed to seeing you with Lance, they might not even notice if one of your little friends took his place.

I don't really have a use for Lance, though I'm sure he's a great guy who will never promise more than he can deliver. But, If you decide not to keep him, please let me know; I'll arrange an adoption. You can't imagine how expensive these things are!

What intrigued Tori more than the doll was its wardrobe, which Cassy had included in the shipment. Although the clothing reflected some odd notions about male fashion, Tori chalked it up to Rachel's sexual orientation. Cassy had often commented on their relationship, but never provided any significant details. Tori had always been thankful for that.

Reyna put both hands on the doll's face, a look of sheer wonder on her own. She exchanged a few hurried words with Mato, who then asked, "Is toy?"

Tori pursed her lips while she pondered her response, then smiled and nodded yes. She removed

Lance from the box and stood him on the table. Mato leaped up beside him. Reyna motioned for him to stand tall, then put her hands on her hips and appraised them both. Mato had begun to look a bit peeved when Reyna finally smiled and said something to him that relieved the tension.

"Mato more pretty," he announced, dropping lightly down to the chair to hug his gal.

Tori would have agreed, but Mato's ego was sufficiently inflated.

Encouragement? No way!

She looked back at Lance. He had the same dark hair as Mato, and it was nearly the same length. His complexion was considerably lighter than Mato's, and while someone had airbrushed a five o'clock shadow on his sharply defined jaw, it didn't do much to alter his basically androgynous features.

Reyna whispered something to Mato, in deference to Tori's feeble grasp of their native tongue, and the two chuckled. Tori suspected Reyna had already determined that Lance was anatomically correct, though undoubtedly not in the same league as her paramour.

Tori handed them both a few items of Lance's clothing. Reyna was quick to try things on; Mato was reluctant. Lance, it seemed, had never spent any time in the gym, while Mato's life in the wild gave him a musculature most jocks would admire, despite his minimalist frame. The end result being that the clothing fit Reyna better than Mato, and she clearly enjoyed strutting around the cabin. She had the poise, presence, and exotic good looks for a runway model, albeit on a significantly smaller runway than usual.

The more Tori thought about it, the more pleased she became with Cassy's gift. Well, she thought, Rachel's gift, and she made a mental note to phrase it that way when she penned her Thank You note. She resumed her place at the computer and had just begun to compose an E-mail message to Cassy when her phone rang again.

"I haven't checked my schedule yet," she said by way of a greeting, assuming Dallas to be on the other end of the line.

"Excuse me?"

She didn't recognize the voice.

"Sorry," she said, clearly embarrassed. "I was expecting someone else."

"This is Nate Sheffield with the Washakie County Sheriff's office."

Wonderful. "How can I help you, Officer?"

"It's Deputy, not Officer."

"Okay then, how can I help you, *Deputy?*"

"May I speak frankly, Mizz Lanier?"

"It won't hurt my feelings."

"Frankly, we aren't gettin' anywhere with our investigation. We know a little more than we did the night your husband attacked you, but since then he's disappeared without a trace. There's no sign of him anywhere."

"I'm inclined to take that as good news," Tori said, knowing precisely what her former husband was doing—decomposing.

"Unfortunately, ma'am, it suggests to us that he could show up just about anywhere. He might try to come after you again."

She wondered if she ought to feign a certain level of fear, just for the benefit of Deputy Sheffield, then opted to go with frontier bravado, a decision made much easier knowing that Shawn was at the bottom of a deep crevasse which ran through a cave beneath her cabin—a cave which had remained a secret from the world, outside of Mato's tribe, for generations beyond count.

"I'm honestly not worried," she said. "I've got a great big dog and a shotgun full of buckshot. If he's stupid enough to come back, I'm still pissed enough to put a bucket-sized hole in him."

"I can appreciate that, Mizz Lanier; I surely can. But we'd like to avoid any further bloodshed, if at all possible. This really isn't the Wild West anymore."

Fearing she may have gone a little overboard, Tori tried to show some remorse. "Of course," she said. "I wouldn't *really* kill him if he came back. I'd be satisfied just takin' off one of his legs." She didn't volunteer which one.

"We try to discourage violence," he said.

"A girl's got to protect herself. I don't have any neighbors I can call on."

"That's what's got us so puzzled. We don't understand how your husband—"

"*Ex*-husband."

"Yes'm. How your ex-husband managed to get clean away without leaving any tracks. It's like something swooped down out of the sky and hauled him off."

She chuckled. "I seriously doubt he has any pals among the angels." His contemporaries occupied a much less desirable realm.

"We'd like to take another look around your cabin, in case we missed something."

"And you need my permission?"

"It'd save us the trouble of gettin' a warrant."

She didn't like the idea of folks poking around her cabin. Granted, the entrance to the cavern was cunningly disguised, yet she had found it. Who could say some enthusiastic crime fighter might not stumble onto it as well?

"I don't want y'all to think I'm trying to hinder your investigation," she said at length. "You're welcome to come out and have a look around, but I'd appreciate knowing when you're coming. The place is a mess. She suddenly realized she'd begun to turn into her mother, unable to resist the urge to straighten up the house before the cleaning lady arrived.

"Would this afternoon be too soon?" he asked.

~*~

A Little More Primitive is available now in paperback and all popular E-book formats.